Vlad
ALL
OVER

BETH ORSOFF

amazonpublishing

Text copyright © 2012 Beth Orsoff
All rights reserved.
Printed in the United States of America.
No part of this book may be reproduced, or stored in a retrieval system, or transmitted in any form or by any means, electronic, mechanical, photocopying, recording, or otherwise, without express written permission of the publisher.

Published by Amazon Publishing
P.O. Box 400818
Las Vegas, NV 89140

ISBN-13: 9781612185989
ISBN-10: 1612185983

"Alas, our frailty is the cause, not we:
For such as we are made of, such we be"
—William Shakespeare

Chapter 1

"You're not wearing *that*, are you?" Zoe asked as I opened my front door.

I glanced down at my outfit—khakis, scalloped-neck T-shirt, and strappy sandals. "What's wrong with it?" I was no fashionista, but I thought I'd succeeded in my goal of neat yet casual attire.

She brushed past me and into my living room. "You are so lucky to have me as a friend."

"You know, I tell myself that *at least* once a day," I said and shut the door behind her.

"Har, har," she replied, and we both smiled. Then she flounced down the hallway in the direction of my bedroom, her black-and-white print dress swishing around her legs, which looked even longer and shapelier in her red peep-toe platform pumps.

Dressing me, or more accurately, re-dressing me, was one of our time-honored traditions. In our fifteen years of friendship, I could only recall two instances when Zoe had approved of my outfit without suggesting even one minor alteration. The first was when I'd donned my high school volleyball uniform. Zoe thought the Westside Cobras' short red shorts and cap-sleeved jerseys made us look hot. The boys in our school agreed, which was why we had such great turnouts for all of our games. Attendance dropped considerably the next year when the school hired a new coach, who replaced our sexy uniforms with the same baggy outfits the girls' basketball team wore. The second instance was the morning of my parents' funeral. Obviously neither of us was thinking clearly that day since I spent the majority of it wearing two different black pumps. I only realized when my mother's former boss asked me why I was limping.

"This'll work," Zoe said, pulling a white sundress with embroidered flowers from my overstuffed closet. To be fair, the closet was original to my 1920s-era Los Angeles bungalow. Even with a monk's wardrobe, my closet would've been overstuffed. Although, admittedly, my wardrobe was much larger and more varied than a monk's.

"I'm not getting dressed up for a seven-year-old's birthday party!"

"Hello. This is not just *any* seven-year-old's birthday party. This is Isabella Romanescu's birthday party."

"And I'm not getting dressed up for a rich seven-year-old's birthday party either."

Zoe glanced down at her watch. "Gwen, we're already late. Can't we just skip the twenty minutes of debate, the eight alternative wardrobe choices, and get to the part where you admit that I know way more about fashion than you do? You know you're going to."

I didn't *always* capitulate. But Zoe did have an amazing sense of style. All of us—her family and friends—had been surprised when she'd chosen to become a teacher instead of pursuing a career in fashion design. Zoe had said it was because once she'd realized she'd have to spend her days with a bunch of spoiled rich people, she'd decided it would be much more enjoyable if they actually listened to her. The truth was she loved the kids as much as I did. As a teacher, you can actually change someone's life. There aren't many careers you can say that about.

I grabbed the sundress from her outstretched hand. "Fine, but I'm wearing the sandals."

She pursed her ruby-red lips as she glanced down at my feet. "Only if you let me choose your jewelry."

"Done." I'd planned on asking her advice on accessories anyway.

We were headed out to Zoe's car when I realized I'd almost forgotten the most important part of my outfit. I ran back into the house and emerged two minutes later clutching my short-sleeve shrug.

"Gwen, it's ninety degrees out."

"You want to wait ten minutes while I layer concealer, foundation, and powder on my shoulder?"

She rolled her eyes and sighed. "Just get in the car."

"That's what I thought." I smiled smugly. Zoe may have known more about fashion than I did, but she also knew better than to argue with me about baring my shoulder. My rule on this topic was ironclad:

No exposed shoulder. Not now; not ever.

Chapter 2

As soon as we arrived at the birthday party, I had to admit that Zoe had been right about the dress. In fact, I probably should've swapped the sandals for high heels too. The Romanescus didn't live in a mansion, at least not by Aaron Spelling standards, but it was larger than any house I'd previously ever entered.

"Six bedrooms, eight bathrooms, over nine thousand square feet," Zoe whispered as we walked through the marble entranceway and passed the graceful curved stairway where I could've easily imagined Scarlett O'Hara descending in a ball gown.

"How do you know these things?" I whispered back.

She flashed her phone at me. "Duh. Internet."

I tried to keep my jaw from dropping as the maid led us past the cook's kitchen, which was the size of half my house, through the great room with its massive stone fireplace and wood-paneled ceiling, to the double doors that led to the patio. We stepped outside and joined the hundred and fifty other guests milling about the sprawling lawn.

I recognized many of the children, since I spent my weekdays teaching them English at *Académie française de la Californie*. Isabella's father had invited the entire first grade class, plus their siblings and parents, as well as all of Isabella's teachers.

"The invitation said no gifts," I remarked as Zoe and I passed a table piled high with elegantly wrapped presents.

"You know how competitive the parents are," Zoe said.

"Do you think we should have bought her something?"

"No, we're her teachers. C'mon, let's get a drink and scope it out."

We each grabbed a mimosa from a passing waiter and commenced our tour of the backyard. We skipped the tennis court, which abutted the tall hedge that separated the Romanescu's property from their neighbor's, and headed in the direction of the infinity pool, where a handful of boys had discarded their shoes, rolled up their pants legs, and were splashing each other on the steps. I recognized the smallest of the four. He was in my second period class.

"Thomas, does your mom know you're in the pool?"

"Yes, Miss Andersen," the blond boy with the angelic face and the devilish personality replied. "She said it was okay as long as I stayed on the steps."

I doubted she had said it was okay for him to get his pants soaked, but I didn't want to interfere. Some parents appreciated it, but others acted as if any attempt to discipline their children undermined their authority. It was a fine line.

"Gwen, it's Saturday," Zoe admonished. "You're off the clock."

"I know, I know." But I couldn't stop caring about a child's welfare just because at that moment in time it wasn't my job.

"You need another drink," she said, and we headed off in the direction of the bar. But before we'd even made it halfway across the lawn, we heard the squeaky shout of "Miss Richards, Miss Richards," and we both stopped and turned around.

Jenny Ko—the only nine-year-old I knew who was fluent in three languages, hosted her own organic food blog, and was such an accomplished cellist that many considered her to be the next

Yo-Yo Ma—stood before us in her perfectly pressed party dress. "Miss Richards, my mother wants to talk to you. She's very upset about the grade you gave me last week."

Zoe sighed. Mrs. Ko was notorious at *Académie française* for fighting with any teacher who dared to give her daughter anything less than an *A*. "Jenny, can you please tell your mother that I have office hours next week and every week on Tuesdays between two and four, and on Fridays between nine and ten."

"She knows," Jenny said. "She told me to tell you it can't wait."

Zoe sighed again. I tried not to smile. "Off the clock, huh?"

She downed the rest of her mimosa in one gulp and handed me the empty glass. "If I'm not back in five minutes, call me," she said then followed Jenny into the throng of parents in the center of the lawn. "Don't forget!" she shouted right before she disappeared into a mass of women in brightly colored dresses and men in slacks and button-down shirts.

"I won't," I shouted back then laughed. All of the parents at *Académie française de la Californie* were high achievers and expected their children to be too. But Mrs. Ko was in a league by herself. It wasn't enough that Jenny's report card have straight *A*s. She had to have the highest grade on every exam, paper, and project in every class. I had no doubt that Jenny would be successful in all of her pursuits—Mrs. Ko would see to that—but I felt sorry for her too. That's a heavy burden to place on a child. When Jenny was my student, I always reminded her that learning was a process and that it was okay to make mistakes. I knew I couldn't counteract her mother's constant pressure, but I hoped that someday if she ever did fail at something, she wouldn't allow it to destroy her self-esteem.

I was about to call Zoe's cell (even though it had only been four minutes) when I saw her approaching. "That woman," she said, shaking her head.

I offered her my still three-quarters-full mimosa.

"That's not going to cut it," she said. "I need a martini."

Yes, they did have a full bar at a seven-year-old's birthday party. Along with hot and cold passed hors d'oeuvres, a buffet featuring beef, chicken, and several vegetarian dishes, and assorted pastries and fresh fruit for dessert, in addition to the three-tiered birthday cake that would've been appropriate for a wedding were it not for the pink icing and princess figurine perched at the top. In deference to the kids, the Romanescus also served pizza and burgers and had set up a sundae bar. And I was not the only adult at the party bypassing the key lime tartlets for a scoop of ice cream with chocolate syrup, whipped cream, and a maraschino cherry.

After an hour and a half of mostly eating and a little mingling, I was about to suggest that we leave when Zoe grabbed my arm. "Who is *that*?" she asked.

I followed her stare to the handsome dark-haired man who had just stepped out onto the patio holding a bouquet of birthday balloons.

"Uncle Stefan!" Isabella Romanescu screamed, then sprinted across the lawn, her pale pink dress billowing around her body and her dark curls bouncing around her head.

"Apparently that's Uncle Stefan," I said. "Can we go now?"

"Not until we find out whether he's single. C'mon," she said and jumped up from her chair. "I want to see if he's wearing a wedding ring."

"What about Evan?" I asked, scrambling to my feet.

Zoe waved her hand in front of my face. "Do you see a ring on this finger? No. And until there is one, I'm a free agent."

"Does Evan know that?" They'd been dating on and off for the last three years.

"Evan's opinion no longer concerns me," she haughtily replied.

Apparently it was an "off" week.

By the time we were close enough to discern that Uncle Stefan was not wearing a wedding ring, he was twirling Isabella in the air, and she was shrieking with delight. Isabella's nanny, Katarina, hovered nearby, trying and failing to convince Isabella to lower her voice. It wasn't until Isabella's father arrived, the only man at the party still wearing his suit jacket in the ninety-degree heat, and said, "Stefan, please put Isabella down," that her squeals subsided into giggles.

"Daddy, did you see what Uncle Stefan brought me?" Isabella said, holding out the armload of balloons that stood a head taller than she did.

"Yes, darling," her father replied. "I'm sure Katarina would be happy to put them on the table with the rest of your gifts." Katarina took the not-so-subtle hint and pried the balloons from Isabella's small fist.

"They're just balloons, Alex," Stefan said, setting Isabella down.

"Yes," Isabella's father responded, "I can see that."

Their words were innocuous, but their tone was not. I elbowed Zoe. "C'mon, let's go."

"And miss the fireworks?" she said. "Not a chance."

"Then you're on your own."

I turned to rejoin the rest of the party when Isabella caught sight of me. "Miss Andersen, you came!"

Dammit. I pivoted back and smiled as she ran across the patio and joined us on the lawn. "Of course I came, Isabella. Did you think I'd miss your birthday party?"

"And Miss Richards came too!" she said.

"*Joyeux anniversaire*, Isabella," Zoe replied in perfectly accented French.

"Show-off," I muttered loud enough for Zoe to hear, but hopefully no one else. Although all of the European teachers at *Académie française* were fluent in French, and were required to be since they taught all of their classes in French, most of the American teachers, who taught in English, were not. Zoe was the exception.

"Did you see my balloons?" Isabella asked.

"We did," I replied.

"And we'd love to meet your uncle," Zoe added.

"Zoe!" The "what the fuck" was implied.

"Why not?" she silently mouthed.

I shook my head but stayed quiet as Isabella led us to the corner of the patio where her father and uncle were huddled. We couldn't hear their words, but it was clear from the expressions on their faces and the way they were leaning into each other as they spoke that they were arguing. When they saw us approaching, they each took a step back and smiled. Only the grin on Stefan's face looked genuine.

"Uncle Stefan," Isabella said, "These are my teachers. Miss Andersen taught me reading, and Miss Richards is teaching me to paint good."

"Paint well," I corrected.

While the family resemblance was strong, Stefan had definitely lucked out in the looks department. Both men were dark-haired with striking sea-green eyes, which Isabella had inherited as well, but that's where the similarities ended. With his height, chiseled jawline, and disarming smile, Stefan could've been a model. Isabella's father was handsome too, but his features were softer, his hair wasn't quite as thick, and he didn't look like he spent two hours a day pumping iron in the gym. Stefan shook hands with Zoe first and then me, and we each told him our first names.

"Alexander Romanescu," Isabella's father said as he offered his hand to Zoe. He'd missed the second parent-teacher conference, and Zoe had been home sick the night of the first, so they hadn't already met. But we had, so I was surprised when he then reintroduced himself to me. "I've heard many wonderful things about you, Miss Andersen."

"Gwen," I said, trying not to be offended that he didn't remember me. "Isabella's lovely."

"Yes. If you'll excuse me," he said, then turned away from us and strode into the house.

"May I get you beautiful ladies a drink?" Stefan asked, obviously trying to make up for his brother's aloofness.

"I would love a drink," Zoe said.

I was hoping we could leave, but I knew better than to try to pry Zoe away from an attractive single man. "I need to find the ladies' room. I'll meet you back out here."

"Do you want me to show you where it is?" Isabella asked.

"I'm sure I can manage, but thank you anyway, Isabella."

"Okay," she said then grabbed her uncle's hand. The three of them headed off in the direction of the bar while I strolled into the house.

The room next to the front door, which I had assumed was a bathroom, was a bathroom. But when I reached it, a woman with two toddlers was ushering them inside. "This could take a while," she said and smiled apologetically. "I think there's another one off the game room."

I thanked her and went in search of one of the house's other eight bathrooms. I found the cavernous space with the billiards table and the pinball machine, which I assumed was the game room, but no bathroom nearby, so I headed to the kitchen, assuming that's where I would find the maid who would be able to direct me. The maid was nowhere in sight, but I did spot Isabella's father, whose back was to me. I called out to him, but he didn't respond, so I tapped him on the shoulder. Big mistake. He spun around so fast, half his red wine flew out of his glass and onto my dress.

"Please forgive my clumsiness," Alexander Romanescu said, staring at the burgundy stain that started at my left shoulder and ended in the middle of my waist. "You startled me."

"I'm sorry, I was just looking for the bathroom," I replied, still gaping in horror at my sundress, which was definitely ruined. My sky-blue shrug was only dappled with wine, so I thought it might be salvageable if I cleaned it right away. "Do you have any club soda?"

"Of course." He crossed the kitchen to the enormous stainless steel refrigerator and returned with a bottle of Pellegrino and an empty glass. He must've thought I was going to drink it.

"And a paper towel?"

He glanced around the kitchen, helpless. I searched too, but there wasn't a spindle or square in sight. "Maybe under the sink," I suggested.

He opened the kitchen cabinet and pulled out a white dish towel. "Will this do?"

"Only if you don't mind if I ruin it."

"After what I did to your dress," he said, nodding at it, "I think it's only fair."

I gave him a weak smile.

I'd just begun rubbing bottled water onto the stain when the maid walked in. "No, no, no," she said, and pulled the towel from my hand. "Take it off."

I didn't have much of a choice as she started tugging the sweater from my shoulders. Isabella's father and I stood transfixed as we watched her combine hydrogen peroxide and dish detergent in a mixing bowl then pour it onto the fabric and start blotting at it with the towel. The stain immediately began to lighten.

"That's amazing," I said and turned to Isabella's father. But he was no longer staring at the maid's handiwork; he was gaping at my shoulder instead.

Chapter 3

Since I couldn't cover my shoulder with the wet shrug, which the maid was still diligently cleaning, I crossed my arms over my chest and hid it with my hand instead. I pretended that I was suddenly chilly and was merely trying to warm myself up, but Isabella's father wasn't fooled. As soon as the three-inch birthmark shaped like a dog chasing its own tail, a dragon spitting fire, or a misshapen doughnut, depending on your point of view, was no longer visible, he jerked his head up and our eyes met, then we each quickly looked away. We both knew he had been staring at the ugly purple mark, and we were each embarrassed—him for his breach of etiquette, and me for its very existence. We spent the next few minutes focused on the maid as she scrubbed at the stain.

"There," she said, holding up my very wet shrug. There were only faint outlines where the wine stains had been just a few minutes earlier. "I'll get the rest in the laundry."

"Oh, you don't have to wash it," I said, grabbing the sweater from her hand.

"It's no problem," she said and looked to Isabella's father for confirmation.

"Yes," he said, "please leave Maria your address and she'll return it to you. Or she can drop it off at the school."

"That's not necessary," I said and tossed the wet shrug over my left shoulder. Although this maneuver was successful in covering my birthmark, it also had the unintended consequence of saturating the top left corner of my dress, as well as my bra underneath, turning both thin white fabrics see-through. We all stared down at my dark and protruding left nipple, and I quickly crossed my arms over my chest again.

"I should go," I said and sprinted to the patio door.

I found Zoe with Stefan. They were seated at one of the small bistro tables scattered across the lawn, deep in conversation. I hated to interrupt, but I didn't have a choice. Zoe was my ride home.

"What happened to you?" Zoe asked as she tore her gaze away from Stefan.

"An unfortunate accident with a glass of red wine," I said. "Can we go now?"

"You don't need to leave," Stefan said. "I'm sure my brother can find you a change of clothes.

Zoe took one look at my pleading eyes and set down her martini glass. "It was very nice meeting you, Stefan," she said and slid out of her chair.

Stefan stood up too. "It was my pleasure. Meeting both of you," he added as he glanced in my direction.

I smiled at him, then quickly turned around. The wet spot on the left side of my dress was slowly spreading. It had already saturated the center of my chest and was closing in on my right breast.

As Zoe and I hustled across the lawn, I apologized for pulling her away from Stefan.

"Don't worry about it," she said. "He's definitely a player."

"How do you know?"

"He asked for my phone number the second you left."

As always, Monday morning arrived too soon. I went through my usual routine of snoozing for an extra thirty minutes after the alarm rang, thereby making myself almost late for work. Luckily, this year I had first period free, so I could arrive at school at eight and still have time to down a latte and review the lesson plan I'd prepared the previous week before my work day really began.

My first teaching job after college was in one of Los Angeles's many overcrowded public schools. I'd had thirty-three students in my class, and I'd taught them all subjects except for art, music, and PE. Although some days I'd felt more like an overeducated babysitter than a teacher. Just keeping thirty-three six- and seven-year-olds quiet, let alone trying to teach them anything, was a challenge.

I transferred to *Académie française de la Californie* three years ago. I now had seventy-five students, but they were broken up into five classes of fifteen students each. I taught first grade English, which at *Académie française* meant letters, words, grammar, and spelling. I missed the variety of teaching different subjects, but I loved being able to give each of my students the individual attention they deserved. It was a trade-off I was willing to make.

Isabella was in my fourth period class, my third of the day.

At the prompting of their French instructor, Ms. Martin, all fifteen students chanted, "Good morning, Miss Andersen," as I walked into their classroom.

This was another difference from my public school experience and one reason I preferred teaching at *Académie française*. In public school, I was assigned a classroom and I remained in that one room for most of the day. At *Académie française*, the students remained in their classroom with their primary teacher for most of the day, and I, along with the music and art teachers, traveled to them. This meant that since I didn't have a classroom of my own, the school provided me with a tiny office instead. It was a minor luxury, but one that made my workday more pleasant. When I wasn't teaching or in a staff meeting, I could retreat to my office to grade tests and homework and plan and prep lessons for the following week rather than trying to concentrate in a noisy teachers' lounge. Growing up as an only child, I was used to spending time alone. As an adult, I craved it.

"Good morning, everyone," I chanted back and smiled at Ms. Martin as she slipped out the classroom door. "Did you all have a good weekend?"

There was some nodding, some giggling, and a few audible yeses.

"Good. So did I," I said and smiled at Isabella, who sat in the front row. "Let's get to work." The next fifty minutes passed in a haze of words, sounds, and picture books. By the time the 11:50 bell rang, I was ready for the only voice I heard to be the one inside my head. Unfortunately, Zoe had other ideas.

"Knock, knock," she said as she barged into my office carrying a huge cardboard box.

"What's that?" I asked.

"You tell me," she said, setting it down in the center of my desk. "And since when did you start shopping at Prada?"

I glanced at the shipping label, which had my name on it with *Académie française*'s address. "This must be a mistake." The only time I'd set foot inside the Prada store was when I'd met Zoe for lunch in Beverly Hills and she'd dragged me.

"Right. They accidentally found your name and address on the school manifest and decided to send you a present."

I rolled my eyes at her, but she said, "Just open it already."

I reached for my scissors and sliced into the packing tape. Inside was a black gift box with "Prada" inlaid in gold lettering. I read the attached card aloud:

Dear Gwen:
Please accept this small gift as my apology.
Sincerely,
Alexander Romanescu

"At least no one can accuse him of being long-winded," I said.

"Who cares about the note," Zoe said. "Just open the damn present already!"

I lifted the lid, unfolded the tissue paper, and pulled out a white cotton sundress.

"Holy shit!" Zoe said. "He bought you a Prada dress. What did you say to the guy?"

"Nothing. I swear." Although it didn't resemble the dress he'd spilled wine on other than that they were both white cotton—this one had buttons down the front, a belted waist, and an A-line skirt—I still assumed he'd sent it as a replacement.

When I shared my assumption with Zoe, she said, "Who buys a Prada original to replace a cheap knockoff? No offense, Gwen."

I wasn't offended. Zoe was right. I'd purchased my sundress on sale at Macy's for eighty dollars. You couldn't buy a pencil at Prada for eighty dollars.

"What do you think I should do?" I asked.

"Try it on, of course," she said. "I'll lock the door."

"I can't keep it!" I carefully refolded the dress and placed it back in the box.

"Why not?"

"You said it yourself. You don't replace a cheap knockoff with a designer original. This had to cost at least five hundred dollars."

Zoe snorted. "Try two thousand."

"Two thousand dollars for a freaking sundress?"

Zoe pulled the dress out of the box and held it up to her model-thin frame. "But look at the detail. Look at the lines. You don't get that kind of workmanship in mass-produced clothing."

Yes, this dress was nicer than my old dress. But it wasn't nineteen hundred and twenty dollars nicer. I would never have purchased a two thousand dollar sundress even if I could've afforded it, which I couldn't.

I held out my hand, and Zoe passed me the dress. When I started refolding it again, she said, "I thought you were trying it on?"

"No, I'm returning it." I appreciated the gesture, but it was too much.

"You can't. It's store credit only."

"Are you kidding me?"

"No," she said. "If you return it, you'll just have to buy something else."

I sighed and pulled the dress out of the box again. "Okay, go lock the door."

I didn't know how Isabella's father (or more likely, Maria or Katarina) knew my size, but the dress fit perfectly. I stood on my toes and twirled once, watching the A-line skirt billow around my legs.

"It's gorgeous," Zoe said. "Now we just need to get you some new shoes and a purse."

"That's not happening." The school year ended in two weeks and I was about to become unemployed. The past three summers I'd worked as a volleyball instructor at a day camp in Santa Monica. But the camp's enrollment was down this year and the owner told me he could only afford to hire one instructor this season, and that position was being filled by his daughter-in-law. I'd managed to score a part-time position at the Starbucks a few blocks from my house, and I figured I could pick up some babysitting gigs too, but I wouldn't be purchasing any new outfits until at least September.

"Then you'll have to borrow mine," she said. "When are you going to call him?"

"Call? I thought I'd just write a thank-you note."

"When someone brings a bottle of champagne to your birthday party you write a thank-you note. When someone sends you a Prada dress because he spilled wine on yours, you call."

I could've consulted Emily Post, but since we'd already wasted half of my lunch hour and I still hadn't eaten, I decided to take her word for it. I pulled the student-parent contact list from my desk drawer and located Isabella's name. "There's a home number, an office number, and a cell."

"Call his office," Zoe instructed.

"What if he's working? I don't want to disturb him."

"That's why you should phone him in the office. If he's too busy to talk, his secretary will take a message, and then the ball will be in his court."

"What ball? He sent a gift. I called to thank him. That's the end of it."

Zoe laughed. "You don't really think this is about your stupid dress, do you?"

I admitted the thought had crossed my mind too. I knew Alexander Romanescu was, if not single, then at least unmarried. Isabella and I had bonded at the beginning of the school year over the fact that we were both motherless, although she had lost hers at a much younger age than I had. "You're forgetting I met him last fall. If he was interested in me, he would've acted a lot sooner."

She shook her head, and the pencil she'd stuck in her hair to hold it in a makeshift bun fell out, causing her thick red locks to cascade around her shoulders. "You're Isabella's teacher. Everyone, even the parents, knows better."

She was referring to the scandal that had erupted at *Académie française* the year before I started teaching there. It was the reason my position had been available. The previous first grade English teacher was asked to resign after the school principal discovered he'd slept with three of his students' mothers during the course of the term. The fact that one of them was still married to her then-current, now ex-husband, hadn't helped either.

"I'm still her teacher," I noted.

"For two more weeks. That hardly counts."

"C'mon, you were there Saturday. Did he seem interested to you? He didn't even remember meeting me."

Zoe shrugged. "Maybe it was the sight of you covered in red wine. Seeing you in distress awakened his protective instincts, and now he wants to ride in like Prince Charming and sweep you off your feet."

I laughed. "You need to stop reading so many romance novels."

"Don't laugh. It could happen."

I laughed again. That's when she lifted the handset from my desk phone and held it out to me. "I'll bet you lunch at Annabelle's he asks you for a date."

She knew I was addicted to Annabelle's gooey, not too greasy, not too dry, veggie sourdough melt. I grabbed the phone from her hand. "You're on."

Chapter 4

"Gwen!" Zoe's mother abandoned the pot she was stirring and bustled around the kitchen counter to envelop me in a hug. I breathed in her familiar fruity scent and smiled. Mrs. Richards was the only woman I knew who wore perfume every day, even if she was just spending the afternoon gardening or straightening up around the house.

"Hi Mrs. Rich—I mean, Michelle." It still felt awkward calling Zoe's mother by her first name, although she'd told me I could when we were still in high school. I'd resisted for years, but once I'd graduated from college, she'd insisted.

"So?" she said, holding me at arm's length. "What's new? How's work? How come we never see you anymore?" It couldn't have been more than six weeks since I'd last visited, but before I could remind her of that, she said, "Zoe tells me you have a date tomorrow night."

"Zoe!" I spun around and flashed her an angry look. It was dinner, not a date. At least, not necessarily a date. When I'd called Alexander Romanescu's office to thank him for the dress, he was, as I'd expected too. busy to talk to me. But his assistant had asked if I was free for dinner the following night. Mr. Romanescu wanted to discuss something with me, she told me. Since I was free, as I was most nights, I agreed. And before I could ask what it was he wanted to talk to me about, she'd confirmed that I wasn't a vegan, a vegetarian, or kosher, then she'd booked us a reservation for eight o'clock at Bistro 66 and e-mailed me driving directions to the restaurant. By that point I was too embarrassed to ask, so I just thanked her and hung up.

Zoe started to defend herself when June, her younger sister, strolled into the kitchen and said, "It's about time you had a date."

"June!" Zoe and Mrs. Richards yelled simultaneously.

"What?" June replied. "You said it first," she added, nodding at her mother. Then she reached for the wooden spoon Mrs. Richards had left on the counter and tried to dip it into the pot bubbling on the stove. But before she could taste what smelled like tomato-basil sauce heavily laced with garlic, Mrs. Richards slapped her hand away.

"How many more days until you leave for college?" Mrs. Richards asked.

"Seventy-eight," June said and smiled as she strode past me on her way to the great room.

"If I let her live that long," Mrs. Richards mumbled, shaking her head at June before turning her attention back to me. "Gwen, you know I only said that because I care. We worry about you spending so much time alone."

"I know." I'd always felt welcome in the Richards's house. But after my parents died, Mrs. Richards had gone out of her way to make me feel like I was part of the family, which meant not only open invitations to dinner, but the right to intrude into my personal life as well. And I loved her for it. "You're right. I do need to make more of an effort."

"Did you hear that?" Mrs. Richards shouted to June, who had flopped down on the couch and was simultaneously flipping channels on the television while texting on her phone. "She said I was right."

June snorted. "That's because you're not her mother."

"Shut up, June," Zoe yelled.

"You shut up," June shouted back.

"Girls!" Mrs. Richards screamed louder than both of them, before patting my arm. "Dinner won't be ready for another hour if you and Zoe want to go out back."

"Excellent idea, Mother," Zoe said and flipped off her little sister.

"Mom, did you see what Zoe just did?"

"Girls!" Mrs. Richards yelled again, even louder this time.

"C'mon," Zoe said and grabbed the shopping bag from my hand.

I followed Zoe out the sliding glass door and across the backyard to the freestanding garage her parents had converted into a guesthouse years earlier. Zoe's grandmother had lived there for a short time when we were in high school. After she'd died, Zoe's father had used it as a home office. Then when Zoe had decided to move back to LA after two years at Parsons, the Richards had converted the one-story guesthouse into a two-story loft. Zoe had been living there ever since.

Some of our friends thought she was crazy to still live with her parents at age twenty-seven, even if it was a separate apartment with its own entrance. But I understood. She paid half as much rent as she would've paid if she lived anywhere else in the city, and the Richards's longtime housekeeper came over once a week and cleaned Zoe's apartment too. Plus she had twenty-four-hour access to a fully stocked kitchen (which usually contained many delicious leftovers) and a laundry room (where she could sometimes guilt her mother into washing her clothes for her). I thought she'd be crazy to live anywhere else.

I followed Zoe up the spiral staircase and sat on the edge of her queen-size bed while she opened all four doors to her closet, which ran the length of one wall. "I'm thinking blue," she said, pulling out a pair of four-inch platform heels. "Or you could go orange," she added, fingering a pair of espadrilles. "But I prefer blue."

I slipped my feet into the size seven cobalt slingbacks with the crisscross straps. I normally wore a six and a half, but I could get by in sevens if they ran small or I added an insole. "What do you think?" I said, holding the dress up in front of me.

"I can't tell like that," Zoe said. "You need to put it on."

I grumbled but pulled off my jeans and T-shirt and slipped the white Prada dress over my head. "Now what do you think?"

"Perfect."

"I still need a—"

"Sweater, I know." She crossed to the double dresser and pulled open both bottom drawers.

"How about the blue one?" I asked, kneeling next to her on the floor. It was almost the same shade as the shoes.

She wrinkled her nose. "Too matchy-matchy, especially if we go with the blue purse."

By the time June texted us to tell us dinner was on the table, Zoe had discarded all of her cardigans in favor of a short, three-quarter-sleeve seersucker jacket, to which she added a dozen silver bracelets and dangling earrings since I'd refused to wear the scarf she'd insisted would "make the outfit." (The phrase "We're not in Paris, Zoe" may have crossed my lips.)

"Gwen, so good to see you," Zoe's father said when we appeared in the dining room.

I shuffled to his end of the table and gave him a hug. "Thanks, Mark." For some reason it was much easier calling Zoe's father by his first name than it was calling Mrs. Richards by hers. I didn't know why.

"Sit, sit," he said, motioning to the chair next to him. "So Michelle tells me you have a date tomorrow night."

I couldn't help but laugh. Did they really have nothing better to gossip about than my next-to-nonexistent love life?

June glanced away from her phone long enough to roll her eyes at her father. "Did it ever occur to any of you that maybe Gwen doesn't want to talk about it?"

"Sorry, Gwen," Mark said, patting my hand. "I didn't mean to pry."

"I don't mind," I said truthfully. I loved that they cared enough to pry. "It's just that it's not really a date."

"Of course it's a date," Zoe said, passing me the platter of chicken parmigiana. Mrs. Richards always cooked it when I came to dinner because she knew it was my favorite.

"Zoe, he didn't even get on the phone."

"Really?" Mrs. Richards asked.

"Really," I replied, then repeated back my entire ninety-second conversation with Alexander Romanescu's assistant.

"Hmmm." Mrs. Richards took a sip of her wine.

"I wouldn't put too much stock in that, Michelle," Mark said between bites of pasta. "He was probably just busy."

Mrs. Richards swirled the wine in her glass. "Too busy to pick up the phone and ask Gwen out on a proper date?"

Mark set down his fork. "He's taking her to a *very* nice restaurant. I'd call that a proper date."

Mrs. Richards placed her wineglass on the table so she could use both hands for emphasis. "He's not even picking her up. She has to drive herself and meet him there. How is that a proper date?"

"Actually, I prefer to meet the guy at the restaurant," Zoe chimed in. "Especially on a first date."

"Why?" her mother asked.

I shot Zoe a silent warning glance across the table. I knew the real reason—because when her dates picked her up at home Mrs. Richards always found an excuse to either drop by Zoe's apartment or be outside when they were leaving so Zoe had no choice but to introduce them. It was one of the few downsides of her current living arrangement. But that wasn't something Mrs. Richards needed to hear. Luckily for both of them Zoe was a quick thinker. "So if he's a total dud I can make an excuse and cut the date short," she lied.

"Zoe! I raised you better than that."

Zoe rolled her eyes. "Mom, it's not that big a deal. It's not like the guy is having a good time with me either."

"You don't know that," Mrs. Richards said. "Maybe he's just shy. Some men are, you know."

They continued their argument, and I thought I was off the hook until Zoe's dad, in a transparent attempt to stop the fighting, said, "Michelle, I'll bet you five dollars Gwen's dinner tomorrow night is a date."

Zoe's habit of wanting to wager on everything was an inherited trait.

Mrs. Richards snorted. "Five dollars! That's not even worth my time. But I did see a lovely cocktail ring at Bloomingdale's this morning."

"I'll just assume I'd rather not know what it costs," he said. "And what do I get if I win?"

Mrs. Richards smiled seductively. "I'll tell you when we're alone."

"Gross!" June yelled at the same time Zoe shouted, "TMI, Mom!"

"Well where do you think you girls came from?" Mrs. Richards shouted back. "Do you think the stork brought you? Because I've got stretch marks that prove otherwise."

I glanced around the table and smiled. Although I always appreciated the solitude when I returned home, I loved the boisterousness of the Richards's house too. Someone was always arguing with someone, and it was even worse when Zoe's brother, Daniel, had lived there as well, but it was equally obvious that they all loved each other and would do anything for one another. Which is what I envied Zoe most. Except for my mother's senile aunt, who lived in a nursing home in Florida, and her children, who I'd never even met, I was alone. If I ever found myself in trouble—real trouble, the kind where one turned to one's family for help—I was on my own.

Chapter 5

I walked into Bistro 66 at five minutes after eight. My lateness was intentional. I didn't want to seem too eager, just in case this was a date. Although I was pretty sure it wasn't. Mrs. Richards was hoping so too (she really wanted that ring). And just so I wouldn't feel bad, before I left last night, she promised/threatened to scour her address book for an eligible bachelor to fix me up with. I shuddered at the thought.

The last eligible bachelor Mrs. Richards had introduced me to turned out to be one of my top five worst dates. He asked me to dinner and then, after spending the entire meal talking about himself, suggested we split the bill. I would've been happy to go home after that, but he insisted we go clubbing instead. I agreed to accompany him for one drink, but he downed three in quick succession then refused to leave the bar. The evening ended when I took a taxi from the club in Hollywood back to my house in Westwood with a stop-off at an ATM first because I didn't have enough cash left to pay for the ride home.

I told the host I was meeting Mr. Romanescu, and he immediately brought me to a table for two where Isabella's father was already seated. He stood up and pulled my chair out for me, which was of course unnecessary but still very gallant. Then the waiter appeared out of nowhere and laid the napkin across my lap before I even had a chance to locate it on the table.

"Gwen, I'm so glad you could make it," Isabella's father said as the waiter handed me the menu. "Do you like champagne?"

"Sure," I replied, although I couldn't remember the last time I drank any.

"Two glasses of the Bollinger Cuvee," he said to the waiter, who immediately disappeared. Then he turned back to me. "You're a brave woman wearing white again."

I smiled at his attempt to break the ice, which needed breaking. I still wasn't sure whether this was a date or a business meeting, but either way, I was a jumble of nerves. I could feel the sweat seeping from my underarms onto Zoe's seersucker jacket.

"I thought you might like to see your gift." As soon as the words left my mouth, I realized my mistake. I was probably supposed to pretend he went to Prada himself to pick it out. Thirty seconds into dinner and I'd already managed to insult the man. "Which was totally unnecessary," I added. "I mean, it's not like you ruined my dress on purpose. I know it was an accident." Geez, could I be screwing this up any worse?

He raised his eyebrows in response, and I thought I saw a slight smile cross his lips, but he remained silent. I think we were both grateful that the waiter chose that moment to return with our champagne.

"To beautiful dresses and the women who wear them," Alexander said and lifted his glass.

Apparently Stefan wasn't the only charming Romanescu. Since I didn't trust myself not to say anything stupid, I smiled in response before gulping down a mouthful of the bubbly golden liquid. It was icy cold and delicious.

Alexander picked up the wine list. "Do you prefer red or white?" he asked.

Champagne *and* wine? Normally, if I drank at all, it was only one. And I didn't always finish that. I'd have to pace myself. "No preference," I said. Beyond red and white, my wine vocabulary was limited to "sweet," "dry," and "good."

"I generally prefer red, but I'm not sure I want to tempt fate. Perhaps a nice Sancerre." He signaled to the waiter and asked him to bring us a bottle of something that sounded very French before turning his attention back to me. "Do you know what you'd like to eat?"

I quickly scanned the menu as the waiter described the specials of the day. After we ordered—pear salad and sautéed scallops for me, gazpacho and grilled salmon for Alexander—the waiter disappeared with our menus then returned with the wine. After Alexander pronounced it acceptable, the waiter poured us each a glass, left the bottle in an ice bucket next to the table, and disappeared again.

I finished my glass of champagne and moved on to the Sancerre, which was neither too sweet nor too dry, but was unbelievably good.

"Do you like the wine?" Alexander asked as I took another sip.

"Yes," I said. "It's delicious."

He seemed pleased.

"So what did you want to talk to me about?" The alcohol had worked its magic; I was already starting to relax.

"That can wait," he said and topped off my wineglass even though I'd only taken two sips. "Tell me about yourself. Are you from LA?"

Hmmm. That sounded more date-ish than business meeting-ish. Mrs. Richards would not be pleased.

"Yes, I grew up here. You?" I asked even though I knew he wasn't from Los Angeles. He didn't speak with an accent, but something about his overly formal manners made me think he wasn't raised in Southern California, and possibly not even the US.

"London," he said, "until I was eleven. Then my family moved to Connecticut. Do you like teaching?"

"I love it." Then I thought about the conversation I'd had with Jeremy Wright that morning explaining why picking his nose in class was not acceptable behavior. "Most of the time, anyway. Do you like"—I realized I had no idea what he did for a living—"what do you do?"

"I run my family's business."

"Oh, what kind of business?"

He waited until the server finished presenting our appetizers and topping off our wineglasses before he answered. "We invest in companies."

"What kinds of companies?" I asked, spearing a candied walnut from my plate.

"Traditionally, manufacturing and natural resources. More recently, financial services, although that's more Stefan's bailiwick than mine. How's your salad?"

"Delicious," I said. "And your soup?"

"Excellent. The key to good gazpacho is to use only the ripest tomatoes, and never, ever tomato juice."

"I'll try to remember that." Although if I didn't stop drinking the wine, I wouldn't be remembering much of anything. The problem was I couldn't tell how much I'd consumed because whenever the level in my glass started to dip, either Alexander or the waiter would top it off again.

By the time we were perusing the dessert menu, I could barely stand upright. I'm not sure how I made it to the ladies' room and back without falling down. If Alexander, or Alex as I was now calling him, noticed how drunk I was, he pretended not to. He even insisted on ordering two glasses of port and a cheese plate when I begged off on coffee and dessert.

The last thing I remembered about the evening was wondering how the hell I was going to get home.

Chapter 6

I rolled over and burrowed my head deeper into the down pillows. Then I remembered I didn't own any down pillows. My eyes flashed open and I stared across the vast expanse of white—snowy pillowcases, milky sheets, pearly comforter. It wasn't until I managed to lift my head that I caught sight of the honey-wood dresser across from the bed and the gilt-framed mirror above it. Early morning light was streaming in through the sheer fabric covering the windows, casting the entire room with a pinkish hue. For a moment, I thought maybe I was dreaming. Then I tried to sit up. My stomach lurched, and my brain pounded against the inside of my head. No, this hangover was definitely real.

I sank back against the pillows and tried to remember how I'd gotten here, then I realized I didn't even know where "here" was. I tossed the comforter aside and staggered to the window happy to note that I was still wearing my bra, my panties, and my dress. I recognized the Romanescu's backyard from the stunning canyon view, which was even better from the second floor of their house than it had been from the lawn below. As I stumbled back to the bed, I spotted my shoes and purse under the chair in the corner and my jacket neatly folded on the seat. On top of my jacket was a note. I tossed the comforter aside (happy to note that I was still wearing my bra, my panties, and my dress), and staggered to the window.

I unfolded the heavy cream paper with shaky hands. Whoever wrote this deserved an *A* for penmanship. I had to stare at it for a few seconds before the elegant cursive writing stopped jumping around on the page.

Dear Gwen,

You were in no condition to drive home last night so I brought you back to my house. You'll find your car next to the garage; the keys on the front seat. Isabella wakes between six thirty and seven, and she leaves for school at seven forty-five. It would be better if you didn't venture downstairs between those times—less explaining for both of us. I took the liberty of calling Simone Lorens last night (she's a friend) and letting her know you were ill and not to expect you today. We'll talk soon.

Alex

"He did what?" I asked the empty bedroom. I knew I needed to act, but the words made no sense to me, and I could barely sit up. I checked my watch, which I happily noted was still on my wrist. It was a quarter to seven, so per Alex's request, I couldn't leave for another hour. I pulled my phone out of my purse and called Simone Lorens, the school principal. Luckily, my call went straight to her voice mail. I left a message letting her know that I was ill and wouldn't be able to make it to work today. I'd have to call Alex later to find out specifically what he'd told her so we could keep our stories straight.

Who does that—calls in sick for someone else? Especially someone they hardly know. But my head was pounding too hard for me to attempt to reason that one out.

I glanced around the room and spotted three doors. The first one I opened led to a huge walk-in closet, which was empty except for an extra blanket and two more pillows. I was luckier with the second, which opened onto an en suite bathroom. Someone had left a bottle of water and a container of aspirin sitting out on the counter. I downed four pills, drank the entire bottle of water, then collapsed back onto the bed.

The next time I opened my eyes it was nine thirty. I still felt horrible, but I was able to hold my head upright so I donned my shoes and jacket and ventured downstairs. I followed the sound of the vacuum cleaner and found Maria in the living room. As soon as she spotted me, she shut it off. "Good morning, Miss Andersen. Can I get you anything? Coffee or something to eat?"

"No, thank you. I just didn't want to sneak out without saying goodbye." Especially not if the house had an alarm system, which I assumed it did. "And thanks for the aspirin and water." I guessed she was the one who had left them for me.

She smiled blankly but stayed silent, which compelled me to continue blathering.

"I really appreciate it."

Blank stare.

"A lot."

Continued blank stare.

Ultimately my curiosity overtook my mortification. "Um, do you happen to know how I made it upstairs last night?" It seemed slightly less embarrassing than asking if she was the one who had put me to bed.

"You walked up."

At least no one had to carry me. "With Mr. Romanescu?"

"Sí," she said.

I just couldn't bring myself to ask the next question. And she probably wouldn't know the answer anyway. "And the garage is that way?" I asked, pointing toward the hallway.

"Sí, I'll show you."

The sight of the black convertible brought forth a snippet of memory—Alex and I speeding along Sunset Boulevard with the top down. One mystery solved. My hair was so knotted this morning, I'd assumed it could only be the result of either horrible bed-tossing nightmares, which I'd frequently suffered from as a child and still occasionally experienced as an adult, or mind-blowing sex, which unfortunately I hadn't been getting much of lately.

I closed my eyes and was struck by a flash of Alex behind the wheel smiling at me, asking me if I was sure, and me telling him I wanted to feel the wind through my hair. I didn't know if I wanted to remember any more.

"Are you all right?" Maria asked.

"Yes," I said, opening my eyes again. "Mr. Romanescu said my car was outside."

Maria tapped a fluorescent switch on the wall, and one of the three garage doors groaned to life and lifted. We stepped out into the sunlight, and I found my Honda parked in the driveway, the keys on the front seat exactly where Alex had said they'd be.

"I'll open the gate," Maria said and retreated into the house.

By the time I'd driven to the end of the long stone driveway, the gate was unlocked, and I pulled out onto the street.

The enormity of what I'd done struck me on the drive home. Not only did I go out on what was possibly a date with the father of one of my students—a definite no-no—but I'd gotten so drunk that I couldn't even remember what had happened. And then, as if that wasn't bad enough, he had to call my boss and tell her about it. I still couldn't wrap my head around that one. I'd be lucky if I didn't get fired.

My cell phone started ringing as I pulled into my driveway. I knew it was Zoe without even checking the display. She'd already sent me three text messages and left a voice mail earlier this morning. I only answered it so I wouldn't have to listen to the obnoxious ringtone she'd downloaded to my phone. "I'm alive."

"Then where the hell are you, and why is Amy covering your class?"

"I called in sick."

She sucked in her breath. "Oh my God, what happened last night?"

"Nothing. I'm hungover."

"Hungover!" She shouted so loud I had to hold the phone away from my ear. "Since when do you drink enough for a hangover?"

"Since last night, apparently. Isabella's father really likes his wine."

"So I was right. It was a date."

I let my silence speak for me, which also afforded Zoe a moment to gloat.

"Did you sleep with him?" she asked.

"Of course not! At least, I'm pretty sure I didn't."

"You don't even remember?"

I slipped my key into the lock and pushed open my front door. "I told you. There was a lot of wine."

"Holy shit! I mean, this is just so unlike you."

My sentiment exactly. What was I thinking? "Listen, my head's killing me, and I feel like I'm going to puke. Can we talk about this later?"

"Sure," she said. "I'll stop by your place on my way home. Just promise me you won't spend the entire day obsessing over this. It's okay to let your hair down every once in a while."

"I promise," I lied. Once my head stopped throbbing, I planned on spending the rest of the day chastising myself for my embarrassingly inappropriate behavior.

Six hours later, Zoe walked into my living room. She plopped down on the side chair, kicked off her high-heeled sandals, and slapped her bare feet onto the coffee table. "Don't worry," she said. "No one knows what you did."

"You can't be sure," I said, adjusting the pillows under my head while maintaining my supine position on the living room couch.

"Trust me, this is good gossip. If anyone at school knew you got wasted and spent the night with Isabella's father, they'd be talking about it."

"Not *with* him, just at his house. And Simone knows. Alex called her." I shook my head. "I still can't believe he did that."

"I'm sure he thought he was helping."

"How could calling my boss and telling her I'm too drunk to come to work possibly be construed as helping?"

Zoe leaned back and sighed. "First of all, he didn't tell her you were drunk, he told her you were sick. Big difference."

"You don't know that." I'd left a message for Alex when I'd arrived home this morning, but he still hadn't returned my call.

"Trust me, if he'd told her you were too drunk to come to work today I would've heard about it. The entire school would've. And I'm sure Simone would've already called you to discuss your *petite indiscrétion*," she said in a perfect imitation of our French principal.

"But why did he call her at all?"

"Maybe he thought you wouldn't wake up in time to call in sick yourself."

"He could've woken me. I was at his house for God's sake." I pushed myself up onto my elbows. "And that's another thing, why did he bring me back to his place instead of here?"

Zoe rolled her eyes at me. "Obviously because he didn't know where you lived."

"He could've asked!"

"Maybe he tried and you were too drunk to answer him."

That shut me up. Briefly. "He could've checked my driver's license."

She threw her arms up. "Yeah, because the first thing everyone does when they move is update their driver's license. C'mon, Gwen, cut the guy some slack."

"I'm telling you, this whole thing makes no sense. You think he drugged me?"

She burst out laughing. "No, Gwen, I don't think he drugged you. I think you drank too much wine, and he took you home. But since you woke up fully clothed in the guest bedroom, I'm assuming nothing happened."

"I wasn't entirely clothed. He took my jacket off. And my shoes."

"So you're thinking what—he has a foot fetish? He got you drunk and took you back to his place so he could fondle your toes?"

This time we both laughed. Then I remembered his fascination with my birthmark when he'd spilled wine on my dress. "Is there such a thing as a birthmark fetish?"

"Eew."

"I know, but you didn't see the way he was staring at it." I shuddered involuntarily. "It was more than normal curiosity. Way more."

While Zoe was Googling fetishes, my cell phone rang and Alex's name popped up on the screen. "Should I answer it?"

"Duh," Zoe said. "How else are you going to find out what happened last night?"

I snatched up the phone and walked into the kitchen. Zoe followed.

"How are you feeling?" Alex asked when I'd said hello.

"Okay," I said. "How are you?"

"Ask him what happened last night," Zoe whispered.

I shushed her and turned away so I could concentrate on Alex's voice instead of hers.

"I was hoping to see you tonight," he said.

"Tonight?"

"He wants to see you tonight?" Zoe asked.

I spun around to face her and put my finger to my lips before telling Alex, "Tonight's not a great idea. I'm not really feeling my best."

"I can imagine," he said and laughed.

"Yeah, about that. I need to apologize. I normally don't drink that much."

"It was my fault," he said. "I never should've ordered the port."

Or the bottle of wine after the champagne, I thought but didn't say.

"Let me make it up to you," he continued. "Tonight, dinner, no alcohol."

"That's not necessary."

"I insist," he said. "Besides, you still owe me an answer."

"An answer to what?"

"Whether you're coming with us to Romania."

Chapter 7

I opened my front door to Alex, who was standing before me with his tie still knotted, his shoes still polished, and an In-N-Out takeout bag in his hand.

"I thought we'd eat in tonight," he said. "You do like burgers, don't you?"

"Sure," I said, inhaling the scent of onions and fried grease. Earlier in the day the thought of food had made me queasy, but now my stomach grumbled. "Come on in."

This time I was glad I hadn't taken Zoe's fashion advice. She'd told me I needed to change out of my sweatpants and into something nice—at least black pants and a cute top, if not a dress. I agreed with her about ditching the sweats, but I'd opted for jeans, a white T-shirt, and a three-quarter-sleeve orange cardigan instead.

Alex followed me into the kitchen and unpacked the food while I set the table. He'd purchased one of everything, which from In-N-Out meant a hamburger, a cheeseburger, a double-double, and fries.

"Good for hangovers," he said and smiled before biting into the double-double.

I'd never seen anyone eat In-N-Out wearing a suit and tie before, but I kept that observation to myself. I took another bite of my hamburger and had to agree about it being a hangover cure. This was the best I'd felt all day. "About last night," I said and wiped my mouth with a paper napkin. "I'm a little fuzzy on the details."

His smile widened. "The sex was fantastic."

My jaw dropped, and I was sure all the color had drained from my face.

"That was a joke!"

I smiled feebly.

"Don't worry, Gwen, I only sleep with women who are at least semiconscious." When I didn't respond, he added, "That was a joke too. Obviously a poor one."

"No, it's just…"

"You don't remember what happened last night?"

"I'm missing some bits and pieces." Pretty much everything between the entrée and dawn. "I know we drove back to your house with the top down, but I'm still a little unclear how my car ended up in your driveway. Obviously I didn't drive it."

"I had the valet drop it off at the end of the night."

"They do that?" I'd never heard of such a thing.

"If you make it worth their while they do. What else?"

"Why did you call my boss and tell her I was sick?" I wasn't trying to be bitchy, it just sounded that way. I really would've preferred if he had not done that.

He dipped a french fry into the pool of ketchup on his plate. "Forgive me if I overstepped, but when you started serenading me with 'I Feel Pretty' on the drive home, I assumed you wouldn't be up to teaching this morning."

Not only did my jaw drop, I'm pretty sure my entire face sank. "I did not!"

"Yes." He nodded, the smile from his lips reaching all the way to his eyes. "You also treated me to a cappella versions of the 'Jet Song' and 'America.' I'm sorry to say we made it home before you were able to finish 'Officer Krupke.' You were having some trouble remembering the lyrics."

I buried my face in my hands, wishing this was all a big lie. But *West Side Story* was my favorite musical, and each time he mentioned another song title, an image of me singing flashed in my head. I prayed for a giant sinkhole to open underneath my kitchen and swallow me whole. It didn't happen, and eventually I had to look up.

He was still grinning. "You have a lovely singing voice."

I buried my face in my hands again. I didn't even know where to begin. "Alex, I——"

"It's all right. I realized fairly quickly you're not much of a drinker."

So why did you keep pouring me more wine? But I was in no position to judge.

"What else can I tell you?" he asked.

I didn't want to hear any more, but there were questions I needed answers to. "What did you say to Simone, specifically? We need to keep our stories straight."

One eyebrow shot up. "Our stories?"

"If you told her I got food poisoning and I tell her I fell off a ladder, I think she'll suspect."

"I wasn't that specific," he said and reached for another french fry. "I told her I thought you were ill and I doubted you'd be able to work today. That's all."

"But she knows we went to dinner?"

"Yes, she knows. But I don't believe I mentioned the name of the restaurant."

That would make it easier. I didn't want to slander anyone.

The BlackBerry he'd set next to him on the kitchen table started vibrating. "Excuse me," he said and picked it up. "*Alo?*"

That's the last word I understood. I spoke some Spanish from having studied it in high school and college, and a little French from working at *Académie française*, but he wasn't speaking either of those languages. It sounded like a cross between Russian and Italian.

He pushed back from the table and ambled into the hallway. Since he'd finished his burger and polished off most of the fries, I cleared our plates and loaded them into the dishwasher. After a few minutes of silence, I ventured into the hallway too. Alex was still holding his BlackBerry, but he was no longer talking. He was staring at the framed photos on my wall.

I used to tease my mother that it was our wall of shame. Disneyland, Hawaii, every school graduation since elementary. If it could be classified as a milestone, my mother had snapped a photo and hung it in the hallway. I'd always wanted her to take them down, at least the really old ones. But after my parents died and I moved back into my childhood home, I left them up. Now that they were gone, I appreciated the memories.

"Your parents?" he asked, nodding at the picture of the three of us from my college graduation. My dad still looked handsome in his dark suit, and my mom was still thin and attractive. And standing between those two ruddy blonds who could've easily passed for brother and sister instead of husband and wife was me in my cap and gown—dark hair, pale skin, and a head shorter than both of them even in my heels.

"Yes," I replied.

"You don't favor either one of them."

A sentiment I'd heard many times before. It used to upset me when I was younger. It didn't anymore. "No, I was adopted."

"Really," he said and turned to face me, his curiosity obviously piqued. "Do you know your birth mother?"

"No," I answered without elaboration. I was used to this question too. Everyone asked, presumably because most adopted children searched for their birth parents at some point in their lives. I'd never felt the need to.

My parents adopted me when I was three days old, and they were the only mother and father I ever knew. One of my earliest memories was of them telling me how special I was because they chose me. Over the years they answered my questions as best they could (they didn't have much information), and when I turned eighteen, they offered to help me search for my birth mother if I wanted to. All they had was her name—Anna Smith, which sounded so generic they questioned whether it was real—and an address in Northern California where she had lived at the time I was born. They also told me she'd had my name and address since the day I was adopted. I think that was what clinched it for me. My birth mother had had eighteen years to come and find me if she'd wanted to. She hadn't. Since she obviously had no interest in me, I decided I had no interest in her either.

Alex continued to stare at the photos until I said, "I think we'd be more comfortable in the living room."

"Of course," he said and followed me to the front of the house. He sat down on the couch, and I took the opposite end, leaving a reasonable distance between us. "You realize you still haven't given me your answer."

I'd been able to piece together the details from our phone conversation earlier in the day combined with comments Isabella had once made in class. She and her father were spending the summer in Romania at the Romanescu family's estate. Her current nanny, Katarina, was getting married in August and didn't want to leave the country for six weeks, so Isabella's father wanted to hire me as a temporary au pair.

"I know Isabella would love to have you," he continued.

"Isabella's great," I replied.

"Is the money not adequate? I thought I'd been generous, but if you disagree I'm sure we can work something out."

"It's not the money." He'd already offered me triple what I'd earn working at Starbucks for the summer. I'd be able to afford to fix the leak in my roof and still have enough left over for a new pair of shoes, several pairs if I didn't shop at Prada.

"You have a passport, I assume. If not, that's easily remedied."

"No, I have a passport." I'd applied for one my senior year in college because Zoe and I were supposed to backpack through Europe after graduation. But that was before my parents had died.

"Then what? You like Isabella, no?"

"I love Isabella. It's just"—how could I tell him I wasn't sure I wanted to spend six weeks in a foreign country working for someone I hardly knew and didn't entirely trust—"a big decision. I need some time to think about it."

"All right." He stood up. "But please don't take too long. We're leaving in two weeks."

Chapter 8

I ordered my men to round up the traitors, and their wives and children too. I watched from across the field as they built the stone structure that would become their tomb. Some of them knew. I could see it in their eyes. The rest thought if they followed my instructions I'd allow them to return to their homes unharmed but for a few days of manual labor. These parasites considered that punishment enough for their misdeeds. Fools. Every one of them deserved the fate they were about to receive.

Once completed, I had my servants set a table inside so the traitors and their families would willingly enter. They cared more for their stomachs than their heads. Once all were ensconced, we locked the doors and set the roof on fire. I breathed in the acrid scent—not just burning meat, but burning human flesh—and listened to their screams. The fire burned so bright it lit up the night sky, the heat so massive it erased the autumnal chill. I sighed with relief. Justice had finally been served. Vengeance was now mine.

I woke up screaming and covered in sweat, and I did what I always did when I had one of my nightmares—I flipped on every lamp in the house and turned on the television, hoping the light and the noise would chase the demons away. It never did.

"Wow, you look even worse today than you did yesterday," Zoe said as she sauntered into my office.

I glanced up from the spelling test I'd been grading and set down my red pen. "Thanks a lot."

"Seriously," she said, plopping down on the chair across from me. "What happened last night?"

"Nothing. I just didn't get much rest."

She shot me a wicked grin. "I thought you said Alex left after dinner."

"He did. I had a nightmare, then I couldn't fall back asleep."

She grabbed an apple from the bowl I kept on my desk and bit into it. I flinched at the *crack* from the crisp McIntosh. If she noticed, she pretended not to. "Like you used to have?" she asked.

"Yes." I reached for the pen again and started doodling on the corner of the test paper. Zoe knew I didn't like to recite details, even though I always remembered them. They were too disturbing. In my daytime life, I was a nonviolent person. But in my nightmares, I routinely slaughtered people. And sometimes, like last night, hundreds of people.

She took another bite of the apple, but this time I was prepared for it and didn't jump at the *crunch*. "It's been a long time," she said. "What do you think brought it on?"

I'd spent the predawn hours pondering that same question. The best explanation I could come up with was anxiety. I'd promised Alex I'd give him an answer to his offer by the end of the week. "I think it's the Romania thing. I know I should go, that I should want to go—"

"Yes, you should. This is a great opportunity for you. Six weeks getting *paid* to tour a foreign country."

"I'm not getting paid to *tour* a foreign country. I'm getting paid to be a nanny."

"Yeah, on an estate with a butler and a maid."

"Zoe, this isn't *The Sound of Music*. It's a couple who work for him and don't speak any English."

She took another noisy bite of the apple and spoke with her mouth full. "You'd be crazy to turn this down."

"I know." Hence the anxiety. I'd already called the manager at Starbucks and asked if he could give me extra hours. It wouldn't close the gap between my hourly rate as a barista and what Alex had offered to pay me, but I thought if I could get it down to double instead of triple, maybe I could find a way to justify saying no. But the manager told me he already had too many employees and not enough shifts and if I had a better offer somewhere else, I should take it.

"I think it'd be good for you," Zoe said. "And not just because of the money. It'll force you out of your comfort zone."

"I like my comfort zone. It's comfortable."

She smiled at the excuse she'd heard many times before. I'd never been overly adventurous, even when my parents were alive. But since their fatal car accident five years ago, I'd become even more risk-averse. Moving back home was a no-brainer. As their only child, I'd inherited everything. I'd used the insurance money to pay off what was left of my parents' mortgage. Mrs. Richards had encouraged me to sell it right away. A single twenty-two-year-old girl didn't need the responsibility of a house, she'd insisted. But I couldn't let it go.

I'd spent the first six months sleeping in my old bedroom, which still had the Bono poster tacked to the wall above my twin-size bed. It wasn't until Zoe and Mrs. Richards invited themselves over for the weekend and forced me to clean out my parents' closets and buy a new bed that I switched rooms. Over the years, I'd redecorated—modern living room furniture, a new kitchen table, a bigger TV—but I'd never been able to part with the wall of shame. And I rarely traveled, despite constant pressure from Zoe.

Every summer the Richards family vacationed in a foreign country for two weeks. Each year they'd choose a different locale and rent a house or an apartment to live in while they explored and soaked up the culture. They always invited me, and I always found an excuse not to go. Usually I was working—even without a mortgage, I still had to pay the taxes, the upkeep, and all my other bills. And until last year, I'd had Chester, my parents' incontinent and almost blind cocker spaniel, to look after too.. But as much as I needed to work, and as much as I loved Chester, that wasn't the real reason. I just had no desire to stray far from home.

No one understood it, least of all James Kessler, my college boyfriend. I'd met James in freshman English, but we hadn't started dating until senior year. By the time we were a couple, he and his buddies had already planned to backpack through Asia after graduation. Since Zoe and I were going to tour Europe at the same time, we all agreed to meet up in Turkey at the end of our respective trips. I'd had to cancel mine when my parents died, but James didn't cancel his. When he returned three months later, he thought we'd pick up where we'd left off. I tried, but according to James, I just wasn't as much "fun" as I used to be, and eventually we broke up. I'd had boyfriends since then, but none of the relationships had lasted longer than a few months.

Zoe constantly teased that I was going to end up as a stereotypical spinster schoolteacher. It didn't sound so bad to me. I liked living alone. I could do what I wanted when I wanted, and the only person I had to worry about was myself. And the less I dated, the less I wanted to date. But for sex, which I did miss, I could've easily given up dating entirely.

It was the knock on my office door that pulled me out of my reverie. I stopped doodling and looked up. Simone Lorens, the school principal, was standing in my doorway.

"Gwen, do you have a moment?" she asked.

"I was just leaving," Zoe said and hurried out of the room.

Simone shut the door behind her then sat down in the chair Zoe had just vacated.

I swallowed hard. Once I'd made it through the school day without being summoned to her office, I'd thought I was in the clear.

"Feeling better?" Simone asked.

"Much," I said. "But I think it'll be a while before I order scallops again."

I smiled. She didn't.

"You look a bit pale. You should go home and rest."

I lifted the stack of spelling tests from my desk. "I will, as soon as I finish grading these."

She nodded and lowered her voice as if she was afraid someone was listening in, which was silly. Zoe had no reason to eavesdrop since she knew I would call her the minute Simone left and repeat back every word. "I wanted to speak to you about Alex. Isabella's father," she added as if there might be another one we both knew. "I hope you're not allowing one bad experience to color your view of his proposal."

One bad experience? Alex swore he hadn't told Simone about my getting drunk and spending the night. Obviously it was my guilty conscience reading into her words. "His proposal?"

"*Oui*. When he told me Katarina would not be accompanying them to Romania, I recommended you. Did he not make you a good offer?"

Ah, now the pieces were falling into place. "No, it was a very good offer."

"Then why have you not accepted? Alex thinks it's because of him, that you don't like him."

He'd told me they were friends, but I hadn't realized they were close enough for him to confide in her. "I don't dislike him. It's just that I don't really know him, and I'd be living in his house." I didn't understand how this wasn't an issue for all the live-in housekeepers and nannies or the families they worked for. I would think it'd be just as weird to have a stranger living in your home as it would be to be the stranger who'd moved in.

"I can assure you, Gwen, Alex is an honorable man. You have nothing to worry about."

She hadn't seen how much wine he'd poured me the night of our dinner. Nor was I going to tell her. "I know, Simone, it's just…I don't particularly like to travel."

"*C'est fou.* That's crazy," she repeated in English. "Travel is good for you. It broadens the horizons. Take the job, Gwen."

I knew it wasn't an order, that it was just her bossy personality, but it still sounded like one.

Chapter 9

"What am I forgetting?" I asked Zoe, who was helping me repack my suitcase for the third time. I was determined to keep my checked bag under the fifty-pound limit, even though Zoe insisted Alex could afford the overweight baggage fee. Although counterintuitive, I discovered the key was to pack the heaviest items in the carry-on bag.

She stopped stuffing socks into every available nook and cranny and looked up. "Whatever it is, you're not going to be able to fit it in here anyway, so you might as well forget about it."

I mentally scanned my checklist. I'd already packed all the clothes—mostly shorts, T-shirts, khakis, and jeans, with two bathing suits, a couple of sundresses, and a pair of black pants that could be dressed up or down as necessary—shoes, and toiletries.

"Camera?" Zoe asked.

"In the carry-on bag."

"Tennis racket?"

"Alex said they have one I can borrow. And the way I play, it won't matter what I use." Isabella had been taking lessons for two years, so no doubt she could already kick my ass on the tennis court.

"Hat?"

"Thank you!" I ran to my closet and pulled my wide-brimmed straw hat from the top shelf.

"Aspirin?" she asked.

"Already packed."

"I meant where are they? All this repacking is giving me a headache."

I pulled the non-liquid toiletries bag out of my carry-on and tossed it to her. All the liquid toiletries were packed in a gallon-size Ziploc at the bottom of my suitcase.

She held up my two vials of prescription sleeping pills. One was past its expiration date but likely still worked. The other I'd just refilled that morning. "I thought you stopped taking these."

"They're for jet lag," I lied.

"You need sixty pills for jet lag? How many flights do you have?"

I grabbed the toiletries bag from her hand, located the aspirin bottle, and tossed it to her. Then I stuffed the sleeping pills back in.

"I'm serious, Gwen. It took you a long time to wean yourself off of these. I can't believe you're going back."

I sighed. I wasn't happy about it either, but I had no choice. "It's the only way to control the nightmares." Ever since Alex had asked me to accompany him and Isabella to Romania, I'd started having them again. Not every night, but often. The only way I could be sure I wouldn't wake up screaming and in a pool of sweat was to pop a pill before I went to bed.

"I think you should find a new sleep doctor."

"Why? They never help." My parents had taken me to half a dozen sleep specialists when I was a kid. The answer was always the same: it's anxiety, she'll outgrow it. They were partially right. The nightmares occurred with much less frequency as I'd gotten older, but they never disappeared completely. I'd tried yoga, massage, warm milk, chamomile tea, and therapy. But the only thing that worked consistently was the sleeping pills. I couldn't swear I didn't have the dreams on the nights I took a pill, but if I did, I didn't remember them, which was good enough for me.

The only downside of the sleeping pills was that they were addictive. Eventually I couldn't fall asleep without them. It had taken months of sleep deprivation before I had eventually weaned myself off the drugs, but I was never able to give them up entirely. I rarely used them anymore, but I liked knowing they were there if I needed them.

"We're not done with this conversation," she said, tossing the aspirin back into my toiletries bag and zipping it shut, "but I need to go."

The moment I'd been dreading. "Are you sure you don't want to come with me?" I asked as I hugged her.

"You'll be fine," she said, squeezing me back. "And I'll be in London for two weeks. Ask Alex for the weekend off and come visit me. It's only a few hours by plane."

"He's not going to give me the weekend off from a six-week job."

"You never know unless you ask," she said, disengaging herself from my grip.

"You should come to Romania for the weekend. I'm sure I can get him to agree to that."

"We'll see," she said, which I knew meant no but sounded better that way.

I walked her to the front door, gave her one more quick hug, then returned to my bedroom to finish packing. I thought I'd packed everything I needed, but I scanned my closet and double-checked all of my dresser drawers again anyway. I found it in the back of my now almost empty underwear drawer. The tiny painting of Saint George I'd had since I was a baby. My family wasn't religious, but my parents told me it came from my birth mother, so I kept it as a talisman. I used to bring it with me to exams for good luck.

I fingered the small oval image, which was half the size of the palm of my hand. It felt like wood under the paint, but it had been sealed with some sort of protectant and mounted on a metal plate, so it was virtually indestructible.

"What the hell," I said to my empty bedroom as I tossed it into my carry-on bag. "You can never have too much good luck."

Chapter 10

Alex and Isabella arrived at one, even though our flight wasn't leaving until six o'clock that evening. As soon as I saw the black town car pull into my driveway, I embarked on a final sweep of the house to confirm that I'd turned off all the lights and locked all the doors and windows. Since I lived in a two-bedroom, one-bath bungalow, it didn't take long. I was down to the last room when Alex knocked on the front door.

"Is that it?" he asked, staring down at my medium-size suitcase and carry-on bag.

"And my purse," I said, grabbing it off the coffee table.

"You pack light."

I smiled in response, knowing he'd retract that statement if he ever lifted my bags. Luckily for him, the limo driver carried them and hoisted them into the trunk.

Alex held open the car door for me, and I found Isabella sitting in the center of the enormous backseat, coloring book open on her lap, crayons everywhere. "Miss Andersen!"

"Hi, Isabella. Are you excited for your trip?"

She nodded. "Daddy says we can go swimming every day."

Ugh. My least favorite activity. It wasn't the swimming I minded so much as the bathing suit it required. There was no way to hide my birthmark no matter what sort of swimsuit I chose.

When I swam in the ocean I wore a rash guard like the surfers did, but those always looked out of place in a swimming pool. Over the years I'd tried various brands of water-resistant foundation, but they couldn't withstand the constant toweling off and reapplication of sunscreen. The only solution was to wear a T-shirt or cover-up and stay in the shade, but I didn't think that was what Isabella had in mind.

"That sounds like fun," I said as I grabbed the crayons and stuffed them in the empty box so I could sit down. "But maybe we can find other things to do too."

Alex walked around to the other side of the town car and slid in, so he and I were on opposite ends of the backseat with Isabella sandwiched between us. And even though I'd called Katarina yesterday and she'd assured me that she would pack Isabella's "plane bag," I'd still stuffed a puzzle, a sticker book, and a deck of Go Fish cards into my carry-on. It appeared they would all be unnecessary. As soon as the driver started the engine, Alex handed Isabella her iPad (yes, she had her own) and the coloring book was soon forgotten in favor of Draw Something and Fruit Ninja. I doubt she would've even noticed if I'd jumped from the car out onto the freeway.

Since Isabella was entertaining herself, I pulled my Romania guidebook out of my purse. Once I'd decided to take the job, I thought I should learn something about the country where I'd be residing for the next six weeks. I skipped ahead to the chapter on Transylvania, ominously referred to by the author as "the land beyond the forest." I was ashamed to say that before I'd purchased the guidebook, I wasn't even sure Transylvania was a real place. I thought it might've been a fictional land dreamed up by Bram Stoker for his infamous *Dracula*. I definitely hadn't known it was located in Romania.

Alex glanced up from his BlackBerry and caught sight of my book. "Ah, Dracula," he said in a voice sounding vaguely like Bela Lugosi. "Are you a fan?"

I shrugged. "I've seen the movie."

"Which one?" he asked.

"How many are there?"

He laughed. "Quite a few."

"I know it's a tourist trap,"—the guidebook had said as much—"but I think it'd be fun to visit Bran Castle." It was known as Dracula's Castle even though, according to the guidebook, Dracula, or more accurately his real-life namesake, Vlad Tepes, had never set foot there. Alex and I hadn't discussed my work hours, but I assumed I'd have some time off even if it was just one day a week. If not, I figured I'd ask Alex if I could bring Isabella to some of the sites I wanted to visit. I thought I could make a convincing argument for their educational value. Even a tour of Bran Castle would be more informative than splashing in the pool all day.

"Sure," he said. "I'd be happy to take you."

"Oh, you don't have to take me." Going with Alex was not part of the plan. "I mean, won't you be working?" I thought that's why I was there—to look after Isabella so he could work uninterrupted. Despite my behavior the night of our dinner, I was trying to keep this relationship professional.

"That's the advantage of being the boss, Gwen. You get to set your own hours."

When we arrived at LAX, I kept Isabella entertained while Alex checked in the three of us and our luggage. After an ice cream cone, a trip to the newsstand to purchase more snacks for the plane (Alex didn't insist on healthy foods, which made life with a seven-year-old much easier), and several rousing games of Go Fish, Isabella was happy to play on her iPad while we waited in the departures lounge. Once we were on the plane, it was even easier. The onboard entertainment system included a choice of several Disney movies, and Isabella contentedly watched one while eating dinner. When her eyes started closing, I helped her into her pajamas while the flight attendant turned her spacious seat into a six-foot-long flat bed. (Yes, Alex had booked three first-class tickets. No cramped coach seating for the Romanescus—or their nanny.) Within ten minutes, Isabella was out for the night.

Unfortunately, I couldn't say the same for me. I was afraid to take a sleeping pill in case Isabella woke up during the flight. But I was too scared to fall asleep without one. If I had a nightmare, my screaming would rouse not only Isabella, but the entire first-class section of the plane. I spent the night watching one mediocre movie after another on the seat's built-in screen, interspersed with brief naps when I could no longer stay awake.

"Did you sleep at all?" Alex asked me when Isabella woke him the next morning. She didn't think he should miss breakfast even though both I and the flight attendant assured her that they'd bring him food later if he was hungry.

"Why? Do I look that bad?" I'd avoided the mirror when I'd used the lavatory. I could barely keep my eyes open, so it didn't require much effort.

"Just tired." He pulled his watch out from under his shirt-sleeve. "We're not landing for another two hours. Why don't you try to get some sleep?"

"No, I'm fine." I planned on hitting up the flight attendant for a second espresso.

I was happy I'd had that extra jolt of caffeine when we landed at Charles de Gaulle Airport. We only had a one-hour layover, and our flight to Romania was departing from the opposite end of the terminal. We barely made our connection. I didn't remember falling asleep on the flight from Paris to Bucharest, but I must've because Alex woke me when the plane started to descend.

We landed at dusk, but by the time we'd traversed immigration and retrieved our luggage, it was dark outside. My first impression of Romania was the airport parking lot. It looked just like the parking lots back home. Alex had arranged for a car and driver, but instead of ferrying us to the Romanescu estate, he drove us into Bucharest.

Forty minutes later, Isabella and I were wandering through the Grand Hotel's marble lobby while Alex checked us in. The bellman stacked all of our luggage on a cart and led us up to the third floor, where he unlocked the door to a two-bedroom suite. Alex claimed the master, which meant Isabella and I would be sharing the room with twin beds.

"I hope you don't mind," Alex said as the bellman flipped on lights and pointed out amenities. "It's just for tonight. You'll have your own room when we get to the house."

Mind? I was spending the night in a European capital in a luxurious five-star hotel. I certainly wasn't going to complain about sharing a bedroom. "No, I'm fine."

"Good," he said. "Are you hungry?"

None of us were, but we were trying to get on the right schedule, so we ordered dinner in the room. After I helped Isabella with her bath and tucked her into bed, I wandered out to the living room section of the suite. Alex was sitting at the desk, typing on his laptop. I didn't want to disturb him by turning on the television, so I opened my Romania guidebook instead.

Although Dracula was a fictional character, Bram Stoker had borrowed the name from a real-life historical figure—a fifteenth-century Wallachian prince known as Vlad Tepes or Vlad III, nick-named Vlad the Impaler for his preferred method of killing people. The Dracula moniker originated with Vlad's father, Vlad II.

In the early fifteenth century, Vlad II was inducted into the Order of the Dragon, a society of European knights whose purpose was to defend Christianity from its enemies, which at that time meant the Muslim-faithed Ottoman Turks. Once inducted, Vlad II became known as Vlad Dracul, or translated into English,

Vlad the Dragon or Vlad the Devil. Since in Romanian, the addition of the suffix "a" signifies "son of," Vlad Tepes became known as Vlad Dracula.

While Vlad Dracula committed many heinous acts, sucking people's blood from their bodies was not one of them. He was, however, infamous for his cruelty. He took pleasure not only in killing, but in torturing his victims. It was this character trait that led to his notoriety, even in his own day, as a "bloodthirsty" despot.

In one of the many horrific tales told about him, Dracula invited all of the city's poor, sick, and disabled to his palace for a royal banquet. Dracula considered anyone who didn't work, no matter what the reason, to be lazy—a mortal sin in his mind. According to legend, when the townspeople arrived at Dracula's castle they were ushered into the great hall, where they were served all the wine they wanted and all the food they could eat. When the beggars had had their fill, Dracula ordered the doors locked and the dining hall set on fire. Every person inside was burned alive.

In another infamous anecdote, Dracula ordered his troops to round up thousands of the city's merchants and noblemen whom he believed were disloyal. He then had them all impaled on the same day. To further relish his accomplishment, he commanded his servants to set up his dining table under the rows of impaled corpses so he and his knights could enjoy the spectacle while they feasted. When Dracula noticed one of the knights holding his nose in an effort to avoid breathing in the horrid smell of disemboweled corpses, Dracula ordered the loyal soldier impaled on a stake higher than all the rest so that he would "always be above the stench."

"What are you reading?" Alex asked.

I jumped. I was so engrossed in the stories I'd forgotten Alex was even in the room. "Nothing," I said and slammed the book shut.

He glanced down at the cover. "The history is fascinating, no?"

"Yes." And disgusting too.

"Well, I'm going to bed. Good night."

I waited until I was alone again before I lay back on the couch and reached for my book. I hadn't been reading long before my eyelids started feeling heavy. I closed them just for a moment.

"Are you sure?" I asked, admiring her full breasts. She was as pleasing in the sun as she was by candlelight.

"I am," she said and placed my hand on her waist. "Your child is inside me."

I grabbed a handful of flesh and squeezed as if in a vise. "The bath woman told me otherwise."

She tried to free herself from my grip, but I held her in place. I enjoyed watching the panic spread across her lovely visage.

"She is wrong, my love. I promise you, I am with child."

I kissed my mistress's warm lips for the last time. Then I pulled my dagger from its sheath and slit her open from groin to breast. Her eyes widened in horror, and she writhed and screamed as I ripped out her insides.

"No, my sweet, there is no child."

I licked her blood from my knife and left her in the dirt. The wolves would enjoy their next meal.

I screamed. Then my eyes flashed open.

Chapter 11

Alex was standing over me, his hands gripping my shoulders. "Gwen, wake up!"

I pushed him off of me and jolted upright. My heart was pounding against the inside of my chest, and my T-shirt was sticking to me.

"Daddy?" a small voice sounded.

We both spun around. Isabella appeared in the bedroom doorway, her hand shielding her eyes from the light. Alex ran to his daughter. "It's all right, Isabella," he said, scooping her up in his arms.

"I heard a bad noise," she said.

"I know, honey, but it's gone now. Let's go back to bed."

I sat on the couch, willing my heart to stop pounding. By the time Alex emerged from Isabella's bedroom, quietly shutting the door behind him, it was almost beating normally again.

"She's asleep," he whispered.

"I'm so sorry," I whispered back. "I never meant to wake her." And I certainly never meant to have that awful dream. I shuddered again just thinking about it. I was always a man in my nightmares, which I'd never understood, and they seemed to take place in the past, but exactly where and when I never knew. Tonight's dream, however, had a new twist. Usually I murdered from afar, ordering others to do it for me. This was the first time I'd actually plunged the knife in myself. And I'd licked the blood off! What was that about? I could still taste the tangy metal in my mouth.

Alex ran his hands through his hair and nodded. "Does this happen to you often?"

"Sometimes," I said. "But I have pills that help."

"Then you should take them."

"I will. I didn't plan on falling asleep on the couch."

He nodded again and glanced down, both of us suddenly realizing he was dressed only in striped boxer shorts and a white T-shirt. This was the first time I'd seen him wearing anything other than a business suit. He had nice legs.

I averted my eyes and stared at the coffee table until he said, "I'm going back to bed. Will you be okay?"

I glanced up. Deep lines crossed his forehead, and he seemed genuinely concerned. "Yes, I'll go take a pill."

The sleeping pill worked. I fell asleep in the bed next to Isabella's and woke eight hours later having no memory of my night. I found Alex and Isabella in the living room eating breakfast at the round table next to the windows.

"Good morning, Miss Andersen," Isabella said.

"Morning," I said and smiled. I wasn't much for conversation before I'd had my coffee.

"Join us," Alex said, motioning to the table set for three. "There's plenty. Or order whatever you like."

I sat down next to Isabella and poured myself a cup of coffee from the polished silver pot.

"Did you hear the noise last night?" she asked. "It woke me up."

That was a conversation I preferred not to have. "Isabella, I'm not your teacher anymore. You really should call me Gwen."

Isabella glanced over at Alex. "*Miss* Gwen," he said.

"Miss Gwen," she repeated, turning back to me before taking a huge bite of her pancakes. After three more bites, she was finished. "Do you want to play a game, Miss Gwen?"

"Sure." I could handle Go Fish even on my first cup of coffee.

"Isabella, I need to talk to Miss Gwen." Alex reached for the hot-pink Nintendo resting on the sideboard behind him and handed it to her. "You can play by yourself for a little while."

She took the video game to the couch and was soon engrossed in the antics of the animated men dancing across the three-inch screen.

"More coffee?" he asked. I nodded and he refilled each of our cups. "About last night," he continued.

Ugh, him too? "I'm really sorry about that. I promise it won't happen again."

"I know," he said. "I was just wondering, what were you dreaming that had you so upset?"

I didn't even have to think about it. Of course I would lie. "I don't remember my dreams."

"Really? I would have thought something that traumatic would stay with you."

"Nope," I said, reaching for the cream and sugar.

"You're sure?"

"Yup," I said, stirring the condiments into my cup.

"Nothing at all?"

Jesus Christ, was he never going to let this go? "I should probably shower and get dressed. What time are we leaving?" It wasn't just about needing to get away from him. He and Isabella were already in their street clothes. I was the only one still wearing pajamas.

"The car should be here in about an hour."

The driver was ten minutes late, so I used the time to take advantage of the hotel's free Wi-Fi. I'd just sent Zoe a short e-mail letting her know I'd landed safely and would write more later when Alex handed me a cell phone.

"For you and Isabella," he said. "It works internationally too, but I'd prefer if you want to call home that you do so from the house."

"Thanks," I said and stuffed it in my purse.

He nodded at my open laptop. "And we have Wi-Fi at the house too."

"Good to know," I said and shut my computer, unsure whether that was intended purely as an informative statement or whether it was meant as a subtle hint that I should be paying attention to Isabella instead of surfing the web.

As we drove out of the city, Alex pointed out the sights—the Romanian Athenaeum, a domed and pillared concert hall with a flower-filled park out front; the National Museum of Art, located in what was once the royal palace; the Odeon Theatre, which from the outside looked like an old-time movie house; and Revolution Square.

"What's that?" I asked, pointing to the triangular marble pillar with what appeared to be a black metal bird's nest impaled on the top. Apparently, impaling was big here in Romania.

"*Memorialul Renaşterii,*" he said. "Rebirth Memorial. It was commissioned to commemorate the Romanian Revolution."

I nodded, recalling what I'd read about it in my guidebook when I wasn't engrossed in Dracula stories. The Romanian people had overthrown the Communists in a violent revolution in 1989.

"It's very controversial," he continued. "Mainly because of its design."

"It's very...abstract." I was trying to be diplomatic.

He grinned. "Yes, some have even called it ugly." He spoke to the driver in Romanian, then turned back to me. "We'll show you a monument that's more attractive."

I was starting to feel guilty for acting like a tourist instead of a nanny, but when I glanced over at Isabella, she was contentedly watching cartoons on her iPad. Alex didn't seem bothered by her addiction to electronics. In fact, at times he seemed to encourage it. So I kept my mouth shut. It wasn't my place to tell him how to raise his child. I was just the well-paid babysitter.

I stared out the car window as we left the city center. The scenery quickly changed from beautiful neoclassical marble buildings to ugly high-rise cement blocks. "The Communists," Alex said, confirming my suspicions.

As we approached the traffic roundabout, Alex pointed to the stone arch in its center. "Do you recognize it?" he asked.

"It looks like the *Arc de Triomphe*." I'd never seen it in person, but we had a poster of it on the wall at school.

"*Arcul de Triumf*," he said, which sounded just like *Arc de Triomphe*, but with a slightly different accent. "*Bucuresti* was once known as the Paris of the East."

I thought it odd that he took such obvious pride in his Romanian heritage since he hadn't grown up there. My father's parents were from Denmark and my mother was actually born in Sweden, but I knew very little about either country.

An hour later, the landscape changed dramatically. Occasionally, we drove through a village with a cluster of houses; otherwise, it was nothing but flat farmland sprinkled with haystacks and the occasional horse-drawn cart slowing down everyone's progress on the road.

Isabella finally looked up from her computer screen. "I have to go to the bathroom."

I was glad she'd spoken up because I had to go too. Alex said something to the driver in Romanian and we pulled into the next gas station. After Isabella and I used the restroom, we returned to the car, but Alex was missing. I didn't know if the driver understood English, but I asked anyway. He pointed down the road. Alex was standing at a makeshift fruit stand up ahead.

"You want to go for a walk?" I asked Isabella.

But the driver motioned for us to return to the car. "I drive," he said.

"Do you like red grapes?" Alex asked me when we joined him. There were bunches of them spilling out of a milk crate, nestled between containers of green grapes, plums, and assorted vegetables. Each crate was stacked face out on an incline of wooden slats, forming a wall of produce.

"I prefer green," I said.

He shook his head. "They're not sweet. Taste."

I glanced at the man behind the fruit stand, who I assumed was the owner. He nodded and motioned for me to test a few. It seemed everyone understood at least some English even if they didn't speak it. I popped a green grape into my mouth and was immediately sorry I had. Alex was right. They weren't sweet.

Alex handed Isabella and me each a few red grapes. "Mmmm," we both agreed. Then I bit into a seed, which surprised me. They only sold the seedless variety at the grocery stores back home. Isabella and Alex spit their seeds onto the ground, so I did too.

Alex purchased several bunches of red grapes, which the man behind the stand split into two bags and handed one each to me and Isabella. (And yes, I did rinse them with my bottled water before I allowed her to eat any more.) Alex also purchased half a dozen tomatoes that were so fresh and ripe they actually gave off a scent, and a few heads of garlic too. "To ward off the vampires," he said and winked at me.

Then we were back on the road again—Isabella watching cartoons on her iPad, Alex reading on his, and me staring out the window at the scenery. Shortly after the fruit stand, the landscape changed again. The flat farmland disappeared, replaced by rolling green hills dotted with trees, houses, and power lines. The drive also slowed as the road steepened and turned into a series of hair-pin turns. For a brief while, we were in the middle of a forest, and it was like driving through a tunnel of trees: the sky was completely blocked out, and the driver had to turn on his headlights. Then the terrain opened up again, and the rolling green hillsides were replaced by forested ones with snow-peaked mountains in the distance.

"Are those the Carpathians?" I asked. I'd read about them in my guidebook, which referred to them as the Transylvanian Alps.

Alex briefly looked up from his computer, said "yes," then returned to his screen.

"Does that mean we're in Transylvania?"

"Yes," Alex replied without glancing up this time. "That's where we live."

Spending six weeks in Transylvania sounded much spookier than spending the summer in Romania. I was glad I'd be home long before Halloween.

I was starting to worry about needing another bathroom break (surprised that no one else, especially Isabella, didn't need one too) when we turned off the main road. Ten minutes later, the driver pulled into the gravel driveway of a three-story house. Although "house" was an understatement. Estate was the appropriate term, or maybe villa. It had six rows of tall windows on either side of an imposing front entrance, a full second story above that, and a third half story with much smaller windows that practically touched the pitched roof. The ground level also contained a row of short windows, which I assumed meant it was a basement of some sort.

I stared at the house open-mouthed as the driver unloaded our luggage from the trunk. Finally I turned to Alex and asked, "Are you royalty or something?"

He laughed. "Afraid not. This house was built by my great-great-grandfather, a very successful politician in his day. One who also married well."

"I'll say."

He laughed again. "You should've seen it when we got it back. Not so impressive then, I assure you."

"Got it back. From where? Or should I say from whom?"

"The government. When the Communists took control after World War II they confiscated houses like these. Many prominent Romanian families were exiled or fled. After the revolution, a democratic government was formed and they passed restitution laws. It took years of legal maneuvering, but we finally got our land back. The condition, however..." He shook his head. "After fifty years of neglect we essentially had to gut the inside and start over."

The front door opened, and an older couple wandered out. The woman immediately started speaking in Romanian. She gave Alex a kiss on each cheek and did the same to Isabella. The man just shook Alex's hand and mumbled a few words. I stood off to the side and watched, unsure what I was supposed to do. The couple seemed unsure too. From the looks darting back and forth between them and me and Alex, I guessed they were asking him who the hell I was.

"Gwen, I'd like you to meet Cristina and Dimitri Popescu." He then said something to them in Romanian, the only part of which I understood was "Gwen Andersen," but I assumed he was introducing me to them too. I shook hands with each of them, which seemed to surprise them. Maybe it was something only Romanian men did.

Alex and Cristina continued talking in Romanian while Dimitri and the driver brought our luggage inside the house and Isabella hopped around enjoying the *crunch* her shoes made every time they hit the gravel driveway. When the driver left, Alex and Cristina walked toward the entrance, so I grabbed Isabella's hand and followed.

The house was even more impressive from the inside. The front doors opened onto a huge vestibule, at the back of which was a double staircase with steps in both directions that led to the second floor. To the right of the entrance was a massive living room filled with a mixture of contemporary and antique furnishings, including an ebony baby grand piano polished to a high sheen. To the left was a den, which looked much more modern with its leather furniture, built-in bookshelves, and large flat-screen TV.

We followed Cristina—who Alex called "Doamna Cristina," but Isabella called "Tanti Cristina," and I hadn't called anything yet because I didn't know which one I was supposed to use—into a high-end kitchen. It looked the same as any you might find in the US with its granite countertops, Viking stove, and Sub-Zero refrigerator. Alex and Cristina exchanged a few more words, some of which I presumed had to do with food because he handed her the tomatoes and garlic he'd purchased at the fruit stand, and she started pulling plates and cutlery from various drawers. Isabella and I had finished the grapes during the drive.

Cristina remained in the kitchen, and Alex, Isabella, and I continued touring the rest of the house, which consisted of a dining room, billiards room, maid's room, and home office on the first floor, and so many bedrooms on the second floor that I lost count. The only ones I had to remember were mine and Isabella's, which were in the same hallway. Alex's room—more of a suite than a bedroom—was on the other side.

My room was modest by comparison. It only contained a queen-size bed with an upholstered ottoman at the foot, a small dresser, two nightstands, a chair and side table, and a huge armoire in lieu of a closet. Although the furnishings—all dark wood and flower prints—had an antique look, the en suite bathroom sported all the modern amenities, including a handheld shower clamped to the wall above the oversized tub.

I accompanied Isabella to her room, which looked like it could've been ripped from the Pottery Barn Kids catalog with its white wood furniture and princess bedding, and I helped her unpack. Then she went downstairs to watch television while I searched for Alex. I found him in his office talking on the phone. He motioned for me to sit down in the chair across from his desk while he finished his call.

"Hungry?" he asked when he'd hung up. "Lunch should be ready in a few minutes."

"Not really." I'd just eaten half a pound of grapes in the car.

"Eat something anyway," he said. "Otherwise Cristina will think you don't like her cooking."

I was glad he'd brought her up. "So she's the housekeeper?"

"For the summer. She keeps an eye on the place the rest of the year when no one's around. Her husband, Dimitri, makes repairs. He'll also drive you and Isabella into town in the mornings for her tennis lessons."

"I can drive us." I assumed Alex housed a car here, although I'd yet to see it.

"I don't think so."

"I can drive a stick shift if that's what you're worried about." I couldn't recall if Alex's car back home was an automatic, but I knew Europeans loved their manual transmissions. I enjoyed driving them too—my dad had taught me—on the rare day when I wasn't stuck in LA traffic. I was looking forward to testing one out on those twisty mountain roads.

He shook his head. "It's not safe."

"What do you mean? Do you get a lot of carjackings here?" They hadn't mentioned that in the guidebook.

"No, nothing like that. I meant the roads are dangerous. I'd prefer it if Dimitri drove."

"If you don't mind, I'd really feel more comfortable driving myself." It's not that I loved driving so much as I loved my independence. I didn't want to be trapped in the house all day and dependent on Dimitri, who I could barely communicate with. I assumed he had other work to do and wouldn't be available to chauffeur us around the clock. What if I wanted to take Isabella somewhere when he was busy? Or what if there was an emergency and he wasn't around? It would be better for all of us if I drove.

"It's not up for debate," Alex said.

It's not up for debate? Since when? I would've continued the argument, but Cristina appeared in the doorway. She said a few words in Romanian, which Alex translated to "lunch is ready" and stood up.

"What am I supposed to call her?" I whispered to him as we followed Cristina into the dining room. "Tanti or Doamna?" I thought my pronunciation was close with the first word, but I knew I'd mangled the second.

"Cristina is fine," he said. "And she'll call you Gwen."

Cristina and Dimitri left after lunch, and Alex gave me a tour of the rest of the property, or at least the part of it I was likely to use. The estate encompassed over thirty hectares, approximately seventy-five acres, much of it mountains. We walked around to the back of the house, where the grassy lawn led to a forty-foot swimming pool surrounded by lounge chairs and umbrellas. Past the pool, the ground sloped downward to a small lake. Surprisingly, there were no other houses on the water. When I pointed this out to Alex, he shrugged, which I assumed meant that he owned the surrounding land too.

Near the lake was a wooden shack that Alex referred to as the boathouse.

"You have a boat too?" I had known from his house in LA that he was well-off. Perhaps even wealthy. I hadn't known until we'd arrived in Romania that he was filthy rich.

"It's just a rowboat."

"What does that mean? Only a fifty-foot yacht instead of seventy-five?" It came out a lot bitchier than I'd intended. "Sorry, I'm just—" I wasn't about to say "taken aback by your wealth," so I said, "jet-lagged."

He stopped walking and turned to face me. "Gwen, this property is owned by my family. My mother, to be exact. She inherited it from her parents. The only house I own is in LA"

Somehow that made me feel better.

The tour ended at the garage, which contained four bays but only one car—a black Audi. "Mine," he said before I could ask. "And no, you can't drive it."

But that didn't mean I couldn't rent one of my own.

Chapter 12

I was the first one to wake the next day. Normally I wasn't a morning person, but my internal clock was off from the jet lag and the time difference—Romania was ten hours ahead of LA The sleeping pills probably weren't helping, but I wasn't about to stop taking them.

I waited until the sun rose before I ventured downstairs to the kitchen because I didn't want to turn on the hallway lights, not that I knew where to find the light switch. I planned on exploring the house further as soon as I was alone. At a minimum, I wanted to count the bedrooms and bathrooms. Zoe would want to know.

The coffeemaker was on the counter, and I located the beans in the pantry, but they were whole, not ground, and I couldn't find the grinder, so I settled for instant. I was sitting at the kitchen table reading yesterday's newspaper online when Cristina and Dimitri walked in the back door. Apparently they had a key, which made sense if they took care of the house the rest of the year.

"*Buna dimineata*," they both said.

"Good morning," I replied, assuming they'd said something similar to me.

Verbal conversation was nearly impossible after that, but we did okay with hand gestures and "*da*," which I'd learned meant yes, and "no," which wasn't pronounced exactly the same in Romanian, but close enough for them to figure out what I meant.

By the time Alex joined us (already dressed for the day in slacks and a button-down shirt, while I was still in my pajamas), I was sipping my second cup of brewed coffee and had eaten a slice of some type of thick bread with sour cream, which was tastier than I'd thought it would be.

"How'd you sleep?" he asked after Cristina brought him a cup of coffee and a plate of sliced meats, cheeses, and vegetables, which seemed more like lunch than breakfast to me.

"Fine," I said. "You?"

"No nightmares?" he asked.

He was like a dog with a bone. "No, I took a pill. Is this a good time to talk about Isabella's schedule? You mentioned something about tennis lessons."

"Yes," he said. "She's already signed up. Ten a.m., Mondays, Wednesdays, and Fridays."

"Where does she play? And when do we need to leave?" We had hours still, but I didn't know what time she usually woke and how long she needed to get ready.

"At the tennis club in Brasov. Dimitri knows where. It should take no more than thirty minutes to get there, but leave forty-five anyway."

"Traffic?" It was Monday morning after all.

"Or a horse-drawn cart."

I would've thought he was joking if I hadn't witnessed it myself the previous day. Even though they used rubber automobile tires instead of wooden wheels, it was still bizarre to see a horse-drawn carriage on the highway. And with most of the roads one lane in each direction, if you got stuck behind one there was nothing you could do but slow down and wait.

I didn't want to start another argument about me driving, especially not since I'd looked online and discovered that I could rent my own car for as little as twenty dollars per day. But I wasn't sure when I'd be able to get it, and Dimitri would be driving in the meantime. And his English was as bad as my Romanian. When I pointed this out to Alex, his response was, "What do you need to talk about? He knows where and when you need to be dropped off and picked up."

"What if we want to detour? Or what if Isabella's hungry afterward and wants a snack? Speaking of which, where can I change money?"

He pulled his wallet out of his back pocket and slapped a couple hundred Romanian lei on the table. I had no idea how much that was in dollars, but I assumed it was enough to cover a week's worth of ice cream cones, and probably a lot more.

"And the language barrier?"

"Isabella can speak a little Romanian."

Enough to get us into trouble, I soon discovered, but not enough to get us out.

Chapter 13

As Dimitri's car swerved around the latest bend in the road, the city of Brasov came into view—steeples, red-tiled roofs, and the word "Brasov" in giant white letters clinging to the side of the cliff. "Hollywood," Dimitri said and pointed to it. He was right; it did look like the Hollywood sign, albeit above a Saxon city dating back to the thirteenth century instead of one built by movie moguls a hundred years ago.

Dimitri dropped us off at the entrance to Brasov Tennis. It definitely didn't look like the tennis clubs back home. This one was made of red brick with wood turrets in the corners, an open balcony where Romeo and Juliet would've been at home, and more spires than a church. If Disney had built a tennis club in Fantasyland, it would've been this building.

"We're not in Kansas anymore, Toto," I said as opened the lobby door for Isabella.

"Huh?" she said. She was lucky she'd inherited her father's long legs. She looked adorable in her pink-trimmed white tennis skirt and matching tank top.

"You know. *The Wizard of Oz.*"

"Oh. I think my Mom read that to me once."

Once? My parents used to read that to me all the time. It had been one of my favorite books. "But you've seen the movie, right?"

"Nuh uh."

"You've never seen the movie? Really?"

"No."

I was appalled, but she seemed unfazed. "We'll have to fix that."

Isabella's lesson was supposed to be for a group of four children, but at 10:00 a.m. she was the only one there. I was watching her lob balls over the net from my seat in the bleachers when a little girl who looked to be Isabella's age or maybe a year older showed up, and another boy and girl shortly after. No one seemed concerned that they'd arrived late. Maybe it was a European thing.

I was surprised none of the other parents or caregivers joined me in the stands. In the US everyone usually huddled together on the bleachers. At first I thought the parents in Romania just didn't stay to watch, but when the lesson was over, they all filed out of the café next to the tennis courts. Apparently I'd been sitting in the wrong place.

Dimitri was waiting for us outside in the car. I asked Isabella if she was hungry, but she wasn't, so Dimitri drove us home. It was going to be a long day.

We colored, played board games, put together a puzzle, and spent many hours in the pool. I was sure Isabella would've had more fun playing with kids her own age, but there were none around. The closest house, which was actually a farm, was miles away. The only other kids I'd seen since we'd arrived at the estate were at the tennis club that morning.

Alex didn't return from wherever he'd been all day until shortly before dinner, which Cristina served in the dining room, even though Isabella and I had eaten both breakfast and lunch in the kitchen.

"So what did you do today?" Alex asked while we ate some sort of hearty meat stew with roasted potatoes on the side.

"Tennis," Isabella said, "then we played games, and swam, and we had a tea party," she continued, counting off the activities on her fingers.

"A tea party," Alex said. "That sounds like fun."

"It was," I said. "I even got to meet Mr. Giggles." Isabella's imaginary friend.

Alex's eyebrows shot up. "We haven't seen him in a while. Did you sneak him on the plane in your luggage, Isabella?"

"He doesn't need a plane, Daddy. He's not real. He can fly himself."

"Oh," he said, seeming relieved. I'd been concerned too until Isabella had told me she knew he was imaginary.

"Since Isabella doesn't have tennis lessons tomorrow," I said, "I was wondering if Dimitri could drive us into town to go shopping." I didn't mention that what I wanted to shop for was a rental car. I'd looked at a map online, and the shopping district appeared to be within walking distance of the rental car company. My plan was to tell Alex *after* I'd driven Isabella home, when it'd be too late for him to do anything about it.

"What do you need?" he asked.

I'd been expecting this question. "I wanted to get some toys for the pool and—"

"Miss Gwen's going to teach me to play water volleyball."

"That sounds like fun," Alex said.

"I could use more sunscreen. And I'd like to find a DVD store. I can't believe Isabella's never seen *The Wizard of Oz*."

"Can it wait until the end of the week? It'll be easier if I take you. Not all the salesclerks speak English."

"Sure, but—"

"I'm leaving for Munich in the morning," he continued.

"You're leaving! But, Daddy, we just got here."

"Just for a few days, honey. And you'll have Miss Gwen to take care of you." Alex turned back to me. "I'll be back Friday, but

Cristina and Dimitri will be here if you need anything, and you can always reach me by phone."

By the time Isabella came down for breakfast the next morning, Alex had already left for the airport. He'd promised to call every night before she went to bed, and he programmed his cell number into the phone he'd given me so I could reach him anytime. He also assured me that if there was an emergency I could dial 112, the Romanian equivalent of 911, and that an English-speaking operator would pick up.

"It'll be fine, Gwen," he said as I followed him out to his car. "If you need anything, call." Then he shut his door and sped away.

It would be fine when I had my own wheels. And maybe an English-to-Romanian dictionary.

Although initially I was terrified—I was responsible for someone else's child in a foreign country where I didn't speak the language—Alex's departure turned out to be for the best. It forced me to become more self-reliant. That morning I discovered a better way to communicate with Cristina and Dimitri beyond hand signals—an online translator. I carried my laptop into the kitchen and typed what I wanted to say in English, and the translator spit the text out in Romanian. This method worked well as long as we remained in the house, which was wired for Wi-Fi. The system fell apart when we drove in Dimitri's car. That's also when we discovered the limits of Isabella's Romanian language skills.

Dimitri drove us into Brasov to pick up the rental car, but the company was not at the address I'd written down. Apparently I'd accidentally mixed up an "a" for a "u" and placed the accent mark over the wrong letter, which led us to a different street. It was luck that saved us. As we stood at the corner trying to figure out where we'd gone wrong, an English-language tour group passed, and the guide was able to direct us. That was the only reason I'd agreed to pony up an extra seven dollars a day for the optional GPS. The woman at the rental car counter assured me that I could type in the street names in English without all the accent marks and the device would still recognize the address and direct me to the right location.

Armed with a paper map, a tourist guide, and a GPS-enabled manual transmission Dacia, the cheapest rental car available, I asked Isabella, "Where should we go?"

"The park," she said. "There's one by the tennis club. Elena told me."

"Who's Elena?" I was hoping not another imaginary friend.

"A girl at my tennis lesson."

"She speaks English?" I knew the instructor spoke several languages, but I didn't know the other students did too.

Isabella nodded. "She learned it in school."

We located the tennis club on the map, programmed the cross streets into the GPS, and spotted the park when we were still two blocks away. Apparently this was where all the kids had been hiding. There must have been twenty of them just crawling all over the jungle gym. While Isabella climbed on monkey bars, slid down slides, and swung on swings, I sat on a bench and read through the tourist guide searching for kid-friendly activities. I found quite a few.

After two hours on the playground, Isabella was hungry. I didn't have enough confidence in her Romanian language skills to chance a restaurant, so I drove us home instead. When we arrived, the house had a new occupant, and one who spoke some English. I was never so happy to see a sixteen-year-old in a too-short skirt and too-tight tank top in my life.

The sixteen-year-old Ivana explained in halting English that she was Cristina's niece's daughter, or her great-niece, and that she would be coming a few days a week to help her Tanti Cristina clean. I was happy to hear it, and not just so she could translate.

The house was too big for Cristina to take care of on her own. Dimitri drove her to work every morning and picked her up every night, and he was quick to fix a leaky faucet and carry anything heavy, but I'd yet to see him wash a dirty dish or grab a dust rag.

The following morning I drove Isabella to the tennis club myself. I'd programmed the address into the GPS the night before, so I knew we'd get there. This time instead of sitting on the bleachers by myself, I went to the café overlooking the tennis courts and ordered a coffee. I didn't particularly want one—I'd already had two cups at the house—but this was what everyone around me seemed to be doing so that's what I did too.

Just like the last time, the three other children in Isabella's tennis class arrived late. When the kids ran out to the courts, the parents headed to the café. I was surprised when one of them stopped beside my table.

"May I join you?" she asked.

"Of course," I said, and grabbed my hat and purse from the opposite chair and set them on the ground.

"I'm Elena's mother," she said as she sat down. "Stela Antonescu."

Apparently every Romanian woman's name ended in "a," and everyone's last name ended in "escu."

"Nice to meet you. I'm Gwen Andersen."

"The nanny," she said.

Apparently Isabella had talked to Elena about more than just jungle gyms. "Yes, for the summer. I'm a schoolteacher the rest of the year. Isabella's teacher, in fact, which is how I ended up here." For some reason I felt the need to explain. Perhaps because I was dressed in cargo shorts, a T-shirt, and sneakers, and she was wearing a black pencil skirt, a silk blouse, and high heels.

She nodded. "I'm a lawyer."

I glanced at the clock on the wall above her head. It was already ten thirty. "You must have a nice boss if he gives you mornings off to take your daughter to tennis." Quite a few of my students at *Académie française* had at least one parent who was a lawyer, and all of them were picked up from school by nannies, and sometimes dropped off by them as well.

"I have my own firm," she said. "It helps in that regard."

Her English was accented but otherwise perfect. When I complimented her on it, she told me she had several American clients, and 90 percent of the documents she drafted were in English.

"What kind of law do you practice?" I asked.

"Business and real estate mostly, but other areas too. When you're on your own you must be flexible."

We chatted about the weather (hot and sunny) and the differences between Romania and the US (many) until the girls' tennis lesson ended. Then we met them at the entrance to the court.

"Do you want to go to the park for a little while?" I asked Isabella. There was no reason to rush home.

She nodded, a grin spreading across her face. "Can Elena come too?"

"That's up to her mother." We all turned to Stela, who was scanning messages on her phone.

She spoke to Elena in Romanian then said, "I'm sorry, not today. I have a meeting. We're going to be late if we don't hurry."

"I can take her with us if you want. You can pick her up after your meeting, or I can drop her off at your office."

"Oh, that's not necessary," Stela said.

"It's no trouble. We're going anyway." I wanted Isabella to have a friend, for both of our sakes.

She looked doubtful; then Elena said something to her in Romanian that I couldn't understand, but from her puppy dog expression I assumed was her pleading to go.

Eventually Stela sighed and said, "If you're sure it's no trouble." I confirmed that it wasn't, and she handed me her business card, which listed her office address, phone number, and e-mail. "What's your number?" she asked. "I'll call you when I'm finished and pick her up."

I read off the number to the cell phone Alex had given me, which I'd taped to the back of the phone knowing I'd never remember it.

She typed it into her keypad, said something to Elena in Romanian, thanked me again, and rushed off.

Isabella and Elena played at the park for two hours, then we all went to lunch at McDonald's (Elena knew the way). Stela called when we were finishing up at the restaurant and met us there. She didn't know where I could find a water volleyball set in Brasov, but she gave me directions to a store that sold English-language books and DVDs.

When we returned to the house, Isabella and I swam until dinner then watched cartoons until it was time for her bath and bed. That was our first argument—bedtime. She thought since it was summer she shouldn't have one. I disagreed. Luckily, when Alex called he backed me up, although with a later time than I would've liked. I suggested 9:00 p.m. for a seven-year-old, but Isabella pleaded with him until he agreed to 10:00 p.m.

Ultimately Isabella and I compromised. She agreed to be in bed by nine thirty if I would read to her for half an hour before lights out at ten. The catch was she had no books in the house. So the next morning our first outing was back to the store we'd visited the previous day. I purchased half a dozen English-language picture books and an English-Romanian pocket dictionary.

I loved having the ability to go wherever I wanted whenever I wanted and was once again so happy I'd decided to rent my own car.

Or I was until Alex returned.

Chapter 14

On Friday morning Isabella threw her first tantrum.

"What about this one?" I said, holding up a turquoise tennis skirt with a matching tank top. "Or this one?" I offered, pulling a hot-pink tennis dress from her closet. Isabella was not lacking for outfits. She'd brought more clothes to Romania than I had.

"No!" she said, tears streaming down her face. "I want to wear the white one."

"You can't. The white one's dirty." She'd gotten a huge grass stain on her butt at the playground on Wednesday and then forgotten to drop it into the hamper, so Cristina hadn't washed it with the rest of her dirty clothes.

"I don't care," she cried again.

I silently counted to ten. If she were my kid, I would've told her she could either change into a clean outfit or skip her tennis lesson and the park afterward and spend her morning in a time-out. But she wasn't my kid, and I wasn't sure how Alex would feel about her missing a lesson, especially one he'd already paid for.

"Okay, Isabella, if you absolutely, positively must wear that outfit then you're going to have to wash it yourself."

"But I don't know how," she blubbered.

"Which is why I'm going to teach you."

I dragged her downstairs to the laundry room to grab the detergent, then back upstairs to her bathroom where I showed her how to pour the soap onto the stain, rub it in, then let it soak in the sink for a few minutes before rinsing it out. It didn't clean it completely, but it was good enough for our purposes.

"But now it's all wet," she said.

"I know," I said and grabbed a towel from her linen closet and laid it down on the bathroom floor. "Now I'm going to show you how to dry it."

I placed the tennis skirt inside the towel then instructed Isabella to roll it up. Then we both pushed down on it together to wring the moisture out.

"It's still wet," she said when we unfolded the towel.

"And now we use the hair dryer." Under other circumstances I would've just thrown it into the clothes dryer for ten minutes, but I was trying to prove a point. When the skirt was merely damp, I told Isabella she could put it back on. I knew once she was outside it would dry quickly in the heat and the sun.

"So next time you stain your favorite tennis skirt what are you going to do?" I asked as I hustled her down the steps.

"Put it in the hamper with the dirty laundry when we get home," she said.

Lesson learned. Unfortunately at the cost of being late. We didn't arrive at the tennis club until ten fifteen. I didn't think it was a big deal since that's when all the other kids in her class arrived anyway, but Isabella liked to be prompt. When I pulled into the tennis club's small parking lot and all the spaces were filled, I thought she was going to have another meltdown. So I told her to go inside without me and I'd park the car myself.

It took me fifteen minutes before I finally found a space four blocks away. When I arrived at the tennis club I went to the café and looked for Stela, but she wasn't there. Then I remembered she'd told me she was taking Elena to Sibiu to visit her father for the weekend (they were divorced). So I sat alone and sipped my coffee as I waited for Isabella's lesson to end.

I'd planned on taking her to the park afterward, and then into town for lunch. Now that I had a dictionary, I was ready to attempt a restaurant on my own. Plus, I needed to find a currency change office or a bank with a US-compatible ATM. I was down to my last ten lei.

The park worked out as planned—we just walked over from the tennis club—but when we went to retrieve the car so we could drive into town for lunch, it was missing. I knew I should've written down the address of the building I'd parked in front of. But when I dragged Isabella up and down all of the neighboring streets too, the car wasn't there either. I couldn't believe someone had stolen it. It wasn't that nice of a car.

"I'm starving," Isabella whined.

"I know, sweetie, and as soon as we find the car I'll take you to get something to eat."

"Can't we go back to the tennis club? They have food."

Yes, but they didn't take credit or debit cards, which I'd learned when I'd tried to pay for coffee with my own money instead of Alex's. However, I sensed another tantrum building and I knew I had to act fast.

"What if we call Dimitri and ask him to pick you up and take you home?" Yes, it was my job to take care of Isabella, not Cristina's or Dimitri's, but I was desperate. It seemed like the best of two bad alternatives.

"Okay," she said and flopped down onto the cobblestone sidewalk with her head in her hands. I had to turn away so she didn't see me laughing at her. Not *too* much of a drama queen. Normally she was a good kid, but she was definitely in a mood today. I suspected it had something to do with Alex vanishing for most of the week. She'd asked me three times yesterday when he was coming home.

I called the house and Cristina recognized my voice and immediately handed the phone to Ivana. I was able to explain to her that my car had been stolen and I needed Dimitri to come and pick us up. I figured he could drop me off at the rental car office and they would be able to help me file a police report. I hoped the insurance I'd purchased covered theft too. If not, I'd be screwed.

"Dimitri's not here," Ivana said.

"Where is he? Can't you call him?" He must have a cell phone.

I could hear Ivana and Cristina speaking in Romanian, then she came back on the line. "He went to Deva. He won't be home until tonight."

Fuck!

I heard more Romanian in the background, and then she said, "Tanti Cristina says Mr. Alex will be back soon and he can pick you up. Or I can call a taxi if you tell me where you are."

I didn't know how much taxis in Romania charged, but I was sure it was more than ten lei, and I doubted they took credit cards. And if Alex beat us home and found out that I let Isabella wither in the heat and starve rather than call him, he was going to be even more furious with me than he probably already would be.

"Okay," I said, "I'll call Alex. Wish me luck."

"You did what!" he yelled into the phone.

I'd explained it all really quickly hoping that would blunt the impact somehow. It didn't.

"I think the important thing at the moment is for me to get Isabella some food."

"Take her to the tennis club," he said. "They have a restaurant."

"I know, but they don't take credit cards and I only have ten lei." Even a bag of chips at the club cost more than that.

"What happened to all the money I gave you?" But before I could answer he said, "Never mind. I have an account there. Tell them my name and they'll put it on my bill."

Nice of him to let me know that now.

"I'll meet you there," he said and hung up.

Isabella ordered the Romanian equivalent of a grilled cheese with french fries and I ordered a salad. We were still eating when Alex arrived. I could tell he was furious. He didn't yell, and he smiled at Isabella when she ran into his arms, but his anger at me was palpable.

When Isabella finished eating, he gave her money to buy an ice cream cone from the snack bar downstairs and told her to wait for us by the tennis courts. I braced myself for the tirade I knew was coming.

Chapter 15

"What the hell were you thinking?" I assumed he kept his voice low because we were still in the restaurant, although it was midafternoon and nearly empty.

"I was—"

"I told you I didn't want you driving here, did I not?"

"Yes, but—"

"And you completely disregarded my very explicit instructions and did exactly as you damn well pleased."

I wouldn't have characterized it that way myself, but I couldn't deny the accuracy of the statement. "If you'd just let me explain."

He leaned back and folded his arms across his chest. "Explain, Gwen. Explain why you disobeyed a direct order."

A direct order? "I didn't realize you were issuing edicts. Am I your subject now?" Yes, I had screwed up. I'd already admitted that and apologized. But no one was hurt, except perhaps for my bank account if the stolen rental car wasn't covered by insurance. But that was my problem, not his. Isabella and I had been doing just fine on our own until this morning. And who leaves their daughter in the care of a stranger in a foreign country with no means of transportation?

"Don't test me," he said between clenched teeth.

Luckily for both of us the waitress, who had been hovering, came to the table. She spoke in a combination of Romanian and broken English and asked if I was finished and if we wanted anything else. Then she cleared away my salad plate and brought Alex the check. The whole procedure took several minutes, which gave us both an opportunity to calm down.

When we were alone again I said, "Why don't we go to the police station and file a report, then discuss this further when we get home. I'm sure Isabella's bored to death, and this isn't really the place."

He agreed.

The three of us were silent on the drive to the police station. Once we arrived and I realized how little English the officer behind the desk spoke, I was glad Alex was with me. I explained and Alex translated. The officer checked her computer and told us the car wasn't stolen, it had been towed. Apparently I'd parked in a restricted zone. Only people who lived in that neighborhood and had the appropriate sticker on their car could park there.

"How was I supposed to know? There was no sign." I'd checked. I was used to parking restrictions from living in LA

"People who live here know," Alex said. "Another reason you shouldn't be driving."

Had Isabella not been standing next to us I would've answered him back. But she was, so I said, "How do I get the car back?"

Alex asked the officer and she told us we had to pay a fine, then we could go to the impound lot to retrieve it.

"How much?" I asked.

That she understood. "Three hundred lei."

It wasn't too bad—less than a hundred dollars. Of course I didn't find out until we arrived at the impound lot that I had to pay an additional two hundred lei separately to the tow truck driver, then an extra fifty lei to the lot for storage, even though the car had only been there for half a day. It was an expensive afternoon. At least for Alex.

"How can no one take credit cards?" I asked after he'd paid the last fifty lei.

"It's a cash-based society," he answered while we waited for the owner of the impound lot to make change. "A few stores and restaurants accept credit cards, but they're the exception, not the rule."

"Fine, then point me to a bank so I can get some get cash." There was no way I was letting him pay for this. It was bad enough he'd had to front the money.

He looked at his watch. "It's too late, the banks are closed. We'll go tomorrow."

"They're closed on a Friday afternoon, but they're open on Saturday?" Call me skeptical.

"The currency converters are open every day."

"Then tell me where the closest one is and I'll go now."

"No," he said. "Tomorrow."

At that point, I think if I'd said I never wanted to drive again he would've tossed me the keys and told me I was his new chauffeur. I decided to take his advice and not test his patience any further.

He pulled his Audi into the garage, and I parked my rental car on the gravel driveway. Isabella scrambled out of Alex's car and ran into the house. I took my cue from Alex. He carried his suitcase upstairs, so I went up to my bedroom too. Five minutes later Isabella appeared in my doorway dressed in her bathing suit.

"C'mon, Gwen, it's time to swim." She knew she wasn't allowed in the pool without me. That was one rule that wasn't negotiable.

"Okay," I said, "give me a minute to change."

"No," Alex said from the hallway. "I need to talk to *Miss* Gwen." Apparently he'd heard her call me by my first name. After

Alex left for Germany I'd told her she could. I knew I'd live to regret that decision.

"But Daddy, we *always* swim in the afternoons. I've been practicing."

"Not today," he said.

"But Daddy—"

"Isabella, go to your room."

"But—" Her lips were already quivering.

"Now," he yelled.

Instantly the tears welled up in her eyes and spilled out onto her cheeks. She ran into her bedroom and slammed the door shut.

I sighed. "You shouldn't have done that. She spent the whole week practicing swimming from one end to the other without stopping so she could show you when you got home."

"Now you're going to tell me how to discipline my child?"

"Of course not. Obviously you know best." My sarcasm did not go unnoticed.

"We'll discuss this downstairs," he said and walked away.

I followed him to his office and he shut the door behind me. He dropped into the wheeled chair behind his desk, the one Isabella loved to spin in when he wasn't home, and told me to take a seat too. When I had, he leaned back and stared up at the ceiling with his hands steepled in front of his chest. "Explain."

"Excuse me?"

In one quick movement he leaned forward across the desk, and I jumped at his sudden proximity. "Explain why you did exactly what I told you not to do."

So I did. As calmly as I could I told him how I felt uncomfortable having to ask Dimitri for a ride every time we wanted to leave the house, and that I wanted the flexibility to take Isabella places on my own. I also reminded him that I'd paid for the car myself (rental car companies were one of the few Romanian businesses that accepted credit cards), so it wasn't costing him anything, even though I knew his objection to my driving had nothing to do with money.

"Except for today, it's been great," I concluded. He glowered but said nothing, so I continued. "I'm a safe driver, Alex. I've had my license since I was sixteen, and I've never gotten into an accident." That wasn't entirely true. I'd been rear-ended once when I was stopped at a red light. But that wasn't my fault, so I didn't think it counted. "And I know you let Katarina drive Isabella." I'd seen her drop her off and pick her up from school. "So why won't you let me drive her too?"

"I would have no problem with you driving Isabella in LA I just don't want you driving her here."

"Why? We've—"

"No, Gwen. No debate. You work for me, and my decision's final."

I crossed my arms over my chest and said, "Fine." What else could I say? He was Isabella's father, and I did work for him, at least for the next five weeks.

"I'll take you into town tomorrow so you can return the car."

"I'm not returning the rental car."

That wiped the smug expression from his face. "But you just said—"

"I said I wouldn't drive Isabella. I didn't say I wouldn't drive myself."

"Where are you going to go without Isabella? You're not quitting, are you?"

"Of course not." I wouldn't abandon her, or him, even though at the moment the notion was very appealing. "She goes to bed at ten. I assumed I could go out afterward, so long as you're home. I also assumed I'd get a day off at some point. Maybe one day a week?" In the future I'd nail down all these details *before* I accepted the job. This was my first live-in nanny gig, so I didn't know.

"Gwen, wherever you want to go, Dimitri can drive you. Or if I'm home, I can. I'll be here all weekend."

"Alex, you can dictate terms to Isabella. You cannot dictate terms to me."

Chapter 16

Dinner was subdued. Alex still hadn't apologized to Isabella, and it was clear she hadn't forgiven him. She wouldn't look at him, and she barely spoke the entire meal. And I wasn't particularly enamored with him either, so I hardly spoke too.

After dinner, Alex disappeared into his office and Isabella and I watched television until it was time for her bath and bed. Her mattress was only a twin size, but I snuggled in next to her so we could read together. I read the book aloud, but I wanted her to follow along in the text so she could learn the words too. We were only a few pages into the first chapter when Alex knocked on her bedroom door.

He held up a beige teddy bear with black eyes and nose and giant paws. It was just about the cutest thing I'd ever seen. "I forgot to give you this earlier," he said and handed it to Isabella. "He just moved here from Germany and he needs a good home."

Isabella hugged the bear to her chest and buried her face in his soft fur. "What's his name?" she asked.

"He doesn't have one yet," Alex said. "I thought you could give him one."

Isabella closed her eyes to concentrate. When she opened them she said, "Peter. His name is Peter."

"Peter it is." Then he kissed the top of her head, wished her good night, and left the room.

The three of us—Isabella, Peter, and I—finished the first three chapters of *Ivy & Bean*, and I shut off the light. When I returned to my own room there was a present on my bed too. I knew it was a book even before I unwrapped it. I could tell from the shape and the weight. Alex had bought me *Dracula: The Man, the Myth, and the Legend*.

I skimmed the table of contents before I turned off my own light. The author's intent seemed to be to highlight the differences between Vlad Tepes, the real man, and Dracula, the character we all knew from books and movies. It looked like an interesting read.

When I straggled into the kitchen the next morning Alex was already seated at the table, fully dressed and reading the *Wall Street Journal*. He must've picked it up at the airport yesterday since I didn't think they delivered this far.

"Good morning," he said. "Coffee's on the counter."

I poured myself a cup and noticed that Cristina's purse and shawl were not on the bench next to the back door where she usually left them. "Where's Cristina?"

"She doesn't work weekends," he said.

If Cristina was entitled to weekends off then surely he could give me one day. "So about my schedule," I said.

"How about Sundays off?" he replied. "And if you need extra time for something you'll let me know."

"Okay, that seems fair." I brought my coffee to the long wooden table and sat down as far from Alex as I could. "And thanks for the book," I added.

"You're very welcome," he said without looking up from the newspaper.

The only sound in the vast kitchen was the ticking of the clock on the wall above the table and the occasional turning of a newspaper page. I didn't normally read the *Wall Street Journal*, but I'd left my laptop upstairs so as Alex finished sections of the paper and set them on the table, I picked them up. Alex didn't speak to me so I didn't speak to him either. I think we were both relieved when Isabella joined us half an hour later.

"Good morning, Daddy," Isabella said in her singsong voice, then she gave him a kiss on the cheek. The bear had worked. Isabella had forgiven him his moment of pique. "Good morning, Gwen," she added when she noticed me.

Alex folded down the top of his newspaper and stared at me across the table. I knew he was annoyed that she was no longer calling me Miss Gwen. "I'd let it go if I were you," I said quietly, "but it's your decision."

He sighed but didn't correct her. "What do you want for breakfast, Isabella?"

"Pancakes," she shouted.

"Pancakes it is," he said and stood up from the table. "Gwen?"

"I'm fine," I said and held up my coffee cup.

"You have to eat something."

"Breakfast is the most important meal of the day," Isabella said with all the seriousness of the surgeon general warning kids off smoking.

I couldn't help but laugh. "Okay, what do you suggest?" I was getting tired of bread with sour cream, which had been my daily breakfast since I'd arrived at the estate.

"Pancakes!" Isabella said.

"I do make the world's best pancakes," Alex said.

"World's best? Are you sure about that?"

"Ask Isabella."

She nodded in agreement, so I relented. Isabella colored at the table while Alex cooked. I wasn't sure if I was supposed to help him or sit with her, so I asked when I got up to pour myself more coffee. Alex told me he had breakfast covered, so I went back to reading the paper.

After breakfast (those pancakes were good, but world's best was an exaggeration), Isabella watched cartoons while I showered and changed. By the time I joined her in front of the television, Alex had planned out our day. The first stop was a sporting goods store on the outskirts of town.

The salesclerk told Alex they didn't carry water volleyball nets, but they could order one from a catalog and have it delivered to the house. I thought we'd leave after that but Isabella had discovered the water sports aisle. We walked out half an hour later with two shopping bags filled with goggles, masks, snorkels, an inflatable raft, a pool basketball net and ball (that sport they stocked), and three water pistols (pink, blue, and green) so we didn't have to share.

The next stop was a DVD store where at Isabella's urging Alex purchased an assortment of animated TV shows. I insisted he buy *The Sound of Music* too, another classic Isabella had never seen. By the time we left the DVD store it was time for lunch.

"Isabella, do you want to go to McDonald's?" Alex asked.

"Yes!" she readily agreed.

I didn't tell him we'd just eaten there a few days before, and neither did Isabella. Not that I think it would've mattered. Today was obviously all about him winning back Isabella's love. It would take more than a Big Mac and an extra-large Diet Coke filled with ice (apparently the only place in Romania where one could get an icy drink) for him to win me back.

Chapter 17

After Isabella finished her Happy Meal, Alex gave her permission to play at the attached playground.

"I'll go with her," I said and stood up.

"No," he said, "she's fine. I can see her from here." We were sitting next to the windows, but I still would've been more comfortable outside, mainly to get away from him. It was too awkward when we were alone.

"I propose a truce," he said when I sat back down.

"I didn't know we were fighting."

He set down his drink. "Gwen, you've barely spoken to me all day."

I shrugged in response. I wasn't *not* speaking to him. I just didn't know what to say. I supposed if I was being completely honest I'd admit that I was still smarting from yesterday's argument. "I feel like you don't trust me, like you think I'm irresponsible or something."

"Is this about the car?"

"Honestly, Alex, until yesterday Isabella and I were doing fine. And Stela let me drive her daughter and she doesn't even know me." Although she hadn't known I'd driven Elena to lunch until after she'd called to pick her up.

"Who's Stela?"

"Elena's mother, Isabella's friend from tennis. She should have friends her own age, Alex. She shouldn't just play with me."

"I never said she couldn't have friends. I want her to have friends."

"That's a little difficult when there are no other kids nearby and no transportation." I'd spotted plenty of buses in the city, but not out by the lake where Alex lived.

"You have transportation. Dimitri can drive you wherever you want to go."

"I told you, I don't want to keep imposing on him."

"Gwen, you're not imposing. He works for me."

This was pointless. I returned to sucking on my Diet Coke.

Alex sighed and drummed his fingers on the table. Eventually he looked up and said, "I think it would help if I told you why I don't want you driving here."

I stopped slurping soda through my straw. "I know already. You don't think it's safe, even though I'm a very good driver."

"My wife died two years ago. Here. In Romania. She was driving home alone one evening and her car rolled down an embankment and landed in a ditch at the bottom of the hill. It wasn't the fall that killed her. It had been an unusually rainy summer and the trench was filled with water. She drowned."

"I'm so sorry," I said, knowing from experience how inadequate those words were. Isabella had told me her mother had died in a car accident, which my colleagues at *Académie française* had confirmed, but I'd just assumed it had happened in LA "My parents died in a car accident too. Drunk driver."

"I'm sorry, Gwen. I knew about your mother from Isabella. I didn't know you'd lost your father as well."

I shrugged. What was there to say?

"So you understand then," he said. "I can't fly home with another coffin."

I still thought he was being irrational—I hadn't stopped driving just because my parents were killed in a car accident—but at least now I understood. I nodded. "I won't drive Isabella anymore, I promise." I knew he wanted me to say I wouldn't drive myself either, but I wasn't willing to go that far.

Our relationship returned to normal after that. After lunch we shopped for groceries and I was able to fill the refrigerator with items that were more familiar to me. Not that I didn't enjoy Cristina's cooking; I did. But I wanted cereal for breakfast, not bread with sour cream, and I wanted something other than stew or sausages for lunch. I'd eaten more pork in the last week than I'd eaten all year.

After the groceries were unpacked we all changed into our bathing suits and headed out to the pool. I considered leaving on my T-shirt to cover my birthmark since Alex was with us. But I hadn't bothered when it was just me and Isabella, and despite the copious amounts of sunscreen I applied to each of us almost hourly, we were both developing dark tans. The puppy chasing its tail/dragon spitting fire/misshapen doughnut on my left shoulder was still noticeable, but the ugly purple mark didn't stand out quite as much against my brown skin, so I pulled off my T-shirt and joined them in the pool.

Alex and Isabella sampled every toy we'd purchased. Isabella favored the mask and snorkel. Her new favorite game was diving down for sunken treasure—coins I tossed into the deep end. Alex preferred the basketball hoop. I was happy to float on the raft all afternoon. I noticed Alex glancing at my birthmark a few times, but he didn't leer at it anymore like he had that first time in LA

That night when I read to Isabella before she went to sleep, Alex joined us. I offered him my spot—both on the bed (we couldn't all fit) and as orator—but he refused. Instead he sat in the rocking chair in the corner and listened as I read aloud. When I shut off the light, he kissed Isabella good night and followed me out.

"You do that well," he said.

I laughed. "I've had lots of practice."

"It's obvious you enjoy it."

"I do." I loved reading to my students. I took great pleasure in watching them get absorbed by stories and fall in love with reading themselves.

"Well, good night," he said.

"Good night," I replied.

I was just about to close my bedroom door behind me when he said, "I'm going downstairs to watch TV if you want to come. No obligation, of course. If you're tired and want to go to bed that's okay too."

I was tired, but I wasn't sleepy. I'd planned on writing Zoe a long e-mail. She'd sent me one this morning demanding to know why I hadn't done so already. But vegging out in front of the television for an hour or two sounded much more appealing. Presumably Alex's tastes ran to more highbrow fare than *Phineas & Ferb* and *Scooby Doo*.

"Sure," I said. "That sounds nice."

Somewhat surprisingly, it was.

When I woke the next morning I realized it was Sunday, my day off, so I rolled over and fell back to sleep. When I staggered downstairs an hour later, Isabella and Alex were already eating breakfast— crepes this time.

"Good morning, Gwen," they said in unison.

I mumbled "good morning" back and headed directly to the coffeemaker.

"Nutella or strawberry?" Alex asked, motioning to their plates.

"You don't have to cook me breakfast," I said. "I'm fine with cereal."

"It's no bother," he said. "The frying pan's already hot."

I begged off twice more, but when he poured the batter into the pan I acquiesced. I procured my own plate and silverware then leaned against the counter as he cooked, even though he told me I could sit at the table and he'd bring them to me.

"These are amazing," I said when I'd taken my first bite. Definitely the sweetest strawberries I'd ever eaten.

"From Satu Mare," he said, "in the north. They grow the best strawberries."

This time I had to agree.

"Can we go to the park today?" Isabella asked, looking at me.

"Ask your father," I replied. "It's up to him."

"If that's what you want," he said. "What about you, Gwen? What are you doing with your day?"

"Aren't you coming too?" Isabella asked.

"No," Alex answered for me. "It's Gwen's day off."

Isabella looked as if I'd just decapitated Peter the bear, who had his own seat at the table and a jar of honey in front of him "because that's what bears like to eat," I was informed by Isabella when I'd asked. "You don't like the park?"

"Sure I do, it's just that I'm going somewhere else today."

"Where?" she asked.

"Bran Castle."

"What's that?"

I was going to tell her a tourist attraction when Alex said, "A real castle where Queen Marie and Princess Ileanna used to live."

"A real princess castle! Daddy, can we go there instead?"

"You have to ask Gwen. It's her day off. She might not want us bothering her."

"Gwen, can we come too?"

I turned to Alex, who tried to hide his grin behind his coffee cup, and shot him a nasty look before I turned back to Isabella. "I don't think you'd like it. It's probably going to be really boring. I bet the park will be a lot more fun."

"No, I want to see the princess castle. Pleeeease can we come?"

"If you're absolutely sure—"

"I'm sure," she said.

"Then of course you can come." I turned to Alex and gave him another angry look. I'd been looking forward to some alone time.

"Sorry," he mouthed.

He didn't look sorry. He looked pleased. No doubt this had worked out precisely as he'd planned.

Chapter 18

Bran Castle looked exactly like what I'd always imagined a medieval castle would look like—perched high on top of a hill with battlements and spires and ancient stone walls. It was definitely not a princess castle. There wasn't a patch of pink or a glittery surface in sight. As I'd predicted, Isabella was bored. But since it was my day off, Alex had to deal with her.

I admit it gave me a twinge of pleasure when he had to run back down to the entrance not once, but twice to buy her a snack after he'd purchased the wrong flavor chips the first time, and when, after an hour of walking up steep steps, she insisted he carry her. I also enjoyed pointing out to Alex that although many of the exhibits noted that the castle was the summer residence of Queen Marie, whose heart was still buried there, there was no mention of Princess Ileanna.

"She inherited the castle from her mother," he said, "and now it belongs to her son," as if that settled the matter.

"But technically the princess didn't live here, right?"

"No," he said, "technically she did not. Although I'm sure she must've spent time here with her mother."

As far as I was concerned, I'd won.

The day didn't turn awkward until an American couple appeared. Alex was taking a photo of me and Isabella next to a suit of armor when the woman noticed us speaking English (most of the tourists were not) and offered to snap the picture for Alex so he could be in it too. Before I could tell her it wasn't necessary, he'd handed her my camera and jumped into the frame. When the woman told us to move closer, he put his arm around my shoulder and leaned in. I knew it was an innocent gesture, but I still found it disconcerting. We weren't a family, as this woman had obviously assumed, and I was uncomfortable pretending that we were.

As usually happens with tourist attractions, we kept seeing the same people again and again as we moved from room to room. The American woman who'd taken our photo next to the suit of armor followed us to the Dracula display. Although it was widely acknowledged by Romanians that Vlad Tepes had never lived in Bran Castle, and likely never even visited there, because of Bram Stoker's novel and the country's desire to have a commercially successful tourist attraction, the castle contained an exhibit devoted to the fictional Dracula and the real Vlad Tepes, the most well-known Romanian outside of the country except perhaps for Nadia Comaneci.

I was studying the Romanian ruler's genealogy chart when Isabella pointed up at the portrait of Vlad Tepes hanging on the wall and said, "You look like him."

This was not a compliment. Besides the long, pointy nose and thick mustache, he had dark circles under both of his wide, deep-set eyes.

"No, I don't," I said a bit defensively.

"Yes," she said and nodded as if the matter was closed. I knew who she'd inherited that trait from.

"Isabella, I do not look like Dracula."

This caught the American woman's attention. She stopped reading the placard listing all of the Dracula films ever produced and glanced from me to the portrait of Vlad Tepes and back to me again. "I can see it," she said, "around the eyes."

That was it. If both Isabella and this woman thought I looked like Dracula, then I needed to start wearing makeup again. Or at least under-eye concealer.

"You're much more attractive than he is," the American woman continued, likely in response to the no doubt horrified look on my face, "but there's a slight resemblance."

That's when Alex abandoned the biography of Bram Stoker placard he'd been studying and joined us. He too glanced from my face to the portrait and back to me again. But unlike the American woman, he didn't say a word. He just took Isabella's hand and moved on to the next display.

"You *should* wear makeup," Zoe said into the phone. "Just because it's summer doesn't mean you get to slack off." I called her from the house that night after Alex and Isabella had gone to bed. I'd been trying not to phone because I didn't want to run up Alex's bill, but Isabella's comment had left me in a foul mood, and I needed cheering up.

"I have a tan. I shouldn't have to wear makeup when I have a tan."

"Obviously you do," she said. "At least eye makeup. You can skip the rest."

"Gee, thanks."

"Hey, I'm not the one who told you that you looked like Dracula. So what else is going on?"

I filled her in on everything that had happened since I'd arrived, and she told me about her first week teaching at an art camp.

"Your life sounds better," I told her.

"No way," she said. "I'm teaching five classes a day. You're spending your afternoons lazing by the pool."

"Not lazing," I said, carrying the cordless phone from the kitchen into the darkened TV room. It was empty so I stretched out on the long leather couch, which felt cool against my warm skin. "Entertaining a seven-year-old. Big difference."

"Whatever. I want to hear more about Alex."

"I already told you everything."

"Not *everything*," she said. "How long do you think it'll be before you two hook up?"

"Are you out of your mind? He's my boss!" And that was just the first of many objections that popped into my head. Sure, he was handsome, and physically I was definitely attracted to him. But he was also Isabella's father, I lived in his house, and he was a control freak. Plus, I wasn't even sure I liked him. He could be quite charming sometimes, but other times he was a total prick.

She snorted. "Yeah, you'd be the first person in history to ever sleep with her boss."

"That doesn't make it right. Besides, what makes you think he wants to sleep with me? I mean, apparently I look like Dracula."

"Oh, please, you know you don't look like Dracula, so get over it already. And he obviously doesn't think so either."

"Why? Just because he didn't say so? I told you, he has good manners."

"No, because he's clearly interested in you."

"I don't see it."

"Oh no? The man can't even go one day without you."

"That's got nothing to do with me. He just doesn't like to be alone with Isabella. He has no idea what to do with her. He thinks quality time is when he's in the same room with her while she's playing on her iPad."

"That's not fair. He's a single parent. I'm sure it's really hard for him."

"One with massive amounts of help," I noted.

"Maybe," she said. "But what about the photo? Not everyone takes pictures with their nanny."

I did think that was weird, but I said, "He was just being polite. Obviously that woman thought we were together."

"Maybe you *are* together and you just don't know it yet."

I laughed. "I think I would know if I was sleeping with him."

"Give it time," she said. "This is just like *The Sound of Music*. You take care of his kid and he falls in love with you."

She started singing the tune to the theme song and I laughed again. Zoe was obsessed with that movie. Her mom was too. They watched it together at least once a year, and they both knew all the words to every song. Once they even dragged me to a *Sound of Music* sing-along at the Hollywood Bowl. It was more fun than I'd imagined it would be, especially considering we weren't drunk as most of the other adult participants were.

"This is so not *The Sound of Music*," I said.

Suddenly the overhead lights flipped on. I sat up and peeked over the back of the couch. Alex was standing under the arched entranceway to the room. "Zoe, I gotta go," I said and quickly hung up the phone. "I'll pay for the call," I offered as I jumped up from the couch.

"It's not a problem," he said.

As his eyes strayed from the phone in my hand to the hem of my pajama top, which had crept up my abdomen leaving my midriff exposed, I wondered exactly how much of that conversation he'd heard. He didn't leave me in suspense.

As I pulled my shirt down, he asked, "What's not *The Sound of Music*?"

Chapter 19

"Nothing," I said. "My friend Zoe loves that movie. I still can't believe Isabella's never seen it."

He smiled and shook his head. "I'd never even heard of it until I moved to the States. It's not well-known in Europe. Probably because it *never* could've happened the way it was portrayed in the movie. If they had walked over those mountains they would've ended up in Hitler's Eagle's Nest, not Switzerland."

"Yeah, yeah." I'd heard it all before. When Zoe's family had visited Salzburg a few years ago their guide for *The Sound of Music* tour had told them the same thing. "Everyone knows Americans are geographically challenged. The point is the movie's a classic."

Either he was too tired to argue with me or decided it wasn't worth the effort. He plopped onto the couch and grabbed the remote off the coffee table. "I couldn't sleep," he said. "I thought I'd watch TV. You're welcome to join me."

While I wouldn't have minded watching some mindless television, I had Zoe's words ringing in my ears. Maybe we were getting a little too friendly here at *casa de Romanescu*. Better to keep some distance between us. "No thanks," I said and ran up the steps.

The following week we all fell into a routine. The three of us ate breakfast together, then Alex either left the house or went to his office to work. Dimitri dropped Isabella and me off at the tennis club, then picked us up three hours later, which gave us time to go to the park afterward, usually with Stela and Elena.

On the days Isabella didn't have tennis lessons, we went to the park in the morning then into town to explore a local site, often a church or a museum. Alex had bought me a handheld electronic translator, which made it much easier to communicate with Dimitri. I typed in English where we wanted to go and he took us there. Sometimes he accompanied us too, and via the translator, he would tell us interesting facts about the place that weren't covered in the guidebook.

Isabella did not enjoy these cultural outings and usually began whining about how boring it was soon after we arrived. But as long as I promised her an ice cream cone afterward and limited the touring to no more than an hour, she went along with it without too much complaining.

Although I was no longer driving Isabella, I kept the rental car. Every day I would tell myself that after she went to bed I would go out somewhere. And every night I was too exhausted to do anything more than watch TV with Alex and go to bed.

And even if I hadn't been exhausted, I had no idea where to go. I considered asking Alex, but I knew that if I did he'd just want to accompany me, which would defeat the purpose. So I asked Stela for a suggestion one morning when we were waiting for the girls to finish their tennis lesson. She laughed at the notion that she would know any of the local hot spots. She said she hadn't been out to a disco in years—apparently they still called them discos in Romania.

By the end of the week I finally decided I needed to force myself to go out, even if I was tired and didn't know where to go. Stela had told me there were always people out at night in the plaza, especially on the weekends, so I decided I'd drive myself into town Saturday evening and wander around until I found a good spot to have coffee or a drink.

I mentioned my plans to Alex on Saturday morning so he wouldn't be surprised when I suddenly left the house that night.

"I don't think that's a good idea," he said as he swerved around a pig that had wandered into the road. He was driving the three of us to the tennis club. He'd reserved a court for an hour so we could all play, even though I'd insisted that I didn't want to. Isabella was only seven and her serve was already better than mine.

And although I knew he objected since it meant I'd be driving, I still asked, "Why not?"

"First, you don't know your way around."

"I know it well enough." After a week of driving Isabella and another week with Dimitri escorting us to various sites, I was starting to get my bearings. The city wasn't that big, at least not compared to LA

"And you know how I feel about you driving here."

"Alex—"

"Especially on a Saturday night. They'll be plenty of drunks on the road."

He knew that would scare me. Stela had warned me that Romanian men enjoyed their brandy. In Romania, she'd said, any man who didn't drink was suspect.

"Then I'll take a taxi." I figured it wouldn't be cheap, but Alex was paying me well. And he'd refused to let me reimburse him for the fines he'd paid the day my rental car had been towed.

He didn't respond, which I thought meant he agreed. Not so.

I was the only one who was surprised when Cristina's great-niece Ivana arrived at the house at seven o'clock. She told me Alex had called her that afternoon and asked her to babysit.

"I thought we'd go to dinner," he said when I demanded an explanation, "and a club afterward if you want."

"I told you I'd take a taxi. You don't need to come."

"I know," he said. "But it'll be better this way."

It wasn't that I didn't enjoy his company—I was beginning to find his charm and dry wit very appealing—it was his making the decision without even consulting me that irked me. He could be so controlling sometimes. Actually, all the time. But I had to admit that going out to dinner with him did sound better than wandering the streets of Brasov alone.

"And what about Isabella?" He'd heard me promise her we could watch *The Wizard of Oz* this evening. I'd planned on going out after she'd gone to bed, not before.

"That's why I called Ivana."

It wasn't that easy. Ivana fed Isabella dinner and helped her with her bath while I showered and changed, but when it was time for Alex and me to leave, Isabella wasn't having it.

"Gwen, you promised!"

I knelt down on the hardwood floor in my black pants and high heels and realized it was the first time I'd worn anything other than shorts, jeans, or a bathing suit since I'd arrived. "I know, Isabella, but Ivana's going to watch it with you instead."

She grabbed my hand. "But you said *you* would watch it with me."

"Isabella," Alex said, "you can watch the movie with Ivana or not at all."

I looked up at his stern expression and whispered, "You're not helping."

He let out an exasperated sigh and walked away.

"How about if we watch the beginning together, and then if you like it, you can watch the rest with Ivana, and if you don't then she'll let you watch whatever you want for the rest of the night?"

"Anything?" Isabella asked. "Even *Barbie*?"

Those were my least favorite of Isabella's many DVDs. I always tried to encourage her to watch something else, normally without success. I hoped Ivana didn't feel the same.

"Whatever you want," Ivana agreed.

When we made it out to the car fifteen minutes later without any tears, Alex complimented me on my skillful maneuver.

I laughed. "Yes, bribery is the key to every successful relationship."

"I'll try to remember that."

Over dinner at a steakhouse in an underground cellar dating back to the thirteenth century, Alex plied me with red wine (or tried to; this time I limited myself to one glass) and peppered me with questions about my childhood. I attempted to do the same to him (with the questions, not the wine) but he always brought the conversation back to me again. That's how I knew this wasn't a date. Guys *always* talked about themselves on dates. Or at least the guys in LA always did. And while I firmly believed that we should keep this relationship professional, or as professional as you can be when you're living in your boss's house and he sees you in your pajamas every morning, there was a tiny part of me that was disappointed too. Besides the charm and dry wit, which were on display in full force this evening, he had a great smile and a confidence I found very alluring. I also hadn't had sex in six months.

After dinner we wandered the cobblestone streets of the plaza, and at my request Alex snapped photos of me under the Bank of Transylvania sign, which, disappointingly, contained no fangs or images of Dracula, and under the awning that declared Brasov "Probably the best city in the world."

"What is that about?" I asked. "I mean, if they think it's the best city in the world, why not just say that? Why equivocate?"

Alex laughed. "I don't know. I never thought about it before."

Luckily we didn't run into any helpful Americans who offered to take our picture, so there were no awkward moments where we had to pretend that we were a couple.

When we arrived home, Isabella was already in bed, and Ivana was asleep on the couch. Alex woke her and sent her upstairs to one of the extra bedrooms because he didn't want her driving home alone in the dark either. Considering she'd arrived on a moped, I didn't blame him.

We climbed the stairs together and stopped at the landing at the top of the steps. Alex's bedroom was to the right; mine was to the left.

"Thanks for dinner," I said, both because he'd paid and because I'd had a nice evening.

"My pleasure," he replied.

Even though this wasn't a date, and we were living in the same house, and we had said good night to each other many times before, it still felt awkward. "Well, good night."

"Gwen—"

Isabella's door creaked open, and she appeared in the doorway in her pink princess nightshirt, Peter the bear in one arm, her other arm shielding her eyes from the light.

"Isabella, what are you doing up?" Alex said.

"I waited for you and Gwen," she said sleepily.

"Sweetie," I said as I joined her on our side of the hallway, "you didn't need to do that."

"Will you read to me?" she asked.

"Didn't Ivana read to you?" I'd specifically told her it was part of the bedtime routine.

Isabella nodded. "But she didn't do the voices."

I laughed. It was nice to know she appreciated the effort. "Okay, but just one chapter."

"Gwen." Alex's tone told me that was not the answer he was hoping for.

"We'll be quick. I promise."

Isabella smiled up at me and Alex sighed. "*Very* quick," he said. Then he kissed her good night before continuing on to his own bedroom.

Isabella saved me from an awkward situation and fell asleep after only two pages. A win-win in my book.

The opposite of the next day.

When I woke up the next morning it was raining. At first I panicked. Rain meant no park, no pool, or any other outdoor activities. Then I remembered it was Sunday, my day off, and I rolled over and went back to sleep.

I ambled downstairs two hours later and was headed to the kitchen when Alex called out to me from the study.

"Good, you're up," he said. "I thought I was going to have to send Isabella to wake you."

"Why?" I replied through a yawn. "What's going on?"

"We're going to the movies," Isabella said, glancing up from her Nintendo.

"Sounds like fun," I said and continued on to the kitchen. They both followed me.

"Don't you want to know what movie?" Isabella asked as Alex lifted her off the stone floor and sat her on one of the counter barstools.

"Sure," I said as I poured myself coffee from the still warm pot.

"Maybe we should surprise her," Alex said. "Let's not tell her until we get to the theater."

My eyebrows shot up. "We?"

"I figured you'd want to come," he said, "knowing what a movie fan you are."

I smiled and shook my head. "Nice try."

"But we're going to see the princess movie," Isabella said.

Of course you are. Sometimes I hated Disney for propagating those princess stories. All the girls were obsessed with them. I almost felt like I had to give them toy guns to play with just to balance it out.

"That sounds like fun, Isabella, but I'm going to let your daddy take you today."

"But what are you going to do?" she asked.

Honestly, I didn't know. Originally I was going to drive to Poenari Fortress, a citadel that the real Dracula had actually stayed in, but it was at the top of a very steep hill, and according to the guidebook the only way to reach it was to climb 1,480 stone steps. I wasn't sure I was up to the challenge on a dry day, but in the pouring rain it sounded miserable. Plus, if Isabella and Alex were leaving, it meant I'd finally have the house to myself. I'd been dying to explore it, but on weekdays Cristina or Ivana were always nearby, and on weekends Alex was constantly hovering.

"Don't worry about me," I said. "I'll find some way to amuse myself."

"Does this involve driving somewhere?" Alex asked. "Because from Brasov you can catch a train to almost anywhere in the country, and certainly all the major tourist sites. We could drop you off on our way."

"Maybe next weekend." If he was never going to let me drive the rental car, and apparently he wasn't, I might as well return it. It was stupid to keep paying twenty dollars a day for it to sit in the driveway. "I think today I'll just catch up on my e-mail and read a book."

"So you'll be here when we get back?" Alex asked.

"Yes." Unless the weather cleared up and I decided to go for a hike in the woods. I hadn't been to the gym in weeks and was long overdue for a workout. Limbering up before I attempted Poenari Fortress would probably be a good idea.

Even after the front door slammed shut I waited until I heard Alex's tires crunching on the gravel driveway before I started snooping.

Chapter 20

I began in Alex's bedroom. It was huge, with a built-in ornate gold-leaf bedframe that must've been original to the house, and tall windowed alcoves on either side. Below each window was a marble shelf with a wooden drawer underneath. Only one side was being used. It held an alarm clock, a lamp, and two framed photos—one of Isabella and another of a beautiful dark-haired woman who I assumed was Isabella's mother both because Isabella resembled her and because I'd seen the same photo in her bedroom.

I hesitated before I opened the drawer underneath. Perhaps that was going too far. But my curiosity got the better of me and I opened it anyway. I'm not sure what I was expecting, but I was disappointed in what I found—a pad, a pen, and a clipped stack of papers. On top was a printed e-mail addressed to Alex from someone at *Universitatea din Bucuresti*, which I assumed was the University of Bucharest. It was written in Romanian, as were the rest of the documents (yes, I admit I flipped through them), so I couldn't read them, but I recognized the names "Vlad Tepes" and "Dracula" even with the Romanian spelling and accent marks. Apparently I wasn't the only one in this house who was interested in the Dracula legend.

I returned the papers to the drawer in exactly the same spot I'd found them and moved on to the giant walk-in closet. Again, one side was empty. The other side was filled with Alex's suits, slacks, shirts, and ties, all pressed and grouped together by color from light to dark. Underneath were several pairs of polished dress shoes and one scuffed pair of sneakers, which I'd seen him wear exactly once—yesterday morning when we'd played tennis.

The bathroom was the true masterpiece. In addition to the enormous stall shower with the built-in stone bench, there was a separate oval spa tub that had to be at least five feet long with jets on all sides. I smiled just imagining myself soaking in it. I'd be covered in bubble bath, aromatherapy candles all around me, per-haps sipping a glass of wine. If I knew exactly what time Alex and Isabella were due home I might've convinced myself to chance it. But since I didn't, I moved on to the next room.

In total there were nine bedrooms upstairs, each with its own bath. There was one more bedroom and full bathroom downstairs next to the kitchen, which were presumably for a live-in maid, and two more half baths. Behind the pantry in the kitchen I found a stairwell that led down to the basement, where I discovered a sec-ond, much larger pantry and the wine cellar. The rest appeared to be dusty storage.

I already knew the first floor rooms pretty well, so I went back upstairs and found the door that I thought might lead up to the third floor, but it was locked. I could've tried to jimmy it open—it was a cheap doorknob lock, not a dead bolt—but I decided that really would be going too far. Besides, I'd asked Alex once what was on the third floor and he'd told me nothing. He'd said a hun-dred and fifty years ago it had been servants' quarters, but now it was a big empty space. He and his wife had talked about turning it into a giant playroom, but she'd died before they'd gotten that far.

At the time I'd had visions of *Jane Eyre* and wondered if his wife wasn't dead after all but really locked in the attic. I laughed to myself now as I thought about it. Alex was much too practical for that Mr. Rochester maneuver. If his wife were insane he would've just installed her at one of the high-end clinics in Malibu.

By the time Alex and Isabella returned from the movies it had stopped raining but was still gray outside. I was lying on the couch in the study reading the Dracula book Alex had given me.

"How was it?" I asked and sat up, making room on the couch so they could sit down too.

Alex grimaced and Isabella synopsized the plot in typical seven-year-old fashion. I stopped listening after "and the princess looked in the mirror." When she finished she said, "What should we do now, Daddy?"

"How about a DVD." It wasn't a question. Within seconds he'd turned on the television, the DVD player, and the surround sound receiver and pulled the basket of DVDs out of the cabinet and set it down in front of Isabella. "Choose."

She pulled a *Scooby Doo* out of the pile. Alex popped the disc into the player and left the room. I watched one episode with her then left too. I didn't think Isabella even noticed.

"You want a beer?" Alex called as I passed the cavernous living room on my way to the stairs. He was lying on one of the three sofas with his iPad propped up on his chest. He lifted his tall glass filled with amber liquid and said, "There's more in the fridge."

What the hell. It was my day off. I grabbed a beer for myself and returned to the entrance to the living room, unsure whether that was meant merely as an offer to help myself to a beverage or as an invitation to join him.

"Take a seat," he said. "There's plenty of room."

I perched on the edge of the couch perpendicular to his. It had carved wooden legs and cushions covered in off-white velvet. I thought it might be antique, so I was afraid to get too comfortable.

"Isabella already spilled juice on it," he said. "Twice. I doubt you could do any worse."

So I leaned back and sipped my beer straight from the bottle.

"I don't know how you do this every day," he said. "Don't get me wrong, I love Isabella more than anything in the world. But if I had to spend all day every day with a bunch of seven-year-olds... well, it wouldn't be pretty."

I laughed. "So I take it the theater was crowded?"

"Overrun. I think every parent in Brasov brought their child to the movies today."

I nodded sympathetically. "It's hard to keep them entertained when they're stuck inside all day. It's better for everyone when they can play outdoors."

"Thank God for DVDs and video games."

He was not the first parent I'd heard utter that sentiment. It was popular among some of the nannies too. I definitely understood. When I was teaching, I followed a lesson plan. Without that structure, it was much harder to fill the day, especially for fourteen hours straight. After only two weeks with Isabella, I had a newfound respect for all those full-time nannies and stay-at-home moms out there.

We chatted for a few more minutes, then Alex went back to reading on his iPad and I opened the Dracula book he'd given me. It was quiet in the living room until I shouted, "Oh my God!"

Alex nearly spilled his beer. "What's wrong?"

"Nothing," I said, shaking my head. "It's just these stories..." I held up the book because I was too freaked out to explain.

"You need to remember, Gwen, he was a product of his time." Alex argued, which the author of the book did too, that while Vlad Tepes was cruel, he was no worse than the other rulers of his era. And unlike some of the others, he actually succeeded in curbing corruption, which was rampant at the time, and keeping the Ottoman Turks at bay. While the Western world considered Vlad Tepes a bloodthirsty despot, Romanians, even now, hailed him as a hero.

Alex droned on, but I stopped listening. I'd just read the section highlighting the most popular tales about Vlad the Impaler.

These stories dated back to the fifteenth century and were circulated in German, Russian, and Romanian pamphlets. Since similar stories were told in all three languages, scholars gave them more credence. The last one was about Vlad and his mistress. Although the details varied a bit, the gist of the story in all three languages was the same:

Vlad had a mistress who, in an effort to cheer him up when he was depressed, told him she was pregnant with his child. Vlad doubted his mistress (he was suspicious as well as vengeful and bloodthirsty), so he had her examined by a midwife who told him the woman was lying. Vlad confronted his mistress, who insisted she was telling the truth. Vlad responded by cutting her open from her groin to her chest and, according to German legend, said, "Let the world see where my fruit lay." Then he left her to die alone and in excruciating pain.

It was exactly the same as that horrible dream I had my first night in Romania.

Chapter 21

I left Alex in the living room and raced upstairs. I would've called Zoe but it was still early in the morning in LA, so I sent her an e-mail instead. I typed out the story from the book and added: *I dreamt this BEFORE I read it. Call me!!!!*

Two hours later she e-mailed me back: *Message me.*

I logged onto Facebook and typed: *I'm freaking out!*

Zoe typed: *Stop freaking out. There's a logical explanation. You must've read it before.*

I typed: *Never.*

She typed: *Then you must've heard it somewhere.*

I typed: *Nope.*

She typed: *Then what's your explanation?*

I typed: *I don't have one. That's why I'm freaking out!!!!*

She typed: *Think, Gwen. Maybe you overheard someone talking about it. Or you read it in a different book. Or saw it on YouTube or Facebook or Twitter. Or maybe your parents used to read you horror stories when you were a baby and they were so awful they lodged in your subconscious. Actually, I think that's it. That's probably why you had all those nightmares when you were a kid. Mystery solved.* ☺

I stopped typing and considered it. No, I didn't think my parents read me horror stories when I was a baby. They never even let me watch scary movies when I was young because they knew I had nightmares so easily. But otherwise Zoe made sense. I must've read it somewhere a long time ago and forgotten it, but it lodged in my subconscious and eventually resurfaced in a dream. There was no other explanation. It was too coincidental that I could've dreamed a story that I'd never read or heard before.

I typed: *You're right, that must be it. Thanks.*

She typed: *My bill's in the mail☺ Gotta go. XOXO.*

Even though I knew Zoe was right about the origins of my dream, I was still on edge. For the first time since I was a child, I was afraid to be alone. I picked up the book, which I was only halfway through, and decided I'd had enough of Vlad Tepes. I pulled down my empty suitcase from the top of the armoire and tossed the Dracula book inside. It landed next to the Saint George painting I'd forgotten I'd brought with me. I picked it up and studied the image.

"I guess you did bring me luck," I said to Saint George, whose sword was perpetually pointed at the dragon's mouth. This job wasn't perfect, but it could've been much worse.

I tossed the painting back into the suitcase and returned it to the top shelf of the armoire. Then I went downstairs and found Isabella in the study still watching *Scooby Doo*.

"You want to play a game?" I asked.

She paused the DVD. "What kind of game?"

"How about a board game? You choose."

We ran up to her bedroom and scanned the bookshelf housing her vast collection of toys and games. Isabella grabbed Sorry and Connect Four, and I pulled out Uno and my personal favorite, although Isabella never showed any interest in it, Rock 'Em Sock 'Em Robots, and I carried them downstairs to the kitchen table. When Alex heard us yelling over good moves, bad moves, and points lost and won, he wandered into the kitchen and joined us. We all played a game of Sorry together and a few rounds of Uno. Then Alex and I played one round of Robots (it turned out he was the one who had purchased the toy for Isabella, which didn't surprise me) while Isabella cheered us both on.

When we had all grown tired of board games I suggested dinner out. Alex let Isabella choose the cuisine, so we ended up at a pizza place. The restaurant was noisy, crowded, and brightly lit, which was exactly what I needed to distract me. By the time we returned to the house I almost felt like myself again.

"Can we watch *The Wizard of Oz*?" Isabella asked before we'd even taken our shoes off and hung up our jackets.

"You just watched it last night."

She shook her head. "Only the beginning. The wicked witch was scary, so Ivana shut it off."

Hmmm. I didn't want to be responsible for giving Isabella nightmares. "Then maybe we shouldn't watch it."

"No, I want to watch it!"

"But the wicked witch is going to be scary tonight too."

"I know, but it'll be okay because you and Daddy will be here."

I wasn't going to take responsibility for this one. "Go ask your father. If it's okay with him, it's okay with me."

Of course Alex acquiesced. He had no restrictions on what kind of content Isabella could watch. So the four of us sat on the couch together—Alex on one side, me on the other, and Isabella and Peter the bear between us. As I feared, the first time the wicked witch appeared on screen Isabella cowered. But Alex pulled her onto his lap and told her when to hide her eyes during the scary parts and she was fine. And even though she had her father to protect her, she insisted on holding my hand too, which touched me.

I knew I'd still see Isabella after the summer ended because Alex had enrolled her at *Académie française* for the following year. But she wouldn't be my student anymore, and even when she had been, I'd only spent an hour a day with her in the company of fourteen other children instead of the fourteen hours a day I routinely spent with her one-on-one now. While I wouldn't miss the occasional tantrums, the constant demands, and trying to comb the knots out of her hair, I knew I'd miss her—all the funny things she said, the way she snuggled up to me when I read her stories, and the random hugs she sometimes gave me for no reason at all. And that surprised me.

On Monday morning Cristina and Dimitri returned and we all went back to our weekday routine. The only two deviations were a trip to the rental car office on Monday morning (I knew Alex was never going to let me drive so I finally returned the rental car) and Elena's birthday party on Friday night. Unlike children's birthday parties back home, in Romania they were much smaller gatherings and the parents and nannies weren't invited too.

"We're free for the next five hours," Alex said after we'd dropped Isabella off at Elena's house late Friday afternoon. "How about the opera?"

"We don't have tickets," I said, praying he wasn't going to pull a pair out of his pocket. It had been a busy day—driving into town for tennis and the playground in the morning, then driving back home for lunch and swimming in the afternoon, then driving back into town again for the party. I wasn't sure I could make it through a potentially boring night at the theater, especially if it wasn't in English, without falling asleep.

"You can buy them the day of the performance. Opera is much more casual here."

"Casual enough for jeans and a T-shirt?" When I'd showered and dressed after swimming, I'd thought we were just dropping Isabella off at the party and driving home. Alex was wearing his standard slacks and button-down shirt. Even when he worked at home, he always dressed up.

"Everyone will write it off to you being American," he said and grinned.

"But I'm not even wearing sneakers!" Stela had told me that was the giveaway, even before I opened my mouth. Once she'd pointed it out to me, I noticed it myself and started wearing them less often.

"*Buna dimineata*," he said, pronouncing it the mangled way I did, instead of the proper Romanian way.

"Hey, at least I'm trying." Dimitri and Cristina had started saying "good morning" to me in English, so I wanted to say it back to them in Romanian. I had "*buna*," down—it sounded like boo-nah—it was the "*dimineata*," I was still having trouble with. Reading the words didn't help because the letters were often pronounced differently in Romanian than they were in English, especially if they had accent marks.

"And it hasn't gone unnoticed," he said. "But I'm sensing resistance to the opera. Is there something else you'd rather do? We could go to Mount Tampa. Best views in the city."

"You want me to hike up the side of a mountain in these shoes?" I dangled my backless sandal from my toes. It figured the one day I wasn't wearing my sneakers I needed them.

"No, I assumed we'd take the cable car."

"Oh," I said. "Yeah, I guess we can do that if you want."

He pulled into an open parking space on the next block and shut the engine. "Gwen, I'm trying to do what *you* want."

"You mean for a change of pace?" I said it with a smile so he'd know I was teasing. On weekdays we always did whatever Isabella wanted to do, which was as it should be. But at night and on the weekends, Alex called the shots. It was his house and his kid, so that was his right, but I resented it a little. At home I was used to doing things my own way. I didn't particularly like taking orders from someone else.

He bit back a twisted grin and looked at his watch. "You've already used up fifteen of your minutes."

He didn't have to prompt me again.

Chapter 22

"The rowboat," he said, as we walked into the kitchen from the back door. I noticed that Cristina's purse and shawl, which had been lying on the bench when we left the house, were now missing. Alex must've given her the night off on the assumption that I'd want to go to the opera. "I offer you anything," he continued, "and that's what you choose."

"I've been trying to get Isabella to go for weeks, but she has zero interest."

"Because the lake's not that interesting."

"For you two," I said, "but I've never had my own lake before."

He laughed. "I don't own the lake, Gwen."

"I know, but you own all the land around it, so it's sort of the same thing."

He looked unconvinced.

"You don't need to come," I said. "But that's what I'm doing. You can do whatever you want."

He ran his fingers through his hair and sighed. "No, I'll come. Just give me a minute to change."

I sat at the kitchen table and played with Isabella's iPad while I waited. He returned a few minutes later wearing tan dress pants and a linen shirt.

"Who the hell are you supposed to be?" I asked, nodding at his ridiculous outfit.

"What?" he said. "This is proper boating attire."

"On a yacht maybe." I'd thought he was going to change into something more casual, like shorts and a T-shirt. I should've known better.

"C'mon, let's go."

"I can't go like this," I said, looking down at my faded jeans and the grease stain on my shirt that I'd manage to lighten with soap and water but hadn't washed out completely.

"Sure you can."

"No, I can't. Not with you looking like Mr. Fancypants."

"Gwen, no one's going to see you except me, and I think you look beautiful."

Whoa. I look beautiful? Where the hell had that come from?

"Give me a minute," I said and ran up the steps.

Was this a date? I could never tell with him. I'd assumed we were just killing time together before we had to pick up Isabella from the birthday party. I considered placing a quick call to Zoe to get her opinion, but it was still early morning in LA

No, I was overreacting, I decided as I opened my armoire and searched for something to wear. He was just being polite. It would've been rude of him to tell me I looked like a slob, even though I did. Alex was a lot of things, but never rude.

I fingered the white Prada sundress he'd given me. "Oh, what the hell," I said to the empty bedroom. If he wanted to pretend we were living in a nineteenth century novel where people actually got dressed up to row across a lake, I could too. I only wished I'd brought a parasol.

"Wow," he said when I'd returned to the kitchen in my sundress, sky-blue shrug, and silver sandals. The white dress really highlighted my dark tan.

"I didn't want to be outdone."

"Clearly," he said, still staring at me.

"What's all this?" I asked, gesturing to the items he'd laid out on the kitchen counter, even though it was obvious what they were. His gawking was making me uncomfortable.

"Refreshments," he said as he pulled the bottle of champagne out of the ice bucket.

I shook my head. "I would've been happy with beer, you know."

"I know," he said, "but this will be better. Trust me."

I grabbed the stack of half a dozen towels Alex had set out on the counter even though I thought two would've been plenty, and Alex carried the bucket of champagne, glasses, and a basket he'd filled with cheese, crackers, and strawberries.

When we reached the lake, I helped Alex maneuver the rowboat out of the shed and tried not to cringe every time he crashed it against the wall. I was used to old wooden ones with chipped paint and mold growing in the crevices between the planks—that was the kind my dad and I used to go out on when I was a kid. My mother hated camping so one weekend a year he would take me to Big Bear himself and we would rent a boat for the day. We stopped going when I turned thirteen and decided camping with my dad was lame. I regretted that now. Alex's rowboat was made of wood too, but it was painted white with polished teak trim and still in pristine condition. It was the most beautiful rowboat I'd ever seen.

I stood off to the side as Alex flipped the boat over onto the grass, then wiped away the dust and the cobwebs with one of the half dozen towels we'd brought from the house. After it was cleaned to his satisfaction, we pushed it to the edge of the lake. I climbed in first, then Alex handed me two towels—one for each of our seats—and the food.

When the only item missing was him I said, "You're still wearing your shoes." But he was looking up at the sky.

"I'm a little concerned about the weather."

I looked up too. There were dark clouds in the distance, but they were miles away and there was almost no wind. "We'll be back before they get here."

"I'm not so sure," he said.

"Alex, I'm in a dress, you're wearing linen, and we have a bottle of champagne on ice. Get in the damn boat."

He laughed. "Relax, Gwen, I'm coming."

I was glad he understood that the point of this boat ride was to relax, nothing more. He slipped out of his shoes and socks and carried them into the shed along with the rest of the towels. Then he rolled up his pants legs, pushed the boat away from the shore, and hopped in.

He rowed us to the middle of the lake, then lifted the oars out of the water. Except for his house on the south shore, we were surrounded by forested mountains on all sides. The air smelled of fir trees, and the only sounds were the water lapping against the sides of the boat, the occasional birds cawing overhead, and the intermittent buzzing of a mosquito.

I closed my eyes, breathed in deeply, then exhaled. I was immediately reminded of Big Bear Lake, except without all the people, and felt my shoulders drop. "Thank you, Alex. This is perfect."

"You're welcome," he said and popped the cork on the champagne. He handed me a glass then joined me on my bench, which surprised me. I'd thought he'd stay on his own side. "Cheers," he said and clinked his flute against mine.

We didn't talk other than to ask the other to pass the crackers or for more champagne. We just enjoyed the fresh air and the solitude. It was the calmest I'd felt since I'd arrived in Romania.

The calm before the storm as it turned out. Literally.

Chapter 23

The first raindrop landed on my head. "Did you feel that?" I asked.

"Feel what?" he replied before the next drop splattered on his shirtsleeve.

"Oh no," I said as I looked up at the darkening sky.

Alex switched back to his seat and pulled the oars out of the water. He didn't row slowly, but we'd drifted to the far side of the lake. By the time we reached the south shore, the drizzle had turned into a downpour and we were both soaked. I jumped out first and grabbed all of our stuff, and he pulled the boat up onto the grass and flipped it over. We both dashed to the shed. The house was much too far to run to in the pouring rain.

"Good call on the towels," I said, grabbing a dry one from the bench where he'd left them along with his shoes. If he'd listened to me they would've been outside on the grass and as drenched as we were.

"Occasionally I am right, you know," he said and grabbed his own towel, which he used to dry his hair.

"Sorry," I said and wrung the water out of my hair with my hands before I peeled off my wet sweater. Then I wrapped the dry towel around my shoulders. "I really thought we'd make it back before the rain."

He shrugged. "It happens."

"Yeah, because I wore this stupid sundress. I'm never going to wear a white dress with you again. It's just asking for trouble."

He laughed. "I don't think you can blame it on the dress, Gwen. Besides, I only spilled wine on the first one."

"And then I got so drunk wearing this one that I passed out in your guest room." I closed my eyes and shook my head in a futile attempt to banish the snippets of memory. "I still can't believe I sang you all those songs from *West Side Story*."

"Don't be embarrassed," he said. "I thought it was cute."

"It's cute when a seven-year-old sings show tunes. When a twenty-seven-year-old who's drunk off her ass does it, it's not so cute."

"I beg to differ."

"I'm surprised you even wanted to hire me after that," I said, but he was giving me that look again, the same one he'd given me earlier in the kitchen. And it made me just as uncomfortable the second time around. I wrapped the towel a little tighter around my shoulders and walked to the doorway of the shed. I stared out at the pouring rain, watching it batter the previously placid lake. "What now?" I asked.

I didn't turn around, but I could feel his presence behind me. "We can wait here until it lets up or make a dash for the house."

I was going to say we should make a dash for the house when a bolt of lightning cracked overhead, lighting up the sky, the mountains, and the lake, before disappearing again. "Let's wait here."

Alex unfurled two towels and laid them on the dusty wood floor, and we both sat down. "More champagne?" he asked and pulled the bottle out of the bucket.

"Sure." I grabbed the two glasses I'd tossed into the basket and held them out to him. He filled each one to the top.

Since Alex was still barefoot, I kicked off my shoes also and sat crossed-legged on the towel. "Good call on the refreshments," I said after I'd drained half of my glass in one gulp.

"I thought you'd like it." Then he topped off my champagne without asking me if I wanted more.

After I finished my glass, I jumped up and grabbed the last dry towel, which I folded into a pillow before I lay down and closed my eyes. Listening to the rain pelting the shingled roof wasn't as soothing as listening to the water lapping against the sides of the boat, but it was rhythmic and the air smelled like damp earth. I'd just started to drift off when another bolt of lightning cracked overhead. My eyes flashed open and I jumped.

Alex was lying next to me on his own towel, his head propped up on one elbow, the glass of champagne in his other hand. "It's okay," he said. "The storm's moving away."

I didn't know how he knew that, but I lay back down and closed my eyes again anyway.

I felt his hand on my forehead, but his touch was so light it didn't startle me. He pushed the wet locks off my face then ran his fingers through the rest of my hair before moving down to my neck. Somewhere deep inside I knew this was wrong, that I should tell him to stop. But that deep-inside voice was drowning under three glasses of champagne. The rest of me just thought it felt good and wanted it to continue. And it did.

When his hand slid down to my breast, I finally spoke. "You're not Isabella's father."

"I'm not?" My eyes were still closed, but I could hear the incredulity in his voice.

"No, because if you were we wouldn't be doing this. It would be wrong for me to sleep with my boss, and wrong for you to sleep with your daughter's nanny."

"Are you sure?" he asked, the incredulity replaced by amusement. "I thought seducing the babysitter was a common fantasy."

I finally opened my eyes. He was leaning over me, his hair still wet from the rain, his linen shirt sticking to his arms and chest. "Maybe, but it's not *my* fantasy."

"Ah." He grinned down at me. "Please continue."

I closed my eyes again. "I'm here visiting for the summer," I said as he began kissing my collarbone and teasing my nipple with his thumb through my uselessly wet dress. "And you're a tourist too. We met on the plaza."

He stopped kissing and let his hand rest on the side of my breast. "Under the 'Probably the best city in the world' sign?"

"Yes," I said, "exactly. And you thought it was weird too. And we became friends."

"Just friends?"

"Just friends. But you're leaving for London in the morning and I'm going back to LA"

"What a pity," he said.

"No," I replied, "it's perfect because this is our last night together. We both want something to remember the other by."

"Ah," he said and resumed his kissing and teasing.

It was amazing how he instinctively knew exactly where and how to touch me. Sometimes, especially when I was with someone for the first time, I felt like I was directing a movie—hand here, lips there, slow down, speed up. With Alex I didn't have to say a word; he knew what to do and my body just reacted.

As his lips and hands moved lower the only sound in the room was our breathing and the rain tapping against the roof. Then he reached for my panties, which were wet from the inside.

I grabbed his hand. "Do you have protection?"

"Protection?" he asked.

"A condom."

A wave of recognition crossed his face, but it quickly changed to worry. "Do I need one?"

I pushed myself up onto my elbows. He was still wearing his shirt, although I'd unbuttoned it, revealing a patch of dark hair that narrowed into a thin line that trailed down to his waist, and he had a huge bulge in his pants. "Of course you need one."

He pushed himself up onto one elbow too. "Is there something I should know?" he asked. "Some problem?"

I wasn't 100 percent sure what he was implying, but I had an idea. "Not with me! What about you?"

"No," he said, "so why do we need a condom?"

Was this not obvious? "Birth control, you idiot."

"You're not on the pill?"

"No," I said and sat up, crossing my legs and folding my arms over my chest. "Why would you assume I was? You think I do this with every guy I meet?"

He sat up too. "No, not at all. It's just...never mind."

"No, tell me." The moment was already ruined; we might as well talk.

"Nothing, it's just my wife was on the pill for years before we had Isabella. I thought it was standard these days."

His wife had died two years ago. Hadn't he been with anyone else since? Or before? I'd assumed someone that skilled at foreplay had been with lots of women.

"I *was* on it," I admitted, "when I had a steady boyfriend. Then we broke up and the insurance company raised the co-pays and the pills got really expensive. It seemed sort of silly to spend all this money on them when I didn't really need them anymore. I mean, whenever I met someone, which wasn't that often, we always used a condom anyway."

He nodded.

"So I guess we're done here." I sighed and stood up. I'd definitely need a cold shower before we left to pick up Isabella. And some clean underwear too.

He jumped up also. "Where are you going?"

"Back to the house. It sounds like the rain's letting up."

"But you said this was our last night together. I'm still leaving for London in the morning, and you're still heading back to LA."

"That was when I thought you were a smart tourist who carried condoms. Unless you have some in the house?" I asked hopefully.

He shook his head. "The last time I was here was with my wife."

Damn. "Then we're done here," I said again and headed to the door.

He grabbed my hand. "We don't need to be done. We can do other things."

That got my attention. "Other things?"

He pulled me to him and kissed me long and slow and deep, and the mood I thought had vanished quickly reappeared. "Tell me about these *other things*," I said when I came up for air.

"I'd rather show you."

This time instead of the floor he maneuvered us against the wall of the shed. I was still wearing my dress, but not my underwear, and he'd peeled off his shirt, but not his pants, although the fly was undone. I was standing and he was down on his knees, and I finally understood why guys liked this position, because it really was a different experience. Well, not *that* different, and certainly no less pleasurable.

I was on the verge of ecstasy from a combination of his fingers and his tongue when suddenly there was more of him inside of me. A lot more.

"What the—"

But he'd stood up and put his mouth on mine, while pushing himself deeper inside me at the same time. I was in such a state, instead of shoving him away as I should've done, I wrapped my leg around him, meeting him thrust for thrust.

It was only after I stopped shuddering from one of the best orgasms of my life that I finished my thought.

Chapter 24

"What the hell was that?" I asked.

He was leaning against the wall next to me, breathing heavily too. "You don't know?"

"Yes, I know! That's why I'm pissed. What happened to *other things?*"

"Sorry," he said, a sheepish expression on his face. "I guess I got a little carried away."

"You think?"

"Sincerely, Gwen, I apologize. It's just..." he hesitated before he continued, "please forgive me for saying this if I'm misreading the situation, but I was under the impression that you enjoyed it too."

I couldn't deny that I had but... "That's hardly the point!"

A quick grin broke through before he could tamp down on it. "Well if it's the other thing you're worried about, don't be. I pulled out."

"Oh, that's helpful," I snorted. "You chose the one birth control method that's caused more pregnancies than it's prevented."

I could see him fighting back another smile. "Gwen, you do realize that this wasn't my first time?"

I rolled my eyes at him. "Obviously." He was skilled at more than just foreplay. "But I thought your wife was on the pill?"

"She was," he said. "But she's not the only woman I've ever known. And I've fathered just one child—Isabella."

"That you know of."

He shot me a withering look. "That was uncalled for."

He'd just fucked me without a condom and *now* he wanted to talk about good manners? But much as I wanted to, I knew I couldn't blame it all on him. Most of it, but not all of it. I could've stopped him and I hadn't. I'd wanted to feel him inside me. It was only now that my desire was sated that I was harboring remorse.

"Promise me you will never, ever do that again."

"None of it?" he asked.

"No, just the no condom part." It was too good to pretend I'd never sleep with him again.

"I promise," he said and held up his right hand as if he was being sworn in.

"I'm serious, Alex."

"So am I. First thing tomorrow morning I'm going out and buying the biggest box of condoms I can find."

We didn't have much time before we had to pick up Isabella from the party, so we ran back to the house and showered quickly then changed into what we'd been wearing earlier in the day.

The music turned on automatically when he started the car, but I was the one who upped the volume. I figured if Alex had something he wanted to say to me he could turn it down. But he didn't, and I was grateful. I was a mess.

On the one hand, I didn't regret what we'd done (except for the unprotected sex part). That was an orgasm I wouldn't soon forget. But on the other hand, *what the hell was I thinking?* He was Isabella's father and my boss for the next three weeks. And we lived together. How were we going to hide this from her? I didn't think a seven-year-old needed to know her father and her nanny were sleeping together when she wasn't around.

I was assuming this wasn't just a one-time thing. It could've been, but I doubted it from the remark he made about buying condoms. Plus, if it had been half as good for him as it had been for me, he'd want to do it again. Although that didn't make it right.

I sighed and glanced over at Alex, who was staring straight ahead, both hands gripping the steering wheel so tightly his knuckles looked like they were about to burst through the skin. He was probably having regrets too. Sex changed everything. Even guys knew that whether they admitted it or not.

I stayed in the car when Alex went to fetch Isabella from Stela's house. Despite the late hour, she was a chatterbox, at least for the first few minutes. Then she fell asleep halfway through the ride home. Once she stopped talking, I leaned my head against the window of the passenger's seat and dozed off too. I woke up when the car stopped abruptly in front of a store blazing under bright fluorescent lights.

"Where are we?" I asked. All I knew was that we weren't home.

"Wait here," Alex said before he ran inside.

I glanced behind me and saw that Isabella was still sleeping and realized we were at a gas station. But we weren't filling up; Alex had parked in front of the minimart. He returned a few minutes later with a brown paper bag.

"What did you buy?" I asked, thinking maybe he had the munchies. Except for the champagne and crackers, we'd skipped dinner.

He handed me the package so I could see for myself. Inside were three boxes of condoms, a dozen in each. "My flight for London's not leaving until morning," he said. "We still have time."

I hoped he wasn't planning on using all those condoms tonight.

Isabella was still asleep when we arrived at the house, so Alex carried her up to her bed and tucked her in. I shut off the lights downstairs and went to my own room, unsure what to do next. Alex knocked on my door a few minutes later.

"Come in," I called.

He opened the door but remained in the hallway. "She's asleep."

"I know." What was the protocol here? Was I supposed to invite him into my bed?

"She's normally a sound sleeper, but it'd probably be better if you came to my room anyway."

"Oh. Okay."

"Assuming you want to, of course."

"Yes," I said.

"Yes, you want to? Or yes you understand?"

"Both. I think. Why? Don't you want to?" There was a reason people got drunk before encounters like these.

"Of course I do. I'm the one who asked, remember?"

"Right," I said and nodded.

"You're not having second thoughts are you?"

Second and third and fourth and maybe fifth. "No. I mean, not really. It's just…I don't know how I'm supposed to act."

"Act like you normally do."

"But what about Isabella? You don't want her to know, do you?"

"I'd prefer that she didn't. At least for right now."

"Okay. And Cristina and Dimitri and Ivana? I assume we want to keep this just between us, right?"

"That's probably for the best," he said.

I nodded again. At least now I knew. And even though I felt the same, that if we were going to continue sleeping together we needed to keep it a secret, somehow I still felt disappointed that he didn't want anyone to know. Like maybe I wasn't good enough to go public with.

When I didn't move, he walked into the room and sat down next to me on the bed. He grabbed my hand in his much larger one. He had beautiful tapered fingers, which I'd just noticed for the first time. "Gwen, I only want to do this if you want to do this. If you're uncomfortable we can stop."

"But you bought three boxes of condoms."

He chuckled. "All right, maybe I went a little overboard. You did make me promise though."

"True," I said and laughed too. "It's not that I don't want to, it's just…what exactly are we doing here?"

"I don't know. This isn't standard for me either."

"You mean you're not sleeping with Katarina too?"

He laughed again. "No, definitely not."

"Well, that's good to hear since she's getting married next month."

He looked at me quizzically for a moment then said, "Yes, I don't think her fiancé would approve."

We sat together in silence for a few minutes until he abruptly stood up. "Gwen, I don't want to pressure you. I'm going to my room. I would love for you to join me, but if you've changed your mind about this, that's okay."

"It's okay? You don't even care?" Really, the poor man couldn't win with me.

"Of course I care! I'll be hugely disappointed that I wasted all that money on condoms." Then he grinned at me so I knew he was kidding. "Seriously, Gwen, I need to know you're comfortable with this. Otherwise everything goes back to the way it was before."

"Really? You think we can do that?" The phrase "you can't unring the bell" came to mind.

"Yes," he said. "I do." Then he walked out of the room and shut the door behind him.

I doubted it. It would always be awkward between us from now on whether we continued sleeping together or not. Perhaps something I should've thought about *before* I had sex with him. I sat on the bed for another few minutes then moved to the bathroom for my nightly routine of washing my face and brushing my teeth. I slipped out of my jeans and slightly stained T-shirt and into my pajama bottoms and a loose-fitting tee, my usual sleep-wear. Then I returned to my bed for another ten minutes before I finally stood up again. Fuck it. It was going to be awkward either way, so I might as well enjoy it. We were only here another three weeks then it was back to self-imposed celibacy for me and who knew what for him.

Alex's light was still on and his door was ajar, but I knocked once before I pushed it open the rest of the way. He was lying on top of the covers in his striped boxer shorts and snowy white T-shirt, reading on his iPad. He glanced up and smiled. "What took you so long?"

Chapter 25

Keeping our relationship a secret was harder than I'd thought it would be. First, I told Zoe. But since she lived thousands of miles away, so I didn't think that counted. Alex was responsible for everyone else finding out. Instead of carrying all those used condoms and wrappers outside to the trashcan and burying them at the bottom, he blithely tossed them into the wastebasket in his bathroom. Of course Ivana was going to notice when she emptied it. And it didn't take a genius to figure out the only person in the house he could be using those condoms with was me. Once Ivana knew, Cristina and Dimitri and probably every person Ivana had ever met knew too.

Not that any of them ever mentioned a word about it to me. But I knew they knew. Whenever Alex and I were alone in a room together and one of them walked in, the smiles and sly looks they shot us made it clear that they were in on the secret. Although none of them seemed to disapprove.

The only one who didn't know was Isabella. And for that Alex and I were both grateful. I made an effort not to even look at Alex if she was in the room. He wasn't as careful. He would often touch my shoulder as he passed or give me a wink or a knowing smile when he thought we weren't being observed. If Isabella noticed I was confident she would've mentioned it. The fact that she hadn't led me to believe she was still in the dark.

Although our daytime schedule remained the same, now that we were sleeping together the nighttime routine changed. Alex usually joined me and Isabella for bedtime reading, where before it had been a rare occurrence. Once she was asleep, he would follow me to my room and lounge on my bed while I washed and brushed and changed into my pajamas.

"Why don't you ever wear nightgowns?" he asked one evening while I was still brushing my teeth.

"I don't know," I said through a mouthful of toothpaste. "I guess pajamas are more comfortable," I added after I'd spit. "Is it a problem?"

"No," he said, but the next night he handed me a gift box filled with expensive lingerie.

I wore them at night when it was just the two of us, but I still wore my pajamas to breakfast in the morning. And I insisted that Alex set his alarm for six thirty a.m., even on weekends, despite the fact that Isabella didn't normally wake until sometime between seven thirty and eight, so I could slip back to my own room unobserved. I was paranoid that she'd see me sneaking out of her father's bedroom in the morning and be scarred for life, or at a minimum it would lead to an uncomfortable conversation I wanted to avoid so badly that I was willing to wake up an hour early every day.

Maybe it was because we had already been living together for three weeks, but the relationship developed quickly. We were comfortable together, both in and out of bed. It was like having sex with a good friend, or what I'd always imagined friends with benefits would be like. Most of my friends were women so I'd never tried it before. Now that I had, I decided I'd have to acquire some new single male friends when I returned to LA It had all the advantages of a real relationship—sex on a regular basis and companionship outside of bed—without any of the messy emotional entangle-ments. It was perfect.

After the first night, I no longer even minded when we would lie together after sex and Alex would trace my birthmark with his fingertip before we fell asleep. He loved that ugly puppy chasing its own tail/dragon breathing fire/misshapen doughnut. But I still hated it.

One night I mentioned that I was thinking about getting laser surgery to have my birthmark removed. I'd read an online article earlier in the day about recent improvements in the technology. Although it wasn't always possible to remove a birthmark com-pletely, the laser could at least lighten it and make it less notice-able.

"I think that's a terrible idea," Alex said. "Why would you even contemplate such a thing?"

"Because I hate it. And if lightening it makes me less self-conscious about it, then why shouldn't I?"

"You shouldn't be self-conscious. You're beautiful."

"Not my shoulder."

He kissed my birthmark then caught my chin in his fingers, forcing me to look at him. "Gwen, it's the imperfections that make us who we are."

"Well I'd rather not be the woman with the hideous purple birthmark on her shoulder."

He shook his head and sighed. "What am I going to do with you?"

"I could think of a few things," I said and smiled seductively.

As it turned out, so could he.

On Saturday night after Isabella had fallen asleep Alex suggested we watch a movie.

"Sure," I said and headed toward the steps, but he stopped outside my bedroom door.

"Aren't you going to change first?" he asked.

I looked down at my jeans and T-shirt, neither of which were stained. "Not unless you'd prefer to see me in my pajamas." Although the lingerie he'd bought me was beautiful, it was too revealing to wear anywhere but behind a closed bedroom door.

He pulled an ivory silk babydoll with black lace trim and matching thong underwear from behind his back and held it up. "I was thinking about this," he said and flashed me a lascivious grin.

"*After* the movie."

He frowned. "Isabella's sleeping. No one's going to see you in it but me."

"What if she wakes up?"

"Has she woken up during the night even once since we've been here?"

"Yes, at the hotel in Bucharest."

"That was your fault. Are you planning on screaming your head off again?"

"Not unless the movie's really scary."

"Don't worry," he said, "it's not that kind of movie."

Against my better judgment I changed into the babydoll and followed him downstairs to the study. He shut off all the lights and turned on the TV.

I paused the screen almost instantly. "I'm not watching porn!"

"Why?" Alex said. "Does it offend you?"

"No, not exactly, it's just…you know."

"I don't know," he said. "You'll have to tell me."

Despite the fact that I was wearing sexy lingerie and we'd been sleeping together for over a week, I could still feel my cheeks burning. "Because it'll put me in the mood."

He threw his head back and laughed. "That's the point, Gwen. I would even go so far as to say that's the sole purpose of pornography."

"Then we should watch it in your bedroom."

"We can't," he said. "I don't have a TV."

"What about your iPad?" The screen was small, but this was not something I needed to watch in wide-screen high def.

"I don't know how to get it from here to there. Do you?"

"No," I admitted. I was a bit of a technophobe.

"Well then," he said and unpaused the television.

"I swear to God, Alex, if you hear the slightest sound from upstairs you better warn me."

"I will," he promised.

It wasn't the upstairs occupant we needed to worry about.

Chapter 26

I was still wearing both pieces of my scanty lingerie when I thought I heard a noise and paused the television.

"What was that?" I asked Alex, who was already down to just his boxer shorts.

"You're imagining things," he said, before unpausing the television and returning to the trail of kisses he was blazing from my chest to my waist.

A few seconds later I heard the noise again, and this time he did too. It sounded like a car door slamming shut, followed quickly by crunching on gravel and then someone unlocking the front door.

We met Alex's brother Stefan in the foyer. He seemed as surprised to see us as we were to see him.

"What the hell are you doing here?" Alex asked.

"Nice to see you too, brother," Stefan replied. "And Gwen," he said, taking in my outfit, "you're looking especially lovely this evening."

I ran back into the study and grabbed the chenille throw off the couch and wrapped it around myself. I also snagged Alex's undershirt off the floor. I tossed it to him when I returned to the foyer, but I couldn't do anything about the bulge in his shorts. I caught him and Stefan mid-argument.

"You said August," Alex shouted as he pulled the undershirt over his head.

Stefan removed his navy blazer and folded it over the top of his suitcase, leaving him in jeans and a striped button-down. "I had a change in plans."

"Then you should've let me know," Alex said.

"Why?" Stefan replied, his voice rising. "I have as much right to be here as you."

"Because a heads-up would've been appreciated."

"If I knew what you were doing," he said and glanced at me before returning his attention to Alex, "I would have. That wasn't part of the plan either as I recall."

These two clearly had a lot of issues that had nothing to do with me and I had no desire to get in the middle of it. "I think I'll go to bed. Good night." Then I ran up the steps without looking back.

They must've moved out of the hallway because suddenly their voices were muffled. And when I closed my bedroom door behind me I could no longer hear them at all.

I e-mailed Zoe about this latest development then played on the Internet for a while before I shut off my light. I'd just gotten my pillow into exactly the right position under my head when there was a knock on my bedroom door. Alex didn't wait for me to answer. "You awake?" he asked as he crept in.

I reached for the light. "What's going on?"

He switched it off again and slid into bed next to me.

"What about Isabella?" I asked.

"Shhhh," he said and snuggled up behind me with his head next to mine and his arm around my waist. "I won't stay."

Then we both fell asleep. It was the first time we'd spent the night together without having sex.

Alex wanted to rectify that oversight the next morning.

"Not here," I whispered. "Not with Isabella next door."

Alex nodded and slipped out of bed. He slunk to the bedroom door and cracked it open. "The coast is clear. C'mon."

We snuck across the hallway to Alex's room without getting caught by Stefan. Not that it mattered. Obviously he already knew. Even if the clothing hadn't given us away, and I was pretty sure it had, I'd forgotten to shut off the television.

"Uncle Stefan!" Isabella called out when he staggered into the kitchen in baggy pajama bottoms, a navy tee, and his hair sticking out in all directions.

"My favorite niece," Stefan yelled back as she ran into his outstretched arms. He spun her in the air until she screamed, then smothered her in kisses.

"I'm your only niece," she said, wrapping her arms around his neck and her legs around his waist.

"That doesn't mean you can't be my favorite too." He returned her to her chair then proceeded directly to the coffeemaker. After he poured himself a cup, he joined us at the table. "Did everyone sleep well?" he asked, glancing from me to Alex.

I felt my cheeks burning and wished I had a newspaper to hide behind. But I didn't, so I stuffed another forkful of pancakes into my mouth and stared down at my plate.

"Play nice, Stefan," Alex said.

"I thought I was," he replied and took another sip of his coffee. "So isn't anyone going to offer me pancakes? Or am I to fend for myself? And where's Cristina?" he added, glancing around the kitchen. "Shouldn't she be here by now?"

"It's Sunday," Alex said. "She has weekends off, remember?"

"You can finish mine," I offered and pushed my plate across the table. "I'm done anyway."

"Gwen, you don't have to do that," Alex said. "I can make more."

"It's okay. I want to go shower and get dressed anyway." And I wanted to get away from him and Stefan before the fireworks started again. It was my day off too. I didn't need to stick around to referee.

Alex followed me out into the hall. "Where are you going?"

"To shower and get dressed, like I said."

"And after that?" he asked.

"I'm not sure. Probably something touristy. Can you drop me off at the train station?"

"I thought you were going to spend the day with me and Isabella."

I had agreed to, but that was before Stefan arrived. "Do you really think that's a good idea?"

Stefan appeared in the hallway with Isabella on his hip. "What's all this whispering about?"

"Daddy, it's not nice to talk behind people's backs."

"Not nice at all," Stefan concurred, presumably just to annoy Alex even more.

It worked. His voice was calm, but he glared at Stefan as he spoke. "I'm not talking behind anyone's back. I'm just asking Gwen about her plans for the day."

"What are your plans for the day?" Stefan asked me.

"I'm not sure. I was thinking about going to Poenari Fortress." It had been my plan last Sunday before it rained. I could go today instead and get away from all of them.

"Ah, Castle Dracula. You know, I've always wanted to go there," Stefan said. "Would you mind if I tagged along?"

I glanced at Alex, who was seething. "Um, no, I guess not."

"Can I come too?" Isabella asked.

"Of course you can," Stefan said. "You don't mind, do you, Alex?"

"Isabella, you have to climb a lot of steps to get to the fortress," I said. "A lot more than at Bran Castle. Are you sure you really want to go?"

"You went to Bran Castle too?" Stefan asked.

I don't know why he was surprised. It was the number one tourist attraction in the country.

"It sounds like you're taking the Dracula tour of Romania," Stefan continued.

"I guess I am. I really didn't know much about Dracula before I came, but Alex gave me a book about him and it's gotten me sort of interested."

"Did he?" Stefan said and turned to Alex again.

"Stop. Right. Now," Alex said. I think if Stefan hadn't been holding Isabella, Alex would've taken a swing at him.

Stefan gave him a twisted smile. "C'mon, Isabella, we have to finish our breakfast so we can go with Gwen to visit Dracula," he said in an imitation of Bela Lugosi.

"Daddy, are you coming too?" Isabella asked as Stefan carried her back to the kitchen.

"Absolutely," he said, glaring at Stefan's back.

If I thought I could've gotten away with it, I would've offered to stay home and let the three of them go without me. But I knew that wasn't possible.

Alex insisted on driving even though Stefan offered to (he'd rented his own car). I volunteered the front seat to Stefan, but he sat in the back with Isabella anyway. She chatted him up the whole ride, telling him about all the things we'd done this summer. I turned up the volume on the music so it wouldn't seem weird that Alex and I weren't talking.

After we stocked up with water and snacks at the store at the base of the cliff (Alex vowed he was not walking down 1,480 steps for a bag of chips when Isabella decided she was hungry), we began the arduous climb. As I'd predicted, by the fourth staircase Isabella was tired and didn't want to walk anymore. At first Alex carried her on his back. But he was sweating so much that Isabella complained that his shirt was too wet for her to hold onto. I thought we were all going to have to give up when Stefan offered to carry her the rest of the way. He must've worked out on a stair-stepper because he was hardly winded at all.

By the tenth staircase even my calves were burning and I was sweating and breathing heavily too. There was a bench at the next landing, so Alex and I stopped to rest. At first Stefan and Isabella joined us, but when Stefan realized we wouldn't be pushing on anytime soon, he told us he'd meet us at the top, and he and Isabella continued on without us.

Alex waited until they were out of sight behind the next bend in the stone staircase built into the forested hillside before he turned to me and said, "We need to talk."

"Uh oh." I was usually the one who uttered that phrase, so I knew it couldn't be good.

"It's nothing bad," he said, still gasping for breath. "I just wanted to know when you have to be back at work."

"Not until the twentieth. Why?"

"I'm not taking Isabella straight home. We're going to London for a week before we head back to LA"

"To see your mother?" I asked.

"Yes, and my sister too."

"And you need me to watch Isabella?" The timing would be perfect since Zoe and her family would be in London visiting her brother that week also.

"No, my sister's already agreed to watch her. She has two boys, four and six, so she won't even notice one more."

I doubted that. "Then what do you need me for?"

He seemed surprised by my question. "I don't need you, I want you. Haven't you figured that out yet?"

"Oh." I didn't know how else to respond. We didn't normally say those sorts of things to one another, and I wasn't sure I wanted to. I liked our relationship just as it was.

"We don't have to stay in London," he continued. "We could go anywhere. Just the two of us."

"Oh," I said again, recognition dawning on me. "You mean like a vacation?" I could definitely get on board with that plan.

"Yes. France, Italy, Spain, wherever you want to go."

Wow, no man had ever offered to take me on vacation before. There were definitely some advantages to sleeping with a rich guy. "That sounds great. Do I need to decide today? I mean, I'm not sure where I'd choose." I would e-mail Zoe as soon as we returned to the house. She'd traveled more than me and would undoubtedly have suggestions.

"Not today, but soon."

I stood up to leave, thinking that was the end of the conversation, but he grabbed my hand. "Not so fast."

"Alex, if we don't keep moving we're never going to get to the top."

"The fortress has been here for eight hundred years, Gwen. It's not going anywhere. Sit down. There's something else I want to talk to you about."

"Oh no. What's wrong?"

"Why do you always assume it's something bad?" he asked.

I laughed, remembering how many times Zoe had asked me that same question. My answer to him was the same: "Because it usually is."

He sighed, then grabbed my other hand and pulled me toward him. When I was standing between his legs, he let go of my hands and slid his fingers into the back pockets of my jean shorts. "I need to know what you want to do when we get back to LA"

Uh oh. This was a conversation I really didn't want to have. I decided to play dumb. "I just told you, I have to be at work on the twentieth. I don't have time for another vacation. Or did you need me to keep filling in for Katarina? When exactly is her wedding anyway?"

"That's not what I meant at all. I'm asking you what your plans are *for us?*"

Dammit. He really wasn't going to let me off the hook here. I answered as vaguely as I could. "I'm not sure I had any plans."

"I was hoping you'd move in with us," he continued.

"Move in with you?" I said, unable to keep the incredulity out of my voice. We'd only been sleeping together for a little over a week! What happened to dating for a few months (or years) first?

"Yes," he said.

"You mean like a girlfriend?" I asked, mainly to buy myself time.

"At this point in my life I prefer the term lover, but yes, as my girlfriend."

Now I did sit down. I was suddenly breathless again, and not from the climb. I wasn't even sure if we were going to continue seeing each other when we returned to LA, or if I wanted to. I liked Alex. A lot. And the sex was great. But he had traits—mostly his controlling nature—that I didn't like too. For a summer fling, which was what I'd thought this was, it didn't matter. But for a boy-friend, especially one who wanted me to move in with him and his kid, it definitely did. "Lover, wow, how continental."

"I thought you enjoyed being my lover." I could tell he was making an effort to sound nonchalant, but a bit of defensiveness crept into his voice anyway. Note to self: never even hint to a man that he is anything less than stellar in bed.

"I do enjoy it. I thought that was obvious." Did I need to start moaning louder?

"Is that a yes then?"

"It's an I don't know." I needed to time to think, but I didn't want to tell him that, or at least I didn't want to admit why I had misgivings, so I said, "I mean, wouldn't Isabella be suspicious? I have a reason for living with you here, but surely she would wonder why I'm living with you in LA too."

Alex laughed. "I assumed at that point we would tell her. In fact, we can tell her now if you want. With Stefan around she's going to find out sooner rather than later anyway."

"No," I shouted and quickly backtracked. "It's just that there's a lot going on right now. Stefan shows up out of nowhere, and now you're going to London and—"

"We're going to London," he corrected.

"Right. We. But we're not staying. All I'm suggesting is that we hold off for a beat. Okay?"

"Gwen, I know this is sudden. But when it's right, it's right. We're not teenagers. There's no reason to wait."

"I know, it's just..." His controlling nature was definitely a problem for me, but he was also handsome, rich, generous, an excellent lover, a decent cook, and I enjoyed his company. Honestly, what more was I looking for?

Chapter 27

"It's fear," Zoe said when I called her from the house that evening.

"It's not fear; it's just too soon. I mean, what's the rush?"

"You're afraid to be happy," she said.

I ducked into the billiards room and shut the door. It was the first time I'd been in there since Alex had given me a tour of the house my first day. It was hard to believe that was only a month ago. "It's not like he told me he loved me. He just asked me to move in with him."

"It's the same thing," she said.

"It is not and you know it. Besides, aren't you the one who's always telling me they don't buy the cow when you give them the milk for free?"

She laughed. "Yeah, but I'd say that ship has sailed already."

I laughed too. "True. I don't know. I'm just not ready yet. I like living alone. I get to do what I want when I want." That would definitely not be the case if I lived with Alex and Isabella.

"Gwen, I say this with love so please take it that way. Will you ever be ready?"

"I'm only twenty-seven, Zoe. Not quite an old maid."

"And every time a guy gets close, you pull away."

"That's not true!"

"Oh no?" she said. "What about James?"

"My parents had just died and all he wanted to do was go out and party."

"And Michael?"

"He left for graduate school."

"In San Diego," she said. "It was only two hours away. You could've seen each other on weekends. And Chris, what was wrong with him?"

"What's your point? That I can't maintain a relationship? I've admitted that already. That's why this friends with benefits thing is so great. If he wants to keep seeing me when we get back to LA why can't we just continue the way we are? Why does he have to screw it up?"

She sighed. "Gwen, friends with benefits *never* works. Someone always wants more. Although usually it's the girl, not the guy. So perhaps it's time you asked yourself *why* you can't maintain a relationship."

"I suppose you have a theory on that too," I said, randomly running my hand along the dark wood trim of the pool table. Ivana must've cleaned in there recently because I couldn't spot a speck of dust anywhere.

"Yes, as a matter of fact, I do. Fear. Ever since your parents died it's like you're afraid to get close to anyone. As if you don't want to rely on anyone because they might disappear and then you'll be all alone again. So you decide you like being alone and then you never have to deal with it."

"That is the biggest bunch of bullshit I've ever heard."

She laughed. "You think so? I thought it sounded pretty good."

I laughed too. "I say this with love, Zoe, so please take it that way. Psychoanalysis has never been your forte." Although I couldn't discount the fear factor completely. It just had nothing to do with my parents' deaths. I hadn't been all that good at romantic relationships even when they were alive. It was the endless sharing of feelings I couldn't abide. Maybe I was just dating the wrong men. Surely football players and construction workers wouldn't want to know my innermost thoughts all the time.

"Fair enough," she said. "So tell me about the fortress."

Finally a topic I was comfortable with. Sort of. "Oh my God, the place was haunted."

"Haunted?"

"Seriously. You know I don't believe in ghosts and spirits and all that hocus pocus, but I'm telling you it was like there was a presence up there."

"What kind of presence?"

"A bad one. It totally gave me the creeps." I shivered just thinking about it. "As soon as we made it to the top I came back down." I searched the room for a blanket or a throw, but I couldn't find one so I plopped down on the leather club chair and hugged my knees to my chest.

"I don't understand," she said. "What do you mean by presence?"

"I can't explain it. There's not much left of the place, at least compared to what it used to be." Eight centuries and several major earthquakes had taken their toll. The fortress that now remained at the top of the sheer cliff consisted of only a few rooms with crumbling brick walls and truly awe-inspiring views of the valleys below. "But there was this one room that was still more or less intact. It's where they tortured the prisoners."

"Tortured the prisoners?"

"Yeah, Vladdy boy just loved to torture people. It was a sport to him."

"Gross."

"I know. But it's not like they left the bones or anything. I'm telling you there was a presence. It was like you could sense all the bad things that had happened there."

"And did everyone else sense this presence too?"

"No, that was the weird part. It was just me."

She laughed. "I think you've been spending too much time reading about Dracula. Next you're going to tell me you've been bitten by a vampire."

Now I laughed. "No vampires, but definitely lots of bloodsucking mosquitoes. I must have twenty bites from that place!"

"It's because you're so sweet," Alex said when were alone together that night.

"Yeah," I said, handing him the tube of anti-itch cream because I couldn't reach the mosquito bites on my back, "that's the same BS my mother used to tell me when we'd go for hikes in the canyon and I was the only one who'd get bitten."

"It's true," he said.

"Alex, you've already got me in your bed. You can stop trying to seduce me."

He smiled and turned off the light.

I glanced down into the valley that stretched out before me. I knew the Turks were there, biding their time, planning their attack. They wouldn't retreat until they had my head on a stake, as I had done to so many of their brethren. Although I preferred entire bodies. Decapitation was too easy. Death was instantaneous. Impalement was so much more satisfying. I closed my eyes and breathed in the fir-scented air, remembering the sights and sounds from a different day.

We used the horses to pull their legs apart, then the servants inserted the stake. But we didn't sharpen the tip. Death would be too quick. Rounded was best, and oiled so it could slide all the way through. One had to be careful not to break the neck. If it was done right, the victim would linger for days. I felt a shiver of pleasure ripple through my body. I could practically taste their blood on my lips; hear their screams. So sweet. So deliciously sweet. I opened my eyes and sighed. There was no time for that now.

I stepped away from the window and followed the stairs to the chamber below. What would it be today? I opened the door and spotted the woman chained to the wall, her clothes tattered, her skin covered in dirt. Ah, now I remembered. She had lost her virginity before her wedding night, the filthy whore. I had the perfect punishment.

"It's said you like something between your legs."

She cowered and shook her head. "No, my lord, it's not true."

I grabbed the poker and reddened the tip in the fire. She would die as she lived, with my metal between her legs.

I tried to scream, but no sound came out. Someone was on top of me, pinning my arms, and covering my mouth. I struggled to push him off, but he was too strong.

"Gwen, stop fighting, it's only me. Honey, wake up."

As I rose into consciousness I recognized Alex's voice, but his hand was covering my mouth and I couldn't speak. When I stopped struggling, he let go of me, then turned on the light.

Alex was breathing heavily too, but not as heavily as me. I couldn't seem to catch my breath. He tried to hug me, but I pushed him away. I managed to croak out one word: "Don't."

"Another dream?" he asked.

I nodded.

"I'm sorry. I didn't mean to frighten you, but I thought you were going to wake the whole house. You have quite a set of lungs."

I tried to smile, but my heart still felt like it could burst out of my chest at any moment.

"What can I do? Can I get you something? Water? Brandy?"

I shook my head and lay back down, but my side of the bed was soaked with sweat so I sat up again. I could speak now; I just didn't want to. Alex reached for me again, but I pulled away. I couldn't stand anyone touching me. Not yet. It was too soon.

"Gwen, tell me what to do for you."

"Nothing," I said. "Just let me be." Then I ran into the bath-room and locked the door. The stone floor felt cool against my naked, sweaty back. I hadn't taken a sleeping pill in ten days. Not since I'd started spending my nights with Alex. The first night I'd forgotten. After that I thought I didn't need them anymore. I thought maybe I'd finally found a cure for the nightmares—sex before bed. Tonight proved that theory wrong.

Alex knocked on the bathroom door. When I didn't answer he twisted the knob. "Please, Gwen, let me in. I need to know you're okay."

I reached up and unlocked the door but I didn't open it. He did that himself and stepped inside. I was seated on the bathroom floor, naked and hugging my knees to my chest. He grabbed a towel off the rack and placed it around my shoulders then sat down behind me. He pulled me to him with my back pressed against his chest. "Tell me," he whispered into my ear, his arms wrapped tightly around my shoulders. "Tell me about your dream."

"I can't," I whimpered.

"Why not?"

The tears slid down my cheeks. I didn't even try to stop them. "Because it's bad."

"Bad how? Did someone hurt you?"

I shook my head.

"Then what?" he said. "Please, Gwen. I can't help you if I don't know what it is."

I tried to laugh, but it came out as a hiccup. "You can't help me."

"I can, but you have to let me. Why won't you?"

The tears continued unabated. I was so tired. Tired of being tormented by these awful nightmares. And tired of being alone too. Even when I was with Alex, I was alone. Not physically—I'd never been more intimate with anyone. But emotionally I kept him at a distance. Zoe was right about that. I didn't like to get too close. But

I knew Alex wouldn't let us continue this way. And I wasn't sure I was ready to give him up. If he really wanted to be with me he should know the truth. I owed him that.

"I'm not a violent person," I said. "Even when I find spiders in my house, I don't kill them. I take them outside and let them go."

"Okay," he said.

"But it's different in my dreams."

"Different how?"

"I kill. Not spiders, but people."

"People who are trying to hurt you? Bad people?"

"No. Not really." I shivered, and he wrapped his arms tighter around me. "I don't know. Maybe they're bad, but not to me. Not directly."

"I don't understand."

Neither did I. "In my dreams, I kill people. Lots of people. And I don't just kill them, I torture them. And I enjoy it. It gives me pleasure. I think I'm a serial killer. Or a sociopath. I'm definitely evil." The tears started flowing again.

"Honey, you're not evil. They're just dreams."

"But if I'm dreaming it, it must mean on some level I want to do it, even though I don't. I swear I don't. It disgusts me. But I keep dreaming about it."

He pulled my legs around so my side was to him, instead of my back, and he could see my face. "Gwen, dreams aren't aspirations, they're fears. Didn't you ever have that dream where you showed up for class naked or overslept and missed a big exam?"

"Yes." I had those sorts of dreams too. "But these are different. I don't just see them, I smell them and taste them. And they don't fade right away like the others do."

"I know, but they're coming from the same place."

I shook my head. "Zoe thinks my parents read me horror stories when I was a kid and now they're all stuck in my subconscious."

He looked skeptical. "That's one theory."

"It's okay, I don't believe it either. Although I think she may have been right about that Dracula one."

"What Dracula one?"

"That was the nightmare I had at the hotel in Bucharest our first night. Don't you remember? I woke Isabella."

"I remember," he said.

"The dream I had that night, I read it in that book you gave me."

"But I hadn't given it to you yet. I bought you the book when I was in Germany."

"I know, but I must've read that story somewhere else. At first I didn't think so, and it totally freaked me out, but then I searched online and found it on a bunch of Dracula websites, so I must've heard it before. It's the only explanation."

He smiled down at me. "Yes, that must be it. Where is that book? I haven't seen you reading it lately."

"In my bedroom. Why?"

"I'd like to take a look at it when you have a chance. There's something I want to check."

"Sure," I said. "You want me to get it now?"

"No, it can wait until morning."

I glanced at the watch on his wrist. I took mine off before bed, but Alex always slept with his. "It's almost morning already."

"Then let's get some sleep."

"I can't. I can never fall back asleep after one of these dreams, not unless I take a pill, and it's too late for that."

"Let's try anyway," he said. "If you can't sleep I'll stay awake with you."

My side of the bed was still damp with sweat, so I curled up with Alex on his side. We talked about Isabella and where we could go on vacation (Alex suggested Paris and I agreed), and eventually I nodded off. When I woke a couple of hours later I felt happy, happier than I'd been in a long time. It was as if telling him about my dreams had somehow unburdened me.

When he started stirring, I propped my head up on my elbow and faced him. "So now that you know I'm really a serial killer, at least in my dreams, have you changed your mind about wanting to live with me?"

He grinned at me. "Not in the least. Knowing your deepest, darkest secret only makes me love you more."

I stopped smiling. "You love me?"

"Yes, Gwen, I love you."

"Good." And before I could think about what I was saying I added, "Because I think I love you too."

Holy shit. Did I just say that? I hadn't told a man I loved him since James, and I'd only said it to him because he'd said it to me and I felt like I should reciprocate. This time I actually meant it. Zoe would never believe it.

It wasn't just the first time I told Alex I loved him. It was also the last.

Chapter 28

"You must tell me what you ate for breakfast this morning," Stela said as we watched Isabella and Elena lob balls over the net from our table at the café.

"Why?" I asked as I added another sugar to my coffee. They brewed it strong at the club.

"Because whatever it was, I want some too."

I shook my head and laughed. "I don't think it was the raisin bran."

"Then what? You're positively glowing." I was still mulling over how much I should disclose—if Alex and I were going to live together in LA then this was no longer a secret relationship—when she asked, "Did you meet someone?"

"Sort of."

"I can't believe you're seeing someone and you haven't told me. What's his name?"

"Alex."

At first she looked confused, then her jaw dropped. "Alex, Isabella's father?"

"Yup."

She just sat there with her mouth hanging open until she finally said, "I don't know what to say. I'm shocked."

"I can tell."

"I didn't even think you liked him. And now you're dating?"

"I didn't like him. I didn't hate him either, but..." I shook my head. "I guess he grew on me."

"Apparently," she said and took a sip of her coffee. "So how long has this been going on?"

I gave her a watered-down version of events, but she kept shaking her head and telling me how shocked she was, and eventually I started to get offended. "Why is it so shocking? Am I not good enough for him?"

"Oh no, Gwen, nothing like that. It's just that you're so nice."

"And he's not?" That was probably my fault. I hadn't painted a flattering portrait of him, especially when she and I had first gotten acquainted and Alex had flipped out because I'd rented that car.

"I don't really know him," she said. "I only met him that one time. But he has a reputation, at least in business circles, for being ruthless. But I'm sure he's not like that at home."

"No, he's not." He could use more patience, especially with Isabella, but I wouldn't call him ruthless.

"I'm very happy for you," she said.

I was too, but I was glowing a little less than I had been when I'd arrived.

We only stayed at the park for an hour today instead of two because Isabella wanted to get home to Uncle Stefan. He'd promised to teach her how to backstroke this afternoon. She started calling his name as soon as we walked through the front door. Stefan didn't appear, but Alex did.

He gave me a quick kiss when Isabella wandered into the kitchen, still looking for Stefan. "I'm glad you're home."

"Why? Did you miss me?"

"Always," he said. "But you also forgot to give me that book before you left this morning. The Dracula book."

"It's upstairs in my bedroom. I'll go get it."

He cocked one eyebrow. "In your bedroom, huh?" He looked at his watch. "How long do you think it'll take her to find Stefan?"

"I don't know. Where is he?"

He shrugged. "I haven't the slightest idea. But this is a big house."

I knew what he was thinking. I could already see the bulge forming in his pants. "No way," I said and dashed for the steps. He ran after me but I was faster, so by the time he reached my bedroom I'd already opened the armoire and had my suitcase half pulled out. He reached over my head, grabbed the handle, and carried it to the bed. I unzipped the top and passed him the book, but he was more interested in what was still inside.

"What's this?" he asked, reaching for my painting.

"Saint George."

"I know that," he said, fingering the image. "I meant where did you get it?"

"From my parents."

"Your adoptive parents?"

That was one of his habits that annoyed me—calling my parents my adoptive parents. "Yes, but they got it from my birth mother. Why?"

"No reason," he said.

"Obviously you had a reason," I snapped. "You might as well tell me what it is."

"Whoa, what just happened here? Why are you mad at me?"

"They were my parents, Alex, not my *adoptive* parents. I don't think they loved me any less because I wasn't their biological child."

"Gwen, I'm sorry. I didn't mean anything by it."

"I know, but you make that distinction all the time, and it bugs me." I sat down on the bed and sighed. Now I felt like an idiot for even bringing it up. "Sorry, I didn't mean to be such a bitch about it. But if we're going to keep seeing each other then you need to stop doing that."

Isabella appeared in my doorway. "Have you seen Uncle Stefan?"

"No," I said, "have you tried the pool?"

She shook her head and ran down the steps. That probably bought us a few more minutes, but Alex no longer seemed to be in the mood. I was relieved since I wasn't either.

Alex waited until breakfast the next morning to announce that he was leaving for Greece. It was just the two of us at the table; Isabella and Stefan were both still upstairs sleeping.

"When did you decide this?" I asked.

"Just now," he said and held up his BlackBerry, showing me the text message. He'd brought it with him to the table, which he didn't usually do.

"So you just woke up this morning and decided you wanted to go to Greece?" Maybe that's what rich people did. Everyone else I knew made plans.

He laughed. "No, it's a business trip. My visitor's permit just came through this morning. I'm going to catch a flight later today."

"Since when do you need a permit to go to Greece?" I knew some countries required visas, but I didn't think Greece was one of them.

"When you want to go to Mount Athos," he said. "They require visitor's permits."

"What if Isabella and I want to join you?" I'd never visited Greece, but Zoe had, and I'd seen her pictures. Some of the islands were beautiful. Even if Alex had to work, Isabella and I could play in the turquoise waters and walk along the sun-bleached shores.

"You can't," he said. "No women allowed."

"Now I know you're lying. You're going to meet your mistress, aren't you?"

He laughed again. "I don't have the energy for a mistress, Gwen. I can barely keep up with you."

"Me? You're the one who's always instigating."

"I'm a man with a beautiful woman in my bed. What am I supposed to do?"

"Go to sleep!"

He leaned over and gave me a chaste kiss on the lips, then stood up. "I will miss you, Fair Gwendolyn."

"Gwendolyn? How did you know my name was Gwendolyn?" My father was the only one who had ever called me Gwendolyn, and even he did so rarely. He'd told me that my name meant "blessed" and that he and my mother had chosen it for me because I was their blessing—they'd tried to have a biological child for years and couldn't, so God had given me to them instead. No one had called me Gwendolyn since he'd died.

He shrugged. "I don't know. I must've read it on your passport. You're awfully suspicious this morning."

"Sorry, I'm just…I don't know." But I did know. It was the relationship thing. I was terrified to be in one again and equally terrified that I was going to screw it up. "Hormonal or something."

He looked at his watch. "I've got to pack and run a few errands before I leave. I probably won't be here when you get back. Give Isabella a kiss for me. I'll call you later." Then he took one last sip of his coffee and sprinted up the steps.

The sky was gray and cloudy when we left the house, but it didn't start raining until we arrived at the park. We waited in the car with Dimitri for ten minutes, but it didn't look like it would be clearing up anytime soon.

I was dreading going home and having to spend the day stuck in the house. I could only take so many hours of board games and cartoons before I started to go stir-crazy. "Any ideas?" I asked Isabella.

"We could go to the toy store," she said.

That worked for me. We didn't want to walk around outdoors, so Dimitri drove us to a shopping mall. I was surprised they had those in Brasov. It seemed like such an American convention. Via the electronic translator he explained that they had several indoor shopping centers in Brasov, all of them new.

Dimitri dropped us off in front of a nondescript three-story building and told us he'd pick us up in two hours. We could've covered it all in one. The shopping mall wasn't big, but it did contain a currency exchange office, which was helpful since I was almost out of cash again.

After I traded in my dollars for Romanian lei we went to the toy store, and I bought Isabella a new outfit for her Barbie doll. Then we wandered through the rest of the shops. Although the names were different, many of the stores were similar to those we had in the US—lots of clothes, shoes, and cell phone kiosks. But this mall also had a casino with slot machines, card tables, and cocktail waitresses in skimpy outfits. I didn't know if there was a minimum age requirement, but I refused to take Isabella inside anyway.

Even stranger than finding a casino in a shopping mall, at least outside of Las Vegas, was passing a fortune-teller. She was tucked into a small storefront between a beauty salon and a shoe store. We still had half an hour to kill before Dimitri was collecting us so I figured it would be good for entertainment.

In heavily accented but understandable English the proprietor told us her name was Madame Olga. She looked exactly like every fortune-teller I'd ever seen in a movie. She held her long dark hair off her face with a brightly colored scarf, and she wore a loose-fitting purple dress. Madame Olga told us to perform a reading she had to meet with each of us alone, but I refused to leave Isabella in the outer room by herself, so she led us both into the back room together.

The only light emanated from a floor lamp in the corner, which didn't offer much illumination. All I was able to discern was a small table covered in a dark cloth with a crystal ball in the center and two folding chairs. Madame Olga sat down in the chair on the far side of the table and motioned for me to sit down in the other. Isabella sat on my lap.

She held my palm in her hand face up and traced the lines with one long fingernail. After thirty seconds of contemplation she said, "You will have a long life with many beautiful children." Then she repeated the procedure with Isabella's palm and told her the same thing.

Isabella took it to heart. I just laughed.

When we returned to the house, we found Stefan in the kitchen. Cristina was ladling a bowl of soup for him, so she dished out two more for Isabella and me.

"Uncle Stefan, guess what we did today?" Isabella didn't give him the opportunity. "We had our palms read. I'm going to have a long life with many beautiful children."

"That's nice to hear," Stefan said. "How about you, Gwen? Did you have your palm read too?"

"I did. And amazingly enough I'm also going to have a long life with many beautiful children."

"Is that so?" he said, and we both laughed.

"That's what I get for going to a shopping mall fortune-teller."

He cringed. "You didn't."

I nodded. "Afraid so. I was looking for some cheap entertainment."

He set down his soup spoon and wiped his mouth with his napkin. "If you're interested, I know someone I could take you to."

"You mean a real fortune-teller?" I waved my hands in the air and added spooky sound effects.

"Yes," he said, but his expression told me he was serious.

"You really believe in all that?" I asked.

"A lot of them are frauds," he said, "but not all. It's a legitimate business here. The witches even pay taxes now."

"Are you serious?" Even in Transylvania, taxing witches seemed far-fetched.

"Yes. I can take you if you want to go."

Had it not still been raining, I probably would've said no. But I thought visiting a "real" fortune-teller sounded like more fun than spending the afternoon playing with Isabella's Barbies.

Chapter 29

After lunch, the three of us piled into Stefan's rental car. Stefan drove toward Bucharest, but long before we reached the city he pulled off the main highway, and we ended up in a residential neighborhood. In some ways the houses in the Gypsy village were much nicer than in Brasov. They were larger, sometimes three stories tall, but they were also garish with ornately carved woodwork and spires on the roofs. With the exception of the giant cement apartment buildings on the outskirts of the city, which had been built during the Communist era, the houses in Brasov were all quaint and picturesque. These homes looked like they could've been candidates for a new reality TV show—*Pimp My House, Gypsy Edition.*

Stefan knocked on the door of a two-story monstrosity painted rose red with white wood trim. The door was opened by a teenage girl wearing black tights, a black miniskirt, and a blue sequined tank top. She had her dark hair pulled back into a ponytail, which made her huge silver earrings stand out even more.

Stefan said a few words to her in Romanian, and she showed us in but left us in the foyer while she disappeared into the back of the house. Another woman, middle-aged and wearing traditional Gypsy garb—a long print peasant skirt with a bright shirt and a scarf covering her hair—led us down the hallway to a dark room with curtains covering the windows, which was a sharp contrast with the rest of the house, which was decorated with bright, often clashing colors.

The woman motioned for us to take a seat on the purple velvet sofa, then she left us.

"Are you sure about this?" I asked Stefan. Even Isabella seemed spooked. She was gripping my hand so tightly I was afraid she was going to cut off circulation to my fingers.

"If you want the real thing," he said, "you have to go to the source."

A few minutes later another middle-aged woman, also dressed in Gypsy garb, walked in and we all stood up. "You're Gwen?" she asked in accented English.

"Yes," I answered.

"Follow me."

Stefan and Isabella walked behind me, but the woman said, "No, just Gwen."

I turned to Stefan and he spoke to the woman in Romanian. After they exchanged a few words he turned back to me and said, "It's okay, Gwen. We'll wait for you here."

"Are you sure?" I asked.

"Don't worry, I'll watch Isabella."

Isabella wasn't the only one I was worried about. I took a deep breath and followed the woman past a curtained doorway into an adjoining room. Inside I found an older woman seated at a round table covered with a black cloth. Only a small portion of her hair was visible underneath her blue head scarf, and it was gray. But instead of a loose Gypsy shirt, she wore a sleeveless V-neck sweater with a gold chain that dropped down into her ample bosom, and huge gold hoop earrings. The flesh on her arms jiggled as she motioned for me to sit down across from her.

The woman who had brought me in sat down in the empty chair next to the older woman. "My mother's English is not so good," she said, "so I'll translate."

"Okay," I said as I sat down in the opposite chair.

The older woman shuffled a deck of tarot cards and began laying them face up on the table. The first one showing was a man with a sword. She immediately began speaking to me in Romanian, which of course I didn't understand.

"You've met a man," the daughter translated. "You like this man."

I didn't know if I was supposed to respond or not, but I said, "yes."

"This man likes you," the daughter said as her mother continued to place cards on the table—a woman, another man, something that looked like crossed swords, or they could've been vines—and speak in Romanian at the same time, "but he is not good for you. He will bring you much pain."

My heart nearly stopped. I didn't believe in this, not really, but Stefan clearly did so I couldn't dismiss it entirely. Plus, the whole "you met a man" thing was eerily on the mark. Although maybe she said that to every woman who wasn't wearing a wedding ring. And who knew what Stefan had told her about me. At a minimum, she knew my name. Plus I'd walked in with Stefan, who was definitely a man. Maybe she was referring to him and not Alex. Once I realized her statement could be interpreted multiple ways, my heart started beating again, only a little faster than usual.

The older woman laid two more cards on the table—a creature with horns and another with a bunch of indecipherable symbols— and looked up at me. She stared directly into my eyes, and it was like she was searching inside me. I finally pulled away from her steely gaze and turned to her daughter. "What?" I asked.

She and her mother started speaking in Romanian again, but it seemed like they were disagreeing. The mother kept nodding and the daughter kept shaking her head. Finally the daughter turned to me and asked, "Do you have a tattoo?"

"No. Why?"

She relayed this to her mother and they continued their exchange. The daughter turned back to me. "A mark of any kind?" she asked. "Maybe a scar you received as a child or something you were born with?"

I didn't answer, I was too freaked out, but the old woman knew. She pointed at my shoulder, the one with the birthmark, and her daughter turned and stared at me too. There was no way they could see it—I was wearing a dark shirt that covered it completely—but the old woman knew it was there. I didn't know how she knew, but she knew.

I grabbed my purse off the floor and ran out of the room.

"What's wrong?" Stefan asked as I joined him and Isabella.

"We need to leave," I said and pushed past them into the hallway. I raced to the front door and out to the car, but Stefan had locked it. I nervously paced next to it while I waited for him and Isabella to emerge from the house. Presumably Stefan was paying the woman, which in my haste to get out I'd forgotten to do. Stefan appeared a few minutes later and unlocked the car remotely. I jumped inside, slamming the door shut behind me as if that could keep whatever that old woman saw at bay.

"Gwen, what happened back there?" Stefan asked as he helped Isabella into the backseat.

"I don't want to talk about it," I said and stared straight ahead.

He waited until he was behind the wheel of the car before he asked me again. "What did she tell you?"

"Nothing," I said, still refusing to look at him. "Nothing worth repeating."

I knew he didn't believe me, and I didn't care. I wasn't about to share what happened in that room with him. I didn't understand it myself. I turned up the volume on the radio and except for the music, we drove home in silence.

But I told Alex about it when he called that night.

"What on earth possessed you to go to a fortune-teller?" he asked. "I told you to stay away from the Gypsies. They're all liars and thieves."

"I'm sure they're not *all* liars and thieves." We'd had this argument before. But apparently everyone in Romania felt the way Alex did. I'd watched stories on the news where every person they interviewed said the same about the Gypsies. "And Stefan must not think so since he's the one who took me."

"Stefan likes to make trouble," Alex said. "Sometimes I think it's his occupation."

"But, Alex, she knew about the birthmark. How could she have known? She couldn't see it."

"Maybe Stefan told her."

"Why would he do that?"

"I don't know," he said. "Put him on the phone and I'll ask him."

"I'm not putting him on the phone so you can start an argument with him."

Alex sighed. "Gwen, I'm sorry you had to go through this. I can't explain what happened, but I'm sure there is an explanation. Now will you do me a favor?"

"What?" I asked.

"Stay away from Stefan."

"Alex, he's your brother and he's living in this house. I can't ignore him. Besides, Isabella adores him."

He sighed again. "Just try. Please. For me."

"Okay," I said, "but don't expect me to be successful."

Chapter 30

After Isabella spoke to Alex, I helped her with her bath, then read her a few chapters of her book before bed. Once she was asleep, I went back to my own room and tried to read, but the novel I'd started wasn't holding my interest so I ventured downstairs to the study. Stefan was already there, lying on the couch, sipping a beer, and flipping channels on the TV.

"You want one?" he asked, holding up his bottle.

"No, I'm good," I said.

He sat up and made room for me on the couch, then handed me the remote. "You choose. I can't find anything."

I clicked up the dial and stopped at one of the nature channels. They were all in English with Romanian subtitles instead of the other way around. Tonight I wanted to listen to the TV instead of reading it.

"So," Stefan said as we watched the host and his camera crew hunt lions in Africa, "you and my brother."

"Yup." I saw no point in denying it.

"How did that happen?"

I had to laugh. We must really be an unlikely couple since everyone's reaction was the same. "You know, I'm not really sure."

Stefan grinned at me. "It happens that way sometimes." After a pause he asked, "Is this serious between you two or just for fun?"

I lowered the volume on the TV. "Originally I thought it was just for fun, but it seems to have changed. Your brother asked me to move in with him when we get back to LA"

Stefan choked on his beer. "Wow," he said when he'd stopped coughing. "I didn't see that one coming."

"Trust me, neither did I."

"And are you going to?"

"I don't know. Do you think I should?" I didn't know why I asked him that. Maybe it was because he'd known Alex his whole life and I'd only known him a few weeks.

"I think you should do whatever makes you happy."

I smiled. "Nice copout."

"What do you expect me to say, Gwen? He's my brother."

I knew it. Even though they pretended to hate each other, deep down they loved each other. Those blood bonds were hard to break.

"What about you?" I asked. "Do you have a girlfriend?"

"I date," he said.

"I'm sure you do." Zoe had pegged him as a player the day she'd met him. "No one special?"

"Why? Is there someone you want to fix me up with?"

"No, you already blew off my friend Zoe. I'm not setting you up with anyone."

"Zoe?" he mused, obviously trying to remember.

"You met her at Isabella's birthday party. Long red hair, perfect skin, nice legs."

"Zoe!" he finally said. "Of course I remember her. I really wanted to go out with her."

"Then how come you never called?" Zoe didn't seem too upset about it, but I still thought it was rude. Why did guys ask for girls' phone numbers and then never call? One of life's great mysteries.

"Because I lost my phone."

"Yeah, right." I would've thought a player could've come up with a better excuse than that.

"It's true! Ask Alex if you don't believe me. It was a major headache. I'm still missing some numbers, your friend Zoe's among them. I don't suppose I could talk you into giving it to me?"

"I'd have to ask her first, and she's currently on a plane to London."

"What's in London?"

"Her brother. He works at one of those huge multinational law firms. Her whole family's going over to visit since he can never get time off work to come home."

"Then maybe I can meet up with her there."

"Oh, are you going to London too?" Alex hadn't mentioned it when he'd asked me. But maybe he didn't know. He and Stefan didn't seem to apprise each other of their plans.

"I take it that means you're going as well?" he asked.

And apparently Alex hadn't told him he'd invited me either. "Only for a few days. Alex is taking me to Paris while your sister watches Isabella."

"Paris? This is serious."

I laughed. "Asking me to move in with him isn't a big deal, but three days in Paris is?"

"No, that's definitely a big deal too. But Paris, well, Alex only takes the really special girls to Paris."

I couldn't tell if he was joking or not.

I was amazed when Stefan joined Isabella and me for breakfast the next morning—both because he was up at that hour and because he was wearing a suit. Unlike Alex, Stefan tended to dress more casually.

He laughed when I expressed my surprise. "I work too, Gwen. Maybe not as much as my brother, but I do have a job."

"I never meant to imply otherwise," I said, afraid I might've offended him.

"But I'll be home early," he said. "Maybe we can all do something together this afternoon."

"Swimming!" Isabella shouted.

"Your wish is my command," he replied, and Isabella beamed. "I cannot deny a beautiful girl," then he turned to me and added, "or a beautiful woman."

Ah, the Romanescu charm. That was one trait both brothers shared. Although on Stefan it appeared more effortless.

Stefan kept his word. He reappeared at the house in the afternoon, and we all went swimming. He taught Isabella to dive, and I captured it on video so we could show Alex when he returned. I was heading back to the house to get us all drinks—beer for Stefan, root beer for Isabella, who wanted to drink whatever Stefan was drinking, and water for me—when Alex called on the cell phone he'd given me.

"Where are you?" he asked.

"At the pool," I said, "or I was. Now I'm walking back to the house. Why? Where are you?"

"Looking out at a magnificent view of the Aegean and wishing you were here."

"Hey, I offered," I said, striding through the back door. "You chose your mistress over me." I was glad Cristina didn't speak English because she was standing at the sink. We smiled and nodded like we usually did, and I headed to the fridge.

He laughed. "Why won't you believe me that they don't allow women on this island?"

"I do believe you. I was kidding." I'd Googled Mount Athos when he'd told me about his trip the other day and was shocked to discover he was telling the truth. It was an island in Greece housing twenty orthodox monasteries. No women were allowed. The justification for this rule was that it made it easier for the monks, all of whom had taken vows of celibacy. Although a few women had managed to sneak onto the island over the years.

"Are you feeling better?" he asked. "About yesterday."

"You mean the fortune-teller?"

"I could kill Stefan for taking you there."

The answer was no, but I didn't want to admit it. "I'm trying not to think about it," I said, which was the truth.

"They're charlatans, Gwen. They say vague things that could mean anything and count on you to interpret it to fit your circumstances."

I agreed with him on the "you've met a man" statement, but not the birthmark. "Can we not talk about this?" I'd managed to put it out of my mind, and now he'd brought it to the forefront again. "Tell me about the island. What are you doing there?" It seemed an unlikely location for a business trip.

"It's stunning," he said. "One of the most beautiful places I've ever seen. Some of these monasteries have been here for over a thousand years and they haven't changed in all that time. It's living history."

"And what kind of business do you have at a thousand-year-old monastery?"

"Research," he said, "for a project I'm working on."

"What kind of project?"

I heard church bells in the background.

"Gwen, I've got to go but I'll call you later, okay?"

I said, "okay," but he'd already hung up.

I asked Stefan about it over dinner that night. He'd arranged for Ivana to stay late and babysit Isabella so the two of us could go out alone. I knew Alex wouldn't be happy about it, but Stefan could be very persuasive. Isabella wasn't thrilled either, but she relented when Stefan agreed to come to the park with us the next day.

"My brother's very mysterious sometimes," he said. "Who knows why he does the things he does."

I waited until the waiter had set down the bread and water and left us alone again before I continued. "But you work together, don't you? Wouldn't you know what sort of project he's working on?"

"We both work for our family's business," he said. "But we try to stay out of each other's way for obvious reasons."

"It's not so obvious to me. Why exactly don't the two of you get along?"

"That's a long story," he said, pouring more red wine into my glass.

"Well I've got nowhere to be tonight. Do you?"

Before he could answer, my cell phone rang. The second time today, which was a lot for me in Romania. The only people who knew the number were Alex, Stela, and Zoe, and I'd only given it to Zoe in case of emergency because we always spoke from Alex's home phone.

"Where are you?" Alex asked when I picked up.

"Having dinner with Stefan. Why?"

"I called the house and Isabella told me you and Stefan had left." It was obvious from his tone that he wasn't pleased.

"Ivana's with her. You let Ivana babysit before."

"That's not the issue, Gwen. I asked you to stay away from Stefan. You promised you would."

I smiled across the table at Stefan. "I promised to try, Alex. That's all. And I can't talk about it right now."

"Put him on the phone," Alex said.

"I'm not putting him on the phone. You're being ridiculous."

"It's okay," Stefan whispered and motioned for me to hand my cell phone to him.

"Alex," he said, then switched to speaking in Romanian. Alex did too, so even though I could hear him yelling through the receiver, I couldn't understand what either of them were saying. Despite that, Stefan still excused himself and walked to the front of the restaurant so he could continue the call in private.

He returned a few minutes later shaking his head. "I'm to have you home by eleven," he said and handed me back the phone.

We both knew that argument had nothing to do with a curfew. "Are you going to tell me what's going on?" I asked.

"I would love to, but it's not my place. Ask Alex. He'll be back tomorrow night."

Stefan spent the rest of the meal regaling me with tales from his and Alex's childhood. According to Stefan, Alex was always the responsible older brother, and he was the one constantly getting into trouble and trying to talk his way out of it. I believed him. It appeared nothing had changed.

The next night I allowed Isabella to stay up past her bedtime so she could greet Alex when he returned, but she fell asleep on the couch long before he arrived. Eventually Stefan carried her up to her bed and tucked her in. It wasn't that late for me, but I was having trouble staying awake too. Stefan and I were watching television, and I closed my eyes just for a minute, but when I opened them again the room was dark and I heard voices emanating from the kitchen.

"You're awake," Alex said as I wandered in. He was still wearing his suit pants, but his jacket was lying on the counter next to his keys, and he'd undone the top button of his shirt and loosened his tie. He was sitting at the kitchen table with Stefan. Each had a beer in front of him. It was the first time I'd seen Alex drink from the bottle.

He pushed back from the table and crossed over to me. "God, it's good to see you." He kissed me as if he hadn't seen me in three months instead of three days.

I was happy to see him too. Stefan, however, was not. Or at least he appeared not to be from the sour look on his face.

"You want a beer, Gwen?" Stefan asked as he headed to the fridge.

"No, I'm good."

He pulled one out anyway and popped the top. "I really think you're going to want a drink when you hear this."

"Hear what?" I asked at the same time Alex said, "I'm warning you, Stefan, stay out of this."

"Alex, she has a right to know."

In one swift movement, Alex pinned Stefan against the wall with his arm on his throat.

"What the hell are you doing?" I screamed, but Alex ignored me. He spoke directly to Stefan, his voice soft and low. "If you value your life you will walk out of this room and not say another word."

Stefan shoved Alex against the kitchen counter and pointed his finger in Alex's face. "You threaten me again and I'll tell her myself. And you won't like what I have to say." Then he stormed out of the room without looking at me. Thirty seconds later a door slammed shut at the other end of the house.

"What the hell is going on?" I'd seen Alex angry before, but I'd never seen him get violent. In the past he'd always been in control. And it was obvious he was hiding something from me, something big.

Alex ran his hands through his hair and sighed. "It's late, Gwen. Can we talk about this tomorrow?"

"No, we can't talk about it tomorrow. I want to know what you're keeping from me."

He sighed again and shook his head. "I wouldn't even know where to begin."

Chapter 31

He wouldn't even know where to begin? My heart started pounding in my chest. "How about at the beginning?"

He wandered back to the kitchen table and took a long swallow from his beer. Then he set it down and stared off into space.

"Alex, I expect an answer."

He turned to me and gazed directly into my eyes. "Promise me that no matter what I tell you you'll remember that I love you."

Now I was really scared. "Alex, just tell me."

He kicked out the chair next to his. "Take a seat."

When I had he reached over to his suit jacket and removed something from the inside breast pocket, which he handed to me. "This is the reason I went to Mount Athos."

I unwrapped the object folded in tissue paper. It was the Saint George talisman I'd brought with me from home and I'd thought was still upstairs in my suitcase. "What are you doing with my painting?"

"It's not just a painting," he said. "It's an icon."

I didn't understand the distinction. "Okay, what are you doing with my icon?"

"I borrowed it. For my research."

"Why didn't you just ask me? I would've given it to you."

"I know," he said.

"Then why didn't you ask? Why did you just take it?"

He paused before he answered. "Because I needed to be sure first."

"Sure about what?"

He reached for his beer and took another long swallow. He had dark circles under his eyes and looked more tired than I'd ever seen him, but I didn't care. I wanted answers.

"Sure about what, Alex?" I prompted again.

"About its origins." He reached for the icon and loosened it from its metal plate. The last time I'd seen it the painting had been attached to the base, but now it came apart easily. He held up the painting with the back facing me. "You see these markings," he said, pointing to scratches in the wood.

"Yes."

"They're numbers."

I peered at the scratch marks more closely. They didn't look like any numbers I'd ever seen. They weren't integers or roman numerals. "Are you sure?"

"Yes. They're ancient Greek. They reference a volume and page number, and below it are the initials of the artist who painted it."

"How do you know all this?" I asked.

"Because I've seen similar ones before."

I presumed he was telling the truth. Why would he lie? "Okay, so what does it mean?"

"I brought your icon to Hilandar," he said, "one of the monasteries on Mount Athos. They have an extensive library with records dating back hundreds of years."

"Why?"

"Because I suspected it was one of their monks who painted it. And I was right. Their records confirmed your icon was commissioned over five hundred years ago."

"Commissioned? By who?"

"Commissioned might not be the right word," he said. "More likely it was given as a gift to a benefactor."

"What benefactor?"

He licked his lips and stared down at the table again.

"Alex, answer me. Who was this painted for?"

"Vlad Tepes. Dracula."

My first instinct was to ask if he was joking, but I knew he wasn't. He looked too upset. My heart was pounding again as I retrieved the small painting from Alex's hand. I couldn't believe I was holding something over five hundred years old that had once belonged to Dracula. The real Dracula, not the fictional one. The bloodthirsty despot who had tortured people for sport. I had so many questions I didn't even know where to begin. "But how?"

"How did it come to be in your possession?" he asked.

I nodded, still staring at the painting. The image was so familiar to me, but now it was as if I were seeing it for the first time.

"Icons like these are inherited. In Orthodox families they're passed down from one generation to the next, normally on the mother's side."

Families? I tore my gaze away from the painting and glanced up at him. "What are you saying?"

"I'm saying that you're a descendant of Vlad Tepes. You're the heir to Dracula."

Chapter 32

I was too stunned to speak. It was too preposterous to even contemplate. Me? The heir to Dracula? This had to be a mistake.

"I know it's a shock," he said, "but it's true."

He pushed back from the table and started pacing the kitchen. I remained dumbstruck and immobilized.

"How did you know?" I finally asked when I'd recovered the power of speech. "I mean, why did you even suspect?" There was nothing on the painting that would've indicated it had once belonged to Dracula. It was a generic painting of Saint George. You could find one just like it in any church. They probably sold similar ones at religious gift shops.

He sighed and ran his hands through his hair again. It was as if he'd been expecting this question and dreading it at the same time. He returned to the table and grabbed my hands. "I love you, Gwen. Please remember that."

I pulled my hands away. My heart was beating so fast now I was sure I could hear it pounding in my ears. "Tell me."

"Your birthmark," he said.

I heard the words before he'd even spoken them. Somehow I knew. Just as the old Gypsy woman had known I had the mark without ever seeing it.

"He had the same," Alex said.

Now I was the one who was pacing. I didn't even realize it until Alex placed his hands on my shoulders to stop me.

"And his eyes?" I asked, remembering Isabella's comment at Bran Castle.

He nodded.

"And my dreams?" They had to be connected to this somehow. It was too much of a coincidence.

"The Gypsies say dreams are memories of past lives. I've never believed that, but..."

I pulled away from him and started pacing again. It was too much. I wasn't just related to this monster but somehow he was inside of me? He was in my dreams and behind my eyes and on my skin. No, this couldn't be true. It had to be a mistake. It had to be. Then I realized. "That book you gave me. It never said anything about a birthmark. It said all that dragon business was because of his father, because he was a member of the Order of the Dragon."

"I know. For years I thought it was just peasant folklore. But there's a professor in Bucharest who's uncovered proof. Dracula had the birthmark, Gwen, and it's the same as yours."

"But birthmarks aren't hereditary." At least I'd never heard that they were.

"Most aren't," he said. "But some kinds are. Yours is."

I grabbed my shoulder. I was sure I was imagining it, but it felt like my birthmark was tingling. Then I remembered all that paperwork I'd found in Alex's nightstand the day I'd snooped. "This professor," I said, "the one in Bucharest. How does he even know what the birthmark looks like?"

Dracula had been dead for over five hundred years, and the only depiction I'd ever seen of him was the one hanging in Bran Castle, the one that had been reproduced everywhere. In it, he was fully clothed. The only skin visible was on his face and neck, neither of which contained a birthmark.

"There are descriptions," he said, "and sketches. When I sent him the photo of yours, he knew right away."

I had to grab the back of the chair for support. I felt like I'd been punched in the gut. "You sent him a picture of my birthmark? Without asking me?"

"I'm sorry, Gwen. I had to. Please try to understand."

"But how did you even get one?" The only photos he'd taken of me were at tourist sites, and I was always fully clothed. I would never have allowed him to take a picture of my birthmark. Never.

He turned away from me, and his voice was so soft I could barely hear him. "In LA That night you spent at my house."

The realizations pummeled me like waves. I felt like I was drowning in a sea of lies. I couldn't speak. I could barely breathe. When I thought I could no longer stand, I collapsed onto the chair.

Eventually I said, "You knew. That day when you spilled wine on my dress and you saw the birthmark." Even at the time I'd thought his interest in it was abnormal. But everyone told me I was crazy, that I was imagining it, that Alex was an honorable man. "You knew, and you've been planning this whole thing ever since."

"It wasn't like that, Gwen. I suspected, but I didn't know. Not until today."

"Why did you bring me here, Alex? Did you really need a nanny for the summer or was hiring me part of the plan too? Is Katarina even getting married?"

He turned away from me. "No, I gave Katarina the summer off. I didn't think you'd come if I just asked you to, so I found a reason."

I couldn't believe I was such a fool. All the lies he'd told me. Lie after lie after lie, and I'd never questioned him. I'd fallen for it all. Even when he'd told me he loved me, I'd believed that too. I'd confided in him about my dreams because I thought I owed him the truth. And the whole time he was lying to me. Everything was a lie. Everything.

I ran into the hall, unsure where to go next. All I knew was that I wanted to get away from him.

"Please, Gwen," Alex said, following me. "You have to let me explain."

"Explain?" I shouted. "You just did. That was probably the first honest conversation we've ever had." I shook my head as I backed away from him. "And to think I slept with you, that I thought I might actually be in love with you…"

He tried to put his arms around me but I pushed him away. "Don't touch me!" I screamed.

Isabella's door cracked open. "Daddy?"

He glanced upstairs then back at me.

"Go," I said.

"Wait here. Please, Gwen." Then he ran up the stairs two at a time. "I'm coming, Isabella."

I wandered back to the kitchen in a daze. I had no plan, but when I spotted his keys on the counter I recognized my means of escape.

Chapter 33

I grabbed Alex's keys and ran. I didn't stop running until I reached his car. When I peeled out of the garage I had no idea where I was headed. I had no ID, no money, not even shoes. My passport was still upstairs in my purse. All I knew was that I had to get away from him. I had to get out of that house.

I drove toward Brasov because it was familiar to me. Dimitri drove in that direction every morning, so I did too. I thought about calling Stela—Elena and her mother were the only people I knew in Romania who weren't connected to Alex—but I didn't have my phone. It was upstairs in my purse too. I was trying to remember her address—we'd dropped Isabella off at her house for Elena's birthday party—when I saw the wolf in the middle of the road. It was staring directly into the car's headlights. I slammed on the brakes and swerved.

The next time I opened my eyes I was staring at a tree, which was closer than it should've been but still on the other side of the Audi's crumpled hood. "Fuck," I said aloud. That's when I tasted the blood in my mouth. I had no idea where it was coming from. All I knew was that everything hurt. I closed my eyes and let the tears wash over me.

It could've been five minutes later or five hours. Alex was standing next to me shouting, "Gwen, are you okay?"

I wanted to lower the window, but I didn't know how. "Go away," I said.

"I've called an ambulance. They're on their way. Just hold on, honey. Please."

I could hear the anguish in his voice, and I didn't care. I closed my eyes and pretended I was asleep. It was easier that way.

The paramedic asked me if I knew my name and where I was. The doctor at the hospital did too. She told me her name was Doctor Ionescu then she examined me.

"No major injuries," she pronounced when she'd finished, "but you fractured your nose, sprained your wrist, and have some bruising on your chest."

I reached up and touched my face with my right hand, the one that didn't hurt. My nose felt bigger than usual and tender to my touch.

"Once the swelling goes down it should be fine," she said. "You can ice it for fifteen minutes at a time over the next two days. That should help. I'll give you a bandage for your wrist. The bruises on your chest will fade on their own. You were lucky. The airbags saved your life."

I didn't feel lucky. I felt like I'd been run over by a truck, or in my case, collided with a tree. "Insurance?" I said. I was surprised no one had asked me. It was always the first question back home. I knew a hospital in Transylvania would be out of network, but I was hoping I would still be covered.

"You can ask for a receipt when you sign out. Mr. Romanescu already took care of the bill."

So Alex was here. I hadn't seen him since the paramedics wheeled me into the ambulance.

"I would've kept you overnight," she continued, "but it's already morning and I think you'd be more comfortable at home." She scribbled something on her pad and handed it to me. "Pain-killers," she said. "Or you can take acetaminophen or ibuprofen. It's up to you. If anything changes, if you start feeling dizzy or disoriented or you start vomiting, come back in right away."

I nodded, and she left the room. A nurse came in a few minutes later. She bandaged my wrist and helped me pull on my bloody clothes. Then she gave me a pair of cardboard slippers because I had no shoes. I sat down in the wheelchair she proffered and she pushed me to the entrance where Alex was waiting. He had drops of blood on his shirt. I assumed it was my blood, but I had no idea how it had gotten there.

"How are you feeling?" he asked.

I hurt all over and was numb at the same time. "Go away."

He spotted the prescription I was clutching in my hand. He tried to take it from me, but I wouldn't let go.

He bent down so we were eye level. "Gwen, if you give it to me, I'll fill it for you."

I closed my eyes so I didn't have to look at his face and handed it over. I fell asleep in the chair waiting for him to return.

He pulled Stefan's car up to the entrance, and the nurse helped me into the passenger seat. The seat belt hurt where it touched my bruises, so I swallowed one of the painkillers dry. For a long time, we didn't speak.

"I'm sorry about your car," I said at some point during the ride. If it wasn't totaled, it would need a lot of work before it was drivable again.

"I don't care about the car, Gwen. I care about you."

I leaned my head against the passenger-side window and closed my eyes. I didn't want to listen to any more of his lies. It was easier to sleep.

I vaguely remembered seeing Stefan and Isabella in the hall as I climbed the steps. Alex was by my side. I didn't want him there, but I couldn't stop him. The painkiller had kicked in and I was barely able to hold myself upright. I didn't bother undressing; I just collapsed onto the bed in my bloody clothes.

I woke briefly that afternoon. I still hurt all over, so I swallowed another painkiller and went back to sleep. The next time I woke it was dark outside but there was enough light shining in from the moon and the stars that I could see I wasn't alone. Alex was sitting in the chair by the window staring out at nothing.

"Go away," I said.

He turned to me. "I'm glad you're awake. I was starting to worry."

"Get out."

"You need to eat. What would you like?"

"I'm not hungry."

"How about a bath? You probably want to get out of those clothes."

He was right about the clothes. The shirt especially was caked in blood and crunched every time I rolled over. "A bath," I said.

He ran it for me while I remained in bed. When the tub was filled, I stumbled into the bathroom and slammed the door shut in his face. He did not get to see me naked. Those days were over. Then I locked it just to be sure.

I eased myself into the tub and let the warm water wash over me. I briefly thought about what he'd told me—that because of the birthmark and the icon that meant I was somehow related to Dracula—but I banished the notion from my mind. It was too incomprehensible. I was an Andersen. That's all I'd ever been and all I wanted to be. My parents were good people, not monsters. I tried to be a good person too. I didn't know why Alex was doing this to me, but whatever his reason I couldn't deal with it now.

For a long time I didn't move. When the water started to cool, I drained some and added more. It felt so good; I closed my eyes and sank lower. I wished I'd brought my iPod with me. Then I wouldn't have to listen to Alex talking to me from the other side of the door. I lowered myself farther so the water covered my ears. I just wanted to be left alone to nurse my wounds. The heartache hurt more than the physical bruises, and hearing his voice only made it worse.

I didn't open my eyes again until the bathroom door swung open and Alex burst in. The door handle was lying on the floor and he was holding a screwdriver in his hand.

"Why didn't you answer me?" he demanded.

"Get out." I closed my eyes and sank back down into the water.

He grabbed my arm and pulled me up. "No, it's time for you to get out of the bath."

"Fuck you," I said and yanked my arm from his grip.

He stood with his hands on his hips and stared down at me. I closed my eyes so I didn't have to look at him anymore. I thought he'd leave but he didn't. Then all of a sudden I had cold water raining down on me.

"What the fuck are you doing?" I screamed even though it was obvious. He was holding the shower attachment over my head.

"Getting you out of the bath," he said and held a towel out to me.

At that point I didn't have much of a choice. The water pouring down on me was icy cold, and I instantly went from toasty warm to freezing. I grabbed the towel and wrapped it around myself, then ran out of the bathroom. I left it to him to unplug the drain and clean up. I quickly dried myself and pulled on pajamas. He'd seen me naked once today; he wasn't getting another opportunity.

Not that I was an attractive sight. I had a diagonal line of black-and-blue marks stretching from my left shoulder to the right side of my waist from where the seat belt had cinched me in. My nose and cheeks were swollen, and I had purple bruises under both eyes. My left wrist still hurt, but it looked okay.

I slid under the covers and reached for the painkillers, but Alex grabbed the vial out of my hand. "You've had enough of these."

"The doctor gave them to me so I could take them."

"Not so you could sleep your life away."

"I'm in pain. I need them."

He opened the medicine cabinet in the bathroom and tossed me a bottle of acetaminophen. "Then take these. They won't put you to sleep."

"I like sleeping."

"I know," he said, "but you need to eat."

"I told you, I'm not hungry."

"I don't care. Now tell me what you want and I'll bring it to you."

"Nothing from you."

"Don't think I won't force-feed you. I will."

After the stunt in the bathroom, I believed him. "Something light. I'm nauseous."

"You've been popping painkillers on an empty stomach all day. What did you expect?"

"Don't lecture me. I'm not your child."

He sighed and rubbed his eyes with his thumb and forefinger. "Toast?" he asked.

"Sure," I said. "And some club soda too."

He nodded and left the room.

He returned ten minutes later with two slices of toast and a glass of club soda and sat with me while I ate. When I finished, I set the empty glass and plate on the nightstand and lay back down.

"We need to talk," he said.

"There's nothing to say." He'd lied to me from the moment we'd met. Betrayed my trust. We were through.

"We're not done."

"Maybe you're not, but I am."

"Not about that," he said. "There's more I have to tell you."

Whatever it was, I didn't want to hear it. Besides, how much more could there possibly be? How much worse could this possibly get?

Chapter 34

I rolled over so Alex couldn't see my face. "Not tonight. I'm tired. I want to sleep."

"Okay," he said. "Tomorrow."

He grabbed the empty plate and glass from the nightstand and headed to the door, but before he stepped out he turned around. "What you did last night. Don't try that again. I expect you to be here in the morning." Then he shut the door behind him on his way out.

I'm ashamed to say it hadn't even occurred to me to try to leave.

I was already stirring when he knocked on my bedroom door the next morning. "How'd you sleep?" he asked.

"Fine," I replied. He'd taken the painkillers with him but not the sleeping pills, so I'd taken one of those instead. He looked like he'd barely slept at all. The dark circles under his eyes were now accompanied by puffy bags.

"You want to come downstairs for breakfast?"

"No."

"Are we going to have to do this again?" he asked.

"Isabella will be up soon. I don't want her to see me like this. It'll scare her."

"She already saw you yesterday."

"I don't care. I'm not going downstairs."

He sighed and ran his fingers through his hair. "Okay, we'll eat up here."

I noted the "we." "I'm not eating with you."

"You don't have a choice," he said and slammed my bedroom door shut. If Isabella wasn't awake already, that would do it. When I heard her moving around on her side of our common wall, I knew I'd bought myself some time. Today was Saturday, which meant Cristina was off. Alex would have to feed her first before he came back for me.

I dragged myself out of bed and into the shower. The hot water felt good, and I stayed under it a long time, being careful to keep it off my face. I hadn't been icing, and my nose and cheeks were still swollen. I'd rectify that today.

By the time Alex returned with two bowls of cereal and two cups of coffee, I was already dressed in shorts and a T-shirt and was fully awake. He sat down in the chair by the window, and I took my bowl of cereal and coffee with me to the bed. When I finished eating, I picked up the novel I'd left sitting on my nightstand. I'd read the same sentence five times and still had no idea what it said when he spoke. "It's time to talk."

"So talk," I said, still holding the book in front of my face.

He yanked it out of my hands. "I'd like your attention."

"I'm sure you would," I said and folded my arms across my chest. "But I've got nothing to say to you." I refused to look at him and stared straight ahead. "I've got one week left. I'll take care of Isabella as usual, but we won't speak. I'd prefer it if you stay out of my way. When we get back to LA, we'll never see each other again." I'd decided this all this morning somewhere between my shower and getting dressed.

"That's not possible," he said. "I need you to do something for me."

I finally looked at him. "You've got to be joking. You actually have the nerve to ask me for a favor?"

"It's not just for me," he said. "It's for you too, and Isabella. For all of us."

"What?" I demanded.

He sat down again. "All this," he said and waved his arm in front of him. "My elaborate plan, as you put it. Didn't you wonder what it was for?"

I had wondered, but I'd worked that out in the shower this morning too. "Obviously you have some sort of sick Dracula fetish. I'd rather not hear the details if you don't mind." I presumed since the real Dracula had been dead for over five hundred years, fucking me was the next best thing.

"No," he said. "That's not it at all. And for the record, falling in love with you was never part of the plan."

"Spare me the lies, Alex. They don't work anymore. Just tell me what you want and get out. Honestly, just the sight of you makes me sick." I was already feeling queasy.

"Did it ever occur to you that as the heir to Dracula you might be entitled to something?"

I still wasn't convinced I was the heir to Dracula. He'd lied to me about so many other things, why should I believe him about this? So we had similar birthmarks and somehow I'd ended up with his icon, what did that prove? Of course there were his memories invading my dreams. Those were harder to explain away.

"Even if what you say is true, I can't prove it and neither can you." There was no Dracula DNA available to test against as far as I was aware. And even if there was, I wouldn't want to. I'd tell Zoe about this, but no one else, and I'd swear her to secrecy. Possibly being related to a bloodthirsty despot who tortured people for sport was not something to be proud of. It was bad enough I knew as much about him as I did. I had no interest in investigating any more of his life. I was hoping in time I could forget this whole waking nightmare.

"You have enough," he said. "Enough to start the process."

"What process?"

"Restitution. Getting your land back."

"I don't have any land."

"You do," he said. "Dracula was a prince. He owned land." He started to explain what had happened to Dracula's property after he died—some of it went to the rulers who succeeded him, but other parcels went to his heirs. By the time he got to the third generation and we were still in the sixteenth century, I'd heard enough.

"Get to the point, Alex."

"Dracula's bloodline died out in the late sixteenth century. At least his legitimate bloodline."

"So you think I'm somehow related to him illegitimately?"

"We know he had mistresses. Illegitimate children were common back then. Some of them became rulers themselves."

"So now I'm the *bastard* great-great-great-whatever of a bloodthirsty monster and his whore?" This just got better and better.

"There's land, Gwen. It's currently controlled by the government, but held in trust for Tepes's heirs—illegitimate ones too. We have restitution laws in Romania. They were adopted after the Communists were overthrown. That's how my family got this house back. We can get your land back too."

"I don't want any land. They can give it to his other illegitimate heirs." Surely I wasn't the only one.

"There are no others. At least none that we've been able to locate. And you do want this land. Or you should."

"Why? I don't want to live in Romania." What I'd seen of the country was pretty and the people (outside of Alex) were nice, but I had no desire to move there. I was an American. That was my home.

"Because that land sits atop a gold mine."

"A gold mine? An *actual* gold mine? We're not speaking metaphorically?"

"Yes," he said, "an actual gold mine. And it's contiguous to my land. We would own it together, along with the state and a small group of investors. Gwen, it's worth a fortune."

I leaned back against the headboard and laughed. Of course this was about money. No one went to all this trouble for a sex fantasy. You hired a prostitute for that. "How much, Alex? How many millions?"

He shook his head. "Not millions, Gwen, billions. So you understand why you can't walk away from this."

"Actually, I can."

I didn't need a gold mine. I didn't want a gold mine. And I certainly didn't want to be business partners with Alex Romanescu.

Chapter 35

Alex leaped from the chair. "Don't be a fool, Gwen."

"But I am a fool. You've already proven that."

He ran his hands through his hair and started pacing the room. "What was I supposed to do? I didn't know you. I had no proof. All I had were my suspicions."

"You could've told me. You could've been honest."

"And if I'd told you that first night back in LA, what would you have done? Would you have agreed to come with me to Romania? Would you have searched for proof yourself?"

"No, I would've told you that you were insane."

"Exactly," he said. "I had no choice."

"Oh no. You don't get off that easy. You had a choice. You *chose* to be deceitful. You *chose* to lie to me to get me into bed."

"I didn't have to lie to you to get you into bed, Gwen. As I recall, you were quite the willing participant."

I reached for the closest item I could find, which happened to be my empty cereal bowl, and threw it at his head. I missed. It hit the armoire then shattered when it crashed onto the wood floor. "Get the fuck out!"

"With pleasure," he said and slammed the bedroom door shut so hard the picture on the wall fell down and the glass that had been protecting the print inside smashed too.

First I sat on the bed and cried. Then I cleaned up the broken bowl and frame.

I was in the middle of typing a long e-mail to Zoe—I had a lot of ground to cover—when someone knocked on my door. "Go away!" I yelled.

The door cracked open anyway. "Don't shoot," Stefan said as he stuck his head inside. "It's just me."

"What do you want?" I had no desire to see any Romanescu right now, although I would've made an exception for Isabella. It wasn't her fault her father was a lying bastard.

"To talk," he said. "Can I come in?"

I sighed. "If you must."

He stepped into the bedroom with his hands up, which made me smile. "I'm unarmed."

I grabbed my empty coffee cup from the nightstand. "Well I'm not, so don't piss me off."

"I'll try not to," he said and shut the bedroom door behind him. He headed to the chair by the window and sat down.

I remained cross-legged on the bed, but I closed my laptop. "What do you want, Stefan?"

"To explain," he said. "Hopefully better than my brother."

I folded my arms across my chest and leaned back against the pillows. "I doubt you could do any worse."

He smiled. "We could hear you two from downstairs. What did you throw at him?"

I smiled back. "The cereal bowl. It was the only thing handy."

"Remind me never to buy you a gun."

"That would be a wise move, unless you want to be the only remaining Romanescu brother." I didn't know how much Stefan knew or when he'd found out, but as far as I was aware he'd never lied to me, so I was willing to give him the benefit of the doubt.

He leaned forward in his chair. "This gold mine, Gwen, it's going to happen whether you're involved or not."

"So let it happen without me. I don't care."

"You should," he said, "and not just about the money, which will be considerable."

"My goal in life has never been to be wealthy. That's not how I was raised. I'm not a Romanescu."

He let the insult slide. "There are two groups vying for control of this project—ours and another being spearheaded by a Chinese company. It's not just money at stake here. The gold deposits are enormous, but getting it out of the ground involves risks. There's no way to get to it without unearthing poisonous chemicals. Romania's had problems with that before."

"So why do it? Why not leave the gold where it is?"

He shook his head. "It's too valuable. Even if it was in the country's best interests, and I don't believe it is, the government has already committed to moving forward. The only remaining question is who will control it. The Chinese don't care about the health and safety of the Romanian people or the environment. You just have to take one trip to Beijing to know that."

"And you do?"

"Yes," he said. "We do. We'll make sure it's mined safely, and twenty years from now when the gold's been extracted we'll put it back to the way it was before. The land will be usable again and no one will be harmed in the process."

"So if your way is so much better, why wouldn't the government just choose you?"

He smiled at my naiveté, and even I realized how stupid that sounded. "Okay, maybe not, but couldn't you win them over somehow? Offer them more money or something?"

"Yes, but we need your land to do it. Right now, they think they own it because it's held in trust for what they thought was a dormant estate. If their ownership is called into question, then that changes everything."

"But I can't prove I own it. Didn't Alex tell you about his 'proof?' " I said, with the air quotes. "A birthmark, a five-hundred-year-old icon, the same eyes, and his dreams."

"His dreams?"

Apparently Alex hadn't told him about that. One confidence he hadn't broken. "No one in his right mind would believe him. If he went to court with that they'd laugh at him."

"In America, maybe, but not here. Remember, this is a country where the witches pay taxes."

I started to run my hands through my hair until I realized I'd picked up the habit from Alex and stopped. "Even it's that true, I'm not the only one."

Stefan smiled. "Been Googling Prince Charles, have we?"

I smiled too. "Maybe." Before I'd e-mailed Zoe, I'd wanted to see if any other potential heirs had come forward. According to a handful of online news sites, Prince Charles of England was related to Dracula too.—although his lineage was legitimate. Supposedly he could trace his ancestry back through his great-grandmother Queen Mary to Dracula's stepbrother.

"You'll note his claim was conveniently timed to promote his latest cause."

"So is this one," I pointed out.

"Yes, but you have physical evidence. You may not think it's enough, and the court may ultimately agree, but it's enough to get an order for *masuri provizorii*, an injunction. The Romanian justice system moves at a snail's pace. This will be tied up in court for years."

"So if the government doesn't want to delay, they'll have to cut a deal with me, which means they'll have to cut a deal with you. Is that it?"

Stefan leaned back in his chair and smiled. "You're a wise one, Gwen."

"Hardly. If I was a wise one, I would never have come here." And I certainly never would've fallen for Alex and all of his lies.

"What do you say?" he asked. "Will you help us?"

"I don't know, Stefan. I need time to think."

"Okay," he said, "but not too long. The Chinese are pushing hard on this. We need to move quickly."

I nodded. I would call Zoe. Her brother and father were both lawyers. They'd know what to do.

Stefan stood up. "And for what it's worth, Gwen, you and Alex, that was real."

I snorted, but the tears welled up in my eyes anyway.

"You know it pains me to have to defend him, but he really does love you. He had nothing to gain by getting involved with you, and everything to lose."

"He had everything to gain! If we were together I would've been stupid enough to do whatever he asked."

He shook his head. "That's not how he thinks. He assumed you'd want the money. Sure, maybe you would've been angry that he hadn't told you sooner, but you'd see reason and come around. He jeopardized this entire project by getting involved with you. Just think about it," he said, then left the room.

I did. But even if Stefan was right, it didn't change anything. I couldn't be with someone I couldn't trust. And how could I ever trust Alex again?

Chapter 36

The next morning I waited until I heard Isabella scramble down the steps before I did too. I didn't want to be alone with Alex. As it turned out, I wouldn't have been because Stefan was already awake. When I walked into the kitchen, they all stopped talking and stared at me. I headed straight to the coffeemaker without saying a word.

"Would you like some pancakes?" Alex asked as I leaned against the counter and sipped my coffee instead of joining them at the table.

"No."

"Gwen, you need to eat."

I spun around, about to tell him to fuck off again, when I caught sight of Isabella staring at me. I'd forgotten how scary I must look to her with my black eyes and swollen face. "I'll have toast," I said and dropped a slice of bread into the toaster. When it popped up golden brown, I joined them at the table. I took the seat farthest from Alex, which happened to be the one next to Isabella.

"Isabella, stop staring," Alex said to her as I buttered my toast.

"Does it hurt?" she asked.

"Not really," I replied, which wasn't entirely true, but four acetaminophen had dulled the pain. At least the physical pain. Although my heartache was morphing more and more into anger.

How dare Alex put me through all of this just so he could gain control of a gold mine that he already partly owned. What kind of person did something like that? It seemed like he should be the one who was related to Dracula, not me. But none of this was Isabella's fault. "Do you want to touch it?" I asked her.

"Can I?" she replied, her eyes wide.

"No," Alex said, but I ignored him and gently placed her hands on my face. I guided her fingers across the bridge of my nose and under my eyes. "See, it just looks bad." Her curiosity satisfied, she went back to eating her pancakes.

I thought the worst was over when she asked, "Why are you mad at Daddy? Did he do that to you?"

"Isabella! I have never hit you and I would never hit Gwen. Apologize right now."

"Sorry," she said without a trace of remorse.

I had to laugh, which felt good but hurt my cheeks and chest. "I drove into a tree. It was an accident."

"And that's why you're mad at Daddy?"

"No, that's not why."

I was trying to figure out what I should tell her if she asked again when Stefan said, "Isabella, what do you want to do today?"

"I don't know," she said. "Gwen, what do you want to do today?"

"It's Gwen's day off," Alex said. "I'll take you to the park."

"I don't want to go to the park."

That was a first.

"I want to go with Gwen," she added.

Alex sighed. "Isabella." The warning tone was unmistakable.

"Isabella," Stefan said, pulling her attention away from Alex, "let's think of something really fun to do today and then maybe Gwen will want to come with us."

I turned around and stared at him. I wasn't going anywhere with Alex, and he should know that.

"Just the three of us," he said, reading my mind.

"I know. We can go to a princess castle," Isabella said, brimming with excitement.

"No more castles!" I shouted at the same time Stefan said, "That's an excellent idea. And I know just the one."

He reached over to the kitchen counter and picked up one of their iPads. With a few taps he pulled up the website for Peles Castle. "They have tours in English," he said, showing it to me. "You can see the whole thing."

It did look like a princess castle with its turrets and spires and beautiful mountain backdrop. "But what about my face?" I looked like someone had beaten me up. "I don't want to scare anyone."

"You can wear your hat," he said. "The one you wore at the pool the other day. And we'll stop at the store and buy you some dark glasses."

"Isn't that a bit obvious?"

"Everyone'll think you're a movie star traveling incognito. They'll probably ask for your autograph."

I laughed. Stefan scored points for trying, which was more than I could say for Alex. He'd been silently glowering at us from across the table. That was half the reason I agreed to go. I knew it would piss him off. The other half was that I knew if I didn't I'd just spend the whole day moping around the house feeling sorry for myself.

Peles Castle was as advertised—a real royal residence with 160 rooms filled with crystal chandeliers and coats of armor and priceless antiques. Stefan signed us up for the full tour, including the family's private apartments. The royal family didn't live there anymore; it was just a tourist attraction. But it was surprisingly modern, with central heating and electricity, indoor plumbing, and even a screening room. Apparently the former king of Romania was a movie fan.

We stopped for lunch on our way to the castle and dinner on our drive home, so I thought I'd be able to avoid seeing Alex for the rest of the day. But he was waiting for us when we returned.

"We need to talk," he said.

"We've got nothing to talk about," I replied as I strode past him.

I don't know what he'd planned to do since by that point my back was to him, but Stefan said, "Alex, don't," and I turned around. Alex was standing between me and Stefan, but closer to me.

"Stay away from me," I said calmly because Isabella was in the foyer too, "or I'll leave tonight."

"I need to talk to you, both of you," he said, and glanced at Stefan. "It's important."

I hung up my and Isabella's jackets, and Alex set her up in the study with a DVD. Then Stefan and I followed Alex to his office. I took the chair in front of the desk and Stefan leaned against the wall.

Alex spoke directly to Stefan. "I received a call from Nicolai today while you two were out *touring*," he said, sarcasm most definitely intended. "The Chinese just closed on another parcel."

"On a Sunday?" Stefan said.

"Apparently they don't value their weekends as much as you do," Alex replied. "We need to act quickly before it's too late." Then he laid two documents on the desk in front of me, both of which were written in Romanian. "This one's a petition for restitution," he said, pointing to the thicker one. "The other asks the court for a temporary injunction, which will halt any further action until this all gets sorted out."

"You mean until you get what you want," I said.

"It's what you want too," Alex said. "Or what you should want. It benefits you as well."

"But I don't want it. I don't care." I knew in time I might feel differently, but at that moment I just wanted him and his gold mine out of my life.

Alex pressed his lips together in a hard line, obviously trying to keep the words he really wanted to say from flying out of his mouth. That's when Stefan stepped in. "Gwen, I know you don't care about the money, but it's going to happen anyway. I promise you, it will be better for the people who live here, for everyone who drinks the water from the river that runs through it or eats the food that's grown nearby, if we're the ones running it."

I picked up one of the documents and waved it in front of his face. "I don't even know what this says. They're not even in English."

"The English translations are attached to the back," Alex calmly replied. "The ones that are filed with the court have to be in Romanian."

"And who translated it? You? You think I would trust you? You think I would sign anything you gave me?"

"If you don't trust me then ask Stefan to translate. Apparently you trust him, although God knows why."

"Shut up, Alex. I'm not the one who did this."

"Right," he said. "You've never lied to anyone, and certainly not a woman. You're Mr. Integrity."

Stefan pushed away from the wall and leaned into Alex's desk. "Well I never lied to Gwen, and that's what matters here."

While I was happy to hear it, he was still Alex's brother, and I knew his loyalties ultimately lay with him, not with me. I set the papers on the desk and folded my arms across my chest. "I'm not signing anything unless my own lawyer tells me to."

"You have a lawyer?" Alex asked.

"Several," I said, even though the only lawyers I knew were Zoe's brother and father, and now Stela as well.

Chapter 37

I called Zoe but couldn't reach her, so I e-mailed her the documents and asked her to have her father contact me as soon as he could. I also brought the papers with me to Isabella's tennis lesson the next morning.

"Gwen, what happened?" Stela asked as soon as I pulled off my dark glasses.

I explained about the car accident first, then I filled her in on the rest. She was as dumbstruck as I had been.

I handed her the documents Alex had given me. "Can you please read these and tell me what they say? Alex wants me to sign them."

"Of course." She didn't look up again until she'd finished reading them both. "The translations are accurate. One's a petition for restitution based on your claim that you're the legal heir to Vlad Tepes's estate, and the other's a request for an injunction to keep everything related to the mine status quo until this can be sorted out." She shook her head. "But I still can't believe it."

"You're not the only one."

"And you really had no idea? All this time?"

I didn't know if she was referring to my relation to Vlad Tepes or to Alex's lies. Although the answer to both was the same. "None. So what do you think I should do? Should I sign these?"

"Oh, Gwen, I don't know if I can help you with that."

"Why not? You just read them. Don't you have an opinion?"

"I have definite opinions," she said. "But it may be a conflict of interest for me to advise you. I grew up near that area and my parents still live there. I've been helping them and some of their neighbors. Many of the people who live there don't want the mine."

"So I shouldn't sign these?"

"I didn't say that." She waited for the waitress to drop off our second round of lattes and leave us alone again before she spoke. "This mine is very controversial. There are lots of competing interests at stake. But I think Alex was being truthful when he said the government was committed to moving forward with it regardless of the opposition. There's too much money to be made and too many corrupt politicians for them to leave it alone. At this point, it's about damage control—who will destroy the area the least."

"And who's that?" I asked.

"I hate to say it, but probably Alex. And now you."

"But I don't want to destroy it at all."

"Then tell him that," she said.

"You think he cares what I think? He always knows best. Even Stefan believes the mine is in the country's best interests. They won't back down."

"A lot of people feel that way, Gwen. It'll bring jobs and money to a very poor area. I'm conflicted about it myself."

"Then what should I do?"

"I can't answer that for you. It's a personal decision. But I can tell you that you won't be doing any damage by signing these papers. If anything, you might help because it'll slow the process down. Keeping the status quo for as long as possible is a good outcome in my opinion."

It was a good outcome in Zoe's father's opinion too. He'd read the English translations I'd sent Zoe last night and called me that afternoon. He told me he needed time to research it further, but if the translations were accurate, and Stela had assured me they were, then he thought I should sign the documents too.

"You swear these are really necessary?" I asked Alex again as I held up the papers. I don't know why I thought he'd answer honestly now when he'd lied so many times before. I supposed I had to try.

He handed me a pen. "I wouldn't ask you if it wasn't."

"And you're going to copy Zoe's dad on everything from now on?" He'd specifically requested it.

"I told you I would."

I shot him a scathing glance that made it clear I didn't believe him.

"You want to see the e-mail I sent to my lawyer?"

"Yes, I would."

"It's in Romanian."

"Send it to me anyway. I'll Google translate."

He pressed his lips together then opened his e-mail. He typed in my address, hit enter, and said, "Done."

I signed the papers and handed them over. Even though both my lawyers had advised me to do it, I couldn't shake the feeling that I'd just made a terrible mistake.

Chapter 38

Isabella and I were at the park—she was climbing on the jungle gym and I was sitting on a bench watching her and the rest of the kids play—when two men approached.

"Are you Gwen Andersen?" the shorter one asked in accented English.

I should've said no, or at least asked who he was and why he wanted to know, but I didn't. I naively said, "Yes."

Within seconds the taller man pointed a video camera at me and the shorter man stuck a microphone in my face. That got the attention of every parent and nanny in the area.

"When did you first know you were related to Vlad Tepes?" the shorter man asked.

"Excuse me?"

"Vlad Tepes," he said again. "Dracula." He waved a set of papers in front of my face that looked like the ones Alex had me sign. "You are the heir, no?"

I shook my head, thankful that I was wearing my hat and dark glasses.

"You are not Gwen Andersen who claims to be the heir to Dracula? The one who wants his property? The one who wants his gold?"

At least some of the people in the park must've understood English because they were staring at me and whispering.

I ran to the jungle gym calling Isabella's name.

"What?" she said as she crawled out from under the giant crisscrossed plastic dome.

"We need to leave," I said. "Now."

"But we just got here."

"Now!"

I don't know if it was my yelling at her, which I'd never done before, or the reporter who'd followed me and was still shouting questions, but she started to cry. I lifted all forty-five pounds of her into my arms and ran as fast as I could to the ladies' room. It was the only place I could think of that the two men couldn't follow.

After I'd calmed Isabella, I pulled out my cell phone and called the house. Cristina picked up, but as soon as she heard my voice she handed the phone to Alex. I would've preferred Stefan, or even Dimitri.

"I knew signing those papers was a mistake."

"What now?" he asked, sounding bored.

"I was just chased into the ladies' room by a reporter who wanted to know when I first knew I was the heir to Dracula."

"Oh no."

"Oh yes." I would've used stronger language if Isabella hadn't been clinging to me. "You need to get us out of here. Now!"

"I'll be right there," he said. "Don't move."

As if I had a choice.

Cristina was better than the cavalry. She and Ivana walked us from the ladies' room to Alex's waiting car, Cristina yelling at the reporters—there was a second one now—in Romanian the whole time. She even swatted one of the cameramen with her purse when he tried to get too close to me.

There was another news van waiting at the entrance to Alex's property. At first I was surprised that Alex had managed to keep them that far from the house—there was no gate to lock or fence to keep them out. Then I noticed Dimitri standing nearby with a shotgun. But I still didn't feel safe until we were inside.

I sat with Isabella in the study while Alex and Stefan plotted our next move behind Alex's closed office door. When they emerged Alex announced that we were leaving in the morning.

"Leaving for where?" I asked.

"London," he said. "This won't be a big story there. It's only here, in Romania, that people care. You should go pack. We have to take the first flight out so you can make your connection to LA"

"I'm not staying in London?"

Surprise registered on his face. "Of course you're welcome. I assumed you wouldn't want to."

"Not with you," I sneered. The words came out harsher than I'd intended. Or maybe they didn't. I glanced down at Isabella to make sure she wasn't paying attention, then lowered my voice. "I was going to stay with Zoe and her family for a couple of days. I told them I would when I thought we were leaving at the end of the week."

"I'll change your ticket. You can go home whenever you want."

"Thanks," I said and turned away.

I was in my room packing that evening when Alex knocked on my door.

"I didn't want to forget to give this back to you," he said and held out his hand.

I knew what was wrapped in the tissue paper before I opened it. "You can keep it," I said and handed the icon back to him. "I don't want it anymore."

"Gwen, I can't keep this. It's your legacy. Your mother gave this to you."

"No, Alex, my mother died five years ago. That other woman, all she did was give birth to me. I've never even met her."

"Do you want to? We could hire a private investigator. Although if we found her she might make a claim too."

I could practically see the gears turning in his head. Would my birth mother coming forward help him or hurt him?

"No!" I didn't care if she made a claim—she could have the land—I just didn't want him to search for her. She'd rejected me once, when I was born; I was not giving her an opportunity to reject me a second time. I sat on the edge of the bed. "I consider myself an Andersen, Alex, not a Tepes, or whatever her name is. That woman is nothing to me. Why can't you understand that?"

He sat on the edge of the bed too, but left some space between us. "Do you miss her?" he asked.

"Who? My mother?"

"Yes."

"Of course. Why would you even ask that?" We'd had our fights when she was alive, like every mother and daughter do, but I loved her and never doubted for a second that she loved me. If she were alive now she would've been the first person I called after Alex's revelation. I was sure she would've told me to fly home immediately and never speak to him again. She had definite opinions about how a man should treat a woman, and she would not have approved of Alex's behavior.

"You never talk about her," he said.

"That doesn't mean I don't think about her." I thought about her all the time. My father too. "I don't talk about her mainly because it makes other people uncomfortable." I almost never mentioned my parents, even to friends, because no one ever knew what to say. They all just looked at me with pity, which was almost worse than the awkward silences and uneasy expressions of sympathy I received from everyone else who knew.

He sighed and lay back on the bed. "When Isabella's mother first died she used to talk about her all the time. She didn't understand and was constantly asking me when she was coming home. It tore me up. Now I wish she'd ask about her, and she never does."

I lay down too. "I don't think that means she doesn't miss her. But I was an adult when my mom died, so maybe it's different. Maybe it's just that she doesn't remember much about her."

"Sometimes I think I should send her to someone—a psychologist or a counselor or something."

"You could," I said. "But if she's not upset about it, I'm not sure it's wise to push her. You might as well wait until she's a teenager and she starts sneaking out at night to meet her boyfriend and telling you she hates you. Then you can push."

He laughed as he ran his hands over his face and through his hair. "God, is that what I have to look forward to?"

"You were a teenager once, weren't you?"

"I never told my parents I hated them."

I shrugged. "I don't know. Maybe it's different for boys." Although I recalled Zoe's brother fighting with their parents too. Maybe it was just different for Alex.

We lay there in silence for a while, both staring up at the ceiling, until he said, "I'm sorry, you know."

"Sorry about lying to me or sorry about how it turned out?"

I thought he'd say "both." He said, "How it turned out."

All the warm feelings he'd engendered in me in the last ten minutes evaporated. I turned on my side to confront him. "You honestly see nothing wrong with what you did?"

He continued to stare at the ceiling. "Gwen, I've been over this in my head a thousand times. I'm not proud of my behavior, but there was no other way."

"Of course there was another way. You could've told me the truth."

"If I did, you wouldn't have come. And I don't regret that, even if you do."

I lay back down again. There was no point in discussing it. If he didn't even think he'd done anything wrong he certainly wasn't going to apologize for it. "But I am sorry for what happened to you," he said. "And I wish I knew how to make it right."

I laughed at the ridiculousness of this entire situation. "And to think two months ago we were strangers. We didn't even like each other."

"I liked you," he said.

"Not the day you found out I'd rented a car and then gotten it towed."

"No," he said, "not that day. But I forgave you."

"Very big of you."

He laughed. "It was a big deal, to me. Don't you think you could do the same?"

"Alex, I'll never think your deceiving me, and not just once but for months, was okay. We're just going to have to agree to disagree on that."

"I can do that."

"Good. Because it takes a lot of energy being mad at you all the time." I was already tired of it. I couldn't wait to get to London so I could put this entire ordeal behind me.

"You mean you don't enjoy throwing cereal bowls at my head? You know, you could've hurt me with that thing."

"Yes, Alex, that was the point. I was *trying* to hurt you."

"And here I thought you were such a nice girl. Well, I did until the boat ride."

"The boat ride? We weren't even fighting then."

"I meant after the boat ride, in the shed. I had no idea you were such a lustful girl."

"I'm not a lustful girl! I happen to enjoy sex. There's nothing wrong with a woman enjoying sex, Alex. It wasn't created just for men."

"I completely agree. I meant I wasn't expecting it, that's all. I'm not complaining."

"Good!"

I was still on my back, but he'd rolled over onto his side. "C'mon, Gwen, say you forgive me."

I folded my arms across my chest. "Never."

"Never's a long time."

"Yes it is."

"I forgave you."

"You're not seriously comparing what I did to what you did?"

"No, just making an observation. I want to move forward, Gwen. I don't want us to be stuck in this place forever."

"Neither do I. I want to move forward too."

"Then we're agreed." He smiled over at me from his side of the bed. "Can we have sex now?"

I knew he was joking, but his comment still annoyed me. I pushed up onto my elbows and faced him. "You really think it's that easy, don't you? You just say you're sorry and that makes everything all right?"

"No, of course not. I realize it'll take us some time to get back on track."

Back on track? "You don't think I'm still moving in with you, do you? That we're getting back together?"

He sat up too. "Well aren't we? You just said you wanted to move forward."

"Yes, move forward with my life. As in without you. This," I said, pointing from him to me, "is over. We're through."

He jumped up from the bed. "You're seriously going to throw away all that we have over one lie? A lie that was as much for your benefit as it was mine."

I leaped to my feet too. "One lie? It was a lot more than that, Alex. You lied to me for months. You took a photograph of my birthmark while I was sleeping—"

"Passed out drunk in my guest room would be more accurate."

"Yes," I said, my voice rising, "passed out drunk on wine you kept pouring me for the sole purpose of getting me in that position. Then you sent the photo off to your friend at *Universitatea din Bucuresti* all so you could get your hands on that gold mine."

"How do you know where he works? I never told you."

Oops. "You said he was a professor in Bucharest. I assumed."

"No, Gwen, you knew. That's the Romanian pronunciation, not the English one. How did you know? Did Stefan tell you?"

"No, Stefan didn't tell me." I wasn't letting him take the rap for this. Let Alex find out I'd been snooping. I didn't care anymore. "I found the e-mails in your nightstand. Too bad I can't read Romanian. I could've put an end to this a lot sooner and saved us both a lot of heartache."

He took a step closer and spoke soft and low like that night in the kitchen when he'd threatened Stefan. "And when, exactly, did you go rummaging through my nightstand?"

I took a step back. "The day you and Isabella went to the movies."

He shook his head and folded his arms across his chest. "So apparently I'm not the only one here who's been lying."

"Not lying, Alex. Looking around the house when you weren't home. Big difference."

"I don't see it that way, Gwen. I'd say we *both* acted in our own best interests."

He was too much. "I think I'm the one who got the raw end of this deal, not you. I couldn't even read the stupid things."

"That's not the point, Gwen. And I hardly think inheriting an interest in a gold mine is a raw deal. You should be thanking me."

"Thanking you? Are you fucking kidding me?"

"No," he yelled back. "I'm not. This victim act you're pulling is getting a bit tiresome."

"Victim act?" I couldn't believe the words that were coming out of his mouth. If I'd had another cereal bowl handy I would've thrown that one at his head too. "We are through, Alex. Done. *Finito. Terminé.* I want you out of my room and out of my life."

"Fine," he said and slammed the door shut behind him. Had the framed picture not still been sitting on the floor sans glass, it would've fallen and broken this time too.

Chapter 39

None of us spoke as we left the house at dawn the next morning. It was a mostly silent ride to the airport, and an equally quiet wait at the gate.

We had four seats in a row on the plane. Alex sat on one end, I sat on the other, and Stefan and Isabella sat between us. I explained to Isabella that I would not be staying with her at her grandmother's house or her aunt's, but that I'd see her again when she returned to school in September.

"Will you take me to the park sometimes?" she asked.

"I'm sure Katarina will take you. But if she's not available you can call me."

"But you'll still come to the house and swim sometimes, right?"

"We're both going to be busy with school. But if you have another party at the house, I promise I'll try to come."

That seemed to satisfy her.

I offered to catch a cab to the flat Zoe's family had rented, but Stefan insisted their driver could drop me off. Alex didn't weigh in. Nor did he get out of the car when the driver pulled up in front of the South Kensington apartment building. Only Stefan did. Isabella and I hugged goodbye in the car. Alex didn't say a word to me, nor I to him.

Their driver set my suitcase on the sidewalk, and Stefan carried it to the apartment building's front door. "As things progress with the mine we'll need to speak," he said. "I can be your contact person if you'd like, instead of Alex."

"Yes, I'd prefer that." I presumed at this point Alex did too.

"Good," he said and gave me a quick hug. "I'll be in touch."

Then he climbed back into the car, and the three of them drove away.

"I can't believe you're really here!" Zoe screamed when she opened the door to the flat.

"I can't believe it either," I said as I wheeled my suitcase into the surprisingly modern living room. From the exterior of the beautiful four-story row house with its imposing portico and giant black door, I'd assumed the inside would be decorated in shabby chic style. Instead it was filled with hip leather furniture and glass-and-chrome tables.

It wasn't until I pushed my dark sunglasses to the top of my head that Zoe said, "Holy shit, Gwen. You look like somebody beat you up."

"Is it that bad?" My face actually looked a lot better now than it had a few days ago. Most of the swelling had gone down and the dark purple bruises under both eyes had faded to a bluish green. "I put on makeup this morning and everything."

"Then we need to get you some new makeup. Are you tired or can we go out exploring?"

I was tired, but I wasn't going to spend my first afternoon in London napping. "Actually, I'm starving. Can we get something to eat first?" They'd served breakfast on the plane, but the smell of all those reheated sausages in that confined space had been so overpowering that I'd skipped the hot food and opted for a handful of dry cereal instead.

"Sure. We can go to Harrods. They have everything."

After lunch at Harrods's food hall, which really did have everything, we walked up to Kensington Palace and toured Princess Diana's former home. It was still being used as a royal residence so we weren't able to see the section where she'd actually lived, but we did get to view a display of her dresses. I hoped Alex would take Isabella there. I knew she would enjoy seeing a real princess's home.

By the time we finished touring and walked back to the flat, Zoe's parents and sister had returned from their day trip to Windsor Castle. We walked to a neighborhood restaurant for dinner, where Zoe's dad insisted that I explain in person how it was that Alex had deduced that I was the heir to Dracula.

"And you just gave him the icon?" Zoe's dad said, shaking his head.

"Yes, Mark," Zoe's mother replied on my behalf. "She just told you that."

"But why?" he asked. "That's your strongest piece of evidence."

"Because she doesn't want it," Zoe's mother answered. "She doesn't want any of this."

Mark set down his wineglass. "Michelle, it's a gold mine. She wants a gold mine."

"But it doesn't belong to me," I replied before Zoe's mom could. "And they'll never give it to me anyway. Stefan pretty much admitted that."

"You don't know that," Mark said. "You never know what a court will do."

"I only signed those papers because Stela told me it was going to happen anyway and it would be better if Alex's company was in charge instead of the Chinese. I don't expect to get anything out of it."

"Oh you'll get something out of it," Mark said. "I'll see to that. This Alex character isn't keeping it all."

I still didn't want it—I had no desire to be business partners with the Romanescus, especially not Alex, and thought the sooner I was out of it the better—but I thanked him anyway. He wasn't my dad, but I still felt like he was looking out for me.

After dinner Zoe's sister, June, begged us to go out clubbing with her. The drinking age in England was only eighteen so she could finally drink legally. Mark and Michelle would only allow it if Zoe went too. And Zoe would only go if I agreed. So even though I was exhausted and just wanted to go to bed, I let Zoe dress me up in a miniskirt and high heels, and we took a cab to a club that was so hip it didn't even have a name, only an address. June had read somewhere that Prince Harry liked to frequent it.

We didn't see Prince Harry (or any other member of the royal family). Just a lot of "tarty girls and footballers," June said, who after only one week in England was already talking like a Brit. But for the accents and the fact that the beer was served warm instead of cold, it was just like the clubs back home—music so loud that you had to shout to the person standing next to you and lots of scantily clad bodies writhing on the dance floor.

I hadn't even finished my first martini when I had to dash to the ladies' room, push past all the other tarty girls in the queue (June had me talking like a Brit now too), and get my head in a toilet before my dinner ended up on the floor.

"Maybe you got a concussion from the car accident," June said when I'd rejoined her and Zoe at the bar. She'd elected a premed track at college and according to Zoe was now spending inordinate amounts of time on Web MD. "Vomiting is a very common symptom."

"Don't be ridiculous," I said and continued searching my purse for a breath mint.

"I don't think it's ridiculous," Zoe said as she offered me the barstool even though she still had five minutes left on her turn. The club was so crowded that we'd only been able to procure one chair, which the three of us were sharing.

"Zoe, my accident was five days ago. I think if I had a concussion the symptoms would've started a little sooner, don't you?"

She considered it. "You did say you weren't feeling well this morning."

"Because the plane hit turbulence. Besides, I think if I had a concussion they would've mentioned it to me when I was at the hospital."

"Maybe they didn't know," she said.

"And maybe I just had some bad prawns." Now that I had puked up my dinner I felt fine.

June said, "I ate the same food as you and I'm okay."

I hated when they double-teamed me. "If I'm not feeling better by the time we get back to LA I'll make a doctor's appointment. Okay?"

They were both satisfied with that answer.

Per Mark and Michelle's instructions, we dragged June out of the club at 1:00 a.m. even though she'd met a cute boy and wanted to stay. She whined for the entire cab ride back to the flat. She was worse than Isabella. I would've offered her an ice cream cone and a Barbie DVD if I thought it would've done any good.

Mark and Michelle were sleeping when we returned so we all crept to our bedrooms—Zoe and I were sharing the larger one next to the master, and June had claimed the smaller room across the hall. They were all still sleeping when I woke up the next morning and ran to the bathroom to puke my guts up again, although at this point I had nothing left to give. I tried to be quiet, but it's hard not to make noise when you're retching.

Zoe's mom knocked on the bathroom door. "Gwen, are you okay?"

"Sorry, did I wake you?"

She opened the door and joined me inside. It looked just like the bathrooms back home except this one also had a bidet. Zoe's mom perched on the edge of the tub. "Too much to drink?" she asked.

I shook my head and leaned back against the cabinet under the sink. "I only had one and I got sick at the club last night too. I thought it was the prawns because after I puked I felt better. But maybe June's right; maybe I really do have a concussion."

"I wouldn't rely on June for medical advice."

I laughed. "Normally I wouldn't, but to be honest I haven't felt right since the car accident. Although last night was the first time I actually got sick."

"Not right how?" she asked.

"I don't know. Just off. All I want to do is sleep, and I'm always nauseous. I thought it was Alex who was making me sick, but I can't blame this on him."

Zoe's mom paused then said, "About him. I know it's none of my business, but when you two were in Romania were you... together?"

I could feel my cheeks turning pink. "Um, yeah, for a little while."

"And did you use protection?"

"Mom!" It slipped out. "I mean, Zoe's mom."

"It's okay, Gwen, you can call me Mom too. I'm certainly acting like your mother. So did you?"

"Of course."

"Every time?" she asked.

"Almost." Then I realized what she was getting at. "Oh my God, you don't think?"

"All I can tell you is when I was pregnant with Zoe I was sick and tired all the time too."

I dry heaved into the toilet again.

Chapter 40

She agreed not to say anything to anyone until we knew for sure. I wanted to forget about it at least until we returned to LA, but she insisted I take a home pregnancy test. When Mark woke up, she told him we were almost out of milk and that she was running to the store to pick up more. She returned with a pregnancy test too, which she slipped to me when he wasn't looking.

"I'll take it later," I whispered.

"You'll take it now," she said and ordered me into the bathroom.

I peed on the stick and we sat together on the edge of the tub while we waited for the window to show a plus or a minus sign. I made her look first.

When she put her arm around me and said, "Oh, Gwen," I knew the outcome.

"But it was only that one time!" Yes, I knew it could happen, but what were the odds that the one and only time in my entire life I'd had unprotected sex I got pregnant? I must've been the most fertile woman on the planet.

"Sometimes that's all it takes," she said and hugged me while I cried. I never missed my mother so much as I did at that moment.

"Now what?" I asked as I wiped away my tears.

"Now you have a decision to make."

"I don't want it." I didn't even have to think about it.

"Gwen, you don't know that. You're scared, which is understandable. This is a huge shock."

My stomach was churning, my head was spinning, and I felt like I was going to puke again. "No, I don't want it. This isn't how it's supposed to be."

She hugged me again. "Sweetie, life never happens like it's supposed to. It just happens."

June banged on the bathroom door. "Are you two *ever* coming out of there? Some of us have to pee, you know."

"Exhibit A," Michelle said, and we both laughed. Everyone, even June, knew she was Michelle's "surprise baby."

Zoe's mom agreed to keep my secret until I was ready to share. I stuffed the pregnancy test back in the box and hid it under my shirt, but June spotted me burying it in the kitchen trash later that morning then pulled it out when I wasn't looking. Once June knew I had to tell Zoe, and then since Mark was the only one in the flat who didn't know, we told him too. Apparently he didn't realize it was supposed to be a secret because when we all met Zoe's brother, Daniel, for dinner that night the first thing he said to me was, "I hear you're knocked up. Congrats."

Everyone but me and Zoe's mom laughed. Neither of us thought it was funny. Nor was I pleased when Zoe's mom refused to let me have Diet Coke with dinner or coffee with dessert.

"But I don't even know if I'm keeping it." I didn't want to keep it. I knew that. But the thought of terminating the pregnancy wasn't sitting well with me either. Being pro-choice is not the same as being pro-abortion. Nor did I think I could have a child and give it up for adoption like my birth mother had done to me. I'd want to know what happened to that child. I'd want to be a part of that child's life. I wouldn't be able to forget about it and pretend it didn't exist. I had no idea what I was going to do. I had no good options.

"Things have changed since you were pregnant, Mom," June said. "You can have caffeine now."

"In moderation," Zoe added.

The three of us had spent the afternoon Googling.

"Not at my table," Zoe's mom said and pulled the empty coffee cup away from me.

After dinner we all returned to the flat and watched television, and Zoe's mom made me take my first prenatal vitamin, which I promptly vomited into the toilet. The next morning she went to the store and bought me ginger ale, ginger tea, ginger candy, and a box of saltines. In combination they helped.

"So when are you going to call Alex?" Zoe asked as we walked through the Egyptian section of the British Museum.

"I'm not," I said as I stared at Cleopatra's mummy. I thought she'd be prettier. I'd always heard she was a great beauty. Then I read the placard underneath the display and realized she was only *a* Cleopatra, not *the* Cleopatra.

"Gwen, you have to tell him. He's the father."

"I don't *have* to tell him. There's no law that says I do." Yes, I'd Googled it.

"You don't think he has a right to know?"

"Zoe, you know what'll happen if I tell him. He'll take over. This is my decision to make, not his."

"He doesn't even get a vote?"

"Not as long as it's inside my body, no."

"Do I get a vote?" she asked and flashed me her pouty smile.

It worked on men all the time, but not on me. "No, because it's not your body either."

"But I'd be such a good auntie. Think of all the cute outfits I could buy."

I wanted to yell at her, but I didn't want to get kicked out of the museum, so I lowered my voice and said, "I'm not having a child so you can buy cute baby outfits. Go have your own kid."

"Someday," she said as we wandered out of the Egyptian section and into Ancient Rome. "But I'm not ready to settle down yet."

"And I am?"

"You don't like going out anyway. This will be perfect for you. Now you'll have an excuse to stay home."

"Thanks a lot," I said and the tears welled up in my eyes. This was the worst part for me—the raging hormones. It was even worse than being nauseous all the time.

She placed her arm around my shoulder and hugged me. "Gwen, don't cry. You know I'm only kidding with you. I support you 100 percent whatever decision you make."

I nodded and pulled a tissue out of my purse. I did know. I just had no control over my emotions anymore. And morally, I agreed with her. I knew not telling Alex was wrong. But I was almost positive he'd want me to have the baby. And since I didn't yet know what I wanted, I was going to postpone telling him for as long as I possibly could.

Chapter 41

I made an appointment with my doctor as soon as I returned to LA She confirmed that I was pregnant and asked me what I planned to do.

"Honestly, I have no idea," I said as tears sprang into my eyes. "The father and I aren't together anymore."

She nodded and handed me a box of tissues. "Well, the good news is you have options. It's still early so you have time, but I wouldn't wait too long. The sooner you decide the better."

I left with a handful of pamphlets, a list of acceptable prenatal vitamins, and instructions to make another appointment for six weeks later if I chose to continue with the pregnancy.

I was still undecided when I returned to work the following week. And the week after that. And the week after that. And the week after that.

"Gwen, you've got to decide," Zoe said as she followed me into the faculty bathroom.

"I know," I said right before I heaved into one of the toilets. I'd overslept and skipped breakfast. That always got me into trouble. "But I don't know what to do." I was no closer to making a decision now than I had been the day I'd found out I was pregnant. I didn't know which bad option to choose.

"Well if you wait much longer the decision's going to be made for you."

"I know," I said again and flushed. Then I stumbled to the sink and splashed cold water onto my face.

A few seconds later a second toilet flushed and Simone Lorens, our school principal, emerged from the last stall.

I froze. Usually I checked to make sure the bathroom was empty before we ever talked in there. But I was in such a rush to reach the toilet before I puked that I'd skipped that ritual today.

"You really need to decide about that gym membership," Zoe said, shooting me a meaningful glance. "I think the cooling-off period's only a week."

"You're right," I said, picking up on her lead. "I'm going to call and cancel today."

"Good morning," Simone said as she joined the two of us at the sinks. "Everything all right?" she asked, glancing from me to Zoe and back to me again.

"Fine," we both said at the same time.

She stared at me in the mirror as she washed her hands. "Are you feeling okay? I thought I heard someone get sick."

"Yeah, I just had some bad sushi last night."

She nodded and reached for a paper towel. "That seems to happen to you a lot."

I shrugged. "Sensitive stomach, I guess."

"Well, I hope you feel better," she said as she glanced in the mirror again, this time to fiddle with her hair. "I may have some crackers in my office if you need them."

"No, I'm good," I said. "I've got my own."

She smiled again and looked me over, lingering on my stomach first and then my chest. I was wearing a loose-fitting sweater over my black pants, so she couldn't see that my abdomen wasn't as flat as it used to be, but my boobs were bigger too. Either that or all my bras had shrunk.

I waited until the door closed behind her before I dared to look at Zoe again.

"You think she knows?" I asked.

"If she doesn't, she suspects. Did you see the way she was staring at your chest?"

I nodded and the tears welled up in my eyes.

Zoe hugged me. "Don't cry, Gwen. She can't fire you for being pregnant."

"I'm not worried about her firing me." I sniffed. "I'm worried about her telling Alex."

Zoe had forgotten that they were friends, but I hadn't.

Chapter 42

I wasn't surprised when Alex showed up at my house that night. I was almost expecting it. I knew it would only be a matter of time before Simone told him. But I played dumb anyway.

"What are you doing here?" I asked when I opened my front door. His anger was palpable, just as I'd expected. I feared this was going to get ugly.

"I think you know," he said and strode inside. He gave me the same once-over eye sweep Simone had given me that morning. I was glad I'd changed into sweatpants and an oversized T-shirt. My boobs weren't as noticeable in this outfit as they had been in the sweater.

"I don't. We're through, Alex. I thought I made that clear in Romania."

"Are you sure there's not something you want to tell me?" he said. "Something important? Something I might like to know?"

We glared at each other for a few seconds before I finally said, "No, nothing."

He glanced down the hallway toward my bathroom, then in the direction of my kitchen, then back at me. "I have a headache. Do you have any aspirin?"

I knew he was up to something, I just wasn't sure what. "Wait here," I said, but he followed me into the kitchen anyway. "Alex, I told you to wait in the living room."

"Why? Is there something in here you don't want me to see?"

"We're in my house now, not yours. If I tell you to wait in the living room, you wait in the living room."

"Get me my aspirin and I'll go."

"No. Go home and get your own damn aspirin."

He reached over my head and opened one of my kitchen cabinets. That one only contained glasses, but it didn't take him long to reach the one with the pills. He pulled out my bottle of prenatal vitamins and shook it in front of my face. "Want to explain these?"

What I wanted was to scream at him to get the fuck out of my house. But I didn't have the energy. Instead I sat down on the floor and cried. Stupid hormones.

He ran his hands through his hair—a gesture I knew so well but hadn't seen in weeks. And despite my hurt and anger at him for all that he'd put me through, I couldn't deny that there was a small part of me that had missed him a little bit too. I had loved Alex, albeit briefly. But I still believed not telling him I was pregnant until I'd made my own decision was the right thing to do. Alex would only support me if I did what he wanted. I knew that.

"Gwen, why didn't you tell me? Didn't you think I'd want to know?"

"Yes." I sniffed loudly.

He sat down on the floor too and put his arm around my shoulder. "It's okay, honey. I know now. You don't have to go through this alone."

"I was going to tell you," I said between sobs. "Honest."

"I know," he said and rubbed my back.

"I just wanted to wait until I'd decided."

He stopped rubbing. "Decided what?"

I realized my mistake immediately. "You know," I said and sniffed.

"Decided what, Gwen?" His tone shifted from comforting back to angry.

"Whether I was keeping it or not."

He pulled his hand away. "You were going to have an abortion and not even tell me?"

"I would've told you. I just wanted to decide on my own first."

He jumped up and started pacing my small kitchen. "I don't believe this. I really don't believe this."

"What don't you believe? It's not like we're together. I'm alone, Alex. I have no family, no one to help me. If I did this and something happened to me that kid would be screwed."

"What about me, Gwen? I'm the father. You don't think I would help you? You don't think I would take responsibility for my own child?"

I pushed myself up from the floor. "It's not the same and you know it."

"How is it not the same? Am I not Isabella's father? Do I not take care of her?"

"She spends more time with her nannies than she does with you. I would know."

"Yes, Gwen, because I'm a single parent. It's not so easy."

"Exactly," I said. "That's exactly why I don't know if I can do this. It's a huge responsibility. I honestly don't know what I'm going to do."

He banged his fist on the counter. "Well I can tell you what you're not doing. You're not killing my child."

"It's not a child, Alex. At this point, it's not anything. And you don't get to make this decision, I do."

"We'll see about that," he said and stormed out of the kitchen and then my front door.

Zoe and I were walking to our cars in the school parking lot the next afternoon when a stranger in jeans and a sweatshirt sidled up to me.

"Are you Gwen Andersen?" he asked.

I'd learned my lesson from the reporter in Romania. "Why?" I asked.

He shoved the manila envelope he was carrying into my hand. "You've been served."

Chapter 43

As soon as we realized they were legal papers Zoe called her dad and he told us to meet him at home.

"Don't panic," he said as all four of us—me, Zoe, Mark, and Michelle—sat together in the Richards's living room. "It's just a Complaint to Establish a Parental Relationship."

"What the hell is that?" I asked.

"It's a way for Alex to establish paternity."

"Why does he have to establish paternity? He knows he's the father. I'm not denying it and neither is he."

"I'm not a family law expert, Gwen, but I assume it's so he can assert his rights."

"What rights? He doesn't have any rights. I'm the one who's pregnant!" I jumped up from the couch and started circling the living room.

Zoe's mom grabbed my hand as I strode past her. "Gwen, you need to calm down. Getting upset isn't going to help you or the baby."

I snatched my hand away and resumed my pacing. "I don't even want this baby."

Zoe glanced up at me. "Are you sure?"

"Of course I'm sure! Whose side are you on?"

She and her mom exchanged a look, then Zoe joined me in front of the living room's big picture window. "Gwen, you've been putting it off for a month. I think if you wanted to have an abortion you would've done it already. I think you really do want this baby."

"But I can't have a baby," I cried. "I'm all alone."

Zoe's mom rushed over and hugged me. "Gwen, you're not alone. You have us."

"I know," I said and sniffed back tears. "But it's not the same. I'm not your kid. You don't have to help me."

"Gwen, we love you like our own. If you decide to do this we'll help you, I promise."

"And we'll make sure this Alex fellow does too," Mark piped up from the couch. "He's not getting off scot-free. He has responsibilities here."

But that was the problem. I didn't want Alex helping me—or taking over, which is what he would no doubt do. Despite my past feelings for him, I knew as a couple we weren't a good fit. I was too strong-willed and he was too domineering. There was no way we could raise a child together. If I did have this baby then I would need to do it on my own.

Mark made an appointment for me with a family law attorney in his firm. The next day he walked me down to Renee Zell's office and introduced us, then she kicked him out so we could talk in private.

"Can I get you anything?" she asked. "Water? Soda? Coffee?"

I shook my head.

She pushed her short dark hair behind her ears and sat down behind her large wood desk with her hands folded in front of her. "First off, I want to tell you that anything you say to me is confidential. Legally, I cannot tell anyone, not even Mark, unless you authorize me to. Do you understand?"

I nodded.

"Good. He told me a little bit about your situation, but I'd like to hear it from you."

I started with the day Alex spilled wine on my dress and didn't stop until I'd recounted how I'd been served with the complaint. She nodded and took notes but didn't interrupt me.

"And do you want to have this baby, Gwen?"

"I don't know," I said and the first tear slid down my cheek.

She passed me a box of tissues. "It's okay. Everyone cries in my office."

I couldn't decide if that made me feel better or worse.

"Well, you have three options. I'm sure you know what they are, but I'd like to run through them with you anyway if that's okay?"

I nodded again.

"First," she said, "you can have an abortion and this whole thing goes away."

"He can't stop me?"

"No, but that doesn't mean he won't try. So if that's the path you want to take you should schedule an appointment for as soon as possible. Second, you can have the baby and give it up for adoption. There are tons of would-be parents out there who would love to give your baby a good home."

"I know. I was adopted."

"Then I don't need to sell you on it. The problem is you cannot give a child up for adoption without the father's consent. And from what you've told me, it seems unlikely that he would agree to that."

"He won't," I said.

"Then that leaves your third option. You have the baby and work out a parenting plan and custody arrangement with the father. He would also have to pay child support, but it sounds like that won't be a problem."

"If I didn't take his money would I still have to share custody with him?"

"Yes," she said. "One thing has nothing to do with the other. He's legally required to pay it. And he's legally entitled to have contact with his child. He could even sue you for sole custody."

"He could get sole custody of *my* child?" This was unbelievable.

"It would be extremely unlikely," she said, "unless there's something you're not telling me. Have you ever had any problems with drugs or alcohol?"

"No, never."

"Have you ever been the perpetrator of domestic violence or been convicted of child abuse or first degree murder?"

"Of course not. I teach first grade."

"Sadly that's not dispositive," she said. "But it sounds like you're fine. The court's only concern is what's in the best interests of the child. Generally that means frequent and continuous contact with *both* parents. The vast majority of my clients work out a joint custody arrangement where the child spends part of the week with each of them. It doesn't have to be that way; it's just the norm."

"What if I don't want to share custody? What if I want to do this on my own?"

"Gwen, I want to be very clear about this up front. You can terminate the pregnancy without his consent, but if you have this child then as the father he has rights. Which means you'll have to find a way to work together. If Alex wants joint custody, you're going to have to agree. If you try to deny him access to his child I guarantee you he will make your life a living hell."

I agreed to meet with Alex and his lawyer at the end of the week. I didn't have a choice. Alex threatened to take me to court if I didn't. Renee had already eaten through half the retainer I'd paid her to represent me—and that was with the friends and family discount Mark had negotiated on my behalf. At this rate, I'd be bankrupt before the baby was even born, assuming I had the baby. I was still officially undecided, although leaning in that direction.

"Another reason to work with him," Renee had said when I told her what I could afford to pay. "Otherwise he'll be hauling you into court every other day."

"But I haven't done anything wrong!"

"It doesn't matter," she said. "His lawyer can just keep filing motions. Even if we strike down every one, you'd still have to pay me to defend you. Trust me, Gwen, it's not worth it. Not financially and not emotionally. Even when you win, you lose. You have to work this out with him. It's the only way."

I followed her into the conference room where Alex and his lawyer were already waiting. Alex was wearing a suit, as I knew he would, so I wore my light gray slacks with a black sweater set. They were the only dress pants I owned that still fit comfortably. The rest were all tight in the waist. I still hadn't gained any weight—probably from all the puking—but my shape had started to shift.

Alex's lawyer, Jim Beckett, introduced himself to me. He and Renee already knew each other. She told me she'd opposed him many times before and that he was the attorney clients hired when they wanted to fight, not when they wanted to negotiate.

I shook his hand and took a seat at the table next to Renee. Alex sat across from me. We didn't speak. Renee told me it would be better that way, that I should let her do all the talking.

"I think we can dispense with the complaint, Jim. My client won't contest paternity. She'll sign a declaration."

"Excellent," he said. "You should know my client intends to enforce his full paternal rights, including seeking sole custody."

"What!" I knew Alex would push for joint custody. Renee had prepared me for that and I was trying to accept it, even though I still thought both the baby and I would be better off if the baby just lived with me and Alex visited sometimes, the way divorced parents used to handle it back in the old days before joint custody became in vogue. But there was no way in hell I was giving him sole custody of this baby. Not in any universe.

Renee grabbed my arm and gave me a meaningful look. "Gwen, I'll handle this."

"Did you hear what he said?"

"Yes, now remember what we talked about."

She'd warned me that Alex's lawyer might try to bait me into an outburst. It was a common tactic, she'd said.

I glared at Alex and his attorney but kept my mouth shut. Alex refused to look at me. He stared at Renee.

"Jim, you know that's not going happen," Renee stated calmly. "You have no basis."

"*Au contraire*," Jim said and slid a sheet of paper across the table to Renee. "Your client has a history of abuse against my client."

Renee spun around to face me.

"He's lying. I swear."

Jim picked up his legal pad and read, "On or about August fourth of this year your client attacked my client with a ceramic bowl."

"You told him about the cereal bowl?" How many more times was this man going to betray me?

Alex finally looked at me. "He asked if you had a history of abusive behavior. That incident came to mind."

"What about you and Stefan? You almost strangled him that night in the kitchen."

Alex directed his answer to Renee instead of to me. "Brotherly horseplay. We've been doing it for years. I've never laid a hand on Isabella and I've never touched Gwen."

"Never touched me! How do you think I ended up this way? Immaculate conception?"

Alex turned to me. "That was consensual."

"Not the first time."

Renee snapped her folder shut. "I think we're done here."

"Goddamn right we're done." I jumped up from my seat and grabbed my purse from the chair next to me. "I would've settled with you, Alex. I would've agreed to joint custody because it would've been in our baby's best interests for us to work this out amicably. But you don't care about this child. You're just out for revenge. Well, guess what, Alex, this is one time you're not going to get your way. You will never get sole custody of my child. Ne-ver." Then I hurried toward the conference room door.

"Gwen, stop," Alex said.

"No, this is bullshit and you know it." The tears were already streaming down my face. "I feel sorry for this child having you as a father. You are a selfish spiteful horrible man, and I wish I'd never met you!"

I was reaching for the door handle when Alex sprang out of his chair and grabbed my arm. "Gwen," he said again and looked down at my pants.

I followed his gaze to the dark red stain spreading below my waist.

Chapter 44

Alex tried to follow me into the ladies' room but Renee barred his way.

"Jim, control your client," she called out to him and locked the door behind us. "Gwen, what do you need me to do?"

"I don't know," I said and ran into a stall. I wasn't in pain, but there seemed to be a lot of blood. "I'm going to call my doctor," I said as I pulled my phone out of my purse. "Just keep Alex away from me."

"Will do," she said and left the bathroom.

My ob-gyn's nurse told me my doctor was in surgery and I should go to the emergency room and the doctor would meet me there. I didn't have a pad or a pantiliner on me and the bathroom only contained a tampon dispenser, so I grabbed a bunch of toilet paper and stuffed that inside my underwear, hoping it would stanch the bleeding. Then I took off my sweater and wrapped it around my waist.

Alex and Renee were waiting for me in the hallway when I emerged.

"What's wrong?" Alex asked.

"I don't know. I have to meet my doctor at the hospital."

They both paled.

"Just because she's already there," I added to quell the panic apparent on both their faces. "The nurse told me bleeding doesn't necessarily mean I'm having a miscarriage. It could be lots of things."

"I'll drive you," Alex said.

"Not a chance," I answered and headed to the elevator.

They both followed.

When the elevator arrived Renee said, "Call me later so I know you're okay."

I nodded and stepped inside. Alex followed. "I swear to God, Alex, if you don't leave me alone I'm going to scream."

"It's my child too, Gwen. You're not going without me."

I drove myself to the hospital and Alex followed in his own car. He also sat with me while I filled out the forms and came with me when the clerk called me inside and showed me to a room. A nurse handed me a gown and told me to undress from the waist down.

I turned to Alex. "Get out."

"Your husband can stay," the nurse said.

"He's not my husband and I want him out of here."

"I'll wait outside while you change," Alex said. "Then I'm coming back."

He gave me five minutes to myself.

A doctor, but not my doctor, walked in a few minutes later. He introduced himself as Dr. Sloan and told me my doctor was still in surgery, so he'd be examining me. "We'll need to do an ultrasound. I'll be right back."

He returned ten minutes later with a nurse and an ultrasound machine. When he asked me to put my feet into the stirrups, I turned to Alex. "Time for you to leave."

"I'm not going anywhere."

"You don't need to be here for this, Mr. Andersen," Dr. Sloan said.

"It's Romanescu," Alex snapped, "not Andersen."

Dr. Sloan glanced down at my chart.

"We're not married," I said. "We're not even together. He followed me here."

"I see," Dr. Sloan said. "Mr. Romanescu, the nurse can show you to the waiting area."

Alex shook his head. "No, this is my baby too."

Dr. Sloan turned to me. "He's the father," I admitted.

Dr. Sloan faced Alex again. "Mr. Romanescu, I understand that you want to be here, but Ms. Andersen's the patient and she's entitled to her privacy. If you won't leave voluntarily I can call security."

Alex looked like he was about to explode, but he left the room.

"Just try to relax," Dr. Sloan said.

Easy for him to say. He wasn't the one with his feet in the stirrups.

First he examined me, then he used the ultrasound, which went inside of me instead of on the outside of my stomach because it was still early in the pregnancy. I heard a sound like sheet metal blowing in the wind. "That's the heartbeat," he said. "The baby's fine."

As usual these days, I started to cry. He smiled sweetly and handed me a box of tissues.

As he moved the probe around he pointed at the blurry image on the ultrasound machine's small screen. It looked like an X-ray of a lima bean with two white seeds inside—one round and one oval. He placed his finger under the round one and said, "That's the head."

It was the first time I'd seen it. I was terrified and excited at the same time. Now it was real. Now it was a baby.

He pulled out the probe and sat down on the wheeled stool next to the bed. He wore metal-frame glasses, and his blue-gray eyes crinkled in the corners when he smiled. I guessed he was in his early to mid thirties, same age as Alex. "Let's talk about what happened today."

"I don't know what happened. One minute I'm yelling at the father, and the next minute I'm covered in blood."

"You think there might be some connection there?"

I shrugged.

"Bleeding during the first trimester is not uncommon. It happens to one in four women, so you shouldn't be concerned. But there's obviously a lot of tension between you and the father. And with this much blood and no underlying cause, I have to wonder if they're related."

"But you said everything was fine."

"It is," he said. "Today. But you're thin, you're pale, and your heart rate's higher than I'd like it to be. None of that's good—for you or your baby."

I closed my eyes and let the tears spill out. "I don't know what to do." How could we have a child together when I couldn't even stand to be in the same room with him? Dr. Sloan squeezed my hand. "Make peace," he said, "for both your sakes."

Alex was waiting for me in the row of chairs outside the emergency room. As soon as he spotted me, he leaped to his feet. "Are you okay?" he asked. "How's the baby?"

"We'll both be fine if you'd just stay away from me."

"That's not going to happen, Gwen. You should know me better than that."

I did know. As long as I was carrying his child he would never leave me alone. "Alex, I swear—" I couldn't finish my thought because his face started to blur. He caught me before I hit the floor. I sat in a plastic molded chair with my head between my knees while Alex yelled at the woman at the front desk until she brought me back inside. This time he didn't leave the room.

"Back so soon?" Dr. Sloan said as he strode into the exam room.

"What's wrong with her?" Alex demanded.

"If I had to guess," Dr. Sloan said, "I'd say you."

That was the moment I fell in love with Dr. Sloan. He was my knight in white lab coat saving me from the fire-breathing dragon that was Alex Romanescu.

"Me?" Alex said, but Dr. Sloan ignored him. He slid the wheeled stool next to the bed and sat down. He reached for my wrist and took my pulse.

"How are you feeling, Gwen?"

"Not so bad," I said.

"Good. When's the last time you ate or drank something?"

"I don't know. Lunch, maybe."

He nodded. "I'll run some tests, but I'm betting it's just dehydration. You may as well make yourself comfortable. You're going to be here a while." He turned to Alex. "Mr. Romanescu, can I speak to you for a minute?"

Alex followed him outside. I didn't know what Dr. Sloan said to him, but when he came back into the room he was a lot nicer to me.

Chapter 45

Alex showed up at my house again on Sunday afternoon. I was still in my pajamas. Dr. Sloan had told me what I needed most was rest, so I was taking his advice.

"What do you want?" I said when I opened my front door.

"To talk. Can I come in?"

"Are you sure that's wise without your lawyer present? You might say or do something I can use against you."

"Please, Gwen. I didn't come here to fight with you."

I opened the door wider and he stepped inside. He sat down in the center of the living room couch, so I took the side chair.

"How are you feeling?" he asked.

"Okay."

"Any more dizziness? Are you eating enough?"

I knew he didn't care about me. He was only asking because of the baby. I was the human incubator now. Once I gave birth he'd probably throw me under a bus just so he could get sole custody. "I'm fine, Alex. Why are you here?"

He looked up toward the ceiling and ran his fingers through his hair. "I've been trying to figure out how we got to this point."

"Really?" I snorted. "Let me refresh your recollection. It all started with a birthmark you just had to photograph and send to your pal in Bucharest while I was passed out in your bed."

"Don't be cruel, Gwen."

"I'm cruel? Who sued who, Alex? Who threatened who with sole custody?"

"What was I supposed to do? I thought you were going to have an abortion."

"So you sue me? That's your solution?"

"You knew you were pregnant for weeks and didn't tell me."

"I didn't tell you because I was scared. Because I knew you'd react this way."

"So you go behind my back instead?"

"I didn't go behind your back, Alex. I didn't *do* anything. I stayed home and cried myself to sleep every night because I didn't know what to do. I still don't." The tears started anew. "You didn't have to sue me, Alex. You could've just talked to me."

"I couldn't, Gwen. I was too angry."

That I understood. Because now I was angry too. "And you think this child should grow up without a mother because you're angry? What happens if the baby makes you angry, Alex? Then what do you do? Or does that not matter because it's all about you?"

"You think killing it would be better? You think that's what your mother should've done to you?"

Sucker punched. I don't know why I was surprised. "Get out of my house!"

He leaned his head back and closed his eyes. "I'm sorry. I shouldn't have said that."

"No, you shouldn't have. You think this is easy for me? You think I'm not struggling with this?" My vision was starting to blur again, which couldn't be good. I dropped my head in my hands and closed my eyes. "Just leave, Alex. Having you here only makes everything worse."

He leaned forward so our knees were almost touching. "Gwen, I didn't come here to fight with you. Honest."

I opened my eyes and looked up at the man that six weeks ago I thought I loved, but now I despised. Alex was right. How did we get here? I sniffed back more tears. "Then why did you come?"

"To give you this," he said as he handed me a small velvet box he pulled out of his jacket pocket.

I lifted the lid and stared at the huge diamond—a round stone set high on a silver-colored band.

"It doesn't have to be this way," he said. "We can get married. We can do this together."

One minute he's suing me and threatening me with sole custody and the next he's proposing marriage? I felt like I was losing my mind, but he'd clearly already lost his. I snapped the lid shut and set it on the coffee table in front of him. "No."

"Gwen, I love you. I would've asked you to marry me even if you weren't pregnant. I was planning to in Paris."

That surprised me. But it didn't change anything. "That was then and this is now. Before you found out I was pregnant we hadn't spoken in weeks. I seriously doubt you spent all of that time sitting around the house trying to figure out how to pop the question."

"You told me you wanted to move on. I was trying to respect your wishes."

"Then please respect them now and leave."

"But everything's changed. Don't you see that?"

"No, Alex, nothing's changed. If we have this child—"

"If?" he said, his voice rising.

"When." Yes, I'd decided. It was time to stop pretending. "But I don't know how to make this work. Do you?"

"Yes, marry me."

I shook my head. "No, that's not a solution. It'll only compound everyone's pain."

He grabbed both my hands in his and gazed directly into my eyes. "Gwen, this is the *only* solution. Please, let me do this for you. I want to be a husband to you and a father to this baby. I want us to be a family. You don't have to be alone anymore. You have me now, and I won't leave you."

Instead of a trickle, the tears rushed out of me in a stream. He made it sound so easy, but it wasn't. Nothing with Alex was easy unless I allowed him to subsume me. This relationship would never work.

"You love me, Gwen," Alex continued. "I know you do. You told me so in Romania. We just have to get back to that place."

"Alex, I don't even know you. That man in Romania, the one I thought I loved, he doesn't exist. It was all just a fantasy."

"Gwen, you're wrong. I'm sitting right in front of you. I'm the same man I always was. I haven't changed."

"Yes, and that's the problem. You're the same man who lied to me. You're the same man who betrayed me. You're the same man who's now trying to take my child away. *You're* the man I can't trust."

He let go of my hands and leaned back on the couch, and I helplessly watched as the look of loving earnestness disappeared from his face, replaced by something colder and darker. "I can't change the past, Gwen. What's done is done. You just have to forgive me so we can move forward. It's the only way."

I wiped at the thick stream of tears dripping from my nose and pouring from my eyes. "No, Alex. I can't. I'm sorry."

"Can't, Gwen, or won't?"

"It's the same thing."

"No, Gwen, it's not."

"Alex—"

"I know you like to think of yourself as an *Andersen*," he said as if the name itself was an insult, "but you're not, Gwen."

"Alex, please don't do this." But I knew I was too late. The anger had overtaken him.

"You're a Tepes through and through," he continued as if I hadn't spoken. "He couldn't forgive anyone either. That's how he ended up with his head on a stake. And you're exactly the same."

He'd sucker punched me, again. And again I was surprised. When would I ever learn?

"Then it's lucky for you I don't like to impale people. Although in your case maybe I can make an exception."

He balled his fists and jumped up from the couch. I could practically see the steam rising off of him. But it was rising off of me too. He thought I was a Tepes, a Dracula, a monster, so I might as well prove it to him.

"Still want to marry me?" I asked. Yes, now I was being cruel. But that's what Vlad would've done.

He snatched the velvet box off the coffee table, shoved it into his coat pocket, then stormed out of my house.

"You realize, of course, that you've just made everything ten times worse by shooting him down like that," Zoe said. Her mom had invited me over for dinner that night and naturally Alex's proposal was the topic of conversation.

I stopped sipping my virgin margarita. "What was I supposed to do? Agree to marry him just so he wouldn't get angry? Besides, it can't get any worse. He's already threatened to take the baby away from me. What else can he do?"

"A lot," Mark said from his end of the dining-room table.

That didn't help calm my nerves. I'd already downed two antacids before dinner. I'd need two more before we were finished. The spicy fajitas probably weren't helping either, but I'd asked Zoe's mom to cook them tonight because I was craving bell peppers.

"Leave her alone," Zoe's mom said and turned back to me. "Tell us about the ring."

"There's not much to tell. It was a big round diamond on a silver band. I'm not even sure if it was white gold or platinum."

"Probably platinum," Zoe said. "How big?"

"I don't know. Three carats, maybe." I wasn't as good at judging stone size as Zoe was.

"Holy cow," she said. "And you just gave it back to him?"

"Well I couldn't exactly keep it if I was telling him no."

"I suppose," she said. "But I would've tried."

"She couldn't have kept it," Mark piped in. "It was a conditional gift."

Zoe's mom waved her hand at him. "Oh, stop being such a lawyer," she said before she turned back to me. "And you really don't think you could ever forgive him? I know he behaved badly, Gwen, but you're having a child together. That's a lifelong commitment."

I shook my head. "After what he did—all the lies and now the threats too—you honestly think I could just forgive him? That I *should* forgive him?"

"I don't know," she said. "But I fear what'll happen if you don't."

Chapter 46

The next time I saw Alex was in my lawyer's office. Our second attempt at negotiation was scheduled for five o'clock, but Renee asked me to arrive early so we could strategize first and she could prepare me.

"Did he really propose to you?" Renee asked as we sat on the couch in her office.

"Who told you?" I didn't think Mark would.

"His lawyer. He's trying to use it as evidence of Alex's willingness to compromise and your bad faith. Don't worry," she added before I could object, "it'll never fly."

I shook my head. "I still can't believe after everything he's done to me he honestly thought I'd say yes. But he did bring a ring. Although, who knows? Maybe it was his dead wife's."

She actually cringed. "Wow, you're even more cynical than I am. And I'm a divorce lawyer."

I chuckled. "I didn't used to be. I used to be a nice person who gave people the benefit of the doubt. But no more."

"You're still nice," she said. "You've just been beaten up. Metaphorically, of course, unless there's something you're not telling me."

"No, he was telling the truth about that. He never touched me and I never saw him touch Isabella either. Only Stefan."

"And that crack about the first time not being consensual?"

Although I dearly wanted to say it wasn't, I couldn't lie. "It was a heat-of-the-moment thing."

Renee's door opened and her assistant stuck her head in. "Mr. Romanescu and his lawyer are here. Do you want me to show them to the conference room?"

"Please," Renee said and stood up. "Don your armor, Gwen. The war is about to begin."

This time Alex did most of the talking and his tone was conciliatory, which really had me confused. The last time I saw him he was calling me a monster for not forgiving him, and now he's suddenly nice to me?

"So you'll agree to stop harassing Gwen?" Renee said.

"I don't think a marriage proposal can be characterized as harassment," Jim responded on Alex's behalf.

Renee smiled. "I'll rephrase. You'll agree to stop dropping by Gwen's home?"

"Unless she invites me," Alex said.

"I wouldn't hold my breath if I were you," I muttered.

Renee placed her hand on my arm, which I knew meant, "Shut the hell up."

"And you'll stop following her to doctors appointments and such?"

"I still think I should be able to go with her," Alex said. "It's my child too. But if she doesn't want me there then no, I won't go."

"But you'll pay the medical bills, to the extent they're not covered by insurance?"

"Yes," Alex said, "that's not a problem."

Renee smiled again, clearly pleased. "We've made a lot of progress here today. Jim, I think we can hold off on negotiations for child support and custody arrangements until later in the pregnancy, don't you?"

"Yes," he said. "We'll agree to that."

"Then we're done," Renee said.

I was about to stand up when Alex said, "No, we're not done."

Renee seemed as surprised as I was, but Alex's lawyer wasn't. Obviously this had been planned.

"I've agreed to everything Gwen's asked for," Alex continued, "but she's given me nothing in return."

"What is it you want?" Renee asked.

"Visitation."

Renee glanced at Jim, who stared down at his legal pad, then turned back to Alex. "Mr. Romanescu, your lawyer just agreed to table the custody negotiations until later in the pregnancy. Are you reneging on that?"

"No, I didn't say custody, I said visitation."

"Visitation?" Renee repeated. "You mean with Gwen?"

"Absolutely not!" After last week's proposal/beat-up-on-Gwen-fest, I had no desire to spend any more time with Alex. I knew once the baby was born we'd have to see each other sometimes. There was no avoiding it with joint custody. But I wasn't due for another six months. I should at least be entitled to this brief reprieve. I deserved that much.

Renee placed her hand on my arm, but I pulled away.

"You think you can bribe me into seeing you?" I said to Alex.

"You were the one who said bribery was the key to every successful relationship," he replied.

"Really?" Jim said and jotted down a note on his legal pad.

"I'll need a minute to confer with my client," Renee said and motioned for me to follow her out of the conference room.

I started yelling in the hallway, but she put her finger to her lips. I wasn't allowed to speak until we were inside her office with the door closed.

"No way," I said. "I'm not doing it."

"Gwen, I can't force you to do anything you don't want to do, nor would I try. But I strongly advise you to hear me out. Will you do that?"

I threw my hands up but sat down on the couch with my arms and legs crossed.

"I've been practicing for over twenty years and I've never, and I mean *never*, seen a request like this before. I've never even heard of one. This man is so desperate to get back into your good graces that he'll agree to just about anything."

"If he wanted to get back into my good graces he shouldn't have sued me."

She waved away my comment. "He was acting out."

"Acting out?"

"He's a man who's used to getting what he wants. That's what they do. But he's finally coming to his senses."

"How is this in any way sensible?"

"Gwen, think. He wants you back. That marriage proposal wasn't a ploy. He really thought you'd say yes. Or at least he hoped you would. My God, this is absolutely perfect."

I'd never seen her so excited. Her eyes sparkled and she was grinning from ear to ear.

"I can get you anything you want, Gwen. Just name it."

"I want him out of my life."

The grin faded. "Except for that. I told you when we started if you had this baby that wouldn't be an option. When you have a minor child together there's no avoiding one another. But this is the next-best thing because you get to dictate the terms."

"What terms?"

"Of visitation," she said.

"You're telling me I have to see him even *before* the baby's born?" This was unbelievable.

"No, and no judge would ever order something like that. I'm telling you that you *should* see him even though you don't want to because it's in your best interests to do so. Let him back into your life, Gwen, and he'll give you anything you want."

"But all I want is to not have to see him anymore."

"We're going in circles here."

"Because you're trying to get me to do something I don't want to do."

"No, Gwen, I'm trying to get you to see reason. If we go back in there and tell him no, everything he just agreed to will be off the table and we'll be back where we started, only now he knows there's no hope and he'll really come after you."

"But there is no hope." I'd already turned down his marriage proposal. How much clearer could I be?

"Yes, but he doesn't need to know that. Just let him believe he has a chance."

"You mean fake it?"

"I'm not telling you to sleep with him, but yes. See him, talk to him, let him feel like he's a part of your life."

"But eventually he's going to realize he's not. Won't that just make everything worse?"

"We don't need to worry about that right now. All I'm trying to accomplish at this moment is to get you a stress-free pregnancy so you can have a healthy baby. Honestly, Gwen, I'm telling you this for your own good. Agreeing to spend time with Alex is the best thing you could possibly do for yourself and your baby."

I followed Renee back into the conference room and returned to my seat.

"Gwen is prepared to agree to your request for visitation on certain conditions," Renee said.

"Anything," Alex replied.

"Alex," Jim said, "can you at least wait until she tells you what they are first before you agree."

"One hour a week," Renee said, "at a time and place of Gwen's choosing. She'll notify you forty-eight hours in advance by e-mail or text message. No contact in between unless it's an emergency."

"Agreed," Alex said.

"And no touching," I added. That was one item I hadn't discussed with Renee. I'd just thought of it now.

"No touching?" Alex said.

"Yes," I said. "Hands to yourself."

He nodded.

Renee smiled her crocodile grin. "Then we have a deal."

Chapter 47

Stefan called on my cell while I was driving home from Renee's office. It had only been ten minutes and Alex was already breaking our agreement.

"Tell Alex having you call me is the same as calling me himself," I shouted into my hands-free earpiece.

"Gwen, what are you talking about? Alex doesn't even know I'm in town."

"He doesn't?"

"No, I just landed. I called to see if you wanted to meet for a drink this evening. I have an update for you about the gold mine. You wanted me to be your contact person, remember?"

"Right. Sorry." I'd been so wrapped up in the baby drama that I'd forgotten about the gold mine. "Tonight's fine. Just tell me where and when."

I pulled up in front of Stefan's hotel and handed the valet my car keys. I'd agreed to meet him in the lounge at eight. I searched the dark interior but except for one couple at the bar, it was empty—it was still early for a place like this. I sat on one of the low couches with a view of the entrance and ordered a club soda with lime. Stefan arrived a few minutes after my beverage.

"Gwen, so good to see you," he said, and kissed me on the cheek. "What are you drinking?"

"Just water."

He seemed surprised, which surprised me. Alex must not have told him about the pregnancy and how he'd made it his life's mission to torture me. On second thought, I wasn't surprised. Stefan wouldn't have approved.

"Do you mind if I go for something a little stronger?" he asked.

"Of course not. Get what you want."

He flagged down the waitress and ordered a dirty martini for himself and another club soda for me.

"So," he said when we were alone again. "How are you?"

"Okay. And you?"

"Are you sure? You look a little pale."

I knew I should've applied more blush to my cheeks. I was going for the natural look, which normally worked for me, but not lately. "I'm fine. Just tired." I would tell him about the baby eventually, but I wanted to hear what he had to say first.

"Is my brother bothering you again? I told him when we were in London to back off, but you know he never listens to me."

"I don't think he listens to anyone."

"True," he said. "So about the mine. There have been some developments. As we predicted, the judge issued a temporary injunction so the entire project is stalled."

"But that's good, right?"

"It is and it isn't. We'd like to move forward, we just want to maintain control. The politicians are going nuts trying to position themselves on this. I know it's not news here, but it's a huge story in Romania right now. I fear this could drag on longer than we'd hoped."

I knew that would make Stela happy, but I didn't share that information with Stefan.

"I think the best way to proceed now is to get you out of it," he continued.

"Out of it how?"

"We said from the beginning we didn't know if you could ultimately win; this was always about leverage. I'm trying to convince a few influential politicians that it's in their best interests for the government to quietly settle out with you. I know you don't care about the money, but—"

"Actually, I might care about the money." Fighting Alex was costing me a fortune. Plus I had a baby on the way. I could use that money now.

"Really?" he said. "What's changed?"

I cracked a smile. "Quite a lot. I'm pregnant."

First his eyes widened, then he grinned at me. "I didn't know Alex had it in him." He paused. "It is Alex's, right?"

"Of course it's Alex's! Who else's would it be?"

He lifted his hands in surrender. "Don't shoot. I'm unarmed."

"Sorry, but I'm not some slut. Before Alex I hadn't slept with anyone in a long time. And we only did it once without protection."

"Hey, at least you made it count."

"That's not funny," I said as the tears welled up in my eyes. God, I hated these hormones.

He slid closer and placed his arm around my shoulder. "I'm sorry, Gwen. It's just that I'm at a loss here. I wasn't expecting this."

"You think I was? It was a shock to me too."

"How about dinner? It's the least I can do for the mother of my future niece or nephew."

"Okay," I said as I wiped my eyes. I'd eaten crackers before I'd left the house, but I was still hungry.

He paid the bar tab and we carried our drinks to the restaurant next door. But when Stefan approached the hostess, she told us they were booked for the evening and if we wanted a table we'd have to wait at least an hour.

He put his arm around my shoulder again and gave the hostess his best smile. "I know we don't have a reservation, but my girlfriend just told me she's pregnant and we're so excited we really want to celebrate. Do you think you could help us out?"

A huge grin spread across her face. "Congratulations! Is this your first?"

"Yes," I said.

She nodded her approval then turned to the interior of the restaurant where every table was full. "Wait here," she said. "Let me see what I can do."

When we were alone again I said, "Something tells me you've used that line before."

He shot me a sly grin. "I didn't think you'd want to wait an hour to eat."

The hostess seated us ten minutes later. Over a pan grilled steak and basil mashed potatoes, I told Stefan what Alex had been up to. As I'd assumed, he was not pleased.

"Do you think you can get him to back off?" I asked.

"Honestly," he said, "probably not. When he decides he wants something, there's no talking him out of it. And what he wants right now is you."

"It's not me he wants, it's the baby. Male ego, I guess. And getting back at me, of course."

Stefan hesitated then said, "Gwen, I would never defend his trying to take the baby away from you. That's a boneheaded move, even for Alex. And I hope in time he'll realize that. But I have to tell you, if I were in his shoes and I thought you were going to have an abortion and not even tell me, I'd be pretty upset."

"The reason I didn't tell him was because I was scared. I knew he'd react this way. And I'm not having an abortion, so he should just back off already. He's getting what he wants."

"I understand that. I'm only explaining his point of view."

We ate in silence for a few minutes, then he said, "I've changed my mind. I'm not going to push the government to buy you out."

"Why not? Now I actually want the money."

"Because at the moment you're the sole heir to the Tepes estate. But once the baby's born, that child will be both your heir and Alex's. He isn't going to want to split up the land. He's going to want to keep it in the family."

What an idiot I was! I couldn't believe I hadn't realized this before. I'd thought his interest in the baby was just about his ego. I should've known there was more to it than that. He wanted the baby because he wanted the land too.

"But it's my land now, sort of. Won't the government still want to buy me out so they can move forward? I don't need a huge amount of money. I'll sell it to them for a lot less than it's worth."

"I can't, Gwen. On this one I have to side with Alex. I'm sorry."

He had to side with Alex, but that didn't mean I had to.

Chapter 48

I e-mailed Stela as soon as I returned home. She e-mailed me back the next day and sent me a retainer agreement to sign. The last time she'd advised me as a friend. Now she'd be representing me officially.

Expect a fight, she wrote. *If Alex wants you to hold onto the land he will block you at every turn.*

I know, I wrote back. *Just do what you can.*

I was expecting Alex to bring that fight to our first weekly visitation session. I'd agreed to meet him at The Grind on Saturday morning, a busy coffee shop halfway between his house and mine. I arrived on time, and he was already waiting. He'd even purchased my latte for me.

"It's decaf," he said as he handed it to me.

"I can drink caffeine in moderation," I replied as I joined him at the table he'd managed to secure despite the line snaking out the front door.

"Sorry, I didn't know. How are you feeling?"

"Fine."

"Would you tell me if you weren't?"

"Probably not." I wasn't in a sharing mood.

We both sipped our drinks and I looked at my watch. Two minutes had passed. Fifty-eight more to go.

We talked about Isabella and about work, his and mine. Anyone listening to us probably would've thought we were a normal couple, even though our relationship was anything but. After forty minutes of meaningless chatter, I could no longer stand the suspense.

"Have you talked to Stefan lately?" I asked.

"Yes," he said.

"Then you know I saw him last week? You know he knows about the baby?"

"Yes."

"And you know I want to sell my land?"

"He told me."

"And you've got nothing to say to that?" I wanted to fight with him. I wanted to scream and yell and run out of the coffee shop, and out of his life for good. He must've realized it, which was why he denied me the opportunity.

"We're not going to discuss it."

"What do you mean we're not going to discuss it? Why not?"

"Because I won't fight with you."

"You mean you'll let me sell the land?"

"No, I mean I won't discuss it with you."

"What if I want to discuss it with you?"

"Talk," he said. "I'll listen."

That wouldn't do any good. It wouldn't even make me feel better. "I really hate you sometimes."

"I know." He sighed. "And it doesn't please me."

"Then stop this, Alex. Please stop this. I'll give you whatever you want. If you want me to keep the land, I'll keep the land. If you want joint custody, I'll agree." That one wasn't a big concession on my part since Renee told me I had no choice. "But you and me," I said, motioning between us, "this has to end."

"Not until we've tried everything. I won't concede until then."

"But we *have* tried everything. It's over. Why can't you accept that?"

He shook his head. "We haven't tried this."

"We just did." I looked at my watch—only ten minutes left. "The hour's almost up and you're no closer to getting me to change my mind."

"That's not true," he said. "You're still here. And you'll be here next week too."

"How do you know? Maybe I just won't show up. Renee told me no judge would force me to see you if I didn't want to. I'm here voluntarily."

"I know, Gwen, and that's what gives me hope. And you'll be here next week too because you know if you're not, our agreement's off. I'll sue you for sole custody and I'll win."

"No you won't. You have no basis. I haven't done anything wrong."

He placed his elbows on the small table and leaned in. "Are you sure about that? Are you really so certain that you'd risk losing custody of your own child rather than spend one hour a week with me?"

I was so angry I had to look away. "You must truly hate me."

"No, Gwen, I love you."

"You have a funny way of showing it."

"You two are scary," Zoe said when I met her at the mall that afternoon. I'd told her it was too early to shop for maternity clothes. All of my regular clothes were tight but still fit. She'd insisted we pre-shop anyway.

"No, he's scary. I'm just scared."

Zoe spotted an empty table in the food court and we sat down.

"You should call his bluff," she said through a mouthful of frozen yogurt. "What's the worst he could do?" she continued after she'd swallowed. "There's no way he'd get sole custody. Even Renee said so."

I set down my chocolate peanut butter swirl with Oreo cookies on top. "No, she said it would be highly unlikely, but even if I win, I lose because he can still drag me into court every day. I'd have to sell my parents' house just to pay the legal fees. It's not worth it. I'd rather suffer through coffee with him once a week."

"You're making me rethink my decision to go out with Stefan."

"He finally called?" I'd given Stefan Zoe's number, but only after getting her permission first. She and Evan had broken up permanently two months ago, and she'd been on a dating spree ever since.

"Yes, I'm meeting him for dinner next week. That's the other reason I dragged you here today. I need a new outfit."

"Good. I'd much rather shop for a new date outfit for you than maternity clothes for me." I'd only gained one pound so far, and that was in the last week, but I was still dreading getting fat. "And don't worry about Stefan. He's nothing like Alex."

"You mean he doesn't lie to get what he wants?"

"Oh no, he lies too. He's just much better at it."

Chapter 49

The next month of visitations with Alex passed without incident. Alex kept to his word—he didn't fight with me, touch me, or try to contact me outside of our weekly meetings. And I kept my word too—I showed up.

This status quo remained until the Saturday I planned to visit my parents' grave. They were born eight days apart, so I went to the cemetery every year on the weekend in between. I preferred to visit on the anniversary of their lives instead of the anniversary of their deaths.

Alex and I strolled out of the coffee shop together, but instead of making a left toward the parking lot, I made a right toward the grocery store.

"Where are you going?" he asked.

"I need to buy something," I said and continued walking.

Alex followed.

"What are you doing? You know the hour's up."

"Technically, it's not," he replied, falling into step beside me. "You were ten minutes late, so I'm entitled to ten minutes more with you."

"I told you, the parking lot was full. I had to wait for a space to open up."

"That's not my problem, it's yours."

I stopped walking and spun around. "No, *you're* my problem. When are you going to get it through your thick head that this is over? Move on with your life already, Alex, and let me move on with mine."

He laughed in my face. "Gwen, the baby's not even born yet. Then we'll have another eighteen years of shuffling back and forth between your house and mine, not to mention all the school functions, and sporting events, and birthday parties. I'm in your life for the foreseeable future. I think you'd be a lot happier if you just accepted that."

God he could be such an arrogant prick. What had I ever seen in him? "I really hate you sometimes," I said as I waited for the crosswalk light to change from red to white.

"I know you do," he replied as he followed me across the street. "But I think you hate me less than you used to, so we're making progress."

It was true; I did hate him less. The only thing I could attribute it to was that I was in my second trimester now and the mood swings seemed to be leveling off. At least I was crying a lot less than I had been the month before. "What kind of sick and twisted relationship is this that hating you less is progress?" I asked as he joined me in the grocery store's flower aisle.

"I don't know, but I'll take what I can get." He looked at his watch. "And I've got six more minutes. You want to tell me who you're buying flowers for?"

"If you must know, my parents. I'm going to the cemetery today."

"Oh," he said, and his tone changed. "Do you want company?"

"Not particularly," I said as I grabbed a bunch of pink tulips. They were my mom's favorite when she was alive.

"Don't you want to introduce them to me, seeing as I'm the father of their first grandchild?"

"Alex, they're dead. I can't introduce you."

"But you must think they're there in spirit or you wouldn't be going."

I wasn't about to get into a metaphysical debate with him in the middle of the grocery store flower aisle. I grabbed a mixed bouquet for my father because I thought the giant sunflower was the most "manly," and headed to the checkout line.

Alex followed, as I knew he would. He still had three minutes left. Then he insisted on paying. I let him because I was learning to choose my battles with him, and paying for flowers was one I was willing to lose.

By the time we reached the parking lot he was down to his last thirty seconds. "C'mon, Gwen, let me go with you. Cemeteries are bad enough. You don't want to go alone."

I normally didn't. All the previous years I'd dragged Zoe with me, but she had other plans today. She and Stefan were driving up to Santa Barbara for the afternoon, their third date. I was shocked. I never thought they'd last this long. I'd thought they'd have dinner once and that would be the end of it.

Zoe knew Stefan was a player, and she normally avoided that type. But she insisted it didn't matter because she was just having fun with Stefan while she waited for The One. Stefan wasn't in town that often and she still dated lots of other men. Plus, Stefan knew if he hurt Zoe I'd cut his balls off—I'd warned him when I gave him her phone number so there'd be no ambiguity.

"Do what you want, Alex. You will anyway." Then I climbed into my Honda and sped away.

Alex followed in his BMW. I tried to lose him on the freeway but he caught up to me. Although even if he hadn't, he would've found me. There weren't that many cemeteries off the 405. He knew which one I was going to.

He parked behind me and followed me to my parents' plot. There was a bench nearby under a tree, which was where I usu-ally sat for the obligatory ten minutes that I stayed. I hated coming here, but I did anyway. What kind of daughter would I be if I never visited my parents' graves?

Alex sat on the bench today, so I remained at the gravesite. The groundskeepers must've watered the lawn that morning because the grass was still wet. I only knelt down for a few minutes, but when I stood up, the knees on both my pants legs were soaked through.

When I headed back to my car Alex joined me. "Did you tell them about me?" he asked.

"No, Alex, they're dead."

"I know that, Gwen. We're in a cemetery."

"Then why are you asking me stupid questions?" Visiting my parents' grave always left me in a foul mood. The anger bubbled up in me every time. Why did they have to die but the drunk driver who hit them survived? It should've been the other way around. But it never was.

He placed his hand on my shoulder. I stopped walking, but I didn't turn around. I didn't want him to see me crying.

"No touching," I said. "That's the rule."

"Unless you want me to," he replied.

"And what have I done to make you think that I want you to?"

"You haven't taken a swing at me yet. I'm taking that as a positive sign."

I jerked my shoulder away from his hand. "This isn't a good day for me, Alex."

"I know, Gwen. That's why I'm here."

He followed me to my car and held me until I was ready to leave. I didn't throw a punch at him then either. I didn't want to.

Alex was the one who showed up late the following week. I arrived at the coffee shop on time and secured our table. I even purchased his cappuccino for him. I was reading the free paper the last patron had left behind when I heard someone call my name. I looked up at the man dressed in green scrubs holding a large coffee.

"Doctor Sloan, what are you doing here?" The coffee shop was only a few blocks from the hospital, but I was still surprised to see him.

"They do let me leave the hospital sometimes," he said. "Not often, but occasionally. How are you?"

"Good," I said and moved my purse off the chair I was holding for Alex. "How are you?"

"Busy," he said then sat down in Alex's seat. "I'm happy to see your color's better," he added before taking a sip of his coffee.

"I feel better. The nausea's subsided and I have more energy."

He nodded. "Most women say the second trimester's the best. That's when they enjoy being pregnant the most."

I smiled. "I can't say I'm enjoying it, but at least it's not as bad."

"And how are things with the father?"

At the mention of him, I checked my watch. It was only eight minutes after the hour, but it wasn't like Alex to be late. "Complicated." I sighed. "As usual."

"I'm sorry to hear that," he said.

Then the door to the coffee shop swung open and Alex strode in. He smiled when he saw me, then frowned when he spotted Dr. Sloan. When he reached the table, he bent down and kissed my cheek.

"What the hell, Alex!"

"I'm sorry I'm late."

"I don't care about that. You know the rules."

"I should be going," Dr. Sloan said and stood up. Alex immediately grabbed his seat.

I glared at Alex then turned to Dr. Sloan. "You don't need to go. We can get another chair."

"No," he said. "I've got to get back." Then he pulled a business card from his pocket, scribbled something on the back, and handed the card to me. "If you need anything, anything at all, call me. You have my cell number too."

"Thanks," I said and stuffed the card in my purse before Alex could snatch it from me. I waited for Dr. Sloan to exit the coffee shop before I turned back to Alex. "Could you have been any ruder? That was my doctor from the emergency room."

"I recognized him," Alex said. "The question is why were you having coffee with him?"

"I wasn't having coffee with him. I was waiting for you when he happened to walk by and being the not-rude person that I am, I offered him a seat. And what was with that kiss? You know you're not allowed to touch me."

"I thought we moved past that last weekend."

"Last weekend was a one-shot deal. You did a nice thing, Alex, and I appreciate it, but it doesn't make up for all the rest."

He sighed and leaned back in his chair. "Okay, Gwen. I don't want to fight with you."

"Good, because I don't feel like fighting with you either."

He grinned at me. "Well that's progress right there."

"Ha, ha. Very funny. You really want to talk about who started us down this path?"

"No," he said, "I want to talk to you about Isabella."

"What about her?" Alex had been filling me in on her activities since we'd started meeting for coffee—she was a safe subject for us. I'd only seen her in the hallway at school a few times since we'd been back.

"We need to tell her about the baby."

"We? I think you're the one who needs to tell her. You're her father." I wasn't prepared to have the where-do-babies-come-from talk, and I didn't want to even attempt to try to explain our relationship to her. I wasn't sure I understood it myself.

"Gwen, she knows you. She should hear it from both of us. Besides, you know if I tell her she'll just track you down at school with questions anyway."

I supposed he was right. "Okay. When and where?"

We agreed to meet for breakfast instead of coffee the following week.

Isabella waved to me as I entered the restaurant.

"Daddy told me you had a surprise for me," she said as I hugged her hello.

"He did, huh?" I glared at Alex, but he just smiled.

I took off my coat and hung it on the peg nailed to the side of the tall booth.

"I don't think it's going to be a surprise for much longer," Alex said and nodded at my swelling belly.

I pulled my shirt down over my bump and quickly slid into the seat next to Isabella and across from Alex. She allowed me to read the menu and order before begging me to reveal her surprise.

"Tell her, Alex." This was his idea.

"Well," he said, "remember how when mommy was with us you used to say that you wanted a little brother or sister?"

Isabella nodded.

"Now you're going to get one."

Her eyes widened and a look of confusion flitted across her face.

"Gwen's going to give you one," Alex answered her as yet unspoken question.

She turned to me. "You're going to give me a brother or sister?"

"Half brother or sister," I said. "Your daddy will be the baby's daddy, but I'm the mommy."

"Does that mean you'll be my mommy too?" she asked.

Alex perked up for that question.

"No, sweetie, I'll just be the baby's mommy. But we can still be friends."

"Will you take me to the park?" she asked. "You said you would."

"Sure. If I take the baby to the park, you can come too."

The waiter arrived with our food, and I thought we were done with "the talk." But then in between bites of pancake Isabella asked, "Where's the baby going to live?"

I glanced up at Alex, who was busy munching on his omelet and fried potatoes. "You want to field this one, Dad?"

"That's up to Gwen," he said.

"Really? I'm making all the custody decisions now?"

"You already know my preference."

"That's not going to happen, Alex."

"What's not?" Isabella asked.

"I want Gwen and the baby to come live with us," he said.

Bastard!

"I want Gwen and the baby to come live with us too," Isabella said and looked up at me expectantly.

In that moment I could've strangled Alex. "I'm sorry, sweetie, but I can't do that."

"Why not? We can read to the baby together. It'll be fun."

Because your father's a fucking prick. But of course I couldn't say that. "There's no room for me and the baby at your house."

"Yes there is. We have lots of empty rooms. Then we can play together all the time."

"The baby will be too young for you to play with, Isabella. But I promise you'll still get to see the baby even if the baby lives with me."

"I don't see why the baby has to live with you," she said and stabbed her pancakes with her fork.

I glared across the table. "You want to step in here, Alex?"

"No, you seem to be doing just fine."

"Because I'm the mommy, Isabella. I have to take care of the baby."

"But you took care of me."

"Isabella," Alex said, "you have Katarina to take care of you. The baby needs Gwen."

"I want a mommy too," she said and started to cry.

"Oh, sweetie." I pulled her onto my lap and we cried together— her for her lost mommy, and me for her. She broke my heart. Alex just sat across from us and looked uncomfortable.

"Isabella, wait here," Alex said as we left the restaurant. "I need to talk to Gwen for a minute."

She played imaginary hopscotch on the sidewalk in front of the café while Alex and I walked a few feet away.

"You bastard," I said quietly so Isabella wouldn't hear.

"Obviously I didn't think it was going to turn out that way," he whispered.

"Well how the fuck did you think it was going to turn out?"

"Watch the language, Gwen."

I glanced over at Isabella, who wasn't even looking in our direction. "She can't hear me."

"The baby can."

"I don't think it has ears yet."

"Well you might as well start breaking the habit now."

"Why? You're going to use that against me now too? I said 'fuck' so I lose custody of my child? But you make yours cry and that's okay?"

He sighed. "Can we not do this?"

"Let's not," I said. "We'll just chalk this up to another one of your bad ideas." Then I spun on my heel and stormed off. I heard him calling my name, but I chose not to turn around. It felt good to be the one in control for a change.

Chapter 50

"I'm sorry," Alex said when I met him for coffee the following week. "But Isabella needed to be told."

"By you, Alex, not by me." My anger at him hadn't lessened over the course of the week. I still felt horrible for Isabella. I waved to her in the hallway the other day and she wouldn't even look at me. She must think I didn't want to be her mother. I wished I could explain to her that I much preferred her company to her father's, but of course I couldn't. "And you just had to tell her you wanted me to move in with you, didn't you? What did you think that was going to accomplish?"

"Obviously I was hoping you'd say yes."

"Alex," I closed my eyes and took a deep breath in an attempt to lessen my fury. "How much longer are we going to do this? When are you going to believe me? You can't force someone to love you."

"I know," he said and sighed. "Trust me, I know."

"Then why are we still doing this? I think you're torturing yourself with this as much as me."

He leaned his head back against the wall and sighed again. "I don't know what else to do, Gwen. I'm at a loss."

"Why won't you just let go? You're a very eligible bachelor, Alex. I'm sure you'll have no trouble finding someone else."

He chuckled. "You know, I think that's the first compliment you've ever paid me."

"I'm sure that's not true."

"It is," he said. "You'll show me how you feel, but you'll never tell me. Unless it's to tell me you hate me. You're very free with those words."

"I'm sorry. But the things you do sometimes…" I shook my head.

We sat in silence for a few minutes until he suddenly said, "Did you know my wife and I were college sweethearts?"

"No." He talked about her as infrequently as Isabella did.

"When she died my whole world collapsed. I still had Isabella, of course, but I thought, 'Well, that's it for me. I've had my one great love and now I'm done.' And then I met you."

"But you were only interested in me because of my birthmark."

"Not *only* for the birthmark. Yes, that was part of it," he said before I could object, "but not all of it. And as I got to know you better it became a smaller part."

"Then why didn't you tell me the truth sooner? Why did you wait for Stefan to practically force you?"

"Because I didn't know how!"

The conversations around us halted as the other patrons turned and stared at us.

Alex lowered his voice and continued. "I knew you'd be angry with me. And everything was so good between us, I just wanted it to last. Don't you see how perfect this is? I love you, Isabella loves you, and now we're having a baby too. It's as if I spilled wine on your dress that day for a reason, like we were fated to be together."

"I don't believe in fate."

"Then do you believe in love, Gwen?" he asked, his voice rising again. "Do you believe in anything?"

"What, now *I'm* the bad guy? I'm not the one who lied, Alex. I'm not the one who betrayed you."

"I can't do this today." Then he pushed away from the table and stormed out of the coffee shop. He still had forty-seven minutes left.

I drove directly to Zoe's house.

"Do you think it's finally over?" she asked as she pulled another shirt from her closet and tossed it on top of the pile at her feet. She was setting aside clothes to donate to the LA Women's Shelter, one of the charities our school supported. I'd dropped off my bag of clothes the previous day.

"I'm not sure," I said and flopped onto her bed. "Maybe I should call him."

"Why on earth would you call him?"

"Because he seemed really upset."

"Gwen, are you listening to yourself? Do you hear what you're saying? I thought the point of all this was to get him to see reason. To make him understand that it was really over between you two and you weren't coming back."

"It is, but I'm not out to destroy the guy."

She yanked a pair of pants off a hanger and tossed them onto the donate pile. "Why not? He's out to destroy you."

I shook my head. "I don't think he is, not intentionally."

"I cannot believe you're actually going to sit here and defend him. Gwen, he lied to you. From the beginning. About everything. And when he found out you were pregnant, instead of being supportive, he immediately slapped you with a lawsuit and threatened to take your baby away."

"I know, but I don't think he'd really do it. I think it's an empty threat."

"Well, bully for him. He's actually going to let you see your own child. Somebody give that man a medal. What the hell is wrong with you? It's like you have Stockholm Syndrome or something."

I laughed. "Except that he never kidnapped me."

"Then what are those weekly 'visitation sessions' about?" she said with air quotes.

"Honestly, I'm not exactly sure."

"Then maybe it's time you found out."

Chapter 51

Alex showed up at my office on Monday afternoon. School had been out for hours, but I was sitting at my desk grading spelling tests because my chair at work was more comfortable than the one at my dining-room table at home. Better back support.

"Alex—"

"I come in peace," he said and pulled a bouquet of red roses out from behind his back.

"You know you're not supposed to be here."

"I know," he said, "but it's a quasi-emergency. Plus you still owe me forty-seven minutes from Saturday."

"I don't owe you anything. You walked out on me."

"I'm sorry about that. It's just—"

"I don't want to talk about it." It had been a long day, and I was tired. All I wanted was to finish grading these tests and go home. "What's your quasi-emergency?"

He placed the flowers on my desk and sat down in the chair across from me. "I have a favor to ask."

"Alex—"

"Before you say no, just listen, okay?"

"Okay," I said and folded my arms across my chest.

"Isabella's barely speaking to me. She thinks I'm the reason you and the baby won't come and live with us."

"Smart girl."

"Yes, she takes after her father."

He grinned, and I rolled my eyes. "I'm surprised you haven't tried bribing her. That's your specialty, isn't it?"

"I have," he admitted. "But none of my usual tricks have worked. I'm persona non grata at the moment."

"So what do you want from me?"

"She has a ballet recital on Saturday morning. I was hoping I could convince you to come."

I didn't answer right away because I didn't know if going to the recital would be sending Isabella the wrong message.

He must've thought I was holding out on him because he said, "I'll give you whatever you want. Name it."

"Boy, you must be desperate."

"I am," he said. "I don't know what else to do."

I considered asking him for sole custody or to end our weekly visitation sessions, but I knew both of those were nonstarters, so I chose the next item on my list. "I want to know the real reason you insisted on visitation with me. Were you trying to hurt me? Or keep tabs on me? Or was it all about the baby? Tell me the truth, Alex. My lawyer said she'd never seen a request like that before. She'd never even heard of one."

He leaned back in his chair and considered my question. "It was a little bit of all of those things, but mostly it was because it was the only way I could think of to get you to spend time with me. It was either that or keep hauling you into court, and after that scare with you in the emergency room, I rethought that strategy."

"Well, thanks for being honest. Assuming you are being honest. You are, right?"

"It pains me that you have to ask that question."

"It pains me too."

I met Alex at the high school at ten o'clock on Saturday morning. Isabella's dance troupe wasn't scheduled to perform until ten thirty, but he wanted her to see me beforehand so she would know I was in the audience watching her. All he'd told her was that he had a surprise for her.

"Where is she?" I asked when I found him pacing the lobby of the auditorium with the rest of the anxious parents.

"In the dressing room," he said. "Katarina's with her."

I followed him down the steps to the backstage area, which was filled with hundreds of little ballerinas running around screaming and their mothers, who were trying to catch them.

"It's the one with the flower," he said, pointing to the second door on the left with a photo of a daisy tacked to the outside.

"Aren't you coming?" I asked.

He shook his head. "No boys allowed."

"That's not fair. This is your surprise; you should get credit for it. Call Katarina and tell her to bring her out here."

"Are you sure?" he asked, but he was already reaching for his phone.

"Yeah, I'll go hide," I said pointing to a row of plastic palm trees. "Come and get me when you're ready."

A minute later Isabella emerged from the dressing room in her pink tights and tutu with her hair pulled back in a bun. She looked so adorable I could've eaten her up.

Alex knelt down in front of her with his back to me. I couldn't hear what he was saying, but when she started running toward the trees I figured she knew, and I jumped out and yelled, "Surprise!"

She threw her arms around me and smacked her head directly into my belly. That hurt.

Alex rushed over. "Are you okay?"

"Yeah, I'm fine," I said, rubbing my stomach.

"Isabella, you need to be careful."

"Is that where the baby is?" she asked, pointing at where she'd just head-butted me.

"Yes, for the next twenty weeks."

"How did he get in there?" she asked.

No way was I answering that question.

"We don't know it's a he," Alex said, smoothly deflecting. "That could be your sister inside Gwen's tummy."

"Actually, we do know." I'd had an ultrasound yesterday morning and the doctor had told me the baby's sex. It was one of the few times I'd wished Alex had been there with me. I'd almost called him when I was leaving the doctor's office but decided not to. I wanted to tell him in person and see his expression. I hadn't planned on having the conversation in front of Isabella, but this seemed like the perfect time. "It's a boy."

His entire face lit up. I figured he'd be pleased. To me it was still surreal. This thing growing inside of me wasn't just an amorphous being, it was an actual person who would someday live outside my body and have his own thoughts and feelings and personality. Despite my swelling stomach and the occasional kick, I was still having a hard time wrapping my head around it.

"Are you okay with that?" he asked, as if I had a choice.

"Yes. I had no preference. You obviously did."

"I didn't," he said. "I would've been happy either way."

If we were alone, I would've questioned that statement, but I didn't want to in front of Isabella.

"Can I name him?" Isabella asked.

"No," Alex and I responded in unison.

Katarina led Isabella back to the dressing room so she could finish applying her makeup, and Alex and I walked to the auditorium to search for seats. Isabella's routine was the ninth out of ten, and troupe number three was currently performing. I thought it would be boring watching endless routines by little ballerinas who couldn't dance, but it wasn't, mainly because those awkward little girls were so damn cute. Plus, I knew Isabella was happy that I was there, which made me happy too.

And Alex was ecstatic. He smiled at me the entire time.

Somewhere between the purple people eaters and the dancing daisies I leaned over and whispered, "I knew you wanted a boy."

"I would've been content either way," he whispered back. "But it's always nice to have one of each."

I met Alex for coffee the following week, and before I'd even taken off my coat, he asked, "What are you doing for Thanksgiving?"

"Going to Zoe's parents' house." After my parents died, Michelle had issued me a standing invitation for all holidays. "Why?"

"I usually take Isabella to see her grandmother, but we decided to stay home this year. I thought you might like to come over and join us."

I toyed with the lid on my coffee cup so I wouldn't have to look at his face. "I don't think that's a good idea, Alex." I still wasn't sure going to Isabella's ballet recital had been the right call. I wanted to be there for her if she needed me, but I didn't want to give her false hope that I was going to be her new mother. I didn't want to give Alex false hope either.

"Why not?" he asked.

"Because nothing's changed. We're still where we always were."

"Not always," he said wistfully.

"You could've invited him," Zoe's mom said when I told her and Mark about it over Thanksgiving dinner. Zoe already knew. "We have plenty of room."

It was only the four of us at their dining-room table, which comfortably held eight. Daniel was still in London working because Thanksgiving wasn't a holiday in the UK, and June had decided to go skiing for Thanksgiving instead of coming home.

"Mom, don't enable her."

"I'm not enabling her, Zoe. He's the father of her child. The better her relationship with him, the better it will be for the baby."

I was surprised Mark didn't pipe up to support Michelle since he constantly told me the same thing. But he was surreptitiously watching the game on his phone. He probably hadn't even heard her. "You can go inside, Mark," Michelle said. "We're done eating."

"Are you sure?" he asked, but he was already out of his chair. Five seconds later, we heard the football game blaring from their living-room TV.

Michelle turned back to me and leaned in. "Now that he's gone, you can tell me what's really going on."

"That's it," I said. "We meet for coffee every Saturday morning, and sometimes we fight and sometimes we get along."

"And has this helped you resolve your feelings for him?"

"Mom, her feelings for him are resolved. She wants him out of her life."

"I didn't ask you, Zoe. I asked Gwen."

I popped another antacid before I answered. I ate them like candy these days. "I suppose it has helped in that we're on better terms than we used to be. I mean, he won't let me do this alone, so I can't cut him out of my life completely. I guess you could say I'm glad we're friends again. It'll make it easier once the baby's born."

"Just friends?" Michelle asked.

"Mom!"

"Zoe, be quiet. This isn't about you." Then she turned back to me. "I just want you to know, Gwen, that if you're having feelings for Alex, or anyone for that matter, *amorous feelings*, that would be completely normal. It happens to a lot of women when they're pregnant. It happened to me."

"Oh my God, Mom, could you possibly embarrass me any more than you are right now?"

This time Michelle ignored her. "It doesn't happen to all women," she continued. "So if it hasn't happened to you, that's normal too. I just thought you should know. Just in case."

"I cannot listen to another word of this," Zoe said. "C'mon, Gwen, we're leaving."

"Where are we going?" I asked.

"I don't care," she said, pulling me out of my chair. "Anywhere but here."

We walked across the backyard to Zoe's guesthouse apartment.

"Sometimes I think I really need to move out of here," Zoe said as she flopped onto her couch.

I glanced around at her spotless apartment that I knew she hadn't cleaned herself, noting the piles of laundered clothes on her dining-room table that I knew she hadn't washed herself, and said, "I wouldn't be so hasty if I were you. You've got a good thing going here."

"I know," she said and reached for one of her hundred-and-fifty-dollar throw pillows that she never could've afforded on her teacher's salary if she had to pay full market rent. "It's just that with June out of the house, I'm the only one left for her to bug. She's driving me crazy."

"She just cares about you, Zoe. It's not such a bad thing."

"I know, I know, I shouldn't complain, especially not to you. But…"

"Yeah, I know. She's your mother so she's a pain in your ass."

"Exactly," she said and we both laughed.

Then it hit me. "Oh my God, Zoe, do you realize that in less than five months I'm going to be someone's mother and they're going to be saying that about me?"

"Well, not right away," she said. "Your kid probably won't even start talking for at least a year."

I grabbed another one of her expensive throw pillows and threw it at her head.

"Hey, watch it," she said, "or I'll tell Alex you're perpetrating domestic violence again."

"Not funny," I yelled as she laughed.

"So was my mother right? Are you having amorous feelings?" she said in a husky voice.

We both giggled at that one.

"As a matter of fact, she is. I swear to God I feel like a teenage boy. It's *all* I think about."

She laughed so hard tears were streaming down her face.

"It's not funny," I yelled again. "It's driving me crazy. I almost wish the nausea would come back just so I wouldn't want to screw every man I see."

When she stopped laughing long enough to speak she said, "I guess you could always buy a vibrator."

"It's not the same. Trust me."

"Oh my God, did you really buy a vibrator?"

"I was desperate!"

This sent her into even more peals of laughter.

"I'm sorry," she said, wiping the tears from her eyes. "I know it's not funny. But honestly, Gwen, look at it from my perspective. Although I do know how you feel. If Stefan were here, I'd totally want to jump his bones right now."

That one I could not understand. Zoe had said she was holding off sleeping with him for as long as possible because she was afraid he was only in it for the chase and once he got what he wanted he'd leave. The fact that he lived in New York helped. They didn't see each other that often. But still. "You have this amazingly hot guy at your fingertips and you refuse to sleep with him. It boggles the mind."

"You want him?" she asked.

I laughed. "Like that wouldn't send Alex over the edge. He'd slit both our throats."

"Gwen, I was kidding. You really want to sleep with Stefan?"

"Zoe, right now I'd sleep with a lamppost if it had a penis."

"Wow, this is bad," she said. "You really do need to get laid."

"What do you think I've been trying to tell you for the last ten minutes? I'm dying over here!"

"Then why don't you go pick up some random guy and sleep with him? You could probably find one online without too much trouble."

I threw my arms up. "Zoe, look at me. No one's going to want to sleep with me. I'm a cow!" I'd only gained ten pounds but my stomach was bursting.

"You're not a cow. You're pregnant. And you're not even that big yet."

"Thanks a lot."

"I'm serious," she said. "Remember when Rebecca was pregnant? Now she was a cow."

"Zoe, she was having twins."

"I know. But she gained sixty pounds. That woman was huge."

"The other night, I was so desperate I actually thought about calling Doctor Sloan."

"From the emergency room?"

I nodded. "He did tell me to call him if I needed anything, anything at all."

"I'm pretty sure that's not what he had in mind."

"I don't know. He's a doctor. He must know this kind of thing happens."

She considered it then said, "Call him. What have you got to lose?"

I let out a laugh. "Only my dignity."

We each grabbed a magazine from her coffee table and read in companionable silence until Zoe suddenly said, "You know there's an easy solution to your problem."

"There is?"

"Two words: baby daddy."

"Two words: bad idea."

"Why? You know he's good in bed. And he's not going to turn down the mother of his child no matter how fat you get."

I shot her a dirty look.

"You said you two are friends now. And it's not like he can get you any more pregnant than you already are. What harm could it do?"

A lot of harm. But she'd planted the seed.

Chapter 52

"Would you mind if we met on Sunday next week instead of Saturday?" I asked Alex over our weekly coffee. "Zoe and her mom want to take me shopping for baby things."

"As you wish," he said.

"As I wish?"

"Yes, as you wish."

He used the same line later when I told him I didn't need his help setting up the crib. Zoe's dad had already offered.

"What's with the 'as you wish' thing?" I asked.

"Nothing," he said. "It's a turn of phrase."

"I feel like I've heard it somewhere before."

"Have you?" He shrugged.

I had, but I couldn't remember where.

The following Sunday morning, I woke up to pouring rain. I dragged myself and my big belly out of bed and checked the dining room. As I'd feared, the roof was leaking. I'd never gotten around to having it fixed. I wiped the floor with a towel and placed a bucket on top. Then I called Alex.

"Would you mind if I canceled coffee this morning?" We'd been getting along so well lately I didn't think he'd make a fuss.

"Why? Is everything okay?"

"Yeah, it's just that it's raining out, and my roof is leaking, and I feel fat, and all I really want to do is go back to bed."

"But how will you get your moderate amount of caffeine?"

I laughed. "I'm capable of making coffee, Alex. I do it all the time."

"I know, but it's not the same. Why don't I bring you coffee?"

"You want to go out in the rain and get coffee and bring it to my house?"

"Sure. I have to drop Isabella off at her friend's house for a play date anyway. You're not that far out of the way. I can pick up breakfast too."

Breakfast did sound good. All I had in the house was cereal and toast, and I was craving a hot and gooey cinnamon roll. "Okay. See you soon."

I answered the door in my pajamas, although in deference to Alex, I did wash my face, brush my teeth, and pull my hair back into a ponytail.

"Good morning," he said and tried to hand me my tall latte with a sprinkle of cinnamon, but I reached for the fragrant bakery bag instead. I didn't even wait for him to join me at the kitchen table, which I'd already set in anticipation of his arrival, before I dug in.

"Oh my God, this is the most amazing thing I've ever eaten," I said as the still-warm icing melted in my mouth.

He laughed. "I'm glad you're enjoying it."

"I should totally not be eating this," I continued as I took another huge bite. "But it's just so good."

"The cravings bad?" he asked.

I nodded. "But it's not half as bad as the horniness." The words slipped out before I could stop them.

His eyes popped.

"Sorry," I said and swallowed hard. "I shouldn't have said that."

"Not at all," he replied. "Tell me more."

I felt my cheeks redden, which was completely ridiculous. I was pregnant with his child. Obviously we'd had sex before.

I set down my cinnamon roll and wiped my mouth with my napkin. "According to Zoe's mom, it's not that uncommon. Something about all the estrogen coursing through my veins. Didn't it happen to your wife when she was pregnant with Isabella?"

"No, I think I'd remember that." We finished our cinnamon rolls in silence. When I was down to sucking the last remnants of icing off my fingers he said, "So what are you doing about this problem of yours?"

"Doing?"

"Yes, to…shall we say, alleviate the symptoms."

I laughed. "Well, I'm not having sex on the kitchen table if that's what you're asking."

His eyes widened and a wicked grin spread across his face. "Would you like to?"

Holy shit. I stopped laughing. "No, Alex. We can't." Even though I very much wanted to. It wouldn't even have to be on the kitchen table. At that point I would've pretty much taken him anywhere.

He grabbed the corner of my glass-topped table. "Why not? It seems sturdy enough to me."

"You know why not."

He gazed directly into my eyes. "I don't, Gwen. Why don't you enlighten me?"

I stared back into those sea-green orbs, which looked darker today in the gray light filtering through the kitchen window. "Because we're having a child together, Alex, and it's taken us a long time to get to this point. Let's not screw it up."

He nodded, which I thought meant he understood. Then he picked up both of our empty plates and set them on the kitchen counter. I wasn't concerned until he reached for my coffee.

"Hey, I'm still drinking that."

"I'll get you another," he said as he set my tall paper cup on the counter too. Then he grabbed both my hands and pulled me out of my chair.

"Where are we going?"

"Nowhere," he said as he lifted me onto the kitchen table. Then he slid his hands into my hair and kissed me long and slow and deep. The man had barely touched me and my panties were already wet.

"Alex, this is a bad idea," I whispered when his lips finally left my mouth and started sliding down my neck.

"Gwen, I'm responsible for your being in this position. I feel it's the least I can do."

I laughed. "Actually, that's true."

He smiled down at me. "I'm glad you agree." Then he returned his lips to my neck.

Every nerve ending in my body wanted this except for the ones inside my head. They knew better. When he brushed his thumb across my breast and I actually gasped, my brain knew the battle was lost, so it switched gears to damage control.

"Promise me, Alex," I said as he kneaded the muscles in my lower back and my whole body turned to jelly.

"Anything," he whispered as he slid his fingers into the waistband of my pajama pants and began gently tugging them down.

"Promise me you're not going to get all emotional about this."

"I promise," he said as he pulled my pajama bottoms off the rest of the way, taking my panties with them. He tossed them both onto the kitchen floor.

"It's just sex, Alex," I said as he gently kissed my belly. "It doesn't mean anything. Nothing's changed."

"It means whatever you want it to mean, Gwen."

He stroked me with one hand while he undid his pants with the other. By the time he was free of his own clothes, I was practically panting. I needed no persuading when he pulled me down to the edge of the table, wrapped my legs around his waist, and entered with me lying down and him standing up.

I'd thought the sex was good before, and it was. But this was even better. It was the best orgasm of my life, bar none.

"You know no good can come of this," I said when he led me to my bedroom next.

"No good?" he said then reached his hand between my legs and I moaned. "I beg to differ."

"Alex, you don't fight fair," I said as he pulled me onto the bed for round two.

"No, Gwen. I fight to win."

This time he decided to torture me. Instead of hurried sex, he kissed and licked and sucked every inch of my body until I couldn't bear it anymore. "Alex, please," I screamed.

"Please what, Gwen?"

"You know what."

"I want to hear you say it."

I couldn't believe he was going to make me beg. "If you don't fuck me right this second I'm never going to speak to you again."

He grinned wickedly. "As you wish, Gwen. As you wish."

I screamed again, but this time from pleasure instead of frustration. At that moment it felt so good and so right, I refused to think about anything else.

The aftermath would come soon enough.

Chapter 53

Our weekly meetings for coffee converted to weekly meetings for sex. They were always at my house, sometimes on Saturdays and sometimes on Sundays, depending on Isabella's schedule and when we could have the most time together. We no longer limited ourselves to just one hour. The sex between us had always been good, but now with all the extra hormones it was mind-blowing. I couldn't get enough.

We were lying in my bed the Saturday afternoon before Christmas when Alex asked, "What are you doing for the holidays?"

"I don't know," I said and started stroking him. "What did you have in mind?"

He moved my hand away. "Gwen, I need a break."

"Oh, sorry." I rolled over onto my side of the bed.

"Where are you going?"

"You said you needed a break."

"From sex. That doesn't mean I don't want to hold you."

Uh oh. Friends with benefits didn't say things like that. But I rolled back to him anyway.

"So returning to my question," he said, now that his arm was around me and my head was resting on his chest, "what are you doing for the holidays?"

"I'm going to Zoe's parents' house Christmas Day. Then I thought I'd start cleaning out the second bedroom to get it ready for the baby." My due date was still fifteen weeks away, but I was starting to worry about getting everything done before I was too big to move. "Why?"

"I thought maybe you'd like to spend it with us."

"Alex, we talked about this. I don't want to give Isabella false expectations." I didn't want to give him false expectations either. I was already starting to regret embarking on our new/old relationship.

"Why do they have to be false? We're having a child, we're sleeping together, why won't you just move in with us already?"

I reached for my bathrobe, which I'd kicked to the bottom of the bed. "I don't want to talk about this."

"Why not?" he asked.

I walked out of the bedroom and into the kitchen. He pulled on his shorts and shirt and followed me. "Gwen, why won't you talk to me?"

If he was looking for a fight, I'd give it to him. I'd received another e-mail from Stela yesterday. As she'd warned, Alex had blocked every attempt she'd made to strike a deal with the Romanian government to buy out my interest in the Dracula land. I'd spent thousands of dollars in legal fees and had nothing to show for it. That was one thing Alex hadn't lied about—he did fight to win.

"Are you ever going to let me sell my land?"

"No," he said.

"Why not?" I demanded.

"We don't need to talk about this, Gwen. Let the lawyers fight it out."

"That's easy for you to say, Alex. You're rich, I'm not."

He sighed and ran his fingers through his hair. "Okay, how about we table this until the baby's born? Then, if you still want to sell the land, I'll find a way to buy you out."

"You mean it?" I asked. "You're not just saying that?"

"Yes," he said. "Now will you come back to bed?"

"I thought you needed a break."

"I've had my break." He put his arms around me and started nuzzling my neck. "Now I need you."

I agreed to spend Christmas Eve with him, but only because he was having a party so it wouldn't be just the three of us. In fact, Zoe would be there too. Stefan was flying into town that morning and was taking her as his date. I asked them to pick me up on their way so I'd have to drive home with them and there'd be no question about me spending the night at Alex's house. Or so I'd thought. Alex just offered to drive me back to my place the next day. I refused. Sex in the afternoon in lieu of coffee was one thing. Spending the night at his house and waking up there on Christmas Day was something else entirely.

Alex mingled with his guests—a few friends and a lot of business associates—and I stayed with Zoe and Stefan.

"A virgin martini," Stefan said and handed me a triangular glass filled with icy cold liquid and a lemon peel. He and Zoe were drinking the non-virgin variety.

"What's in it?" I asked.

"Bottled water," he said. "But it looks more festive this way."

I laughed. "Yes it does."

He placed his arm around Zoe's shoulder and she slipped hers around his waist. I never would've imagined them as a couple. Love was so unpredictable. Although she claimed it wasn't love, just the thrill of the chase. But it looked like love to me.

"So how are things with my brother?" he asked.

"He's an ass," Zoe said. "But he's fulfilling her needs."

Stefan arched one eyebrow. "Your needs?"

"Zoe, you need to stop drinking," I said and grabbed the martini out of her hand. It was her second, or maybe her third. I gave her my virgin drink and trudged to the kitchen for more water. I wasn't waddling yet, but it was only a matter of time.

"There you are," Alex said just as I was about to snag the last bottle of Pellegrino from the back of the fridge. "I've been looking all over for you. Come with me."

He pulled me into the corner of the family room where the Christmas tree twinkled with tiny colored lights. Then he reached underneath and grabbed a small turquoise box with a giant white bow. I recognized the Tiffany's colors even before I read the name. "Merry Christmas," he said as he handed it to me.

"Alex, I didn't know we were exchanging. I only brought something for Isabella." I had no idea what to get for the child who had everything, so I bought her a new Barbie doll. I'd never even considered buying a gift for Alex too.

"It's okay, Gwen. I didn't expect you to. I just spotted this while I was shopping and it made me think of you. C'mon, open it."

"But Christmas isn't until tomorrow." My parents had strict rules about opening gifts on Christmas Day and not before.

"I know, but I won't be with you tomorrow and I want to see your face. Please."

He didn't have to push too hard. I was dying to know what he'd gotten me. I untied the ribbon and lifted the cover. Inside was a black velvet box. For a moment I thought it might be another engagement ring and I panicked. Then I realized it was the wrong shape. This box was flat and rectangular, not a cube. I raised the lid and found a heart-shaped diamond pendant on a white gold chain. It was beautiful, and definitely the nicest piece of jewelry anyone had ever given me.

"Do you like it?" he asked, his face expectant.

"Of course." Who wouldn't like a necklace from Tiffany's?

"Because if you don't you can exchange it. I wasn't really sure which one to get. You don't wear a lot of jewelry so it's hard for me to know your taste."

"Alex, it's beautiful. Really. I have no doubt you chose the nicest one in the store."

His shoulders relaxed and he smiled with obvious relief. "Do you want me to help you put it on?"

"No!" I should've said yes. I'm not even sure why I didn't. Actually, I did know. I just didn't like to admit it, not even to myself. Tonight was the first time I'd been back to Alex's house since he'd gotten me drunk so he could photograph my birthmark. I was glad I didn't remember that part. Just thinking about the parts I did remember made me angry enough. Usually I was able to put it out of my mind. That was the only way we could become friends again. But I'd never really forgiven him, and I definitely hadn't forgotten. We'd just agreed to disagree.

"No?" he said.

"I don't think it really goes with my outfit," I replied, which was a lie since this necklace went with everything and certainly would've matched my plain black maternity cocktail dress.

"Oh, okay," he said. "Well, try it on whenever you like."

"Why is it I'm always catching you two off in a corner whispering?" Stefan asked, and we both looked up. He and Zoe were standing a few feet away.

"Because you don't know how to mind your own business," Alex snapped and marched out of the room.

Stefan's gaze followed him out. "Something I said?"

"No, something I said." I shut the jewelry box and hid it in my hand. "And I think it's time for me to go."

"You've should've seen him, Mom," Zoe said to her mother the next day. We were standing in the Richards's kitchen helping her mom stuff the turkey, which meant she stuffed the bird and Zoe and I stood next to her and chatted. "He was crushed."

Zoe's mom turned to me and frowned. "Oh, Gwen."

"He was not crushed," I said.

"He was," Zoe said. "You should've seen his face."

"I was standing right there, Zoe. I saw his face." She was right. He was crushed. I felt like a heartless shrew. Maybe Alex was right. Maybe I really was a Tepes. But I didn't like to admit that, not to Zoe, not even to myself. "Besides," I said, "since when do you defend Alex? When I tried to you accused me of having Stockholm Syndrome."

She ignored my question. "You've got to cut him loose, Gwen. What you're doing to him, it isn't fair."

I sighed and looked away. "I know. Sleeping with him again was a huge mistake. It's only made everything worse."

Chapter 54

I didn't want to spend New Year's Eve with Alex, but he'd caught me at a weak moment. Zoe told me Stefan was taking her out to a club, and Mark and Michelle had plans with friends. Even June, who was home for Christmas break, was going to a party. I just didn't want to sit home alone and watch the ball drop on TV.

"We can watch it together," Alex said. "It'll be fun. You, me, and Isabella. I'll let her stay up late and we can all drink sparkling cider and toast the New Year."

I was feeling lonely, so I agreed.

"And this time you're spending the night," he said. "I'm not letting you drive home on New Year's Eve with all the drunks on the road."

I agreed to that too..

Isabella fell asleep at eleven. While Alex carried her up to her room, I flipped channels on the TV. I paused at a rerun of *The Princess Bride*.

"'As you wish' is just a phrase, huh?" I said to Alex when he returned. Wesley had just repeated it to Buttercup. According to Peter Falk, it meant "I love you."

"Um."

"Alex—"

"Not tonight, Gwen. It's New Year's Eve. Whatever you want to say to me can wait until tomorrow."

He was right. One more night together wouldn't make a difference. I knew when I told him we couldn't sleep together anymore he was going to start hating me again. The fact that we were still having a child together wasn't going to matter. If I refused him what he wanted, which was apparently still me—in his life, in his bed, and maybe even as his wife—he would find a way to exact his revenge. I knew that. Alex played to win.

I nodded and flipped the channel back to Dick Clark's New Year's Rockin' Eve. We watched the revelers in Times Square until the ball dropped, then we shut off the television and went to bed. We had sex once before we fell asleep.

"What do you want for breakfast?" Alex asked, smiling over at me.

"I don't care," I said, burying myself deeper under the covers. I was in no rush to start the day. I was dreading the conversation I knew I had to initiate.

"No cravings?"

"Not yet."

"What's wrong?" he asked and snuggled up to me. "You look upset." He put his arm around my belly and the baby kicked. I'd felt him move before, but that was the first time Alex had. He smiled over at me. "Is that what I think it is?"

"If you think that's your son beating me up from the inside, then yes." This kid wanted out.

He kept his hand on my stomach and the baby kicked a few more times then went back to sleep, which was what I hoped to do too.. Alex had other ideas.

"So have you given any more thought to the name?" he asked.

We'd already agreed that we would name the baby after my father. But my father's name was Dirk, and neither of us liked that one, so we'd decided to only use the "D," and Dracula was definitely out of the question. "Yes, I'd like to name him David, if that's okay with you."

"David Romanescu," he said, testing it out. "I can live with that."

"No, Alex. David Andersen."

"No, Gwen. David Romanescu."

I pushed his hand off my stomach and pulled away. "We're not married, Alex. The baby doesn't automatically get your last name."

"My son is going to have my last name."

"Your son?"

"I'd feel no differently if it were a girl. *All* of my children will have my last name."

"And I get no say in this?"

"You're choosing the first name."

"And has it ever occurred to you that maybe I'd like to have the same last name as my child too.?"

"Marry me, Gwen," he said, his voice rising. "Then we can all have the same last name."

I threw the covers off of me and pushed myself out of bed, stomach first. "How many times do we have to have this conversation, Alex? I do not want to marry you."

"Why? What would be so terrible about being married to me? You'd get to live in a beautiful house, you wouldn't have to work, you'd never want for anything. What is so terrible about that?"

"I like my job. I don't need you to support me. I just need you to stop suing me every time I don't do what you want."

I wasn't referring solely to the battle over the Dracula land, but he took it that way.

"Don't throw that up in my face again. You'd be a fool to sell that land."

"But I am a fool, Alex, as you constantly prove to me. And it all started right here in this very house."

"Are we back to this again?"

"When did we ever leave this? It's been between us from the start. And you should know since you're the one who put it there."

This wasn't how I'd wanted it to end. But we were past the point of calm, rational conversation where I could've explained why we needed to go back to being just friends. And in truth, there was no good way to tell someone you didn't love them. Not when that person loved you. So I gave in to my anger and frustration.

"You're the reason this will never work, Alex," I continued, tears now streaming down my face. "You're the reason we can never be happy."

"No, Gwen, you are. Because you can't find it in your heart to forgive me." He tore out of bed and started pacing the spacious bedroom. "I actually thought this time was different. When you wanted to sleep together again I thought *finally* we're getting somewhere."

"It was just sex, Alex. I told you that. You promised you wouldn't get emotionally involved."

"Gwen, I love you. I *am* emotionally involved. The only one who isn't is you!"

"Jesus Christ, Alex, can't you just be a fucking man for once?" I froze, regretting the words as soon as they'd escaped my lips.

"Be a man?" he roared. "What do you think that means, Gwen? Come to your house and fuck you and not care?"

"I'm sorry. I was wrong. I shouldn't have said that."

"But you think it. You think because I love you that makes me weak." He shook his head and smirked. "You are such a Tepes. Even without the birthmark, there'd be no doubt whose genes you were spawned from. You might as well be his clone."

He knew exactly what to say to hurt me the most. I grabbed my overnight bag off the floor. "I'm leaving."

"I think that's an excellent idea."

"And don't think I'm showing up for coffee next week, because I'm not. I'm done playing this game with you."

"Agreed. You win, Gwen. I concede. I hope that makes you happy. God knows nothing else I've tried has."

It should've made me happy. It's what I'd wanted all along. But it didn't.

Chapter 55

Three and a half months later, my water broke at 7:55 p.m. I called Zoe as soon as it happened. She and Stefan were at a restaurant, but they left their entrees uneaten and their wine undrunk and drove to my house to collect me. Stefan must've called Alex from the road because he was waiting for us at the hospital when we arrived. It was the first time I'd seen him since New Year's Day.

The plan was that Zoe would stay with me in the delivery room. She was my "birth partner." We'd taken all the classes together, and she was the one who supposed to feed me ice chips and hold my hand. Alex wouldn't allow it; he insisted on doing it himself. I didn't object. I was terrified, and I wanted him with me. He'd been through this once before. Zoe was as clueless as I was. Plus, he was the one who'd gotten me pregnant, so he was the one who deserved to be cursed at every time I had another contraction.

Our son was born at 5:45 p.m. the next day. It was just like in the movies. The baby came out all covered in gunk and they placed him on my chest. We both cried and the doctor let Alex cut the cord.

"He's perfect, Gwen. Absolutely perfect."

I wanted to see for myself but my vision was blurring. Then I closed my eyes and the room disappeared.

When I opened them again the room was dark. I had no idea if it was night or day. I reached for the light, and Alex turned it on for me.

"What happened?" I asked. "Where is everyone? Where's the baby?"

"He's fine," he said. "He's in the nursery. You're the one we were worried about."

"Me? Why?" Except for being incredibly sore and extremely thirsty, I felt okay.

"Your heart rate dropped and your blood pressure soared. The doctor was afraid you were going to stroke out."

"Well, I guess that would've solved the custody issue once and for all."

"Please, Gwen, don't joke about this. We were all really scared."

"Sorry." I couldn't wrap my head around what he was saying. It was incomprehensible to me that I wouldn't be here to see my baby grow up. "So what now?"

"They'll probably want to keep you an extra couple of days to make sure you're okay."

"When can I see the baby?"

"He's sleeping," he said. "Which is what you should be doing. It's the middle of the night."

"Then what are you still doing here?"

"You think I'd leave you like this?"

"I thought you hated me." After our blowout on New Year's Day, Alex reignited the custody battle. We let the lawyers fight it out without us this time, but no matter what I agreed to—nights, weekends, fifty-fifty joint custody—Alex wanted more.

"No," he said, "you hate me. I still love you."

I closed my eyes and sighed, and the tears slid out from underneath. There was no middle ground with Alex. Everything had to be his way.

"Don't cry, Gwen. We'll work it out."

I turned to face this man I'd once loved, however briefly. He was capable of great kindness, but also cruelty. "Will we?"

"You just have to forgive me."

If I could've, I would've. God knew I wanted to. This was an unwinnable war for both of us. I think even Alex knew that. But as incapable as I was of forgiving him, he was just as incapable of letting go of his fantasy that we were destined to be. I closed my eyes again thinking there was no way I'd be able to sleep, but I did. Maybe it wasn't just fluids they were pumping through that IV.

The nurses woke me the next morning and brought me the baby. I was going to try breastfeeding, but my doctor advised against it because of the medication they were giving me to keep my blood pressure down, so I gave him a bottle instead. Alex was right. He was perfect.

Before he was born I'd been a little concerned that if he looked like Alex I might hate him. Now I couldn't imagine how I ever could've felt that way. I fell in love instantly, even though he did have Alex's eyes. And my birthmark. It was a miniature version of mine, no bigger than a quarter and under his right shoulder blade. The doctor told me it was no big deal and might even go away. I knew it wouldn't. I knew what it meant.

Alex was the first to arrive. He'd never really left. He'd just run home to shower and change while I was sleeping. I was dying for a shower myself, but I couldn't tear myself away from the baby. I couldn't believe this was what had been growing inside me all those months, that despite all the hurt and anger, Alex and I had managed to create this perfect being.

And despite holding my child in my arms, I was still having a hard time believing that all of this was real, that I was actually this tiny person's mother and forevermore I'd be responsible for another human being's life. It was still surreal.

Stefan and Zoe arrived an hour later with Isabella in tow. She was supposed to be in school; they both were. Isabella told me they were playing hooky today. I figured Simone Lorens would understand. Mark and Michelle arrived not long after them, and that's when Stefan whipped out his camera. But Zoe made him wait to take pictures until after she'd brushed my hair and applied mascara and concealer to my eyes. "You'll thank me later," she said. I did.

We were making so much noise that the nurse came in and yelled at us to keep it down and chastised us for having too many people in the room. Stefan charmed her into allowing everyone to stay and even conned her into taking a few group photos. The man had skills.

But after lunch exhaustion overtook me, and the nurse kicked everyone out. I knew they were feeding me more than just fluids through that IV because I rarely napped in the afternoons, and never for four hours.

When I woke the next time, it was early evening and I was alone again except for Alex. He was dozing in the chair beside my bed.

I roused him and asked, "Where's the baby?"

"In the nursery," he answered through a yawn. "They wanted to give him a bath."

"I could use one of those."

He gave an exaggerated sniff. "You are a little ripe."

"Fuck you," I jokingly replied.

"Hey, no more cursing. I have visions of 'fuck' being our son's first word."

I laughed, but the lightheartedness didn't last. "Alex, we need to decide where David's going to live."

"You don't need to worry about that right now."

"Yes, I do. I'm not going to be in here forever. We need to resolve this."

"He's going to live with you, Gwen. He was always going to live with you. At least at the beginning."

"You mean that?" I could feel the tears stinging my eyes, but I held them back.

"You think I want my son's first weeks of life to be spent sitting in traffic driving from your house to mine?"

I smiled at him, and the tears spilled out onto my cheeks. "Thank you, Alex. Really. Thank you." I had no idea when my hormones were going to return to normal, but it couldn't be soon enough for me.

He looked away. "I got you a present," he said and reached down into a shopping bag I hadn't even noticed at his feet. He handed me a white cardboard shirt box. "Sorry, I didn't have time to get it wrapped. But I really think you're going to like this one."

"I liked the other one too., Alex, it's just..." I'd wanted to hurt him like he'd hurt me. Not my proudest moment. "I'm sorry. About the necklace, about everything."

"It's okay. Unlike some people in this room, *I* don't hold a grudge."

I laughed. "No, you just call your lawyers and sue me. That's so much better."

He laughed too, then the smile faded from his face and he grabbed my hand in both of his. "It's not too late for us, Gwen. We can start over. You, me, Isabella, and David. We can be a family."

I shook my head and more tears spilled out. As enticing as that thought was, and it *was* enticing, I knew it wasn't possible, at least not in the way he wanted it to be. "Can't we just be friends again? I know that's not what you want, but it's all I can offer you. I promise I'll always be there for you. And Isabella too.. I'm a good friend, Alex. Just ask Zoe."

He chuckled. "You mean you come with references?"

"Yes! Please, Alex. Just try this my way. That's all I'm asking."

For a long time he silently stared down at my hand, the one he was still holding in both of his. Eventually he spoke. "Friends for David's sake?"

"Yes," I said, "for David Andersen Romanescu."

He squeezed my hand and looked up at me, and I saw one tear slip out, but he quickly wiped it away. "Thanks, Gwen. That means a lot to me."

"Alex, I do love you. Just not the same way you love me."

He let one harsh laugh escape. "You mean you love me as a friend?"

"Yes, if you'll let me."

He let go of my hand and nodded toward the heavy box that was sitting on my lap. "Then open my present."

I lifted the lid and pulled back the tissue paper. Inside was a beautiful silver picture frame surrounding a familiar image—the photo Stefan had asked the nurse to take this morning. We were all in it: me with David in my arms; Alex and Isabella to the left of me; Stefan, Zoe, Mark, and Michelle to my right.

"Do you like it?" he asked.

"I love it." I couldn't tear my gaze away. Everyone I cared about was forever captured in that moment. He'd chosen the perfect gift.

"Good," he said, relief evident in his voice. "I thought you might like to add it to your wall of shame. Then you can have your parents and the baby all in one place."

That's when the tears overtook me. At first Alex just held me, but I was bawling so hard he got scared and called the nurse, who made me take a sedative.

When I woke up the next time it was dark outside. This time I was truly alone—Alex wasn't dozing in the chair next to me. I flipped on the light to find the call button and discovered another package on my bed. This one was a small gold box with a note attached. I recognized Alex's elegant handwriting immediately.

For David Andersen Romanescu—

Gwen, you should be the one to give him this, not me. It was your legacy, and now it's his.

I opened the box even though I already knew what was inside—the icon my birth mother had given me. Saint George was still fighting his demons, and so was I. But I was no longer fighting them alone. Now I had David, and Alex and Isabella too.. We weren't a traditional family, but we were a family nonetheless.

My family.

Turn the page for a sneak peek at the next installment of Gwen and Alex's story...

Chapter 1

"Did you hear that?" I asked.

My boyfriend, Robert, rolled over onto his side. "Hmmm," he mumbled, still half asleep.

"Pancakes!" I heard my two-year-old son, David, shout, then collapse into giggles.

Dammit. I knew I shouldn't have moved him into a toddler bed so soon. At least when he still slept in a crib I had a modicum of control over his early morning activities.

I slipped out of bed and hustled down the hallway, afraid of what I might find. Last week he'd gotten into the baby powder while I was in the shower and made it "snow" all over the house. I didn't think my vacuum cleaner would ever recover. Hopefully David woke his stepsister, Isabella, before he started exploring. The two of them could certainly get into trouble together, but since she was almost ten it was much less than what he'd get into on his own. What I found in the kitchen shocked me even more than the baby powder.

"Alex, what are you doing here?" He was standing barefoot in my kitchen stirring batter in a mixing bowl. David was sitting cross-legged on the counter—something I never allowed him to do, but Alex routinely did—trying to grab the spoon out of his father's hand.

"Good morning," Alex said, taking in my outfit with one eye sweep. If I knew my ex was in the house, I would've grabbed my bathrobe. The days of wearing sexy lingerie in front of Alex had ended years ago. "Pancakes?" he asked.

"Mommy!" David yelled and held his arms out to me, which always brought a smile to my face. Apparently I was still more interesting than a bowl of pancake batter. How much longer would that last?

"Good morning, baby," I said as I lifted him off the counter and inhaled. He still smelled of baby shampoo from last night's bath, a scent I never tired of.

"I'm not a baby. I'm a big boy."

His new mantra for the last few weeks. I didn't know where he'd picked it up. Maybe from another kid on the playground when he was with his nanny, Katarina.

"Big boys don't grab Mommy's breast," I said, removing his hand from its favorite resting spot. I'd never understood this habit since I'd bottle-fed him from day one. Alex insisted it was instinctual. Or perhaps he just took after his father.

"They don't?" Alex asked, then grinned at me.

Smart ass. "You still haven't told me what you're doing here. I thought you weren't picking up the kids until this afternoon."

"I took the red-eye home so I decided to get them earlier. I didn't think you'd mind."

"I don't," I said as I set David on the kitchen floor with two of his toy trucks, which usually bought me ten minutes of peace. "But you should've called first. I gave you a key for emergencies, not so you could waltz in here whenever you wanted." Giving Alex a key to my house had been a huge issue for Robert. But since technically he didn't live with me—he just slept over four or five nights a week—I overruled him.

"I didn't use the key," Alex said. "Isabella let me in."

At the mention of her name I glanced around the kitchen. Even though she was Alex's daughter, not mine, some weeks she spent more time at my house than at his, especially when he was out of town on business a lot, as he had been lately. I didn't mind. She was a huge help to me with David. They were so close, sometimes I felt like she was the mother and I was the interloper.

"In the living room listening to music," he said, reading my mind. "And I didn't call first because I didn't want to wake you."

"You didn't think I'd wake up when you started banging around my kitchen at seven o'clock in the morning?"

Alex sighed. "Gwen, I've spent the last twenty-eight hours traveling and I haven't seen my kids in ten days. Can we please not fight about this?"

I nodded and turned away from him, choosing to busy myself with making coffee instead. Alex and I had a good relationship these days and I wanted to keep it that way. It was better for all of us when we got along. We hadn't always.

After our bruising custody battle while I was pregnant, I'd been expecting the worst. But Alex softened once David was born. He let him live solely with me for the first three months even though we'd agreed to fifty-fifty joint custody. In exchange, I allowed Alex to come over to my house and visit David whenever he wanted. That set the tone for all future custody negotiations.

When David turned three months old Alex insisted we abide by the joint custody agreement. I was devastated. When I dropped David off at Alex's house that first morning I'd felt like a piece of my heart had been ripped from my body. I was so distraught that Alex let me spend the day with them. And even after I put David to bed that evening, Alex offered me the guest room for the night because I didn't want to leave. The next two days I only spent the evenings with them. I went back to my own house after David fell asleep. Over time it became easier. Two years later I could last the requisite three or four days without seeing David, but I always began missing him after a few hours.

Alex and I set up a schedule: David was supposed to spend Sunday, Monday, Tuesday, and every other Wednesday with me, and Thursday, Friday, Saturday, and alternate Wednesdays with Alex, but it almost never worked out that way. In reality, we shuttled David back and forth all the time depending on our respective schedules. I returned to teaching in the fall after David was born so on weekdays he was always with the nanny, either at Alex's house or mine. And in the last year Alex had started traveling for business a lot more, so I kept David and sometimes Isabella whenever Alex was out of town. When he returned, I always let him have David for a few days even if he was technically supposed to be with me.

Being flexible with the schedule worked out better for me since I ended up with David more than 50 percent of the time. Plus, I was able to see him even on Alex's days because I had an open invitation to Alex's house. After that first awful week of joint custody, Alex told me I was welcome to come over and spend time with him and the kids whenever I wanted, which I sometimes did, much to Robert's consternation. This, however, was not a reciprocal arrangement, much to Alex's consternation.

"So was that a yes on the pancakes?" Alex asked, pouring batter into the frying pan.

"No," I said, pulling two mugs from the cabinet even though the coffee was still brewing. "None for me, thanks."

Alex sighed again. "Gwen, you need to eat."

"Why are you always pushing food down my throat?" He'd been doing it practically since the day we'd met almost three years ago. "Do I look too skinny to you?"

"Yes," he replied.

"Really?" I glanced down at myself, still in my cream silk babydoll. It was loose fitting so Alex was unable to see the pouch in my abdomen, which I couldn't eliminate no matter how much weight I lost or how many crunches I did. After a year of trying everything I finally accepted that my stomach was never going to be as flat as it had been pre-baby, at least not without a tummy tuck, which was a step further than I was willing to go. But for my belly, I thought the rest of me looked pretty good. I was thinner now than I'd been before I'd gotten pregnant, which I attributed less to my attempts at a healthy diet and more to my constantly running after David and not having time to eat.

"Robert likes me this way," I said.

Alex rolled his eyes. "Of course he does."

I let the comment slide.

"I like you a little rounder," Alex continued.

I laughed. "Then you must've loved me when I was pregnant. I was very round then." I'd only gained twenty pounds, but my stomach was huge.

"I did." He stared at me through those familiar sea-green eyes. David had the same ones—inherited from Alex—although David's eyes were a few shades darker.

I turned away. Yet another conversation I didn't want to have.

Alex finished cooking breakfast and I set the table and rounded up David and Isabella. When Alex passed me the platter of blueberry pancakes I grabbed one to keep the peace. It wasn't a major concession—they smelled delicious.

"Isn't this a lovely family portrait," Robert said from the kitchen doorway. He was dressed in my favorite of his scrubs—the dark blues—the same ones he'd been wearing the day I met him. The doctors weren't supposed to wear their scrubs outside the hospital anymore, but occasionally he did anyway, usually when he was too tired to change into street clothes before heading home.

"Sorry I didn't wake you," I said, jumping up from the table. "I figured you'd rather sleep." Robert hadn't crept into my bed until almost three a.m., even though his shift was supposed to end at midnight. The ER was always busy, and he often worked longer hours than he was scheduled to.

I poured him a cup of coffee, added two sugars, and handed him the steaming mug. "Thanks," he said and took a sip.

"Good morning, Doctor Bob!" David waved to him between bites of pancake.

Robert crossed to the table and ruffled his hair. "Good morning, champ. Morning, Isabella."

"Good morning, Doctor Bob," Isabella said. She wasn't quite as fond of Robert as David was. I suspected Alex had something to do with that.

"Good morning, Doctor Bob," Alex said too..

I shot Alex a don't-make-trouble-for-me look.

He knew Robert didn't like the nickname "Doctor Bob." He accepted it from the kids, and from me on occasion, but not from Alex. David was the one who had started it. When he first began talking he couldn't say "Robert" and instead called him "Baba." But "Baba" was too close to "Dada" for Alex's liking, so I tried to get David to call Robert "Doctor Robert," which eventually became "Doctor Bob."

"Alexander," Robert said because he knew Alex preferred the shortened version. "What brings you here so early on a Saturday morning?"

"Breakfast with my children," Alex said without looking up from his plate. "Obviously."

"Yes, your children," Robert derisively replied before turning back to me. "Sweetheart, don't you think you should put some clothes on?"

I glanced down at my lingerie. "Yeah, I guess I should go change."

"Why?" Alex gave me another eye sweep and smiled. "I was always quite fond of that outfit."

I shot him another stop-making-trouble-for-me look, even though the damage was already done.

Acknowledgments

A big thank you to my beta readers—Al, Allie, Elaine, Natasha, Vickie, and Win. Your input, even when you didn't like something, perhaps especially when you didn't like something, was invaluable. And a big thank you to my agent, Marlene Stringer, for encouraging me to write this book when it was no more than a vague idea, and then selling it off of a two-page synopsis. Impressive indeed.

I'd also like to thank everyone at Amazon Publishing who helped bring this book to fruition, especially Eleni Caminis for never saying no, and Charlotte Herscher for tirelessly battling with me over Gwen and Alex's "unwinnable war," which I have no doubt made this a better book.

And no acknowledgments section would be complete without a thank you to all of the Back Roomers (you know who you are) for their fun, friendship, and support. You guys are the bestest.

Finally, a big thank you to my husband, Steve, who's always my first reader and my biggest fan.

About the Author

Photo by Steven Bingen

A native of New York City, Beth Orsoff has long sought to return to her primordial roots by refusing to live more than an hour's drive from the ocean. She spent her formative years working as a lifeguard, thrilled to be paid to work on her tan, until her parents forced her to get a "real" job. And so she headed to law school—conveniently near the beaches of southern California—and launched a career as an entertainment attorney. Today she lives in Los Angeles, dividing her time and energy between writing fiction and drafting Hollywood contracts.

Made in the USA
Charleston, SC
23 December 2012